Praise for *Architects of M...*

"A thrilling labyrinth of plot twists exploring loyalty, trust, and promises." —Sue Burke, Arthur C. Clarke Award finalist and author of *Semiosis*

"A nonstop dystopian space opera adventure that screams F*** CAPITALISM at the top of its lungs. Equal amounts sweet and painful, but 100 percent human, this is a mystery and a treatise and a nail-biting kick to the stomach all in one."
—K. A. Doore, author of *The Perfect Assassin*

"Kick-ass and poetic." —Emily Devenport, author of *Medusa Uploaded*

"Far-future corporate dystopia plus deep-space mystery plus powerful character drama. For fans of *Firefly*, *Killjoys*, and *The Wrong Stars*." —Michael R. Underwood, author of *Annihilation Aria*

"Completely heartbreaking. Utterly brilliant."
—K. B. Wagers, author of *A Pale Light in the Black*

"An absolutely stunning debut . . . razor-tipped and diamond-sharp. A deadly first shot from one of the most incisive new voices in the genre." —Tyler Hayes, author of *The Imaginary Corpse*

"*Architects of Memory* is the queer, nail-biting love child of the humanity of *The Expanse* and the action-fast pulse of *Die Hard*, and I loved every minute of it." —A. J. Hackwith, author of *The Library of the Unwritten*

"A plot-twisty, heart-stealing delight . . . It's a safe bet that this debut is the start of something really special."
—Bryan Camp, author of *The City of Lost Fortunes* and *Gather the Fortunes*

ALSO BY KAREN OSBORNE

Architects of Memory

KAREN OSBORNE

ENGINES OF
OBLIVION

TOR

A TOM DOHERTY ASSOCIATES BOOK

NEW YORK

ENGINES OF OBLIVION

Copyright © 2021 by Karen Osborne

A Tor Book
Published by Tom Doherty Associates
120 Broadway
New York, NY 10271

www.tor-forge.com

Tor® is a registered trademark of Macmillan Publishing Group, LLC.

The Library of Congress Cataloging-in-Publication Data
is available upon request.

ISBN 978-1-250-21550-5 (trade paperback)
ISBN 978-1-250-21549-9 (ebook)

Our books may be purchased in bulk for promotional, educational, or business use. Please contact your local bookseller or the Macmillan Corporate and Premium Sales Department at 1-800-221-7945, extension 5442, or by email at MacmillanSpecialMarkets@macmillan.com.

First Edition: February 2021

Printed in the United States of America

0 9 8 7 6 5 4 3 2 1

For Claire
who was always with me

ENGINES OF
OBLIVION

Caught between heartbeats, a single breath skelterways in her hurling lungs, Natalie Chan wondered if operating the proxy rig herself had been such a good idea.

The boneheads in R&D hadn't sent up the people she needed for this mission—real soldiers with real combat experience. Instead, her rig operator was to be chosen from a trio of shivering indentures, too young and too stupid to have any real combat experience—lab rats sent to do a soldier's duty. She'd stared at their skinny bodies and sleepless eyes, remembering a time when she was the one stuck in front of a frowning citizen with director's tabs, terrified down to her bones and trying her best not to show it.

"You're not in the military branch at all? Any of you?" she asked.

The tallest one—young, dark-haired, exhausted—blinked. "I'm a janitor," he'd said, stammering it out. "We're all janitors."

Another boy lifted his chin. "Are we getting upgrades finished today?"

She took one more look at the exterior cameras: *Vancouver* was still losing the battle over Bittersweet, and orders were orders. She thought about the twelve yawning minutes it would take to get decent infantry replacements, muttered an epithet against cost-effective savings, then marched to the proxy rig herself.

"Strap me in."

"This isn't a good idea, sir. It's not like they need to *shoot* anyone." App-K's head researcher frowned from behind a curtain of fashionably slashed bangs.

"That's not the point, Mx. Ascanio," Natalie said.

"It's just a half-mile walk!"

The proxy rig looked like something straight out of a holovid—an open black cube hung with spiderlike cables, straps, and neural interfaces. Applied Kinetics had been working on the project all year, using the guts of captured and defused Vai devices to elevate the formerly simple infantry helmet-cam into something far more useful. Natalie stepped inside the assemblage, picking her way to the center.

The techs hovered around her, making sure the cold, sticky neural patches lay flush against her sweaty temples. They drew the straps supporting Natalie's chest harness tight enough to sting, then tested her balance. Natalie jabbed the button that tightened the thick, shining support cables above, lifting her feet off the floor. She heard the same quiet whine she always did—a whine the techs swore they couldn't hear. She hadn't wanted to use the rig in combat before eliminating that annoyance, but it was too late now.

Natalie stretched her fingers, kicked her feet, felt the give. She checked her center of gravity, feeling the tug of *Vancouver*'s antigrav on her feet, making sure the Vai-slippery cables were gathered far away from where they could catch on her elbows and ankles. The harness dug into her belly. *We really should be doing this in zero gravity*, she thought, but while Auroran R&D could stick her consciousness in a puppet drone thousands of kilometers away, artificial gravity was still a ship-level constant. Nearby, the janitors wavered, their eyes wide, their faces more confused than grateful.

Natalie sighed. "What were you doing during the Vai war, Mx. Ascanio?"

"I was completing my robotics degree."

"Right. You were basically sitting on Europa Station eating candy with your thumb up your ass," Natalie said. "Infiltration is a specialist's game, and I don't care what the board says—you can't just drop unconditioned indentures down the chute and expect them to do a good job. I'm the only one here who can."

Ascanio bristled. "Ms. Chan, if the board finds out—"

Natalie sighed. Her head researcher's blatant brown-nosing was exhausting. She made a mental note to deal with it later. "I'm sick of the board getting in my face on this. No other directorate on *Vancouver* gets this kind of oversight. Just me. Just Applied Kinetics."

"They must have their reasons."

"And this is mine—people are dying, Ascanio. Drop me."

Natalie caught some hesitation in Ascanio's stance—she wondered about it, briefly, because the engineer was always so confident—but before Natalie could ask about it, Ascanio's hands slipped clean and quick into the now-familiar motions that activated the proxy rig. After that, it all came very quickly, exactly as Natalie expected: the prick of the needle, the rush of the meds, the ache of being poured into the proxy puppet pancreas-first, followed by the silence of her beating, thrashing heart and the sheer animal panic of *death death this is death*—

—until the puppet's HUD matrix smashed straight into her prefrontal cortex, jerking her awake, bringing her boggled senses back online. Sunlight wailed around her as if she were actually on Bittersweet, her feet covered in its thin golden dirt.

Natalie struggled to stand and walk, feeling sudden, stabbing adrenaline spike behind her sternum. *Something's wrong,* her adrenals shouted, and she spent a few precious seconds searching for hostiles before she realized the *wrongness* was wrapped around her tongue, was the half-sweet filtered air of *Vancouver* rather than the tin-strong tang of a tank on her back. A view of the Applied Kinetics lab—Ascanio, the techs, the lab rats—flashed in front of her eyes for a moment, unstable and withering.

"Ms. Chan. Please check in."

She heard Emerson Ward's wry, granular voice in a broken half echo, as if he were both six inches from her face and six thousand klicks away. He was all business on shift, of course, tight-shouldered and blanched, his sallow hair drawn up in ribbons, his rawboned frame steady at the interface. He was good at business, good at separating his role as her operations officer from the things he did to her with his hands in the middle of the night.

Her vision blurred, and she stumbled to a halt.

"You're messing with my immersion, Mr. Ward," Natalie said, feeling a sudden, saber-sharp headache. "Can you use the interface on the other side of the room so I don't hear you twice?"

He went quiet for a moment. She heard faraway bootstrikes, and his voice adjusted to fit the tinny suit speaker she was used to.

"Better, sir?"

"Somewhat."

"Acknowledged. Mx. Ascanio and I would like to go through the pre-engagement tests."

"No time," Natalie said. "My head feels like someone's put a spike through it. I want to get this done."

More silence, like he was using the haptics to communicate with the other scientists in the room so she couldn't hear. Typical.

"Proceed, Ms. Chan," Ward said.

She swallowed. Immersion. She needed to stay immersed in this. *I'm the one on the ground, I'm on Bittersweet, there's only a half inch of fabric and plasteel between me and sucking down certain death,* she lied to herself, and she marveled at how similar the interaction felt to querying the memory device she was wearing—*no,* she reminded herself, that her *body* was wearing—back on *Vancouver.* It was going to be hard enough to keep everything straight as the rig's actual project manager, and the board thought *janitors* could do it?

She rolled her neck and started walking, relishing the strange, shiny weight of the mech paired with a momentary pride. The puppet drone was a triumph of Auroran scientific design, sporting cruiser-quality sensors paired with advancements in Vai kinetic weapons research. Here on Bittersweet, working the puppet, she felt more like herself than she had since joining *Vancouver.* She felt like a soldier, not a pencil-pushing lab rat.

It was hard not to feel a little cocky. After all, it was partly her soldier's skin that Aurora wanted for Applied Kinetics. She was the only one in the company with the required experience, mixing a gunner's eye for tactics from the war with an engineer's knowledge of Vai bomb guts from her time as a salvager on *Twenty-Five.* Even her half-forgotten pre-corporate life was useful here—even though she'd left the Verdict collective years ago, she still knew enough about off-brand biocoders and their work to guide the rig from concept through reality.

If her proxy rig worked as advertised, Aurora would be able to deliver Vai weapons to the battlefield without killing the soldiers who brought them. Her tactician's heart imagined drones, tanks, entire cruisers driven from haptic rigs, her body writ large in metal and flame, invincible, her blood safely inside her skin where it belonged. There'd be another promotion, honorifics, maybe an important chair on a starship bridge.

Unless—

Wait. Something's wrong.

She was familiar with that scratching *something* from being on the battlefield—it was her own version of a proximity warning, a sixth sense between her shoulder blades, a delicate metal sliver thrust under her fingernails. Beyond that, she could hear the crashing wails of equipment moving at the Baylor-Wellspring airfield, sirens and grav-engines and the rumble of rovers being scrambled to check out the transport crash.

She could handle Baylor-Wellspring. She could handle anything human hands could throw at her. She could even handle

Vai kinetics in the puppet rig. Bullets were nothing compared to the weapons she'd seen during the war: the wild, alien light that rained from alien ships and mechs, turning human lives to soup and flame. The screaming, insane city-killing moleculars only the aliens could use.

She could walk straight through all of it.

Natalie pushed away the worry. She paused, tracing her sudden surge of adrenaline to the space where her stomach should have been. She took a deep, calming breath, her heart banging in her ears, the sweet battlefield music of *you're alive you're alive you're still alive.*

In the puppet's belly—*her* belly—App-K had installed a *kicker,* a particularly useful kinetic Vai electromagnetic pulse weapon. Her old salvage crew on *Twenty-Five* had found a dozen in the wreckage over Tribulation, and just one could take out every single piece of modern technology at the Baywell headquarters. The problem with the kicker was that it also disrupted electrical signals in the human body that set it off, and previous weapons tests had scattered a dozen unintentional suicides in their wake. With the puppet drone, she'd be able to disable the entire Baylor-Wellspring military airfield at once. Aurora could sweep in and interrogate Baywell executives, and—most importantly—secure the lab where Wellspring technology had turned her former shipmate Ashlan Jackson from an indentured miner into the most desired weapon in the world. It was the most important day of Natalie's career.

During testing, the kicker had sung cold and quiet and blue, a razor's whine married to an understated buzz. On Bittersweet, it worried her already-frazzled nerves with a rattle and howl, humming bright and frightening where her guts should have been, spilling up past her brainstem into her mouth. This felt like wet ashes on spoiled toast: slippery, ungracious, the Cana kind of wrong, the kind of wrong that got people killed.

She cleared spit from her throat. "What the hell, Ascanio? Kicker doesn't feel right. Did you make sure to check the install?"

Ward answered, his voice even. "The executives are watching, sir, so your language—"

"I don't give a fuck. The weapon's active. If I fall on my face because I'm distracted, this all could be over before I get close enough to engage."

"You built the quarantine system yourself, sir. Trust yourself."

The humming in her head crescendoed, lancing behind her eyes like a particularly shitty migraine. "I do. I do. Stop arguing with me and figure out why my molars are rattling before we lose the element of surprise."

Ward's voice went darker. "R&D is holding the position that nothing is wrong."

"Oh, *fuck* this—"

"The executives, sir. *Amberworth* is on the other end of the feed. *Aulander.*"

"Hi, guys," she quipped. "You wanted janitors to do this? They'd be shitting their pants right now."

"I'm sure the board had their reasons, sir."

Natalie bit her bottom lip to stop her next response. There was no reason to torpedo her chances at a new promotion by being nasty to the board, no matter how she felt. The executives wanted actionable data, so she sucked recycled air between her teeth to staunch the ache, rolled the suit's faceplate to face the woozy gray sky, and swallowed every single black opinion she had.

"Acknowledged," she said, and started walking.

The whirling dirt of the Bittersweet planetoid had already found its way into the puppet rig's joint mechanism, making it harder to pull her adopted legs toward the target. The buzzing of the weapon inside the puppet's quarantine belly was behind her eyes now, in her bone marrow, under her fingernails, rattling around just underneath her skull. It was fucking with her immersion.

Lose immersion, lose control. The last thing the eggheads hadn't really been able to solve with their crappy drug cocktail. Losing control led to capture. And if that happened, the Baywell specialists might be able to defuse the kicker, rendering moot everything she'd done with Applied Kinetics since returning from Tribulation a year ago.

Natalie looked down at her puppet body, concentrating on being in the suit, being on the planet. She imagined it eating her alive, even though that was impossible, even though her meat and bones were nowhere nearby. She imagined her feet in the boots, her esophagus sucking down air from the puppet's useless airpack.

Next time, she'd ask for canned air.

The ship's air she was breathing was a reminder that she was safe, no matter what happened to the suit, a reminder that she was a walking miracle, bilocating like an actual fucking saint. That she was the reason for all of this, that the future of warfare would soon spring cursed and screaming from her belly. War without a body count, victories without sacrifice—humanity could learn more than just killing from the Vai.

Natalie's vision went blurry again, and she fell back against a large rock.

"Status report." Ward, worried.

My feet are on the ground, she thought. *On the planet, on Bittersweet, above the tunnels where Ash used to live.*

Ash.

The memory device in her brain helpfully brought up a memory, and not one of the good ones. Her former shipmate and friend Ashlan Jackson, her black hair in sweaty, dark strings, hovered for a moment in the death-cold ache of the *London* bridge, her eyes red, her shoulders shivering. Ash had been sick, sick as poison, although Natalie hadn't known it at the time.

"I'm fine," she said through gritted teeth. "I reached the last beta point. I need the final go order."

Natalie felt suddenly nervous, the pressure of the cameras heavy against the back of her neck. An angry shiver skated like a bright current through her shoulders. She licked the desert from her lips and placed the puppet's fingers against the rock formation, feeling the clatter in her fingertips.

"Go order is given," Ward responded.

And there it was: the singular stab of focus that came right before battle, the breath in her chest like a hot coal, the awareness in her feet, her hands, her very core. The puppet crashed in around her, feeling like her skin, like her bones.

She pushed off a nearby rock, hauling herself to her feet, stride-stumbling her way toward the airstrip. The enemy saw her almost immediately, which was the whole point; the puppet was a black, crackling scar against the bright horizon, all arms and legs with a barrel torso and a blank, curved helmet, the heavy armor painted in rivulets of sand and dust.

She couldn't quite see the battlefield above, hidden by the green-gold lights from the base and a curtain of thin atmosphere. She couldn't see the damaged Auroran ships running pell-mell from the Baylor-Wellspring cruisers. But she knew people had already died for this, for her, for the end of the war with the Vai and the end of this *entirely stupid* new war. She was a warrior, a soldier, a delivery system for the kicker EMP inside where her stomach should be—*no, in my stomach, in the quarantine box, hot and whirling, bouncing against my mucosa like a sick little pinball.*

The feeling of a Vai weapon exploding was blue, the memoria remembered for her, *blue like the Hudson River should have been, like a sapphire in a nuclear blast—*

—like Marley's bones had been when the screamer took him, skin first, then the blood, then his eyes and his tongue and his

fingernails. For a bright second the memory device put her back in a blackening forest on Tribulation one year ago, running from a Vai kinetic with Ash, trying to get away from the thing that had just killed her team.

Her vision twisted. Natalie stumbled to an embarrassing stop, then gulped down acid-sour spit-up, tasting the bitter remnant of her breakfast. She blinked. She banished the memories of the red-dirt Tribulation for the yellow stone of Bittersweet. *I'm here,* she thought, *I'm here, I'm here, I'm here.*

"Your heart rate is increasing, Ms. Chan," Ward said. He sounded a lot more concerned than he should have been. "Is immersion still an issue?"

"The memoria is interfering."

He whistled. "I'll have the doctors push you another dose of ester."

"No. That'll just make it worse."

He ignored her. "Ascanio agrees with me. Injection in three, two, one—"

She wanted to spit, but she swallowed instead, as the rush of *here and now* hit her brainstem on a tidal wave of intravenous medication. The executives were watching. They were always watching, especially now that they'd wired Ingest into the fabric of cruiser life. They'd examined the edges of her existence since she was dragged from her molecular-induced coma after the Second Battle of Tribulation and given a memory device. They might as well have followed her around with a camera drone, she thought. The Natalie Chan Show, live and in tri-D, just in case she gets any ideas.

She felt blood at the back of her throat.

"I'll have a visual of the airstrip in three, two, one," she said.

Bittersweet was a celestium-rich planetoid. Ash spent years working the mines here before Baylor-McKenna's merger with her old employer Wellspring Celestial, and the kind of airstrip she'd described warred with the tactical map currently hanging on Natalie's HUD. Ash's tales had included squat transports, cargo ships with swollen bellies, slow vessels that made reliable, lumbering trips back and forth to the transfer station above.

What Natalie saw were sharp-edged fighters, aerodynamic craft meant to slip in and out of planetary atmospheres, and pilots running to board them. She saw troop transports bristling with railguns and spinal lances. Celestium mining continued here—that much was certain, from the silver particles kicking up in blank little tornadoes around the mine's exhaust vents—but the airstrip itself was packed with combat mechanics and pilots, missiles and quarantine boxes like a proper spaceport.

"*Vancouver,* I'm seeing military assets. They're expecting us. Tell the board they'll need to beef up the frontal attack," she said.

"Sounds like we're in the right place."

Natalie examined the airfield. She thought of Ash again and wondered if her friend had ever been allowed up to the surface while she'd been indentured here, if Ash ever thought for one bare second that Bittersweet might be home to the biggest unintentional weapons development in the history of human warfare.

"Of course it's the right place," Natalie said. "You think I did all this for fun?"

She continued forward. Beyond the fighters and troop transports were the massive doors that led down to the mine. She imagined the hundreds of miners that lived there, and God knows how many executives and scientists this time, all of them working on the technology that had given Ash her terminal illness—as well as her strange, alien powers. Whoever held Bittersweet held the future. And now that future was up to her: Natalie Chan, one of seven survivors of the Battle of Tribulation, war hero then and now.

Time for the feint. Her attention narrowed, her eyes set only on the task ahead. She walked: left foot, right foot. Dragged a little, added a limp, making it look like she was just one crashed-out soldier from the battle above, hurt and unarmed. It didn't stop the closest guards from pulling three boltguns on her, or forming into teams, two to flank and one to approach from the center, all of them holding automatic bullet guns that looked powerful enough to punch through the puppet's armor.

The weapon rattled. She felt it rot her teeth. Yank at her kidneys. She'd expected guns in her face. Welcomed them. She wasn't going to die here. The Baywells weren't going to die, either, if they knew what was good for them. This was Aurora's clean win, and Natalie Chan's star-bright, post-indenture apotheosis.

All of this, and something still felt very wrong.

2

The Baywell forward team flanked Natalie easily, forcing her down to her knees, their coldsuit gloves slamming into the shoulders of the puppet drone. She felt the impact of hard metal on stony ground, teeth rattling, chatter from her brand-new memoria grasping at the space beneath her skull. Elsewhere, Ward had gone quiet; she could hear his ragged and nervous breath echoing hers in the earpiece, and a crackling from inside the suit, a loose violent rattling, a brokenness she couldn't fix now.

"Auroran soldier." She heard the whine of line-of-sight comms engaging, the crackle of a voice across the distance. A male growl, probably belonging to the leader occupying the mech at the center of the formation. "Are you surrendering?"

She said nothing. Saying *yes* would make this a war crime. Saying *no* would give Baywell the chance to retrieve the kicker. She could hear her old captain's favorite phrase bouncing around like Kate Keller was here, and not dead: *Space plus bullshit equals death. And this is bullshit, Nat.*

The response to her silence was accompanied by the crack of the barrel of the leader's boltgun against her helmet. *Clang.* For a moment, her animal hindbrain panicked, and the immersion cracked. The white walls of the lab flashed before her eyes, causing a splitting headache.

Clang. "Answer me, you Auroran shit." The captain's voice had gone venom-sweet.

Natalie licked her lips and tasted blood. *Hell.* One of the rig connections must have slipped.

"I crashed," she said.

"Really," the captain's voice spat, then he turned to a person nearby. "Can we get a team to check out the crash site?"

Natalie let the words settle. In her ear, Ward was counting down. *Eleven. Ten. Nine.* In her belly, the kicker howled in impossible, twisting phrases.

Clang. "You have indenture tags, but nobody lets an indenture drive a fighter. You have two seconds to tell me who you really are, or I blow your head off."

Her mouth went dry. She wasn't supposed to say anything else. The board hadn't said anything about getting the puppet rig's unoccupied head blown off. If that happened, Natalie would still be alive, but Baywell would discover the kicker. Aurora would lose the weapons labs—and the war.

"I don't suppose *you* want to surrender," she said.

He snorted and raised the gun, flicking off the safety. "Plenty of space below for POWs, friend."

Eight. Seven.

"Okay. You're right. I'm not an indenture. I'm a birthright," Natalie lied. She had to keep him going for another seven seconds, and the best way to do that was to convince him that she might have actionable intel. Seven seconds was a fucking *year* when you were dealing with automatic boltfire. It was a lifetime with a bullet.

"What's your line, then?"

"My family is—" The memoria showed her a picture she'd seen on Tribulation, lit by flashlight in a dark, destroyed office. People with their arms around each other, a small girl wrapped in a rainbow blanket. Words. *"This Is My Family,"* scrawled in black marker, like a reminder. Reva Sharma had been on Bittersweet during the war, while doing work for the Sacrament Society, hadn't she? Could she eke a few more seconds out of that? The memoria whirred against her forehead. The words came out before she could stop them, pushed out by the sheer force of the memory and the strong immersion drugs.

"I'm from the Sharma line," she said.

Ward's voice crackled. "Six."

She saw the captain's gun waver for a moment. "Holy shit," he said.

"She's lying," said the soldier next to him. A woman. "Intel says Sharma died on *Phoenix,* and her entire line in the war."

"Intel's full of pinheads, Susan," said the captain.

Five. Four.

Susan growled. "My sister died on *Phoenix.* I should know."

"Really? For sure? The Aurorans didn't return her body, did they? What do you think we're *fighting* for?" She turned back to Natalie. "Look, what do you know? You give us something good, we can chat about your accommodations."

Natalie chose a version of the truth. "Reva Sharma lied to me. That's what I know. It stands to reason she'd lie to you."

One.

"You lying to us too?" Susan said.

As an answer, Natalie slipped her little finger into the trigger she'd set in the haptic rig, and pulled.

Most people assumed that Vai weapons were radically different from conventional bolts, bullets, and bombs. They were mostly correct—the powerful moleculars that did most of the killing in the war were incomprehensible, operational only when in direct contact with the Vai. The aliens' lesser kinetics, though, still responded to the laws of physics, to vectors and triggers, to impact and intent. Natalie expected the yawning ache she'd last felt when the blue screamer went off at Tribulation, the silent, terrible wash of bright green light that meant *detonation.*

The light was *red.*

It took her less than a moment to realize what was happening, and another moment to realize she couldn't do a thing about it.

"Run," she whispered.

"What the hell is that?" said the captain.

"Run," she repeated. The word choked against the panic in her throat, and any other answer would have been moot, anyway. It was too late. Within seconds, the puppet was drenched in blood-scarred radiance. The light crawled down her stolen arms, whipped up skeins of golden dust, careened out from the ground zero of her body—a red twist that torqued together like some devil's idea of rope.

Someone had switched out the kicker EMP with *Vancouver's* only redshift star.

"Mr. Ward—"

"You're fine," he responded.

"Disconnect me!"

"We're trying."

But she didn't disconnect. She closed her eyes, but the Ingest-quality renderbots Ascanio had recommended for the suit slammed the visuals straight into her brain. The drugs dragged her deeper into eyes-wide consciousness. She'd seen some shit working the ordnance teams in the Vai war: catareactors making peach fuzz of people's eyes and redoubt stars sending unholy fire through carotid arteries. She'd seen the gas of the greenhouse bomb on the battlefield at Cana snacking on soldiers' lungs and making soup of her bunkmates' bones. She'd seen the blue screamer itself, and the way it slipped up the spine, twisting the person apart at the vertebrae. She'd seen her friends die like this, on planet after planet, and on Tribulation itself.

But the redshift star.

Nobody had seen a redshift star work.

Nobody lived that long around a redshift star to know *how* it worked.

Natalie shook—violent, nauseous. Somewhere inside, she knew this had been inevitable. Applied Kinetics was all about the hope that wild Vai kinetics could be controlled and used in conventional warfare. But this—murder—hadn't been the plan. Her mission was supposed to go a completely different way. The plan had been to take the base with the EMP, then use the ready platoon to secure the weapons labs. Even now, that seemed off, stupid—boltfire could damage the labs' operational capacity. But the redshift star—

The star rolled out from the puppet's stomach cavity onto the ground with a muffled thump, like a badly aimed soccer ball. The roughly spherical weapon had a pockmarked surface more like an asteroid or a stone than a ball of gas. It bumped to a stop at the foot of the leader, and split in half.

He was the first to go, and he went screaming: the red light slipped out from the weapon and shattered in sixteen directions. Red light shot up his leg, slithered under his fingernails, flayed his skin, turned him into strips of meat, and finally into a fine red dust that twisted in a hot electric current.

The others turned to run. She watched from her knees, calling to *get me out, get me out, get me out,* but they'd pushed more drugs into her IV, and the thrum of reality was *so fucking loud,* banging around in her ears like gunfire. Rooted to the spot, she watched the Baywells die, cracked by red light, twisted apart into dust.

Above, she gulped down sweet air.

Vancouver air.

She was losing immersion. She knew was on the planet, at the center of the furnace, standing in the middle of a tornado of red and gold dust. But she was also back home staring down her father on the winter-swept plaza, and occupying a tiny slab bed on a troop transport going to Cana, and breathing back on *London* with Ash and the dead and the dust, and smiling across the *Twenty-Five* mess at a man she didn't recognize. Which was fucked up, because there hadn't been a man on *Twenty-Five*—

—but the break didn't last, *goddamn estrefurantoin.* The

humans before her turned from skin and bones into blood and dust, brief flares and candles, little explosions that burned bright and burst into darkness, the small bursts of wind sending the dust that was left into fading spurts around the landing gears and tail-pieces of the abandoned fightercraft. They were dying below her, too, the indentures who worked this mine, the innocents and the misfortunates, the Ashlans, the Natalies, people who knew that going corporate was the only way to get off starving Earth.

She remembered the alien on the concrete floor of the bugout bay on Tribulation, Ash telling her that *there's no such thing as a single Vai,* even as her gun spun hot, even as the inhuman silver blood swirled around her feet. *They didn't know we could die,* she'd said.

But Natalie knew.

Natalie should have known this, too—

She swayed where she stood, choking on a helpless anger hot enough to burn, struck with the inevitability of it all. Here she was, messing around with proxy rigs and kinetic weapons and other expensive bullshit, when Aurora had simply chosen the rawest of Auroran solutions—one that was efficient, effective, and cheap. Natalie would have thought of it herself, except she'd been to Tribulation. She'd *seen* efficiency when Ash triggered the *London* weapon—seen the blank-eyed bodies spinning in their tombs, just alive enough to breathe.

She'd *been* efficiency down in that bugout bay, the Vai that had attacked Ash bleeding out at her feet—

—and it had been stupid, stupid, stupid of her to think the Auroran executive board would actually leave the outcome of this battle up to a platoon of soldiers with guns when a more efficient solution was offered.

The noise tapered after a moment, and she placed her bor-rowed fingers against the ground, imagining what was happen-ing below.

"You're a monster."

A new voice. She whirled. The voice belonged to a man with brown eyes, close-cropped black curls, blue work pants, and an *Alien Attack Squad* swag shirt tight around his arms. He'd been standing behind Natalie the entire time, bare-handed and bare-headed, as if he weren't afraid of the proxy and the power crackling around her stolen body at all. The air on Bittersweet wasn't breathable, but he stood without a coldsuit, his chest rising and falling.

Her own suit still crackled with bright red light, fizzled and snapped with it. *He wasn't real. He couldn't be real,* she thought. *Unless*—

The last time she'd seen a human being survive the demolition of a Vai kinetic, it had been Ash, back on Tribulation. She'd been lined in blue, the light shoved down her throat, sparkling death at her heart. She'd *lived*. She'd lived because of what was done to her here on Bittersweet, below the surface of this cursed world.

"Who are you?" she croaked.

The man met her eyes across the distance. "You're a monster," he whispered, again.

"It's not my fault. I didn't do this." Her stomach crawled with unwanted guilt.

"It's never your fault, is it?"

Natalie's world twisted, and a liquid knot under her skull snapped, as if enough of the drugs had worn off to make her finally realize that *this was wrong, this was wrong, this was not her body, that they'd hijacked it to commit a war crime,* that she'd just—she'd just—*oh god, she'd just*—and the scratching yellow dust of Bittersweet spun away from her, fading from gold to black. The last thing she saw was the man still watching as she collapsed, still alive even as an entire world turned to dust.

3

Natalie landed back in her skin with a stumbling, half-caught scream. The mechanized arms of the rig scrambled to keep her upright, tweaking the IV in the port on the back of her neck. Pain settled between her shoulders like someone had inserted a fork and twisted her rhomboids like spaghetti.

Familiar hands freed her from the rig, helping her to the floor. She clawed at her face, unhooking the oxygen mask. A coarse wetness at her temples and her neck dripped into the hollow between her shoulders.

She tried to speak, to tell Ward and Ascanio that she was fine, because she was *always fine* in front of other citizens—but her mouth had other sounds in it, and her teeth were grit-choked with gold gravel and red death. Her stomach heaved, and she spat out chunks from her breakfast onto the floor of the lab. A headache as bright as a star clogged her vision. One of the doctors was yelling at Ward. Something like *it's immersion medicine, not a superhero cocktail.*

She spat on the ground, to rid herself of the taste of bodies and Bittersweet. "What—what happened?"

"The redshift sun caused a surge that severed our connection to the proxy," Ward said. "You started seizing in the suit. We lost your pulse, so I made the choice to bring you out before the drugs wore off. You nearly died."

Her tongue felt like cold rubber. "Turn on the feed."

Ward exchanged glances with Ascanio. "The proxy's fried, sir,"

Ascanio said. "We're just waiting for the infantry from *Savannah* to land right now. And you need medical attention."

"I'm fine."

"You were dead, sir," she said. "In fact, I'm not sure you're not—"

"Just stop." Natalie took a deep breath, then dragged herself to her knees, then her feet, shaking away an attending doctor's helpful, unwanted hands, choking down the indenture's typical refrain: *I don't want care, please, I'm fine.* That wasn't the case anymore, of course. She could get whatever *care* she wanted, but tradition was tradition.

The lab was clogged with people—mostly her techs, clustered around the interface controls, but there were also R&D brains she didn't recognize. The three janitors were still inexplicably present, quiet and swaying in the corner like they were too scared to ask to be dismissed. Ward hovered nearby, his forehead furrowed with wildly unprofessional worry. He tried to grab her hand, but she slapped it away.

"Hey." He blinked. "Take it easy."

Natalie shook her head. "In a minute," she said. "Right now, you're going to tell me why someone replaced the kicker EMP with my only redshift sun."

Nobody spoke.

"Anyone?"

She felt a frisson of nervous energy in her staff as they quieted. She cleared her throat, trying to channel her old captain, Kate Keller. "At least *one* of you useless fuckers can get me the infantry feed."

They were all dead silent now: her entire staff, doctors and techs and indentures. Even chatty Ascanio. One of the staff at the main interface waved a hand, and suddenly she was staring at Bitter-sweet, smoothed out by the suit's 2D renderbots on the screen in front of her. Flat as a pancake. Quiet as a desert.

She had been hoping it had all been a bad dream.

Natalie wiped the corner of her mouth with her sleeve and came back with a smear of blood. Her jaw ached. The view had changed. Instead of the puppet's view, she saw a multi-camera feed from the raid that followed. The puppet lay cracked and dead where she'd left it. Nearby, red dust kicked up in swirling, circular patterns, filling the quiet little indentations where people used to be.

One of the techs whooped.

"That's a one hundred percent kill zone," Ascanio said. "Far better than the war committee expected. You did it, sir. It's a win."

"You call that a *win*?" Natalie said, in the Keller voice, the one that brooked no room for an answer. She still expected someone else to be "sir," for someone else to stand up and give her orders.

But *she* was the one with the director's tags here.

The soldiers reached the front door of the Bittersweet mining complex, kicked it in, and shoved themselves into an orange-beige hallway decorated with photographs of smiling miners showing off the underground celestiumworks: machines that dug the rocks from the walls and sucked the precious mineral from the stone. There were no workers in sight.

Ash never smiled like that, she thought.

"Tech only." Natalie's voice was ice. "The plan called for a kinetic assault on base electronics using a kicker EMP, with soldier-to-soldier engagement to come when reinforcements landed. The plan was not to commit a fucking *war crime*."

Ward cleared his throat. "There was a call from the board about twenty minutes ago. Mr. Solano requested a different tactic, and the decision was made above our heads."

Natalie felt something black and wild ignite just behind her heart. "Why was I not on that call? This is *my* department. I make the decisions here. Who implemented the change?"

"I did," said Ascanio, in a near-whisper.

"They said we were going to lose *Savannah*," Ward said. "So—"

"Did they instruct you not to tell me?" she said, tasting blood on her tongue.

Ascanio expelled a shaky breath. At least two indentures exchanged glances.

"Not, ah, in those words, sir." Ward paused and stood beside her now, offering her gauze, and Natalie took it from his hand, spitting into it, still tasting blood.

The indentures in the corner swayed. A dark-haired girl choked back a sob, and one of the boys rubbed her back. She gulped, her face faintly pale, reflecting the stinking red suddenly crawling up in the corners of the camera. The dust of human life.

This is war, Natalie wanted to tell her, *and war ruins everything it touches. This is war and this is Aurora and this is who you are. It never gets better. Welcome to the rest of your life.*

"The rules of engagement don't cover this," Natalie said. "There were hundreds of indentures down there. Miners. Innocents. People who made the wrong choice when they took the long walk to their local recruiting offices. We want to fight, we fight human. We fight fair. We aren't the Vai. We don't *massacre indentures*. Someone is going to answer for what we just did, and it isn't going to be me."

Silence.

"Being as the decision was made over all of our heads, perhaps now isn't the time for a moral discussion we're not exactly allowed to have, Director," said Ascanio. "Expected or not, this mission just took down Baywell's major celestium depot and weapons development facility, and that's a major win. They were just indentures."

Natalie thought of Ash, smiling in the mess on *Twenty-Five.* Her old team. "Just," Natalie repeated, and the words were poison on her tongue, were every red drop of blood in her body. She ran a sweaty hand through her hair, and it came back drenched and stinking. God, she needed a shower. She needed a drink. She needed to prevent the memory of the redshift sun from scabbing over her entire future.

The memory device kicked in again. She remembered Ash's face, her friend's hands slicked with blood and silver, standing over the dead alien on Tribulation. Her words. *There's not just one—they don't live just one life—*

No. That had been impossible then. It was impossible now. The death of the alien colony wasn't her fault. Natalie couldn't have known. She still didn't quite believe it.

The redshift star wasn't her fault either.

Natalie focused on the transmission from the ground, watching the soldiers get off at an elevator, seeing the red dust pull into tiny swirls as the doors slid open. The soldiers waded through ankle-deep swaths of it, wondered aloud what it was. She thought of toggling the comm and telling them, then stopped in her tracks. Maybe it was better that they didn't know the dust used to be *people*. They could figure it out later.

She swallowed her growing anger. "The next time I hear you talking about innocent people like that, Mx. Ascanio, I'll have you sent back to Europa. This isn't some sort of bullshit assignment. The math is fucking *sacrosanct,* and nobody's disposable. *Just indentures.* God."

One of the cit techs jumped slightly, her shoulders hunching under her white coat, but she said nothing. Nobody met Natalie's eye except for Ward, his hair catching the ocean-blue colors of the lights above, his skin reflecting the yellow-red hell on the planetoid below. He wiped sweaty hands on his skirt.

"Em," she said, knowing she shouldn't use his nickname, knowing what it meant, knowing she didn't quite care. "Who on the board gave the order?"

He lowered his voice, clearly concerned for her. "Mr. Solano is still watching, sir."

"Let him," she said, louder, adjusting her jacket. "Maybe he saw the survivor, unlike the rest of you."

Ward blinked, the first slivers of doubt pushing into his voice. "There were no survivors, sir." He ran a shaking hand through his hair and turned to Ascanio. "I told you not to give her the whole syringe."

Ascanio stiffened. "We were well within the dosing guidelines."

Natalie's mouth was dry. Her lips tasted like bloody plasteel. She touched the memory device at her temple, felt the warmth, queried for something calming. It gave her an afternoon's break a few days before the Battle of Grenadier, sitting on the beach with her teammates, smoke in her mouth, the touch of salt air, the feeling of sand in her toes and the taste of contraband liquor on her lips, some citizen's stolen rotgut. *Calming. Right.* As calming as that Sacrament Society abattoir back on Tribulation.

"You wouldn't survive one day on a salvage craft," she said. "Corporate rules are fine until they try to kill you. And they will try to kill you. You goddamn *birthrights*."

Ascanio's mouth flattened in confusion. "Corporate rules—"

"—are the thin red line between civilization and anarchy, yes, you said that yesterday. And last week. And—" Natalie's stomach heaved. She retched, and Ward rubbed her back. She allowed that little comfort; it felt too good to ask him to stop. "There *was* a survivor. At least of the initial blast. He called me a monster. We know Bittersweet was the center of the Wellspring weapons program. And they've had a couple years without Alliance oversight. Who knows what they've accomplished?"

The room was silent, and she caught at least one or two of the techs raising their eyes toward the corners, where the black circular renderbots recorded everything in the room, sending it to the newly formed Ingest Department to be processed and used for development and discipline. The programming team had said Ingest wasn't panopticon surveillance—that Aurora was too big and too varied to run everything through an algorithm that wouldn't understand nuance—but Natalie had grown up in a software cult, and knew that it wasn't the programmers you needed to worry about, but the users. The users were executives. Assholes by definition.

At any rate, it didn't matter. She was a citizen now. Dissent was no longer a crime. A problem, yes. But not a crime.

Ward's hand finally lifted, and he waved at the indenture running the feed. The view shifted to earlier, to the last few seconds taken by the puppet camera, lying half-kilter on its side, facing the airstrip. She watched the last few runners pop like cherries, their skin turning to flags, their liquid blood dropping into trails of dry dust. She saw nothing else: no footprints, no bodies, no survivor.

"He was right there," she said. "Is the footage corrupted? Nobody saw him?"

Silence. Her hands shook.

"We're not doubting you," Ward said.

"You'd better fucking not." Natalie licked her lips and savored the tension in the room. Sometimes having a known temper was a good idea. She wanted to give in to the sudden rage she felt, the anger that burned constantly beneath her breastbone these days, the thing that curdled and wailed and shoved up her throat whenever she wanted to speak, but she'd had enough incompetent commanders to know she didn't want to be one herself. But Natalie couldn't invent a survivor if there wasn't one on-screen, and she felt the angry pang of having lost some sort of high ground with her staff before she even knew the battle was joined.

Was she hallucinating, then? Natalie went cold. Hallucinations were the only other reasoning Auroran science might accept.

They could be from the drugs she took, or—*impossible*—they could be celestium-induced hallucinations like Ash had described a little over a year ago on *London*'s freezing bridge. It made sense that a hallucination might occur on the planetoid that spat out broken citizens with debilitating neuropathies on a regular basis. But Natalie had never left *Vancouver.* And she'd certainly never voluntarily exposed herself to celestium.

"Nobody has any grand ideas?" she said, after a moment.

Ascanio winced. "Sir, nobody could have survived that."

"Yes, but—"

But there was another explanation, Natalie knew, one the others couldn't know. She felt a sudden breathlessness and an overwhelming exhaustion, and she started breathing quietly, steadily, trying to center herself. She thought of Ash, of the way the blue screamer had twisted around her spine on Tribulation, the way she'd come out of certain death with her skin clear and her eyes wet. The way that had been impossible before Natalie saw it happen with her own eyes. Natalie hadn't mentioned this before, hadn't wanted the department to know about Ash, hadn't wanted her sacrifice to be in vain.

But.

She took a breath.

"It's possible to survive Vai detonations, with the right exposure to celestium and the right medical tweaks. Those tweaks were developed here on Bittersweet. I've seen it."

Ascanio's mouth widened a bit. "Is that how you survived Tribulation? That's why you're wearing a memoria?"

"No," she said. "I thought you got over the 'I survived the alien superweapon and only lost half the memories of my life' bullshit."

"Of course, sir, but—" Ascanio licked her lips. "It's just that you might be overlooking the simplest, most obvious explanation. Since you've had exposure to this kind of Vai-based brain injury before, I'm actually concerned the memoria itself was the cause of your seizure. It might explain what you saw. I'm worried that you'll put yourself at risk for further brain damage if you use the rig again. And I really suggest you go to the medbay."

Blood welled between Natalie's back teeth. *I've had worse,* she wanted to say. She'd been hauled screaming out of an alien-induced coma and lived to tell the tale, even if her temporal lobe resembled a pasta colander. But Ward's eyes were dark and concerned, and even though their relationship was largely casual, she still hated to disappoint him.

"Fine," she said. "And someone take these poor bastards back down to Janitorial."

"Don't you remember?" said Ascanio. "We were told to send them to R&D afterward. For the upgrade."

"Whatever." Natalie turned to the indentures. They were young, all of them, as young as she'd been when she thought going corporate was the best way out of her shitty tiny life. They held each other, stared at the floor or the wall or anywhere but at her. If she hadn't stepped in, it would have been one of them in the suit, and they knew it. They owed her, and knew she could collect. Somehow, the weight of that responsibility made her feel worse than any of the drugs burning their way out of her system.

Best to do what citizens did best and pass it off up the chain.

"Just—" she said, licking her dry lips. "Sorry to muck up your entire day, but I don't have any control over this. It's really the board's fault."

I don't have any control over this. The worst thing you could say to an indenture, the absolute worst thing. She steadied herself on the back of a chair, dizzy-woozy and angry and embarrassed, and strode off to the medbay without another word.

4

The anger was back.

No. The anger was always there, making barbecue of Natalie's heart, rattling around in the space between beats. This time, however, it barged in holding hands with guilt and wearing a garland of ruin, pushing her through the busy corridors at a brisk pace. It made her old *talk to me and I'll end you* face easy to pull off.

It was nice that the news cycle had largely moved on from its inexplicable focus on Natalie Chan, Genius War Hero. There were regular photographs of her on the Company announcement stations—the ones where they'd made her up in lines of thick black eyeliner, blue lipshade, and—ugh, the worst—heavy matte powder for her topaz skin. This was *Vancouver*, where she was the war hero who destroyed the Vai infestation on the planet and uncovered the work of their human collaborators.

That wasn't entirely true, of course. It was the story the board told, and she supposed it was true enough. *True enough* was easy to swallow but would choke her if she spent too much time with it.

She bit her bottom lip until embarrassment distracted her long enough to drag the sudden tears away from her eyes—tears, like an absolute fucking *child*. When she felt composed enough, she checked the optikals above, as if daring Ingest to send security after her, and moved down the corridor that led back to her small apartment.

She still had pride; an indenture's pride, a pride in being independent even when her entire life was ruled by the contract

she'd signed. Natalie lived through the Vai war, walked off battlefields so full of slaughter that she was glad the alien weapon
ripped those memories from her mind. Going to the medbay for
getting knocked around a bit in a puppet rig felt like overkill.
Her hands flew up to touch her cit tags; as a citizen, health care
was affordable to her now. Citizenship was the very thing Ash
had desired most. Going to the medbay was what Ash would
have wanted her to do.

You had a seizure, Ward said, only it felt more like a *flashback,*
and damn that man for lying to her, and damn the stupid Company psychologist who'd told her what that word meant. She
pressed her fingers against the memoria and it gave her Marley's
spine torn apart by a blue screamer, gave her the darkness of Ash's
weapon dissolving her mind back on the battlefield. Gave her
the choice once more: kill the alien or lose Ash.

That choice. Her finger on the trigger in the bugout bay, placing Natalie between what was and what would be.

She'd chosen Ash. She'd chosen right.

Of course she'd chosen right.

And here was the other thing she couldn't stop thinking about:
that she might be the only soldier in the entire war who had
actually *killed an alien.* She hadn't known that when she was on
Cana and Grenadier, wading knee-deep through the dust and
viscera, doing her part to save humanity. Nobody knew then that
the alien constructs she and her fellow soldiers gave their lives to
cut down were no better than broken hard drives.

She and Ash had discovered that the Vai themselves were
made of light and memories, collective beings that colonized
bodies like humans occupied starships, moving in and out of
a shared consciousness of sorts through the weapon Ash had
found in the wreckage of *London.* Natalie had kept her secret
all these months: that the thing wasn't a weapon at all, but an
organic consciousness-transfer machine that took its charge from

the environment around it, from planets and stars and batteries and living things and everything the Vai didn't need to survive. To the Device, as Natalie had come to think of it, ordinary, un-infected humans were just another power source to draw upon. The detonation at Tribulation had nearly killed her, leaving her mind pockmarked with aching black swaths where her memories should be.

She had not killed. Not one Vai, not the entire time. She'd been just another victim in the galaxy's bloodiest con job, until she'd killed the alien on Tribulation.

Until she'd killed human beings this morning.

The black, broken clarity grabbing her throat couldn't be guilt. Natalie didn't allow herself to feel guilt. She was a soldier. An ordnance engineer. Death was her job. They'd scrubbed guilt out of her neocortex during training, and if any was left it had been tossed aside with her friends' bodies on burning Grenadier.

No. Whatever this was, it was worse than guilt.

She was breathing hard. Too hard. Ingest might pick that up, flag it, and a messenger would be dispatched from the medbay to check on her. Ash would have laughed in shrieking gales at that level of attention. Natalie had been flagged more than once in the last month, so maybe they'd send security, too, just to make sure she wasn't too broken. She was a Company investment now. She was important, important enough to monitor, important enough to care for. Thinking about Ingest felt like spiders crawling up her back; she'd had much less surveillance during her wartime indenture, but that was before haptics, before *superhaptics*, before renderbots as ubiquitous as stiletto heels.

A commotion of corporate security officers in newly printed blues stepped through the nearest hatch, and her old instincts found her back flat against the wall before she remembered she didn't have to do that any longer. They rushed by like they were on a mission, four of them in quick succession, flanking a duo of quiet, confused cargo workers wearing indenture tabs. She watched them all stop before a door labeled SUPERHAPTIC UP-DATE LAB, and Natalie blinked. Had that door even been there before? Hadn't that been a biologics lab? Had that been before the last mission? Was she forgetting new things now?

A mission. Natalie's mind seized on that thought. She could do that. She imagined her own door as the mission target, searched for her old armor in the memoria, saw how it clapped around her shoulders and her chest, felt the weight of a gun in her hand, set back out on her way to her compartment. *Eyes on the prize, stay on target. Don't cry. Don't err. Don't let them see you bleed.*

And then she was through her compartment door, the burning knot in her chest unraveling as soon as she was alone.

Alone.

She'd had her own space on *Twenty-Five*—barely more than a cot and a cubby, and only because of the disastrous early journeys that made it clear that having some privacy on long-haul salvagers was a psychological need rather than a want. But, otherwise, she hadn't ever really been alone. Not with Verdict. Not in the barracks later on. Certainly not on *Twenty-Five*.

Verdict. She felt an unwelcome pang of nostalgia. She still wanted to call the hacker collective home, because she had been born there, because it had been just about ten years since she'd walked off that gray plaza in the snapping November wind, the weight of snipers in the skyscrapers above no longer a comforting one. *When you leave,* her father had said, *you don't come back.*

I get it, she'd said, hope in her heart. *That's the whole idea.*

Hope.

In the corporations, *hope* was a citizen's privilege. So was being alone. The stupid shit she'd wanted her entire life. *A fucking palace,* Ash might have called her room. A real bed. Cold storage for food—food she could save, food she could choose, could stuff in her mouth while stretched out on the aforesaid real bed. A gray couch, a dark blue table, a place to keep her things, now that she could have things. Cits called it *tiny*, muttered about the *shit accommodations* on these big new flagships, but to Natalie, the compartment was too big, rattling with shadows and silence.

The only thing missing was all of her stuff—the stuff that mattered, at least. That had all disappeared with *Twenty-Five*. Her favorite boots. The picture of her old fire team on the beach after training. The other photos she'd printed on Europa because she couldn't have cloudspace out here. Her father's sweater, which didn't really fit her anymore, but still smelled like concrete and flame.

The best part of her new room was the lack of optikals and renderbots in the ceiling, tracking how Natalie slept, what she ate, who she talked to. She had a bath closet of her own. Her very own interface.

Which was blinking.

Natalie tossed her jacket over the couch, collapsed there, told the interface to play her messages, and unhooked the front plate of her memory device. It was blinking, as always. She poked it, not expecting much. It responded by humming against her skin. She didn't see anything wrong with it, but then again, she wasn't a neurotech, and the memory device wasn't a Vai bomb. She didn't really know how it worked—the faceplate she held or the parts buried in her brain beyond the plate screwed into her skull. Natalie had done what she could to rejigger the device's code to increase the speed of recall or the memory storage, but biohacking techniques had progressed since her days in Verdict, and she always stopped short of breaking it.

Natalie had been given the device a few days into her recovery after Tribulation, when she was still half-drugged and shaking from the rescue, unable to keep a thought in her mind for over ten minutes. The memoria was a more complicated version of a citizen's info-implant, modified by R&D to keep her alive. *Average citizens probably won't be able to tell the difference,* they'd said, *and you can still decorate it,* like they thought that would have been at all a thing she'd be interested in.

She knew having the memoria installed was a risk, but the alternative was forgetting everything she'd ever known. It was one of just a few experimental prototypes, and she imagined those usually went to people the company wouldn't miss too much if the experiment went wrong. But she'd done this kind of thing before—you had to test your own tech on yourself, to keep respect in Verdict—and Natalie figured if she ended up frying her brain for good, it wouldn't feel any worse than the time she couldn't remember her own name.

The installation was done while she was awake, like most neurosurgery, and she'd seen the faces of the scientists gathering around her cracked-open skull, heard their whispers. It was strange to think that she was at the center of their hopes and dreams, that she got to carry and use this brand-new, lifesaving technology without having to pay anything for it. Not one credit. Not one extra day of her life. No smuggling of questionable painkillers, no backroom trades, no suffering through injuries not accrued "in the line of duty." No Dr. Sharma pushing the hatch closed in her face instead of treating her nausea. The memoria was hers because of the simple, plain fact that she was now a citizen and worthy of the company's money and time.

The memoria was supposed to help her feel secure about the memories that still remained in her hole-punched head, as well as knit together thoughts that had been torn apart. It operated like an old-style search algorithm of sorts, calling up fading memories when she needed them—but it didn't always behave, and it would sometimes offer up visions and thoughts she didn't want at all. Sometimes it would try for a memory she'd lost entirely, return a blank, and her field of vision would swim and scatter and go gray. She'd slammed into more than one pylon that way, like an embarrassed human pinball.

It's in beta, the doctors would say when she complained, and yeah, she'd grown up in a software cult, she *knew* beta like a prayer, but the Verdict hackers had been better at beta with shittier technology than the supposedly cutting-edge Auroran R&D.

A few weeks into their relationship, Emerson would give her info-diamonds as a courting gift, and she'd try to install them near the memoria and end up in the medbay with horrible flashbacks. She spent a few days supposedly stuck in the mud on Cana, blood in her mouth, her skin tearing, watching her platoon burn behind her. It was at that point that R&D told her that upgrades and decorations needed to be done in the medbay, that they were *sorry,* which was odd, because Emerson and Ascanio loaded updates on their own.

No doctor had ever told her they were *sorry* before. You didn't tell indentures you were sorry. It was tongue-snapping delicious, that *sorry.* Almost worth the pain.

Natalie flagged the thought to remind herself to see about routine neuromaintenance, then started paying attention to her messages, slapping the memory device back into her face. She rarely received personal messages. This one was from Node 73, Arpeggio Station, the last *fucking* thing she wanted to deal with today. She thumbed the play button anyway.

The older man on the other end—her father, who had been going by a codename, Xie, when she left Verdict—smacked his thin, wrinkled lips together, and began to speak. His hair was a slushy gray run through with void-black vestiges of a lost youth, and he'd kept the wrinkles on his forehead and his cheeks despite the aesthetic offers that had doubtlessly been made during his Auroran onboarding. Xie had been planetborn to the core, a Verdict sniper since he was fourteen. He'd inexplicably entered Armour three years after Natalie left, despite a lifetime of screaming *fuck the corps* at the skyscrapers by the river and refusing to eat the rations distributed by the area's Auroran sponsor. She knew this not because she *remembered* much of it, or of him, but because of the notes still in the central file from Natalie's own onboarding interview.

Fucking Tribulation.

The years had spotted Xie's face and arms with brown smudges and smears. Natalie wondered about the curves of his face, flattened into shadows over the ansible video connection, wondered if he would hug warm and hard or long and loose, or not at all.

Natalie, he said. *It's been a year. I don't understand why you paid to stick me here if you weren't going to talk to me. I traded six days for this call.*

He sighed, looked off-screen, then continued.

They tell me you're okay, that you're on Vancouver, *that you're doing important work. Life is fine here. The food is fine. Everything else is stupid. I can't work on anything without having to turn it over to the fucking company. I did this for you, Nati. What the hell do I have to do to get you to talk to me?*

A second sigh.

I'm ready to talk about your mother, if that's what it takes. Call me.

Natalie paused the recording. Reached up to the memory device, tapped it, waited for the blank answers that just weren't there. Looked at her own reflection: her face, her fingers, the long, straight white scar on her neck.

She just didn't know what she would say to Xie if she called back. She'd found her father's name in the Armour uncitizen rolls, paid off his indenture debt with her bonus from Tribulation, and used the rest to secure him a warm place to sleep, because Armour was a terrible place to be old. The memory device told her that he'd spent most of her childhood getting drunk because of Natalie's mother, aside from the brilliant sober moments when he'd taught her how to shoot, to code, to swear. He was the one who told her she couldn't come back if she left Verdict, then left himself.

Hypocrite.

Xie was wrong. Natalie didn't want to know about the mother who had walked away when she was too young to remember her. Natalie had rescued Xie for a far more selfish reason.

She wanted to know about *herself.*

Natalie knew she was one of the lucky ones. When Ash's weapon was triggered at the end of the Second Battle of Tribulation, she'd been on a shuttle hurtling away from *London,* empty-handed and lying like a rug to her team of combat engineers about killing Ash. She didn't even know she'd been caught in the area of effect until she woke up in a Company medbay for the nth time, the ache of the memory device newly drilled through her skull.

In the days that followed, she put herself back together like a puzzle with a hundred missing pieces. She spent days scrolling through Auroran corporate records for her name, or references to Verdict. Her unhelpful linksave list (why *had* she marked so many *Alien Attack Squad* jokes?). She trolled through news holos from the war, filling her eyes with the death and destruction she'd forgotten. The memory device helped shore up what was already there, making connections, filling in details, noting blanks. The curved outline of a teammate at mess. The metal tang of a ship's recycled air. The rough fabric of an EVA suit. She'd lost whole chunks of stuff she'd learned as a kid, like coding in ellis-b and the layout of the Concourse (although she still knew C-kalibre and starslip). Losing that was almost a mercy.

But there were some things only Xie would know, and she was still too scared to ask.

The doorbell chimed. She felt a sudden, embarrassed flush, and walked over to the door, palming the lock. Her visitor was Emerson Ward, his smile crooked, his brown eyes and jagged nose hiding behind a shock of too-long saffron hair, and oddly symmetrical birthright's lips regarding her from an angle. His collar was loose and his jacket unbuttoned, and one hip canted slightly against the doorjamb.

"You said you were going to the medbay," he said.

"I did say that," she said, deadpan, moving to close the door in his face.

"Wait." He pressed his palm against the door to stop her. "You were pretty hard on the staff today. And me. We're not indentures. You can't just swear at citizens like that."

"What, do you want me to apologize? After—after—" She couldn't say it. She couldn't swallow. All she could do was keep herself from shaking. "After. You let Ascanio push me way too much ester. You *ordered* it."

"It was dangerous to disconnect you. You know this."

The memory device helpfully supplied a rush of red dust, and for a moment she felt it choking her, coating her tongue. She shook the cobwebs away from her head. "They made me do it. But you made me *watch*."

He shoved his hands in his pockets and looked away. "I get why you're angry. That was a shit move by the board, Nat."

"I'm not angry. I'm furious. Do you understand why they wanted a full indenture for the mission now? They needed someone who couldn't say no."

Ward pushed in slightly, blocking the light from the corridor.

"Like I said. Shit move."

"Is that all you're going to say?"

"Let me in."

He crossed his arms, leaning on the doorjamb. She felt a tight truth loosen in her chest. She wanted to tell him no, to *fuck off*, but he had that unguarded look he usually had post-shift, the last time they'd had a close moment. Not that she could afford close moments as a recently turned cit with everything to prove.

It was the kind of look that could shake down her walls in seconds.

"Fine," she said, sighing. "Come in, as long as you leave your ulterior motives outside."

"I never have ulterior motives."

Natalie grinned. "Fuck you."

"I live in eternal hope," he quipped.

She stepped aside. As he walked in, Natalie noticed the sweat beading slightly at his temples, his fingers fiddling with the zipper hovering at the base of his jacket. *No ulterior motives, my ass*, she thought.

They'd met six months ago in the hot, crowded darkness of one of the citizen lounges. He'd leaned in, smelling of sweat and cologne, and she'd felt wrong and indentured and lucky and drunk as hell. She'd tilted her chin, appreciated the slight curl to his hair, enjoyed the way he walked. She'd liked how he made her feel human again. Their relationship was everything she wanted in the wake of Tribulation. Casual. Quiet. A little hot.

Natalie ran her hand through her own shorn hair. An indenture's style, still. She couldn't let it go. Short hair was comfortable, easy to wash, manageable. She should let it grow out, learn how to twist it up into buns and curls and whatever spiky bullshit the bridge officers were into that season, like Ward's long, curling sweep down the edge of his whip-curve jaw. "Did they get to the weapons wing?"

"They did," he said, collapsing against the sofa, ignoring the fact that he was crushing her jacket. "We're securing the labs right now. And it's all because of you."

Her shoulders seized. She imagined soldiers getting off at an elevator, the red dust pulling into smoky, glistening swirls on a helmet HUD.

"I need a shower," she said, slapping her thighs and standing.

"Stop walking away from this," he said.

"I'm not."

"You won. Take the win."

"I—" Her throat seized. "That was winning?"

"Nat—"

The words came out before she could control them. "At least with the Vai, the war was just. The war was necessary. What happened this morning was just plain murder."

He sighed. "Aren't you the one who told me that the tactic that wins is the tactic we should use?"

"That was during the Vai war. We are not the Vai. We don't wipe out innocent people because they happen to be in the same vicinity as a hard target."

"Then why did you agree to run Applied Kinetics?"

She had no immediate answer for that; her mouth worked, and she dropped angry hands into her lap, expelling a quick breath. The conversation was rapidly passing her threshold of casual, and she didn't like how uncomfortable it made her feel. "That's not fair."

He joined his hands tight enough for his knuckles to go white. "The purpose of Applied Kinetics is to develop technologies based on Vai weaponry, which exists to kill human beings. And right now, Baylor-Wellspring exists to kill *us*."

"I know," she sighed, giving up.

"Maybe you should talk to someone about this."

"I'm talking to you."

"We're . . ." He pressed his lips together, then patted the couch next to him. "Complicated. Which is what I actually came here to talk to you about."

She sank into the space next to him. "I stink. Your funeral."

"You're fine." He took a deep breath and made a face. "Look, you're not used to this, which is why I'm going to explain. You're going to get a lot of personal contract proposals over the next few weeks, once everyone in the Company learns you were behind the raid. I just . . . want you to consider mine first."

"You're *proposing*?" She flushed, suddenly nauseous. She felt a crashing, overwhelming desire to kick the earnest look on his face into the nearest trash chute.

"You know we'd be good together," he said. "Our work is just going to get more important from here. With my connections and your visibility, we could easily parlay this into the executive track. Both of us could—"

Dizziness roared, and she blinked, unable to listen. Her jaw slowly opened, in shock, and she found she could barely look at him. "You think that question is appropriate right now? This is literally how you're going to ask?"

"Just think about it. You can have kids, now that you're a citizen. With me involved, they'll be birthrights. They can go to a proper school on Europa while we crack the executive track. We can go places, Natalie."

"*Children*? I thought we were just having fun."

He tilted his head in surprise and reached for her hand. "We are, which is why we should go ahead with this."

"I can't even believe you."

"I know it's not what you're used to where you come from, but—"

She sighed, rolled her eyes, and pushed off, leaving him standing by the couch. She shoved her hand in her pocket. "Out."

His eyes widened. She thought she registered genuine surprise. "I thought you'd be happy," he said.

"It's nice of you to ask," she lied, hoping it would make him leave.

It did not. "There's someone else. Ascanio? I mean, we only have to contract for a year or two if you want—"

"That asshole?" she said, frustration building. "Okay, the answer's not no, but it's just—not a good time for me to discuss this. Maybe when Baywell surrenders. It's not you. It's not anything you've done. And we are . . . I'm just . . ."

"I get it," he said, after a moment, with a dark look on his face that said he most certainly did not. "But I'm not going to wait forever."

"I get it. You're going places."

"And so are you. We could go together."

"I know."

He kissed his fingers and brushed them against her shoulder as he walked to the door, and she stiffened at his touch. He paused, as if he wanted to say something else, then pulled the door open. She wanted to feel something, wanted to feel heat, a spark, anger, disgust, love or lust. She wanted to *feel*.

I should be happy he's interested, she thought, closing the door. *He's a nice guy. I should just say yes for a year, forget to tell him I'm never going to get my reprocontrol removed, go to all the Ward-line parties, squeeze what I can out of it.*

But all she could think about was that his skin was the wrong color, his laugh the wrong shade, that his wrists were thin and his chin too *different,* that his humor lacked a particular edge. That he wasn't—someone else. Someone faceless, someone forgotten. Someone lost.

The door rang.

She popped up, apologies on her lips, and opened the door again.

"Em, I'm sorry—"

"Tell the executives."

When she looked up, her belly unclenching, she found herself face to face with Cora Aulander, the board's tight-lipped personnel director.

"Come with me, please," Ms. Aulander said.

"I was going to take a shower," Natalie replied.

"Sorry," she said, shrugging slightly, as if Natalie's filthy state wasn't her problem. "They want you right away."

5

Aulander's info-implant was an understated matte gold—awfully drab, compared to the screeching embellishment usually favored by Auroran executives and their striving hangers-on. As they walked, Natalie stared at the executive's tight-fitting, ruby-studded jacket, her briarpatch eyes, the ship-pallid hands that had lost any sense of planetside glow. She dredged through her memoria to find some appropriate small talk that would be both practical and complimentary, some of the quietly obsequious shit she learned from her former ship's exec, Alison Ramsay, back before Ramsay had betrayed *Twenty-Five* to Baywell. The personnel director remained calmly unmoved through the walk, responding in polite half statements, until she turned a corner, palmed an unassuming door lock, and ushered her bodily into a boardroom.

Any thoughts that Natalie would be taken up to the executive level died as soon as she saw who was inside.

"Be welcome, Ms. Chan. Please, sit down," said Joseph Solano, Aurora Intergalactic's CEO.

The boardroom itself looked fairly executive, plush in that rich, Earthbound way she was still becoming accustomed to, drenched in wooden accents, comfortable seats, and a kind, yellow glow, light-years away from the bare metal and bright rooms of her indenture and the charcoal concrete and crumbling marble of her childhood. It made her itch, made her grind her teeth. How had they arrived here? Had this room been here the whole time? What else was hidden behind *Vancouver*'s quiet gray doors? Was the executive level so sacrosanct that the entire fucking board had put this room here just to talk to citizens? Natalie cast her gaze around, suddenly aware of the tightness of her muscles, the twist of her spine, the half-hunched position of her back, and met the calm eyes and blank faces of the Auroran executive board.

The men and women who had thought switching out her perfectly good plan with a last-minute war crime would be a fabulous idea.

The rig-induced kinks in her back flared up, and Natalie winced in response. If cits were lucky, they met the CEO once or twice in their lives, at promotion ceremonies or recognition luncheons. Never so close. Never in a boardroom like this. And never in front of the *whole fucking board*.

She thought of the kowtow crap she'd tried on Aulander earlier, and pushed it to the side. That wasn't going to get her out of this because nobody was brought in front of the entire board to be praised. Her cit tags lay heavy against her throat.

Citizens didn't have to bow.

So she stared instead.

At Solano, at his dark brown hair, at the way the wrinkles crowding his eyes grew darker with the deepening of his frown. At the fact that he was gaining wrinkles at all, in a roomful of people who looked like they spent half their day getting anti-aging treatments. He wasn't like the others—*and maybe it was the height of power, to know you could let yourself go a little,* Natalie thought. To be secure enough to allow the existence of the lines creasing the corner of his mouth as he gave her a solemn battering ram of a smile.

"You will want to sit," he repeated.

Natalie slid into the offered chair exactly like her old captain Kate Keller taught her, swinging one ankle over the other, folding her blood-cracked palms over the nearest knee, feeling hot and nauseous. This was a trap. It was almost certainly a trap.

The executives—eight of them, skinny fuckers in blue suits, their diamond rings catching the starlight outside—stared right back, clearly bored. She thought that they'd be happier about her involvement with the afternoon's "win," but maybe permanent bitchface was the price you paid for becoming an executive.

"Do you know why you're here?" said Mr. Solano.

Stop this patronizing indenture bullshit and just tell me, Natalie wanted to say. Instead, she twisted her lips like she'd just sucked down a lemon. Her hand flashed up to brush her cit tags again, to remind herself that she had license to speak.

"Let me guess, sir," she said. "You're going to apologize for what you made me do this afternoon."

One of the executives—Vidal, she thought, her thick yellow hair drawn up in a complicated pile—laughed out loud, then exchanged glances with Solano. "That's an . . . interesting theory, but no."

"The operation was properly planned between Applied Kinetics, Ground Operations, and Fleetcomm," Natalie said, hoping she sounded more stable than she felt. "We all agreed that an EMP kicker would have taken out threats while leaving noncombatants alive, which was the goal."

Raynor Stephenson, the host of *Corporate Idol*—spindly fingers, sharp chin, eyes so blue they might have been newborn-gray, the most recognizable of the others—spread his fingers palm-down against the table. "The goal, Ms. Chan, was to control Baylor-Wellspring facilities on Bittersweet. The *only* goal. I understand you don't agree with what was done. There was a reason we sent down a set of perfectly capable full indentures to run the suit. Was it our fault you chose differently?"

"They weren't capable."

Stephenson opened his mouth to respond, but Solano lifted his hand, ostentatious rings glinting in the overhead light. "Was it our fault you chose to go of your own free will?" he said.

Natalie winced. "I didn't know about the change in plan. It was manipulative."

"We followed Company policy. Did you?"

"No, sir." She wanted to disappear into the shining floor. "But—"

"And that's the problem with you, Ms. Chan," Solano said. He sighed, then brought his hands together in a loud clap that made her nearly jump in her chair. "You don't trust Company policy to guide your decisions."

"That's not true, sir," she said. "Shipboard Company policy is that experienced personnel should take lead on crucial matters."

Solano's eyes narrowed on her; his left index finger tapped out a quick, bothered tattoo on the desktop. "Shipboard Company policy is that you follow directions given to you by the captaincy, shipside officers, and members of the board," he said. "We're not having this discussion, not when you've refused treatment for ester intoxication, and you're technically still *high*."

Natalie recoiled as if she'd been slapped. "Was it Company policy to inject that much ester into my system in the first place, and then call me to a meeting in front of the entire board when they knew I just needed to sleep it off?"

"You would have made a different decision, if you'd been in command of the mission?"

"Of course."

He smiled, mirthless. "But you weren't in command. And here you are, still complaining about it like you don't know any better. I thought I could trust you. I had you on tap to be elevated. Instead, I find—" He shrugged, trailing off, and Natalie realized, with growing horror, that she'd said all the wrong things. "We'll send some detox tea with you on your way to Tribulation."

All Natalie could manage was a quiet, shocked "What?"

"We're sending you to Tribulation."

"No, sir," she said. Her cit tags felt like anvils. "I'm a citizen. I can refuse."

Solano traded a silent glance with Aulander. The blond woman glided over to the interface. She reached into her pocket, located a small personal drive encrusted with diamonds, and activated the drive reader.

The room burst into light. On the table interface before her was a scattering of stars in a pattern even the Earthbound knew: the famous view from the most important building in human history, the intercorporate comm station that monitored the White Line. Beyond it lay the roiling violet-white nebula and Vai space, where humans had never gone.

Ships gathered there.

Alien ships, Vai ships, wearing clammy silver hulls, their sharp lines tracing the thin arc of a dancer's outstretched arm. Ships humming the hulking beat of *vvvvaaaaiiiiiiii* and bristling with the kind of death that she could never forget, the kind of bright fear etched into her being at the cellular level even as the memory weapon ripped everything else away.

She felt a stab of inchoate terror. "Is that real? That—that can't be real."

"It's quite real. We could not afford to lose Bittersweet today, Ms. Chan. The survival of our company is at stake. We need people who can fight the Vai, and for that, we need the technology that made Ashlan Jackson. We need to fight them on *their* terms this time, with weapons that can deal actual damage to their ships and soldiers. Unless you would trust Baylor-Wellspring to lead the fight that will come?"

"No, sir," she whispered.

Solano nodded. "I am glad we agree. Because this, Ms. Chan, is real as well."

He waved his hand, and the interface changed, from wild, un-believable photographs to a standard medical interface—similar to something she'd last seen when recovering from hypothermia on *Rio de Janeiro* after Wellspring agent Alison Ramsay's be-trayal of *Twenty-Five.*

Natalie's heart banged fast and wild in her ears. She felt like the others could hear it echoing through the room, rattling the floor under her boots, and flushed—until she realized that they could, and that it wasn't her heart at all, but a recording fed through the renderbots above.

"I don't understand," she said.

Solano nodded. "You thought you would get away with it. You thought you could ascend to citizenship while protecting one of the worst criminals Aurora has ever known—a human being, if we can even call her that, who murdered hundreds of Auroran citizens and indentures in one remorseless breath to rob us of what we legally owned."

"I—criminal? Sir, I—"

The CEO raised his hand, and Natalie's stammered protest died behind her teeth. Her confusion was replaced with a nau-seous certainty. The heartbeat in the recording thrummed, dragged at her molars, echoed her own heart. It was ragged, half-pathetic, sick. She knew who it belonged to. She'd heard it before, on the bridge of *London,* wrapped in a blanket as they waited for *Rio de Janeiro* to answer their distress call, her arm linked in Ashlan's, her frostbit thumb pressing tight against the outside of her former friend's wrist.

"Our cruiser working the Tribulation battlefield picked up this broadcast coming up from the planet. Ingest identified it as the heartbeat of Ashlan Jackson, transmitted by the monitors we installed the last time she was on *Rio.* Ms. Chan, you told us she was dead by your hand on *London* due to an accident and that her body could not be retrieved. That's the story you gave your team, at least. The funny thing about that is that none of them saw it happen. You sent them away."

"Sir, I—"

"Save it," he said. "You lied."

Natalie straightened her back. "I did what was best for the Company."

"It's not for an indenture to make that decision," Solano said. "Misrepresentation is cause for termination. Think very carefully about what you want to say next."

Natalie fought an electric shiver that made her want to bolt, to fight, to drag herself up and gash the pretty wooden table with her diamond-bright fingernails. Instead, she nearly bloodied her tongue with a bite from her back molar and let the mounting dread paste her body to the chair. Solano was leaning on her old indenture's instinct to tell the truth, but *which* truth? Watching Ward and the executives had taught her that truth only went one way. What they fed to her was more like a *story*. Perhaps she could get away with her own *story* now that she was a citizen. Part of the truth. Enough to pass the test he was presenting her with.

Enough to help Ash.

"I did what was best for the Company," she repeated. "She wasn't going to come along quietly and I wasn't going to shoot her for it. But you wouldn't give me a direct order to *murder* a shipmate, would you, sir?"

A nasty frisson went through the board at this, their heads looking this way and that, at this member of the board and the next without even the courtesy of a whisper, and Natalie realized that the executives were talking to each other somehow— maybe through the new superhaptic upgrades the Company was in the process of installing everywhere. She flushed, sitting up straighter. Her old drill instructor's voice came out of nowhere. She jumped in her chair. *Show 'em you're Auroran, you fucking niblets.*

Solano pursed his lips again, his eyebrows raised. "That's not the order I gave you, no." He paused. "Unfortunately, we no longer have time to figure out the arcane and archaic technology below. We need a template. We need Ashlan. *Now.*"

"If I'd been allowed to use the kicker today, we'd have people to interrogate about that. We might even have an actual template body to work from."

The youngest board member, Aileen Amberworth, wore coarse black hair ribboned so tightly Natalie thought she might be trying too hard. She cleared her throat and tapped on the table.

"Ms. Chan," she said. "It's very clear even from our earliest investigations that Baylor-Wellspring wasn't able to reconstruct the experiments that led to Ashlan's continued existence. If they did, there would have been survivors. There were not. So you'll take a small team to Tribulation, retrieve Ashlan Jackson, and bring her home."

"Sir, I have the puppet rig project to finish—"

Solano nodded. "Mr. Ward can do that. You are the only one who can command a mission to Tribulation. Nobody else knows the area like you, and on top of that, you have military experience. We have actionable intelligence from our cruiser *Beijing* that both Baylor-Wellspring and InGen are already present on-planet. *Everyone* has seen the ships massing at the White Line. With that kind of threat, the exclusion zone might as well be a fairy tale."

Natalie resisted the urge to roll her eyes. "Intelligence couldn't keep the spies out?"

"Nobody can keep the spies out, Ms. Chan. Not with something this big. You can only attempt to get ahead of the game." He sighed. "No matter why she chose to flee with that weapon, Ashlan is still one of ours. We need her more than ever, and she needs us. And—"

"She's not going to want to come."

Solano cleared his throat. "That does not matter. And *you* need us, unless you'd like to be reassigned to another seven years of indenture to make up for what you took from honest, hardworking Aurorans."

Natalie's shoulders felt wire-tight as she cast around for a way out. "She might be too sick to move."

A third board member clapped his hands together—Alistair Coriolis, she guessed, from the distinctive tornado-tight birthright tattoos that spiraled up the left side of his neck and around his long fingers. "We're sending a medic with you. She's part of the team that developed a—what did you call it, Joseph? A treatment?—for her condition. With the memory device and our recent superhaptic developments, we can keep her alive long enough to develop a real cure. Which we will give her free of charge."

"She won't believe that."

"She will if it comes from you."

Natalie stayed quiet for a moment before responding. "How long is 'enough'?"

"Four months. Five."

Natalie nodded. Her eyes went back to the video from the White Line playing on the interface, the slivering, frightening Vai ships collecting there like a necklace of misshapen pearls, and felt a halting, unwanted hope. "How am I supposed to convince her to come back if the promise of a cure isn't enough? Because I worked with her for a long time, and I know that sure as *hell* won't be enough."

The CEO shrugged. "That's up to you. Just get it done."

"I imagine I'll be given a fire team?"

"You'll pick them up in-system. *Beijing* will be there to provide material support and extra manpower if you need it, and two other cruisers are due to arrive within the week—but to be

honest, Ms. Chan, we don't want to spook her. Ash will respond
to a friendly face. *Your* friendly face."

Natalie hauled in a breath and held it. Back on dead *London,*
she'd told Ash she was going to come back. That hadn't been a
lie—at least, not then. She'd meant to return, meant to stage
some sort of rescue, but simply hadn't found the right way to do
it. Or maybe that had been the lie. No. By staying quiet, by staying away from Tribulation, Natalie was just protecting a friend.
Keeping everyone safe.

Wasn't she?

Was she lying to herself?

Natalie tossed aside the thought. There was only one lie here
that mattered, and that was that she had any choice in this matter
at all. She pressed her lips together and worried some dirt from
underneath her left thumbnail, noting Solano's frown growing
deeper with each passing second. There would absolutely be consequences if she refused this assignment. For herself. For Ash.

For everyone.

"I'll bring her back, sir," Natalie said, and stood.

6

Natalie swung from *Vancouver*'s spine into the cruiser's transport deck, wiping her hands on her pants to rid them of their crust of sweat and blood. She shook with a strange kind of anger, a bright shiver wound with a tight thread of disbelief. After all she'd accomplished—earning her citizenship, driving the work of Applied Kinetics, ensuring the Auroran victory on Bittersweet—the idea that the Board could manipulate her so easily left a foul taste in her mouth. On top of that, her memory device was on the fritz again, throwing up visions of Tribulation, of blue death and humid, choking air. The glitch caused her to walk face-first into a wall.

Natalie peeled herself away from the bulkhead, massaging her nose. She could feel a sharp ache still clutching at the place her IV had gone wrong, resting itchy and dark in the hollow at the bottom of her brainstem. God, she needed a shower.

Vancouver's main transport section—a wide hallway painted the color of a darkening sky, dotted with airlocks and emergency-access hatches—was full of citizens and indentures alike, shoulder to shoulder, cheering the end of the battle and moving from their airlocks toward the exits. A quick scan on her tiptoes identified the only evidence of imminent departure: stevedores silently loading crated equipment, with Ascanio, of all people, supervising. The younger cit waved as Natalie approached.

"I thought you'd be in App-K," Natalie said, nursing a slight disappointment that Ward hadn't shown up instead.

"Nah," Ascanio said. "Technical section's taken over my station for the rig upgrades, and, besides, I wanted a chance to apologize for shooting you up with so much—"

"Rig upgrades?"

Ascanio frowned. "Yeah, the new superhaptics. That, and the body upgrades."

Natalie wrinkled her nose. "Right, I forgot. *Body* upgrades. Tell Ward that I don't want them installed on you or any of the other personnel until we have the puppet rig fully tested. I don't want to fry anyone's cerebral cortex. That includes him. And you."

The roboticist's face fell slightly, and Natalie caught the flustered twitch of her lips as she flipped through her tablet. "Fine. So, your medic's already aboard. She's an executive. I'm supposed to make sure you have everything you need, so take a look at the load list and tell me what else you want added. What are you doing that they're sending an *executive*?"

Natalie pursed her lips, running her hand through her still-dirty hair. She grabbed the flimsy Ascanio offered. The board had certain advantages in this situation. Natalie had others—namely, that they could not make her disappear entirely, as long as the proper Auroran shipboard gossip routine was being maintained. Anything she told Ascanio would be all over the cit lounge by daybreak, a mantra against being forgotten.

"Dark-edge stuff," she replied, giving the other woman a knowing smile. "Research and retrieval related to my last assignment. You know if there's a shower on board?"

Ascanio took this in, wide-eyed, and it took a moment for her to process the abrupt change of topic. "It's a midrange yacht. No shower."

Natalie grimaced, then scanned the flimsy she'd been given, momentarily relieved that most of the equipment she wanted was there. The quartermaster had gone light on the weaponry, which irked her.

"This is not a full fire kit. Please tell the quartermaster that I want a full fire kit. I'm not trusting these people I don't know on *Beijing* to have it ready to my specs. Boltguns, ranged weapons, a backup long-range portable ansible, and make sure the railguns are charged. I am not going back down to that steam bath without a way to shoot some bastards and then call home."

Ascanio whistled. "So. You *are* heading back to Tribulation."

"Can't possibly confirm that," she said, flashed Ascanio a wide-toothed smile, and ducked through the airlock.

The yacht felt stiffly comfortable and was painted in shades of calming Auroran blue—the kind of lush austerity she'd come to expect from cit-level status. The cabin was slightly longer than the average salvage shuttle, with a proper long-distance drive, ergonomic bunks in a private back compartment, a thick kinetic web at the side for cargo, and a pilot's seat that wouldn't make her rear end go numb after an hour. Natalie had registered for and passed her official pilot's certification after returning from Tribulation, but knowing she was meant for the open seat up front still made her stomach flip. Instead of dwelling on it, she looked around to find and introduce herself to the medic, who was securing tubs of cargo in the back.

Her pleasant greeting died in her throat.

The medic was an older woman, small of stature, wearing a white coat over her Auroran executive's uniform. Her black hair was gathered behind her in a simple queue, her familiar lined hands tying off the web with businesslike flair, a new info-implant clipped above her eyebrow. She'd seen those hands on a render-bot recording on Tribulation, limned in orange. She'd worked next to those hands for six months. These were the hands that traded two weeks of her indenture time for amoxicillin. That had refused to play rummy with Ash and Kate in the mess. That had witnessed the horrors on Tribulation.

That had perpetrated them.

The corners of the medic's mouth tipped up slightly as Natalie stopped cold.

"Hello, Ms. Chan," said Reva Sharma. "It's delightful to see you again."

"Oh, *fuck* no," Natalie said, wavered for a moment, and walked out of the shuttle, slamming straight into Ascanio.

"Hey, I need your authorization for the quartermaster—" Ascanio said.

"I'm not going if she's going," Natalie said.

Dr. Sharma followed her out, looking as calm as a born executive usually did, while poison butterflies collected in Natalie's chest. The hum of the bay dimmed slightly as her blood ran hot and loud in her ears; the nearby indentures caught the tension immediately and shuffled off to find somewhere else to be.

"Ms. Chan," Sharma said, wiping her hands on a towel. "We had our differences on *Twenty-Five*, but I am one hundred percent the only person here who has any chance of saving Ashlan."

"We had our *differences*? Oh, fuck right off."

"We must have, for you to react like this."

"Um." Ascanio stepped forward, scratching the back of her neck. "I would like to remind you both that they've made the Ingest upgrades in here, so anything you say will be processed through—"

"I don't give a shit," said Natalie.

"And I don't need to," Sharma said. "Don't you have something else to do, tech?"

Ascanio muttered something under her breath, then pulled away, clearly put off. *Don't you know what she is,* Natalie wanted to say to her, *don't you know what she's done, how has she not been imprisoned, interrogated, tortured,* but the words stopped on her tongue, remembering the early morning in the puppet, the swirling red dust that had once been human, and the fact that the board had installed the redshift star in the puppet knowing exactly what it would do.

They know about Sharma, she thought, and the memory device helpfully supplied Ash's voice. *Solano was down on the planet before Ash set off the weapon. He saw the experiments. And now she's back and working in R&D like nothing happened? Shit, how else do you think they made the redshift star work?*

They know. They just don't care, as long as she's working for them this time.

The smallest of smiles touched Natalie's lips, and she stiffened. "Don't you need to be at some sort of victory party, or planning your next genocide? What's your angle?" she said.

"No angle," Sharma said. "I'm here because I care about Ashlan and what happens to her. I'm the only person in this entire company who can possibly understand what has happened to her and how to keep her alive. Of course I'm going with you."

"And they're just *letting* you?"

"There are mitigating circumstances keeping me with Aurora at the moment," Sharma said, tapping a bright flash of silver on her forehead. Not an info-implant, she finally saw, but a memory device just like hers.

Natalie's mouth shut against a glut of sudden questions. Sharma had disappeared shortly after their original camp on Tribulation had been raided by Baywell troops. Natalie assumed that she'd been taken by the same Baywell heavies that had grabbed her, and when Sharma hadn't been listed among the seven survivors of the Battle of Tribulation, Natalie had just assumed she'd died in the final blast—or was one of the terrifying few that didn't die, their husklike, half-breathing bodies languishing in a storage facility somewhere like bags of frozen vegetables.

And it had been a relief, hadn't it? For Natalie to know she was the only one left, the only one who knew where Ashlan was. To know that the monster behind the Sacrament Society horror show was gone, in soul and in body, and that everything had tottered on back to the way it should be.

She should really have known better.

"How many memories did you lose in the blast?" Natalie pointed to Sharma's implant.

The doctor stiffened. "Enough," she said.

"And you're doing this because—what, because they gave you a memory device too?"

Sharma looked surprised, and then made a fist, rapping her leg just above the knee with her tight knuckles. A damp, metallic sound returned. "After our lab site was raided, I was taken to the Wellspring ship and forced to continue my research on the Heart for their use. My femur was crushed in the battle, so it was a couple months of rehab and a bone replacement for me. And then there were the interminable re-onboarding interviews, and very few breaks in all the work afterward. Most importantly, of course, there's the cortical bomb."

She said the last few words in such a plain, everyday tone that Natalie's brain went straight past them, stumbled, and blanked. "I'm sorry, the *what*?"

Sharma inclined her head. "The board put a cortical bomb in my head, so they wouldn't worry about my wandering off to betray Aurora to my old friends."

"That's—" The word danced near the tip of her tongue, was replaced by a dire, more fitting silence. *Inhuman. Inhumane.* But to say that to mad, inhumane Reva Sharma sounded like a cop-out. "That's certainly a choice."

"It's completely expected, given my behavior." Sharma sighed, and her smile contained an insolent edge. "I kept on defeating all of the devices they used to try tracking me, so I suppose I did it to myself."

"You're just going along with this so they don't curbstomp you before your old friends pick you up. You don't give a fuck about Ashlan."

"And you're here because you made your own shady deal with the board. No—" She raised her hand to stop Natalie from speaking. "Don't deny it. If I bring Ashlan back, safe and hale and healthy, the bomb comes off. If I divert in any fashion from the mission, if I make contact with the Society or give Auroran assets to anyone outside the Company, this will turn my brain into chutney. And I do care about Ashlan."

Natalie shook her head. "You don't care about anything but your bottom line."

"That's completely unfair. I believe that both of us care about Ashlan—"

"*No*, you care about what Ashlan can do—"

"If that's all she meant to me, I wouldn't be here."

"I'm not going to let you near her. You're a—"

Sharma sighed. "Yes, I know. I'm a terrible human being." Her tone was almost mocking.

"A murderer."

"As are you. If you want to keep on punishing me because of your own self-righteous delusions, you may proceed. The only person you're truly punishing is Ashlan."

Sharma turned away. The conversation was clearly over. Ascanio, in the corner, had the pursed, deliberate look of someone who had been trying hard not to be caught listening.

"I'm going to take a shower," Natalie said, waving her hand over the last of the gear—the last thing in this world she could control. "You guys get this packed."

7

Natalie showered in a nearby pilot's ready room. By the time she returned, scrubbed clean and smelling like soap, the cargo was loaded and both Sharma and Ascanio were elsewhere. She paused in front of the open airlock. Glanced around at the rest of the small-craft bay. She saw indentured mechanics everywhere, of course, and Ingest would be a problem, but it still might not be too hard to drop into one of the other yachts when no one was looking, hotwire the thing like Ash had taught her, and go—

—go where?

Where could she go?

Sharma would take another yacht to Tribulation, of course, alongside some other cit—a climber like Ward, someone on the fast track to promotion and willing to do whatever it took to get there. And meanwhile, Natalie's own achievements would cease to matter. Her department would be given to someone else. She'd starve. She had precisely as many options now as she did when she signed her indenture.

She tightened her fists and stepped in.

The doctor was already sitting in the copilot's chair up front, the safety web loose behind her, reading flimsies. She wore her familiar white coat over a blue Auroran jumpsuit, the light from the warming interfaces reflecting against her topaz skin, just a few shades darker than Natalie's. Natalie dropped into the pilot's seat and went through preflight without saying a word, grateful for the relative silence. She was halfway through checking fuel flow when Sharma laid her flimsies to the side and cleared her throat.

Natalie looked up. "If we could get through the next few days without having an unnecessary conversation, that would be great."

"It's a very small bomb," Sharma said, in a smirking tone that made Natalie wonder if she was being condescended to. "It's located between the folds of my frontal lobe. From what I can tell, it will turn my brain to slurry and crack my skull in a few places, but that won't create a problem for you or the ship."

Natalie watched the fuel flow test come back green, then moved on to the environmental subsystems. She confirmed oxygen levels, integrated antigrav, and the head mechanic's inspection. "Maybe we should just get it over with, then."

The doctor's lips pressed together. "I don't understand where this hostility is coming from."

"I suppose you're going to say you *don't remember* two months into the Tribulation contract, when I had a UTI and you wouldn't give me antibiotics because I hadn't gotten sick 'in the line of duty.'" Natalie stabbed the air in front of her with her thumb to sign off on the inspection, then switched over to the release forms.

"I don't."

"You don't remember that I had to defuse six zappers while fighting off a kidney infection, huh?" *Stab.* "Oh, and then there was that time I tweaked my back cracking open a crate for Ms. Ramsay and was in pain for a week, but *you* reminded me that my indenture released the Company from any medical liability 'when not engaging in activities that are directly related to my job description.' Because that was her *personal* crate and not the Company's." *Stab.* "That was before we figured out that you were just using us."

Sharma nodded slowly. "Ah." She paused. "It's just Company policy."

"Oh, sure," she said, stabbing her agreement one last time and closing the HUD. She turned in the chair, fixing Sharma with her coldest gaze. "You know, where I grew up wasn't heaven. But we took care of each other. That was *Twenty-Five*, too. Except for *you*. You fucked it up."

The doctor paused. "Where did you grow up?"

"A noncorp in the North Atlantic protectorate. You'd call it a software cult."

Sharma's chin lifted imperceptibly. "I didn't know you were a coder."

Natalie frowned. "It wasn't one of my skills. One of the reasons I left."

"Along with the constant war with the townie governments over Company-issued rations, the climate—"

"You sound like you're speaking from experience."

"I spent some time in a software cult when I was in my twenties, just after medical school. The Society used a lot of hacker-cult framework from Earth to build our earliest experimental processes, mostly because it didn't interface with corporateware."

"Of *course* you did. You know what?" Natalie exhaled. "I don't need to hear about the summer you slummed it in the Manhattan warrens or whatever."

Sharma breathed out. "No, I suppose you don't," she said, in a tone that suggested a grudging concession. "I honestly don't begrudge anyone wanting to leave. Although it must be very hard to be away from your family . . . ?"

"Nah." Natalie thought of her father, the way his hair ruffled in the cold November wind as she walked down the hill to the river. *If you go, you can't come back.* He'd finally taken the long walk down the hill too, when things got bad enough, and now she didn't even remember enough about him to make a conversation worth a damn. Her stomach flipped with a rush of sudden anger, in a blast of cold wind across the marble plaza of her childhood, and Natalie cleared her throat, making an attempt to change the subject.

"So the bomb's controller is in your memory device?" she asked.

Sharma looked mildly disappointed at the conversational shift, but she didn't stop it. Instead, she tapped her temple. "Yes. It sorts through everything I file away in there each day, flagging anything that might be concerning to the board. I can't betray you or work against the purposes of the mission, which is to keep Ash safe. I have some latitude there, so you don't need to worry."

"I really don't honestly care if your head explodes."

Sharma raised her eyebrows. "This isn't just about the kidney infection."

One last release form popped up. Natalie stabbed it. "Aren't you smart?"

Sharma flipped the memory device over, placing it in her lap, knitting her fingers over it, going quiet for a few seconds too long for Natalie's comfort. "I never betrayed you. You and the others were never supposed to be involved at all."

"So you could profit all on your own."

Sharma's gaze sharpened. "We're not out for profit. After seeing what happened at Tribulation, I'm sure you can agree that nobody who *is* should have access to zero-point Heart technology."

"Everybody's out for profit."

Sharma's silence was coated with a crackling annoyance. "I sincerely doubt you're here simply out of the kindness of your heart, *Ms.* Chan."

Natalie clenched her teeth, making it through the end of the major-systems checklist, moving on to the guidance system. She was running out of status buttons, of lists, of rechecks, of things that could take her attention off the conversation. She felt stiff and angry and tight, like someone had wrapped her chest in a wide rubber band.

"And I suppose they forced you to make the redshift star work," she said.

Sharma's smile thinned. "Is that your guess?"

"It makes sense to me." Natalie shrugged. "I'm pretty sure you're the only one with the skillset to figure out a way to set off a molecular without a trigger."

Sharma nodded slowly, then exhaled. She picked up the flimsies again, placing them in her lap, smoothing them with an open palm. "I was just as surprised as you that it succeeded. I told the board that the task was impossible. I still don't honestly know what I did right."

"Don't fucking lie."

"I wish I'd gotten it wrong."

Stab. God, preflight had gotten *long* since the Company had to start acknowledging her personhood. "Maybe you did get it wrong."

Sharma paused, pursing her lips, considering that. "I don't understand."

"It worked because there was a trigger present on Bittersweet."

"That would be the most logical thing, except that Wellspring never really knew what they were doing in those labs." Sharma shook her head. "Ash, her friend, the others—those human triggers were by-products of the weapons development process, not the original goal. They never even knew what they had."

Stab. "They had years afterward to figure it out."

"True." Sharma still didn't look convinced. She shuffled the flimsies, then smoothed them again. "That would still mean that a traitor on their side knew what Aurora was planning and triggered the star exactly when and how we wanted it triggered. Other scientists would find that unbelievable."

Natalie shook her head. "Well, I saw something."

Sharma clapped the nearby tablet-top shut and stowed it. "I believe you. We'll figure it out together."

Natalie snorted. "You make it sound so *fun*."

"We're a lot alike, you and I."

"Right."

"Just because the corporate system in which we are all trapped is the only system that seems to work out here doesn't mean that it's infallible. Or right. Or good." She paused. "You agree with that."

"You're a birthright. You can say that. You can do whatever you want."

"Ha. If you think I get any more say about my destiny than you do, then you're—"

Natalie tore her eyes away from the last release form. "You're a *Sharma*."

"And they still put a bomb in my head." The doctor's words were pointed, loud, forward. "We do what we can, where we are, with what we have. You need to stop feeling guilty about what happened on Bittersweet. Concentrate on *Ash* now."

Natalie had very little to say to that. Instead, she watched the computer logic subsystems come in as green, and moved on to navigation backups. "Maybe you can just wave your hand and make it go away. I can't."

"You don't have a bomb in your head, but you might as well." She smiled. "Unlike me, though, you can choose to do something about it. Do you think Joseph will stop at Applied Kinetics, Ms. Chan? They triggered a redshift star without a trigger. *Everything* is a possibility now, and if we don't work to control the narrative and the science as best as we can, what we saw this morning is just the beginning of a new and frightening world."

Natalie tensed. "And how can you control the narrative when you're doing their dirty work?"

"You *do* know how infiltration works?" the doctor said, clipped and annoyed. "We need resources to live out here, and the corporations have those resources. Inside Aurora, inside the boardrooms in other corporations—that's where change can begin. And things will change. The Vai are so beautiful, Ms. Chan. They're cooperative in a way humanity could never achieve. Do you think a society that exists only to compete, like ours, could develop a thing as beautiful as the Heart? With what we learn from the Vai, we don't have to burn the corporations to the ground. We can change them for the better. If you could just see—"

A sudden wild anger twisted a knot in the center of Natalie's heart, and her fingers closed on the edge of the pilot's interface, tight enough to make her knuckles go white. She tried to breathe. "Are you trying to recruit me? After everything I saw?"

Sharma's hands twisted together once more, then dropped to her sides. "We can help you, Natalie."

We can help you. The doctor's words stoked the old rage, the old helplessness, the part of her that was dead on a battlefield somewhere, and she slammed silent and shaking through the last of the cross-check, then sent the signal to detach from the airlock. Guilt was an ungrateful guest in her head, cropping up when she least needed or wanted it to, whispering *it's your fault it's your fault you've ruined everything* even when she knew she hadn't. Saving Ash's life by shooting the alien hadn't been a choice. Living through the war had been pure luck. And the redshift star—that was Sharma's doing, hers and Solano's and Aurora's. Natalie had been fresh out of choices when she'd taken her place in the puppet rig.

This time, Natalie was going to get to choose.

She was going to claw it out of the fabric of the universe if she had to.

Sharma focused on Natalie as if she were expecting a response, then picked up a flimsy when she realized one wasn't coming. Natalie brightened the HUD lights, drowning out her companion's presence. If she could pretend the doctor were elsewhere, she could breathe easily. She could relax. The departure could be all business, and for a few glorious moments, Natalie could let the information from her HUD flow in and out of her ears, could pretend that Sharma was a person she actually liked—Ash, perhaps, or Keller, who had been the first to encourage her to learn the pilot's trade. She could calm down.

The doctor was quiet during the glide to a safe distance, the confirmation of the vector plot, and the nauseous twist of the long-range engines spinning to life. She worked on a tablet tilted toward the ceiling, and Natalie caught glances of chemical formulae and long, incomprehensible strings of numbers.

Natalie concentrated on the hum of the ship beneath her feet, thought of Kate Keller, the way her old captain would place her hands gently on the console, as if the ship were a friend, a lover, a family member, ceding herself over to the white noise of the engines building up the gravity fields that powered the yacht's movement through space. Natalie understood now. How Kate had held herself alone for so long, how even then her walls could crumble. When the star-studded black of ordinary space ceded to the total darkness of the distance drive, Natalie slumped in her seat. Thought of the yacht as a friend. Her only friend. Her fist closed in on itself. She felt a delicious ache in her joints as she settled in, kicked her legs up on the dashboard, and closed her eyes.

8

The trip to Tribulation took three strained days. They talked, when they had to, and Sharma attempted numerous times to get Natalie to open up. Natalie would respond in monosyllables, followed by stuffing her mouth full of whatever ready-to-eat travel meal was on the top of the pile.

Natalie spent most of the time planning the rest of App-K's superhaptic upgrade on a tablet, with Sharma scrawling medical nonsense on the backs of old flimsies. Ingest had already placed most of the renderbots it needed to process daily feeds from her department, and she felt mildly peeved that they seemed to be getting along quite well without her. After reading a whiny petition from Ascanio and half the department about how much the Ingest rig updates would increase their productivity, she sighed and finally signed off, allowing the interface tattoo appointments to go forward at Ward's discretion.

Natalie wondered how the birthright class was taking it, this gate-crashing of one of their favorite haute styles. She giggled under her breath. Tattoos used for direct connection to devices didn't sound Auroran. It sounded like a software cult idea, a *Verdict* idea. She imagined Aurora's richest and brightest sailing through the parties Natalie was still not allowed to attend, boasting about their biohacks, not knowing they'd been developed on forgotten, starving Earth. The more she thought about it, the more the wild idea made sense. She barely remembered that her father had been working on biohacking issues when she left—and what was laying down tattooed paths for computers to pass orders directly in and out of a brain if not the purest form of biohacking? Had one of her old buddies gone corporate in the meantime? She made a note to search the Company directory when she returned to *Vancouver*.

Natalie was asleep in one of the transport's thin bunks when the autopilot disengaged fifteen minutes earlier than scheduled. Her dream—there had been blood in it, and something sweet and violent—disappeared in the bleary twist of the descent from fulldrive. She pushed herself upright, shrugging into her rumpled jacket, leaving behind the vat-beef sandwich she'd put next to her shoes for breakfast.

In the copilot's seat, Sharma sat dull-eyed but awake, her tablets tossed to the floor, her fingers flicking at the haptic controls with the half-graceful talent of someone who knew just enough about what they were doing to be dangerous.

"They didn't teach you to take a ship out of fulldrive in human sacrifice school, did they? Lemme at it," Natalie said, stifling a yawn.

"An alarm sounded," said Sharma, her eyes traced with the beginnings of exhaustion. She abandoned the pilot's seat with a grateful lift of her left hand. "I reacted, and it—"

"Read your reactions. Right. It does that."

As Natalie sat down and reached for the haptic crown, she noticed that the faceplate of Sharma's memory device lay unhooked on the interface nearby, next to a bag of half-used tools. The doctor grabbed it as soon as she saw Natalie's attentions, snapping it back into place above her left eyebrow.

Natalie cleared her throat. "We're just inside the asteroid belt, where we should be. Did you check for sensor glitches?"

"I—" Sharma paused. "No. This is a late-model yacht. It's too new to have sensor problems."

Natalie narrowed her eyes. "You're awfully trusting for a traitor to the brand."

Sharma's lips widened slightly. "I'm a pragmatist. Mr. Solano is not going to send out two of his most important stakeholders in the kind of rustbucket he gives to everyone else."

"Oh. Right. Is that the kind of expertise you get from running covert organizations that rip the hearts out of people?"

Sharma smacked her lips in annoyance. "Do you ever get tired of trying to get a rise out of me?"

"Never," Natalie said.

She put on the haptics and felt the stir of the neural patches against her fingers, her wrists, her temples. Numbers and lines in blue and gold erupted in front of her eyes as the HUD settled in next to her irises, humming hot and sure where it interfaced with her memory device. Fancy as hell, but not really anything different from the kind of hand-flown ship that had taken her away from Earth for the last time ten years ago.

And that was the thing about haptics, she thought, buckling the safety mesh at her shoulders and waist. War. Piloting. Science. It was all process and checklists and muscle memory just like it always had been, and as helpful as haptics were, gravity did not forgive, even the grav-drive. If you didn't know what you were doing, the reduction in lag was no help.

They spent some time in their now-familiar silence, watching Tribulation's sun blossom from tiny speck to riotous mass, the asteroids passing them by like stones in a river. Natalie accessed the engine, antigrav, and navigational settings. She sent out an approach ping to the *Beijing* comms, but received nothing in return, which set tiny, loud alarms ringing inside her skull. Her stomach churning, she focused on the long-range sensors as soon as they came online.

"Well, *shit*," she said, a second later.

"What?"

Natalie switched the HUD to combat view, then pushed the information to the main interface so Sharma could see it. The doctor's eyes widened at the sight of ships settled in tight orbit of the dead colony planet, around the wrecks of *London* and *Mumbai*. None of them displayed the safe blue IFFs of Auroran friendlies.

"Where's *Beijing*? Our salvagers? They're supposed to be enforcing the no-fly zone," Natalie said. "Those IFFs near the wrecks are InGen, and the ones hanging by the moon? Penumbra. I don't read any Auroran signals at all. This is really strange. Confirm that for me?"

Sharma's fingers waved. "I don't see *Beijing*, either," she said. "There has to be a good explanation. Maybe it's patrolling the other side of the system?"

The unease stirring up Natalie's sour stomach became stronger, and her hands hovered for a moment over the fire controls. She was tempted to warm up the railguns.

"Yeah, well, I don't know if it'll be a good explanation."

"Jumping to conclusions is bad science."

"Sticking with the previous plan when conflicting evidence is presented is bad *recon*."

Sharma considered the battlefield, the tiny ships displaying InGen gold flickering like honeybees between the picked-over Auroran wrecks. Her hand clenched for a moment, and she dragged it away from the keyboard, as if stopping herself. "Maybe an emergency? They could be offering assistance to *Beijing*. Most of these companies are still bound by the rules of the Corporate Alliance, even if Baywell dropped out."

The adrenaline was back, the twist at the back of Natalie's neck, the huff of short, stolen air in her lungs. Dismay. The birth of panic. She'd felt this shatter her body so many times she knew exactly how to breathe through it. *In. Out. In. Slowly.* "I don't think so."

"No?"

"Fuck no. We'll take a long arc behind the dark side of the moon, hide in the radar shadow, then slip into the atmosphere hidden by the glint of the sun. They won't even know we're here," she said, drawing up a vector plot as she said it.

Sharma smiled knowingly. "You're going to be a good executive," she said.

"And have to answer to people born with their thumbs up their asses?"

"Well," Sharma said. "Birthrights have their uses, as you'll find out soon enough."

"Aren't *you* a birthright?" Natalie responded, keeping her eyes on the HUD, skirting asteroids with a practiced hand. The fact she could do that made her proud. Just this time last year, she'd still been training with Ash in a pod, still unsteady with the math, the force of the grav-drive, the pitch and the yaw. Now, with haptics training, the transport felt like an extension of her body, exactly like the puppet rig, and it was *fun*. This exhilaration must have been what Ash had loved: the kick of freedom in a life that was a cage, a taste of flight in a life spent underground. She could understand wanting more. Getting addicted to it.

"I suppose," Sharma said, again.

"What do you mean, you suppose?"

"I don't entirely remember."

Natalie pushed the tiller, charting an arc out of the asteroid field. "That's convenient. You remember what you did in your death cave."

The doctor's face settled into stone. "I worked with the Heart for years. You get used to losing things. You get used to navigating around the holes in your mind, even without the memory device. You're doing it right now. You've obviously figured out how to live without Len."

"Who?"

The doctor's face settled, the barest hint of sadness smoothing out the lines under her eyes. "Well. That's unfortunate." She paused. "Or maybe it's for the best."

"Stop trying to bait me." The anger was sudden and inexplicable, riding the back of Natalie's tongue, and she swallowed it. "Just watch for *Beijing*, okay?"

They rode in unfriendly silence through the asteroid belt, Natalie mentally listing off of how many ways she could abandon the doctor without killing her—not that she would, of course, but she couldn't deny that fantasizing about it made her feel better. Tribulation gobbled up the horizon on the other side, wine-soaked and graceful; its star hovered small and far to port, lighting the battlefield in fits of sparkling silver. As they grew closer, Natalie identified the familiar shattered hulks of *London* and *Mumbai*, black against black, the backdrop to the worst three days of her life.

Around them was the wreckage of the *Second* Battle of Tribulation, the one she'd barely escaped: nearly a dozen massive cruisers, their lines cut and shattered. Around the scattered chaff was a buzz of unwelcome industry—squat, half-square ships in formation just outside the battlefield, salvage pods glimmering in the Tribulation sunlight. But they weren't working the older wrecks, the familiar, bent curves she'd grown to understand last year.

They were working a new wreck—the quiet carcass of *Beijing*, black and dead and cut down the center in a slithering swipe by the nastiest lancefire Natalie had ever seen. She could still see the echoes of light shimmering through the windows and breaches in the hull.

"This just happened. They're probably still alive over there," Sharma said, swallowing audibly.

"We have to help them," said Natalie, her hand going for the ansible controls.

"No," said the doctor. Her fingers rapped against the back of Natalie's hand, pushing it down and away. The shuttle twisted and shuddered in response, and Natalie spent a moment coaxing it back to the original vector.

"What kind of doctor are you?"

Sharma's mouth settled into a serious line. "If they knew about *Beijing*, they might know about Ashlan. In that case, we need to get down there as soon as possible."

Natalie licked dry lips. "Spies. Of course there are spies."

"There are always spies."

"You'd know."

Sharma paused. "Can we get a more comprehensive look?"

Natalie brought up the overlay map of the battlefield, dragging the pads of her fingers over the space the *London* weapon had harried. The whole place was registered with the Corporate Alliance as an exclusion zone, watched over by Aurora, which owned the nearby space. Natalie narrowed her eyes, magnified the view on the ships. They were short-range Armour-made salvagers, stocky like *Twenty-Five* had been, with not one single plasma lance between them.

"Where's their cruiser?" Sharma said.

Natalie chewed the inside of her cheeks. She heard Ash's heartbeat thudding in her memory device, and she slid her hand up, increasing the velocity. "Probably out past the asteroid field, making calls? They won't dare use the Auroran ansible."

Sharma inhaled. "Let's assume we're the only proper Auroran presence in the system for the foreseeable future."

"Probably a good idea."

They shared a moment of solemn quiet, and Natalie watched the stars wheel beyond the graveyard, watched faraway *Beijing* in its death throes, felt the thrum of the ship hauling hard for the planet she never wanted to see again.

The memory device was firing quietly in the back of her mind, connecting the local stars—*the Ballerina, that's what Captain Keller had called that constellation*—with a hundred other memories, things that continued to distract her even as they passed into the radar shadow of Tribulation's malformed moon.

The darkness of the space between the stars became the sky above the Verdict plaza back on Earth. And then she was thinking of her father, of his hair moving in the cold November wind, his eyes as flinty as the weather—

"You have to control it," Sharma said, quietly.

"Control?"

"The memoria. You have to tell it what's important, which threads to pursue and which to file away, or else it'll give everything equal importance and you'll get hit with a bunch of memories at once. Like what's happening now. I've seen that look before. I can teach you how to do it."

"Fuck off. I'm fine."

"I had a hand in developing it, so I know how to—"

"Damn it!" Natalie saw the enemy cruiser only moments before its spinal lance shot hot death toward the yacht, emerging from the pitch darkness of the drapery of the moon. Her haptic response wasn't nearly fast enough—she swerved bodily to the side and the ship bucked and heaved in response. The ship shook around her—three great concussions, rattling the walls. She felt a tearing under her feet, heard the shattering sigh of plasteel tearing apart, and the whining horror of the engines spinning down.

That's okay, she thought, *that's okay, we have secondary systems on this yacht.* The memory device was already feeding her fingers Ash's flight-training tactics, and Natalie felt the heady haptic rush of *doing* before *knowing.* She yanked the transport to the side, leaning into the extra velocity from the hit to peel away toward the planet.

"Tell me what to do," the doctor hollered.

"Railgun!"

"How?" Sharma was already scrambling for the targeting array, her hands dancing as it came up.

"Think: combat HUD to copilot. Concentrate to grab a target, then fire. Aim for the engines; stopping your enemy or keeping

them on a consistent vector makes your job easier. Think of it
like robotic surgery."

"I don't know—oh. *Oh*."

It's basically telepathy, Natalie remembered her old CO saying, as Sharma's hands grabbed at the battlefield like a child at
a toy giveaway, her eyes glassy and darting from side to side, the
back railgun ripping suppressing fire just milliseconds later—
wide and wild at the start, but more targeted as the doctor's
breath settled, wrapping her mind around her new task.

The cruiser was squarely behind them now, coming around
in a tight arc, and Natalie knew it would be easy to mistake the
lumbering mass of the moon for relative safety. They'd be easily
pinned there and eventually chased in-system, toward the sun.
She gunned the engine, shoving celestium through the grav-
drive's engineering matrix, using the resultant power to send the
yacht into a wild spin, to push and pull just long enough to con-
fuse the cruiser's plasma lance.

Sharma scattered fire against the enemy railgun points, giving
Natalie enough time to whirl the ship around toward the safety
of the asteroid field beyond, adrenaline convincing Natalie that
she'd make it, that they'd be able to hide, that she'd—

—*incoming*, she felt, more than heard; Sharma's voice ripped
through the memory device in a crackling, double-blind chorus.
The cruiser fired its plasma lance before she could do anything
else. The lance impact hit a millisecond later, and even the cit-
quality safety web didn't stop a jolt that had her screaming, a
violent push forward that threw the breath out of her body, that
made blood-blisters of the skin on her shoulders. Then: a second
impact, one that caused a sick wind to lick at her hair, her chin,
her hands, to howl like a hurricane, and she didn't need the red
alarms to know the ship had been breached.

Natalie looked over her shoulder. It was a small breach. The
smallest of mercies. She saw movement to her left; it was Sharma,

throwing off her web and securing a tether, her chin resolute, the lines in her face growing deeper, her voice calling out breach sealing protocol. The doctor hung suspended in the rushing air, slapping sealer on the breach, then crashed to the floor like a sack of bricks. As gravity returned, Natalie sucked in a shocked breath, a breath that barely held oxygen. There wouldn't be enough air to take them to safety—

—she hauled in another breath—

—but there *would* be enough air to take them to the planet.

If she were a good enough pilot. If she could do the math fast enough.

Tribulation wheeled below, spreading its bloodstained welcome.

Natalie plotted a vector with a quick twist of her hand. She knew it was a bad plan. It was the panicked thought of a worm who didn't want to die, but that didn't matter: the yacht computer translated her thoughts into flight as fast as she could feed them into the haptics, taking her panic for gospel. The lack of oxygen stealing her breath, she called to Sharma to strap in, because *we're going down to where they can't fucking follow*. With one last shuddering impact direct to the engine, the ship gave up control like a soldier bleeding out, and she allowed gravity to suck them down into a darkening planetary atmosphere intent on chewing their ship into hot coals.

It was all Natalie could do to keep the damaged yacht from corkscrewing, and the land was coming up fast, too fast, and her thoughts came like gulping shadows, the panicked commands through the haptic a prayer to the god she didn't believe in, over and over again, slow down, slow down, *slow the fuck down*—

—*I'm sorry, Ash*—

9

Natalie's first conscious breath was hot with the humid tang of Tribulation on her tongue. The doctor's hysterical laughter rang in her ears.

She blinked away the bleary, dizzy twist of her returning vision, and before she could even determine up from down, she pulled at the safety web digging into her shoulders, fumbling with the fastenings, ripping it aside. The motion was agony; since the crash foam hadn't deployed well on her side of the cockpit, it hadn't stopped the fire stemming from the sputtering gravdrive, which had committed suicide to save them from becoming carbon-based smears on the forest floor. Half of Natalie's safety web was burned away, and some had melted into her skin. Above, the dark Tribulation wind cast itself through the flags made of a spare flightsuit, lighting her nerves from the inside. The memory device ran hot with panicked scenes from her past—

—*fire, fire in the forest, blue fire tugging at her legs, at her hair, teasing at her ankle, the scent of bright death in the air, the scattering of Marley's body, I hate this goddamn planet so much*—

Damn thing was still glitching.

She grounded herself in the familiar pull of the planet's tight gravity, and clambered to her feet, a headache rioting behind her eyes. The pilot's visor had been ripped from her head in the fall, and the haptics lay, sparking and useless, by her feet. The ceiling was open to the burgundy sky, and a toothpick-sharp tree had punched its way through the cargo space. Even if they'd had a crack mechanic, the yacht would never fly again.

Sharma groaned from the copilot's seat. Her head lolled to the side, eyes closed, lips parted, laughing.

"Doc," Natalie said, pulling herself closer. "Doc. Ship's fucked. Can you walk?"

"Glory," Sharma breathed, and laughed again.

"What, is your memoria glitching too?"

Sharma's broken fingernails dragged a logy line to a dark place near her shoulder where a piece of shrapnel stuck out like a broken pencil. Her laughter trailed off, the wrinkles at the corners of her eyes slackening slightly, her brown eyes unfocusing, but she didn't move. The wound was actively bleeding, a dark, seeping red swirled with a silver sheen reminiscent of oil skating over water. Ash's blood had looked like this when the Vai was bleeding her dry in the bugout bay, a fact that stopped Natalie short. If Sharma had the same sort of celestium sickness—

—but that was impossible, she *couldn't*, she'd be sick like Ash, *dead* by now—

"The crash foam was supposed to work," Sharma said, "*executives* ride shuttles like these," then dissolved again into a paroxysm of giddy laughter.

"I'll get the shrapnel out," Natalie said, wondering if it would be appropriate to punch her companion in the face and call it anesthetic.

"Just toss me the medkit," the doctor responded.

"You're not at the right angle to—"

"The *medkit*," Sharma barked. "You take care of those burns. There's areprazin in the back, if the foam didn't ruin it."

Natalie wanted to protest, but she reached for the medkit instead, threw it open, and tossed it in front of the doctor. Sharma found a plastic tube, held it in her mouth, and then used a surgical tool to remove the shrapnel, resulting in a gush of blood and a quick slap of an autobandage. By the time Natalie found and smeared on a helping of the burn cream, Sharma was shoving things in a backpack.

"How far are we from the ag-center?" she said. "Should we fortify or run?"

Natalie grabbed her own pack. "We run. We left a contrail fancy enough to be seen from Europa."

Sharma frowned. "I don't know how badly your burns will interact with the atmosphere outside."

"Doesn't matter. Let's go."

"You're the boss, I suppose," Sharma quipped, quick and clipped.

Stung with a sudden, crystal-clear annoyance, Natalie tied her jacket around her waist and leaned over toward the door, releasing the lock. She cracked the door, tasting dark smoke and the tough, meaty heft of the alien soil outside. And then they were tumbling out into the Tribulation forest, into the blood and the burgundy and the memories, as the sun dropped further into the swaying treetops.

Just like the first time.

The air was heavy, the very taste of it redolent with sulfur and scorched plasteel, soaked with the humid weight Natalie remembered entirely too well from her last time here. Her lungs labored from the very first moment she hit the air; she felt out of breath, permanently scarred from the inside.

Natalie shook away the echoes. *Run,* she'd said.

—*the blue screamer lapping at her ankles*—

—*to have come so far, to have given so much, to die like this*—

Her muscles ached to the bone. Her eyes focused on the twisted, bloodred brambles on the forest floor. Her vision went blurry and blank.

The doctor grabbed at her wrist. "Where's your rebreather?"

She'd forgotten. Natalie skidded to a stop and turned around, fumbling in her pocket, finding the rebreather, then shoving the thing over her mouth. She felt winded already, like she was a kid again and had been playing tag in the dirt basin of the Wash-park amphitheater. The doctor was right—with the planetary atmospinners almost entirely dead, there was very little oxy-mix. A long walk meant toxic claw marks inside her lungs, a delicate spatter of blood. A longer walk might be fatal.

Natalie took a shallow, painful breath, her hands resting on her aching knees. She could almost feel every single one of her cells on fire, like the atmosphere itself was a twisted Vai weapon intent on taking a torch to her very cytoskeleton. She looked back at Sharma, who was breathing heavily, her mouth open to the air.

"Where's yours?"

"In the ship. Probably."

"We'll share, then," Natalie groaned. "Two minutes on, two minutes off."

"Didn't think you would."

Natalie straightened. She forced the words out. "You're on my team."

The doctor was behind her, strands of black hair loosened from her typical tight bindings. "It'll only buy us some time, any-way. Colonists weren't even allowed down here until the oxy-mix ratio was at least eighty-eight percent in the settled areas. This tastes like sixty. If we're lucky."

Natalie wiped her nose with the back of her hand. It came back bloody, and she swore, immediately regretting the wasted breath. The memoria flashed again, and she whacked her head with the butt of her hand. *Distracted again.* "It'll be fine. Ashlan will have the atmospinners running at the ag-center. She was a miner; clean air is gonna be pretty high on her to-do list."

Sharma's alarm flattened into obvious suspicion. "It's not fine. Do I need to tell you what a mix of forty percent methanethiol does to the human lung?"

"Walk," said Natalie, shoving the rebreather at Sharma.

The doctor's jaw worked, momentarily speechless, and Natalie took the compass out of her pocket, recalibrating it for Tribulation's magnetic field. The thing whirled and fluttered before it settled on a direction. Natalie sighed, checked for the direction of the lowering sun, and spun around, stomping deeper into the forest. Sharma followed, her breath ragged and audible in the rebreather.

"Okay, let me see."

"See what?"

Sharma huffed and pushed around to block Natalie's path. "Your memoria. You're glitching. You've been glitching for hours. And it just got worse when we crashed. Trust me, I can tell."

"Because you're glitching too?"

"Because I care about you."

Natalie coughed. "You care about getting off the planet alive. Let's not make this any more than it is."

The doctor fumbled in her backpack for the tools she'd been using earlier. "I'm just concerned that they put a bomb in your brain, too—"

"They didn't put a bomb in my brain."

Sharma raised her eyebrows. "Are you willing to bet your life on that?"

Natalie's slight hesitation was enough to send her memoria wheeling toward distraction again. The doctor's face disappeared, replaced by the unwelcome memory of waking up in the medbay after the Battle of Tribulation to a splitting headache, a smiling nurse, her own name disappearing into the haze. Sharma tapped Natalie's shoulder, tilting her back into the world. She blinked, and the doctor shoved the rebreather against her mouth. "Take this," she said, "and sit down."

They ducked into an overgrown copse of trees that Natalie deemed defensible enough. She sucked plain, sweet air through the rebreather while Sharma's hands slipped underneath the device and removed the control-module faceplate, and Natalie felt the dry scratch of her fingers against her skin, the loss of the slight weight that had become the most important part of her body, the tight invisible skein that was the wireless connection between the portion of the memoria embedded in her brain and the control module. Sharma knelt on the wet forest floor, spreading out her tools on a handkerchief, and told her to close her eyes.

"Are you done?" Natalie complained, closing them until they were barely slits. "If they were monitoring my memories, they would have known Ashlan was alive months ago."

The doctor's hands came up again, this time with an unknown tool, to hover over Natalie's head. She felt a warmth at her temple, a clicking sensation as the doctor peeled back the safety cover, and a full minute of relatively terrified silence as Sharma poked around inside the other half of the memoria's workings—the neurotech that interacted directly with the rest of her brain, where her memories were stored. When she pulled back, the doctor's voice was bright and curious. "No bomb," she said. "But I do think I can assist. The circuits leading into your cerebral cortex are almost fried from overuse, and the connectors are corroded. I'm going to install something that'll help."

Natalie snorted, keeping her eyes closed. "So you're a neuro-tech now?"

"Been one." She rustled in her tool bag, drew out a spanner and a few more tools Natalie didn't recognize, then spent some time drilling around under her skull, which wasn't painful, but still made her teeth rattle. Natalie grabbed at the rebreather, took a long draught like in the old holos, and then dangled it in Sharma's direction.

"Are you done yet?"

"Almost."

"Let's go."

"Calm down," Sharma said. "If you overclock from stress—"

"—if you reprogram the memoria to wipe every single memory I have—"

The doctor looked hurt, then handed back Natalie's faceplate. "You just don't stop, do you?"

"I'm not known for it, no." Natalie flashed a smile, and clicked the faceplate back against her forehead, feeling a rushing relief as the buffer caught up with the long-term memory in her meatbrain. She thought she saw a green light behind her eyelids as she did so, something bright and shivering, but when she blinked her eyes, it was gone again. *Probably nothing.*

The doctor swept up her things as Natalie checked the compass for directions to the location of the signal tied to Ashlan's heartbeat. The woods out here were a tangle of burnt umber and sulfur, of underbrush that clutched at the trunks of trees. It was a hard hike—just on the edge of doable, even with the rabid sting of the burn on her neck, even though she was *so hungry*. She found herself craving a very large sandwich, or a can of protein, and was distracted enough that she almost missed the unmistakable, almost imperceptible whir-whistle of a drone.

Natalie hissed *get down, don't even breathe,* grabbing wildly at the doctor's suited shoulder. To her credit, Sharma crumpled alongside her, dropping to a hunch behind a twisted fallen log, folding her frame into the space behind a loamy stump.

Natalie wrapped her palm around her cold boltgun, her index finger sliding in just next to the trigger guard, slowing her breath, trying to match the aching wheeze in her chest to the wind that had kicked up after sunset.

The boots showed up seconds later: InGen boots, big, shiny black groundwhackers with wide yellow stripes, meant for wading through rivers and intestines and blood. Natalie knew InGen wasn't even supposed to be anywhere near Tribulation, didn't have an official statement on the hostilities, preferring instead to work through more underhanded means, corporate espionage and merger destruction. They didn't put troops on the ground unless they had to.

She pressed herself up against the log, slivers pressing into her forehead as she stared through the knothole, checking for shadows, for an exit. No doors and corners here—just fat hardwood trees clumping around the edge of the clearing, and tight brambles fit to trip over. Not the best place for a fight, but beggars couldn't be choosers. There were only three men, which was strange, because InGens walked in fours.

Have you fought, Natalie wanted to ask Sharma, *because we're going to have to fight,* but she nearly gave away her position with the skinny laugh that followed. A birthright like Sharma, a scientist, a surgeon, risking her birdbone fingers on something as risky as a wild punch? No. Natalie couldn't count on her. What's worse, she'd have to factor Sharma's uselessness in to any physical decision she made, because the doctor was right: she was the only person in the universe who had any chance of understanding what was happening to Ashlan. She was baggage. She was *worse* than baggage.

Reva Sharma was irreplaceable.

A boltgun spun up nearby, and a skewed, sour note slithered into her left ear. *Ah,* she thought. *There's the fourth.*

"Stand up. Slowly."

The voice belonged to a young man with a dull, ship-bound complexion, wearing InGen cit tags and a dirty yellow uniform. His voice bent around gravel like he'd started drinking backhouse moonshine twenty years ago, and his face, slathered with three days' worth of a salt-and-pepper beard, wore the angry, bored gaze of a functionary whose already annoying day had just become much worse. His gun hovered close enough to Natalie's head that she could feel the heat of the spinner against her forehead, and his bulky backpack blocked out the afternoon sun.

No, she thought. *That's not a backpack.*

The gun was the least of her worries.

Sharma's hand closed on Natalie's wrist a second later. Of course the doctor would recognize a transport isolette as quickly as Natalie—fat, tough things meant for hauling Vai kinetics, wrapped with layers of woven fabric and topped with triple-milled titanium. But these weren't strapped on antigrav dollies or safely stashed in some proper armory; these were set on the burly shoulders of the InGen soldiers. Each of the four men carried one, like pack mules hauling a small apocalypse.

Natalie slid up, the blood clammy against her chest, and remembered what it was like to fear. She let her shoulders drop. Imagined the confidence leaking from her veins like blood from Ash's wrist.

"Please," she whispered. "Please, help us."

"Unlikely," the leader said, mirthless.

"It's just me and my boss," she whispered, throwing herself into the role. She remembered the retreat at Grenadier, the terror in her throat, the fire in her lungs, and let it wrap around her tongue. "We crashed. Someone—someone shot at us. We need help—"

The man tilted his head. "Are you Auroran? *Shit.*"

Sharma had figured out the ploy by now. She moaned, her fingers dropping from Natalie's wrist to claw at her dirty ankle. When she spoke, her voice softened into a pale version of itself. Natalie knew she shouldn't feel so surprised that the doctor was so good at acting.

"Of course we're Auroran," she said. "This is *our* planet. We're terraformists. And if your company was responsible for shooting us down—" Sharma huffed for air, and this time it was obvious she wasn't quite faking it, that the atmosphere had taken up residence in her lungs. She gulped again, almost as if she were daring the planet to kill her.

Natalie leaned over, pressing her bloody hand to Sharma's

forehead. "Look," she said, trying to sound as worried as possible. "She might care who you are. I don't. She needs help, she—" *Think of Ash. Think of everyone who died. Cry. You know how to cry.* "Do I need to tell you what a mix of forty percent methanethiol does to the human lung? She needs a rebreather, bandages, a *doctor*—"

The man's hand shook on his boltgun. "We're going to take you in."

Sharma let out a theatrical groan, and Natalie scrambled to her feet. "Seriously? This is an Auroran planet, asshole. I don't know who *you* are, but you're not even supposed to be here. When *Beijing* notices we didn't make our checkpoint, they'll fire on whatever can of shit you have in orbit. You either help or you let us go."

She didn't expect the lie to work. She expected to be stunned, shoved face-down into the brig of some foreign cruiser, perhaps dragged in front of some yellow-shirted InGen interrogator. But the man harrumphed, holstered his boltgun, and nodded. "I meant *help you*," he said. "We have food and meds at the camp. We'll have the commander fire up the ansible to *Beijing*, and then we'll go get the rest of your people."

His smile was a shark's.

Natalie smiled back, wide and with teeth. *A feint in return,* she thought. *They know* Beijing's *dead. They want us to lead them to other Aurorans on Tribulation so they can clear their path to Ashlan.*

"I appreciate it," Natalie whispered.

"Just try to keep up," he said, turning away.

"We'll make an attempt," Natalie said, picking her way through the brush and brambles. Just behind her, Sharma favored her right ankle like she'd actually rolled it in the crash, letting out entirely realistic cries of agony at completely appropriate times.

"So, you're terraformists," said the team leader, looking over his shoulder. "We didn't know Aurora was looking to recolonize so soon."

"We didn't know InGen was coming to help," said Natalie.

The team leader paused for a moment, using a long knife to slash a set of tight-knit vines blocking the path. "Well, you know," he said, "our executive board was entirely shocked by what happened here. We're still proper members of the Alliance. Were you making your survey in the area of the old colony?"

Why? Natalie thought. *Are you looking for a particular ag-center too?*

"The southern continent, near Tanner Point. A new site." Natalie's eyes snagged on the man's long knife, which was catching the violent, late-afternoon light as it minced the brambles, and Natalie moved to loosen the safety on her boltgun while he wasn't watching. Nearby, Sharma's eyes widened in warning. She sent a dark look back in the doctor's direction—*I know what I'm doing.*

"Ah," he said. "Too many ghosts here, huh."

"Something like that."

Snick. The long knife sliced throuth the brambles again, opening their path, and the man's eyes drifted toward Natalie's waistband. "I didn't know scientists needed boltguns."

"War is a science," Sharma said.

The man's eyes narrowed as he walked.

"The battle plan: the hypothesis," Sharma continued. "The battle: the experiment. The aftermath: the data, examining what you need to change for the next time."

"Interesting," he said, in a voice that said he considered it anything but.

"Human blood," said Sharma, interjecting before Natalie could get a word in edgewise. "Soldiers' blood. Their sweat, their loss. Those are the reagents in the chemical reaction that is war. Violent, yes, and all too often necessary. Hopefully, the research bears it out for the betterment of all. If not, well. You still have data to analyze."

The man grunted, unimpressed, and Sharma went on for a bit while Natalie tried to figure out how to turn a possible fight to her advantage. She wondered if the men even knew what they carried, if they felt the humming hubbub against their shoulders, cackling like needles under her fingernails, breaking open behind their eyes like birds against a dark sky. She was even more sure now that if she and Sharma made it back to the InGen camp they wouldn't make it back out again. But one against four? That was a risky move.

"Do you know what you have?" Sharma finished.

"Excuse me?" said the man.

"On your back," she said. "Do you know what's in there?"

Hah. You can't stop poking either, Natalie thought. *She's right. We may have more in common than we think. Ugh.* "Boss, let's not bother our hosts."

"Ssh, dear," said Sharma. "We all know one against four is a rotten ratio. I'm just evening the field."

"Excuse me?" said the man.

Natalie's tight shoulders took on a tighter knit. She didn't want to follow Sharma's lead—the lead of a genocidal freak, like her, impaler of hearts, skewerer of livers, but then, wasn't she the same? Hadn't she pulled the trigger on thousands, too? And if they were both lucky, nobody would die here. She could dial down the boltgun setting. The InGens would dream about knives in their lungs until they were found, but she didn't have to kill them herself. She didn't have to make that leap right away.

The memoria whispered to her. *Ash, bleeding out, her blood pooling on the concrete—*

She could do it right this time.

Right. What was right? There was no reason to play happy

houses with the very company that shot them down. This would not end up with established prisoner of war treaties; the corporate engagement rules had already been thrown out when *Beijing* died and these InGen assholes lied about it. If they made it back to InGen's camp, their next destination was an InGen brig.

Natalie balled her fist, taking a breath, smelling death and ozone and lemonade, as the man's gaze hit her waistband again and he realized that the weight of the equation had shifted. His hand hovered near his own weapon.

"Don't even try it," he said.

Sharma cleared her throat and spoke before Natalie could think of a comeback. "I'm very much a lover of science," she said. "Shall we see if you are, as well?"

The leader blinked. "What the hell?"

"I have a hypothesis," Sharma responded. "You were sent here on a suicide mission. You didn't know that until just now. When I told you."

"I will shoot you if you make that necessary."

"You've been told *not* to," Sharma said, "or you would have thirty seconds ago when you saw that my companion's safety was off. No. They told you that you couldn't shoot, but they didn't tell you why. They probably told you to just stay away from plasteel, and that they didn't know if energy discharges would affect your cargo."

The man's boltgun wavered. "How did you—"

"*Hypothesis*," said Natalie, feeling a stab of cruel confident fire. "*You're* the ones who are going to need a medic."

Natalie was already in motion before the man could respond. The fight was quick and dirty, the kind of scrap she'd enjoyed back at Verdict, her fists fast with the bloody talent that got her fast-tracked to the Auroran military division. Men who relied on barrels and triggers forgot about fists and feet and the force of metal. She slammed down on the man's foot, smashed his nose and his eye, cackled at the jelly giving way under her hand. Gross, but effective.

He stumbled, clawing at his face. The other three advanced, their focus entirely on Natalie, and Sharma took advantage of the moment of distraction to pop the leader's backpack open.

A light emerged, violet and sodden and wilding like a bleeding child. The four soldiers froze, and the fight ended as quickly as it had begun. The leader knew what that meant in an instant; he panicked and shoved the pack off his shoulders, backing away. It fell to the ground. Inside, behind the light, Natalie could see a round silver-violet ball large enough to rest inside her palm, wrapped in golden isocloth, nestled in the center of the isolette.

Natalie, who understood these things, reached in and fished it out.

She felt her teeth start to rattle on contact. Something felt wrong—the same kind of *wrong* she'd felt in the puppet rig. All of the Vai weapons had cutesy Auroran pet names: *poppers* and *jammers* and *clippers,* nicknames that might have been used for viruses distributed on a Verdict hacknetwork in her previous life; she recognized this as an evaporator, and felt a rushing relief. It was a kinetic, and kinetics stayed dormant until they hit the right trigger—in this case, coldsuit fabric. It was also fairly easy to outrun. All in all, not the worst thing to be up against.

But this evaporator wasn't dormant.

She saw traceries of light surrounding the cool silver sphere, flash-flickers of intense violet and stabbing red, of boughs and blood and little whining trout with their poison bones. She felt the tingling heat of alien energy beneath her fingers, heard it crackling in the air around them like flames licking at the insides of a computer or acid souring her fingertips. She knew that old twist of her stomach, that wild beat of her heart, that caustic anticipation of death—but the whisper behind it felt new.

Sister, she heard.

"Doc," Natalie whispered. "Doc. That's a *molecular.*"

"Don't be silly, Ms. Chan. It's clearly an evaporator kinetic."

"I know what I'm talking about," Natalie snapped.

"So do I."

The leader tightened his grip on the boltgun. "We were carrying *Vai* weapons?"

"Let's engage in the scientific method," said Sharma, who might understand what Natalie meant, quite possibly more than any other person in the universe. She fished a piece of broken plasteel hull from her bag like she'd grab a bandage or a hairbrush. "Is it a kinetic or a molecular? The only way to find out is to run an experiment. Let's set it off."

Natalie's chin snapped up. *What?*

The man's eyes were wide, and it was obvious he hadn't thought for a second about what he was carrying, and didn't understand how Natalie could just stand there holding a Vai weapon like a holiday trinket. Natalie glanced at the others, who were equally rooted to the ground. She felt for them. She really did. Every single person alive had been there at some point during the war, staring down a short, hot, violent future.

Natalie breathed out. Looked at Sharma. "They could always run."

"They could," the doctor replied. Her eyes were wide and warning, Sharma-speak for *follow along.*

"I mean, I run pretty fast," Natalie said, sweating. "There was that time at Grenadier, then here on Tribulation—"

"And you're not encumbered," Sharma said, and smiled.

The leader shivered. "Yeah, but you are. Your ankle—" he said.

Sharma shifted her whole weight on it. "What about it?"

Natalie turned back to the others, swallowed her terror, and slid the thing into the crook of her arm like a murderous infant. It sang, sang, sang—"Gentlemen, it's been lovely. But I think that if you enjoy your skin on the outside of your body, you'd better run."

The man at the back was the first one to break. He'd been trembling since the violet light first appeared. The other two followed. The commander hollered, turning his attention away; Natalie could almost see him doing the math delineating exactly how screwed he was in his head: *four lost weapons and three lost indentures.* Shitty math for the InGen commander, but it worked out in Natalie's favor.

Natalie and Sharma whirled, hurtling into the underbrush, heading in the path of least resistance, losing themselves once again in the anonymous embrace of the darkening forest. And that was a problem—a major problem—but Natalie was used to Kate Keller's salvage motto of *one fucking problem at a time,* and right now she only had eyes for the horizon.

Once Natalie was sure it was safe, she wheezed to a stop, her lungs sucking down the oxygen that grew more plentiful the closer they got to the ag-center.

"I have to say," Sharma said. She closed her eyes and leaned against a tree. "I'm proud of you."

"Ah. You still think we're friends." Natalie coughed.

"We're not?"

"That was a performance."

Sharma kicked away a vine. "And a good one. You've come a long way in a year. The Natalie I knew when I first boarded *Twenty-Five* wouldn't have thought of that gambit."

"I'm not sure that's a compliment."

"You've developed a sense of subtlety since you've become a citizen."

"Yeah, fuck you, too." Natalie watched her footing as she pushed up and away again, striding through a particularly soggy patch of ground, trying to stifle a wet cough. She tasted salty mucus at the back of her throat and thought about how much she hated subtlety. "It's not a kinetic. I didn't activate the thing. *They* didn't activate the thing. Which means it was you."

Sharma blanched. "It wasn't me."

"Bullshit."

Natalie dropped off into a spate of hard coughing, spitting congealed, greenish liquid onto the back of her hand. It was traced with red blood—clear evidence the atmosphere had found its way into her lungs and started to curdle her bronchioles. Fantastic.

"Don't be silly. They wouldn't have sent me to Tribulation with you if I were *infected*," said Sharma.

Natalie snorted, pushing some brambles out of the way, letting the branch whip back into Sharma's face, and heard the satisfying snap of wood against skin. Sharma made sense, which annoyed her. The doctor grumbled slightly, but kept up behind her, and Natalie felt a little burning satisfaction under her sternum, next to the evaporator, still hot and white against her skin, unexploded and unexplored.

"Well, it's not behaving like one. This is something new."

Sharma stepped on a gathering of dry twigs, sending a series of staccato snaps that dragged Natalie straight back to gunfire and Grenadier. "It's a kinetic."

Natalie stopped, then spat on the ground, centering herself, ridding herself of the taste of Tribulation's tight, rotten air and the aftertaste of iron. She stopped again, allowing the weapon to slide carefully into her right hand. She turned it around in her palm, feeling the warmth of its silver skin, hearing the song, extending it toward Sharma.

"Can't be. It's *on*."

"I don't need to tell you that Vai weapons are either bloodlocked or impact-locked. We already know the rules."

The air felt like sandpaper in Natalie's lungs, dragging pointed nails down her throat, harassing her memoria for feelings she hadn't had in years. "No, we don't. There's the Tribulation weapon, which is neither molecular or kinetic, and—"

"You mean the Heart, and that's only because it's not actually a weapon." Sharma walked closer, hovering in the white weapon-light, a craggy tree throwing shadows across her face.

"You named it." Natalie's voice came out flat.

Sharma shrugged. "I'm not sure who came up with it. I've forgotten. Ms. Chan, the Vai are living beings, bound by the rules of physics and biology. We know how their weapons work." The edges of Sharma's mouth turned down, and she crossed her arms.

"Maybe you don't know as much as you think you do." Natalie watched the weapon spin and whirl, heard the energy inside whisper and howl, chaotic and wordless and blank. Wondered what Ashlan heard when she held this kind of death in her hands, if it felt more like music or terror or blood. Like a promise, perhaps.

The doctor shook her head. "I've been studying this for years. I know what I'm talking about."

"Enlighten me, then," Natalie said, gritting her teeth.

Sharma turned, then stubbed her toe on a large fallen log. She let out a pained hiss. "Not here."

Natalie coughed again, wiping her mouth. Her hand came away smeared with blood. "No. Now. We are having a very bad day. If you know something that can fix this, or explain this, or make it a very *good* day, then you'd better be out with it."

Sharma sighed. "My research concluded that—"

"Don't worry about it," said a third voice, accompanied by the whine of a boltgun. "It doesn't matter what she says. She lies."

Natalie heard the gun fire from the trees, and she whirled; she saw the flashing glint at the muzzle and the bolt that followed, casting vivid, bright light against the tall trees. The bolt hit Sharma right below her left knee, and the doctor fell back against a tree, clutching her leg, her ragged, angry call echoing against the leaves

twirling in the evening wind. Natalie thought she caught a glimmer of silver through her grabbing fingers, but lost it in the weaponlight, in her scramble for a response and a boltgun.

The dark shadows of the dim forest hid the figure, enveloped
in the long, wine-dark fronds of a stunted alien bush, her gun
black against the evening, completely unmoved by Sharma ripping a tourniquet from the sleeve of her jacket.

"She lies, Natalie," the woman repeated. "She lies, and she
takes, and she uses, and you brought her *here*?"

The shooter was a familiar, near-skeletal woman in a worn,
ill-fitting indenture's jumpsuit, her dishwater hair tied up out of
her face, her skin streaked with burgundy dirt in an unprofessional attempt at camo. A shaking recognition hit Natalie, and
she stopped in her tracks.

"You can give me that," said Kate Keller, extending her hand
for the evaporator.

"You shot her. You fucking *shot* her."

Sharma gasped. "That was my good leg."

Keller waved her hand, and the molecular died, leaving the
noisy evening forest preternaturally quiet. "Oops."

Natalie focused on the dead evaporator. Keller's hand. The
impossible presence of Keller herself. "What the *fuck*," she
said.

Her presence was impossible, and what she'd done to the
evaporator even more so. The captain—who had been one of
the first supportive citizens she'd ever met, who had reached
out, been her friend, gave her dozens of new chances, new desires, new hope, had redirected her energy—had most certainly
died, either on *Twenty-Five* or when Ramsay had taken her prisoner. That Keller had been kind and funny, with a warm, devious
smile. That Keller had mediated, navigated, supported.

This Keller was barely alive.

Gone was the constant ponytail, the bias-cut bangs, the reliable shoulders. This doppelganger's skin had turned from bright to wan, the whites of her eyes muddied and darkened, her muscles gone to waste. Her dirty-blond hair had been cut to her ears, and thin, sweat-soaked strands peeked out from under a dishrag that served as a bandanna.

Natalie had always thought that Ashlan's fragile constitution had been left over from her time at Wellspring Consolidated, but now she saw the truth of the illness: the alien silver just below Keller's skin, the whisper of death in the tremor of her hand, and a ghoulish darkness around her eyes. The joy at seeing Keller—the joy at knowing her captain had made it out, that she'd found Ashlan, that she was safe—died immediately, because she'd seen that look before. It's just that she'd never recognized it for what it really was.

"You're sick," Natalie whispered.

Keller laughed, but there was no mirth in it—just the hollow, meaningless, cracking sound that lived in Natalie's own throat. "Come on."

"But the evaporator—"

"I'll explain inside. InGen's still around."

By now, Sharma had shredded her jacket to make a bandage and a tourniquet, covering the burned, bloody boltgun wound, mopping up the edges with what used to be a sleeve like she was still worried about offworld contamination protocols. Natalie saw the glimmer hiding under the doctor's sleeve again, playing against the weaponlight, and began to suspect that she was the only one in the little group who would die if the evaporator she was carrying went off.

"I can't exactly walk," the doctor spat.

"Not you," Keller said. Her eyes flickered back to Natalie. "Her."

"She'll die. You can't leave her," said Natalie.

"It's a flesh wound," Keller said. "Sure I can."

"You *meant* to shoot her?" Natalie said, aghast.

"All of this," Keller said, her hand making a wide arc around the space, the trees, them, "is her fault."

"And that's why I'm here," the doctor continued, fixing her eyes on Keller, breathing hard. "That's my lab you're living in. Your illness is my field of research. I can help her. I can help you. I might even be able to save you both, and you thank me by shooting me."

"Yeah, well," Keller said. "We didn't start this to be saved. You of all people should understand the idea of sacrifice."

Sharma's mouth jawed open like an offended fish. Some dark emotion played across her face, as if she'd just been outplayed in some game Natalie couldn't quite understand. She swallowed. "I've made a lot of mistakes, Ms. Keller. *Twenty-Five* was the first place I thought I could change. Let me make it up to you."

Keller's eyes darkened, but Natalie could see her wavering slightly. "That's a lie."

"Are you going to stake Ashlan's life on that?"

"Doesn't matter. You're too late."

"Nothing is ever too late."

Keller narrowed her eyes. "I know you're working for Mr. Solano. We saw your yacht IFF register on the ansible when you arrived."

Sharma laughed. "And you're going to care about that when she's dead? Do you want InGen to have the Heart? What about Armour? Baylor-Wellspring? Are they any better?"

Her former captain's lip twisted. "I sure as hell don't want *you* to have it."

Natalie cleared her throat, feeling the conversation lingering close to the edge of a massive cliff she was quite sure she didn't want to step off. "Well, we can't stay here," Natalie said, looking over her shoulder. "InGen will have drones in the air by now. We need to go."

Keller played with the safety on her gun, her eyes migrating to the pale, dead evaporator in Natalie's arms. "I'll let *her* decide."

Keller reached into her pocket. Natalie expected a gun—it was always guns, these days, bullet guns and boltguns and the violence of the gun's simple request. Instead, she brought out a bog-standard walkie and thumbed the transmission button, asking the question, then pressing it up to her ear to listen to the response.

And for a moment, stupidly, Natalie wondered who *her* was.

The growing darkness underlined Keller's illness; her hat-shaded eyes turned toward the sounds in the distance, the increasing clanks and clatters, the signifiers that InGen was getting closer.

"All right," Keller said into the walkie, after a moment spent listening. There was a tight and terrible thing in Keller's eyes, then, a light and a darkness, and she slid the walkie back into her pocket. "You fuck anything up, Doc, and I mean anything, you drop a fucking *spoon,* and I'll shoot you in a place it isn't going to be so easy to fix."

Sharma's eyes had gone narrow and lambent and, for a second, suspicious, but when she spoke, it was with a tiny smile. "Fair," the doctor replied. "Let's go."

10

Natalie followed her former captain into the vine-choked remains of the agricultural center's main plaza. As they walked, Keller explained that she and Ash had moved the atmospinners closer to the main dormitory and barn, increasing the percentage of breathable air there while allowing the native forest to encroach on the outer buildings, creating natural camouflage. This resulted in brambles circling the broken maglev, trees weaving themselves through the wooden buildings, and sharp, hardy Tribulation grasses invading windowsills and doors.

Otherwise, it was exactly as she'd remembered: a scene straight out of a colonization holo, with plain-walled barns and dorms set squat and square around the mud-choked plaza, the whole place scattered with shredded festival banners. Rusted trucks and tractors lay where they'd been left after the war; doors to indentures' cabins jawed wide open, their bright tattered curtains flapping in the sulfur breeze. This was the other way to citizenship—working Auroran land you'd eventually lease as a citizen, supplying the Company's assets in space with food and resources. Boring as hell. Maybe it was the dream of people who grew up on stations, Natalie supposed, or people who cared about what Earth was like before the biosphere tanked. Not her.

Ash and Kate—calling her captain by her first name just felt curious and wrong, even though Kate now insisted on it—had removed all evidence of their post-battle presence: the leftover comm tent, the ansible equipment, anything that would point at current human habitation. She could see halfhearted stone fortifications in the west but recognized them as new only because she'd been here before.

New, too, were the solar-powered sensors on the east end, covered with artistically arranged burgundy scrub grasses to make it look like the machines had been there awhile. Ash and Kate hadn't bothered to hide the impact crater where the escaping transport had gone down; they had been too weak at that point to do heavy shoveling, Kate explained. Natalie half-listened to her former captain talk, remembering how this was where everything had started to go wrong: where the blue screamer had gone off, where her team scattered like they hadn't even been trained, where she'd lost the men and women of her very first command to a Vai kinetic the Sacrament Society had left lying around in their haste to get off-planet.

Natalie swallowed down memories: the fireball's stunning heat, the fear, the pounding of her feet on the ground, the screamer wrapping around Ashlan's chest and tearing her apart before it spat her out breathing. Of all the terrible memories the Heart could have taken from her, it left Natalie the empty, screaming loss of the people she was supposed to protect—the men and women of her first real command. She blinked away a sudden tightness in her chest, padding across the expanse, trying to keep up with Kate, who was walking faster than any woman as sick as she was had a right to.

"You're in danger," Natalie said.

"No shit," said Kate. Her mouth twisted. "I was hoping we'd have a few more weeks. It's fine. We knew we couldn't hide forever. We've done most of what we came here to do, and if the rest of it fails, at least we have a plan to kill the Heart."

Natalie could hear Sharma hacking up a lung behind her, gasping at the spun oxygen as it slithered closer, leaning on her makeshift crutch. Natalie coughed herself, feeling an absurd stab of gratitude for the change in the air, and then swallowed the last clot of thick mucus in her throat.

"You can't," Sharma said, gasping for breath. "You can't kill the Heart."

Kate opened a side door to the barn. "Watch me." She paused. "You know, I actually hope you do."

Sharma shook her head. "It's my life's work. I should know."

"Is it?" Kate ducked into the barn, and it swallowed the sound of her voice. "Do you know, or are you just hypothesizing? There's one thing about dying from celestium toxicity in an underground test site that's actually quite fun: you get time to *practice*."

"If you think you know so much, how do you plan to disable it?"

"The same way you defuse any molecular. The same way we neutralized the stash of weapons stored here."

Natalie interjected. "You can't *defuse* most moleculars. You can only set them off."

Sharma's eyes gleamed. "You mean—all the others—you—" She paused. "Everything we stockpiled is gone?"

"Yep."

"Then you're ready for the fight." The doctor struggled to catch up, limping, while Natalie struggled to understand. "The Vai are massing at the White Line, Ms. Keller. We don't know why. We need the Heart."

Kate smirked and continued on like Sharma hadn't said a thing. "Do you honestly want to find out what it *really* does?"

"Yes," Sharma breathed.

"Then *shut up* about your goddamn research."

Sharma's eyes grew wide. Kate simply smiled and moved forward, the sound of her footsteps echoing against the wood and plasteel floor.

Natalie pulled away from the doctor's eyes burning a hole in her back, disappearing into the darkness of the barn. She expected to see the crates of Sacrament-stored kinetic weapons that were inside last time, as well a dusty cot and some old, rusting farm implements, but the crates were missing, quite possibly relocated elsewhere. A polished wheelchair sat in the corner. She pursed her lips, casting another glance around, and then hurried to catch up with Kate, who was already clattering down the staircase to the Sacrament lab.

"Wait," Natalie said, leaving a boiling Sharma in her wake. "Captain. You're infected too. How?"

Kate paused on the staircase. "The price of a kiss."

"How long do you have?"

"A couple months," said her former captain. "Not long enough."

"The doc has a treatment," Natalie said.

Kate's mouth flattened, and she took in Natalie's information like she always had, back on the ship—with the same calm face, the same unlined forehead. The only sign Kate had felt anything was her knuckles whitening against the railing. "Doesn't matter," she finally said.

"If she can save you, it's worth hearing her out."

"*If*," Kate said, her eyes darting over Natalie's shoulder.

Natalie straightened. "You wouldn't believe what we've been able to accomplish back home. I believe them. You should, too."

This caught Kate by surprise. "Never."

"Do we really have any other choice?"

"*We*." The former captain repeated the word, then frowned. "There's no *we*, Natalie. There could have been a *we*, but you brought *her*. Maybe you'll understand once I show you—"

"Is Ashlan downstairs?" The doctor's voice, and her shadow, draped over Natalie's shoulders, and Kate turned, continuing toward the underground facilities.

Sharma limped down the staircase behind them; she'd fashioned a splint of sorts from the hilt of some old farm tool. Kate rolled her eyes, fired up a solar torch, and shone the beam toward the metal door at the bottom of the stairs. They passed through the small reception room—the dead body was gone, but the stink remained, scrubbed into the walls like sin—and passed into the cavernous underground chamber where the Sacrament Society had once stored their nauseating experiments.

Natalie's boots hit the dirt following Kate's, and she wiped sweaty palms on her uniform top before looking around. The quarantine boxes were gone, replaced by five old mattresses surrounded by improvised medical equipment. Nearby was a generator, whirling power into intravenous poles and dialysis machines. Lying on the mattresses were five men, sleeping.

She recognized them.

Cables obscured their faces, and blankets their legs, but Natalie saw enough to cue the memoria. These twisted, wasted bodies belonged to Solano's staffers; they were members of the team the Company had landed on Tribulation to inventory the Sacrament atrocities. She'd left with a fire team to find Ashlan, leaving behind men with clipboards and cameras. They must have still been below when Ash triggered the Heart in orbit.

They were undernourished, despite the obvious care to keep intravenous drugs flowing. They had the beginnings of bedsores, yellowed teeth, and lungs that inhaled and exhaled with the dregs of a ragged instinct. Natalie couldn't stop staring; this, she knew, would have been her fate if she hadn't listened to Ash.

Take this away, she begged the memoria, but for the very first time, the damned thing seemed to be working as advertised. She saw them hauling equipment down the stairs, their eyes wide with excitement. Heard their voices saying how honored they were to be here, to be trusted by the board. They must have still been poking through the isolettes when the Heart went off, ripped through ships, through space, through their bodies, their pasts, and their futures. She didn't even know their names.

"You're reusing IV bags?" Sharma's voice at least had the respectability to sound shocked.

Kate heaved a sigh. "It's not like we get regular shipments of saline solution down here. What the hell else was I supposed to do?"

Natalie thought of the yawning black chasm of the things she should have known, the things she could have done for the five young men. How much worse would it have been without the memory device? The words came out before she could stop them. "Bullet. To the head."

"Oh, is that your best idea?" said Kate, the sarcasm thick.

"Did you expect them to wake up?" said Natalie.

Kate sighed. "I kind of hoped they would."

Sharma didn't respond right away; she moved from patient to patient, her hands lightly touching the improvised IV bags, resting her fingers against the inside of a wrist, checking the temperature of another. "They're not going to wake up," she said. "Natalie's right. A bullet would be better."

Kate breathed out. "I can't *believe* you two."

"What about the memoria? Could that help, if we could get them back to *Vancouver*?" Natalie said.

Sharma's voice soured. "The memory device has to contain some reference to who you used to be. These poor men, well. There's nothing left to save. The memoria would provide, at best, a programmed fantasy, not that they'd understand it, because they don't even have the experiential touchstones of a newborn baby—like a mother's heartbeat, or light and darkness. I feel for them, Ms. Chan, but there's nothing I can do."

"We can take them home," Natalie said.

"I think it's interesting that you're suddenly a humanitarian," Sharma said.

"These people are *Auroran*." Natalie's face reddened. "But I wouldn't expect that to be important to you."

Sharma shrugged. "It's not important to the executive board."

"There was a lockout—"

"Come on." Sharma's laughter took on a bitter edge. "*Beijing* was here the whole time. They could have sent search parties down at any time."

Kate cleared her throat, stepping between the two. "So do you want to see her or not?"

Sharma cleared her throat, tore her eyes away from Natalie, and hobbled away. It took Natalie a few more moments to leave; her hands brushed the palm of the body closest to her. She shivered when she found the pads of his corpselike fingers were still warm.

The administrative wing was still a mess, still choked with papers and clutter from the Sacrament Society bugout. Kate explained that as their disease advanced, she and Ash focused on making updates to Sharma's lab, which had morphed from an alien abattoir into a hospital, if a hospital could be cobbled together out of scraps and trash by minds and hands more used to working on engines and ships.

Natalie's vestigial Verdict brain saw the proliferation of wires and tubes and interlaced computer parts first, fastened together with wire and shoelaces, running to and from a set of blinking, jury-rigged servers in the corner. These were innards ripped out of quarantine boxes and old colony terminals, tied into repurposed power sources running pumps where blood-dark medicine dripped in regular intervals. All of it served the central surgical bed, where what was left of Ashlan Jackson lay battered and dozing, lost in a drug-induced haze.

The mattress nearby belonged to Kate, from what Natalie could tell. The captain's belongings had always been impeccably sorted and cared for aboard *Twenty-Five*, and here, she saw even meal wrappers folded and stacked in a rubbish bin nearby in some fantasy of control. She counted eight days' worth of uneaten pasta dishes, one fork, and no obvious change of clothes. Kate lived here. Natalie felt a quick pull at her heart, a quick thought of *nobody would do that for me.*

"*You* did this?" Sharma whispered, sounding impressed.

"I followed your manuals," Kate said. "Whatever else you are, you're not a half-bad technical writer."

Sharma ignored the dig, then moved toward the familiar stranger on the surgical bed, checking her vitals. Ash still had her dark hair cut into the ragged, knife-slash edges of a busy indenture, but that was where the resemblance to the friend she'd known on *Twenty-Five* ended. This Ash lay withered, exhaustively thin, breathing irregularly in a low, congested rattle. Her fingers twitched as the doctor approached—not that she looked at all conscious.

"This," Sharma said, waving her hand over a set of diodes on Jackson's feverish forehead. "This is wrong. Do you *want* to fry her frontal lobe?"

"That was in your instructions—"

"I wrote that years ago," Sharma said. She licked dry lips, shaking her head. "There were so many things I didn't understand back then, knowledge I didn't have regarding the way the human brain interacts with Vai physiology. Let me fix this. Please."

Kate hesitated near Ash's head, then leaned over, lifted the sick pilot's fingers, and pressed her lips soft and light to Ash's bony knuckles. She took a few quick strides toward the door, settling in the space just outside the room, her shoulder lingering against the doorjamb and her arms crossed. Sharma moved in, stepping in front of the readings on the monitor. Natalie followed Kate, a thousand questions bubbling behind her teeth, but when she arrived, it was the ex-captain who spoke first.

"*He* sent you, didn't he?"

Natalie considered telling her otherwise, but the truth had always been the best option when talking to Kate. "Solano? Yeah. He figured out that I lied and let Ash go, during the battle, so—"

"—so now you're back to fix your . . ." Her lip curled. "Mistake."

Natalie took a breath to respond but was caught instead in a wreck of a cough, the lingering mucus in her throat clotting her air intake. Inside the room, Sharma darted from the computer to the bed, checked Ashlan's pulse, tied a tourniquet on her upper arm, and fished out a lancet from a nearby drawer like she hadn't spent years and years away from the lab.

"You know I don't think letting her go was a mistake. I told her I'd return as soon as I could."

Her former captain's lips settled into a full, derisive twist. "Once they put your shiny new citizenship on the line, I'd imagine. I know how this works, Ms. Chan. Everyone has their price. What was yours? A directorship?"

Natalie winced. "That's not—"

"A directorship, then."

"It's complicated."

"You know, Nat, I always thought you were going places. That you were going to be better than the rest of them. But now I know I can't trust you, either. The old Natalie would know not to dangle false hope in front of me like a fucking executive." Her osprey eyes fixed cold and angry on Natalie's.

"Just talk to her," Natalie said. "She has no reason to lie."

"Dr. Sharma has *every* reason to lie. Never forget that," Kate said. She pushed off the doorjamb and entered the lab, effectively ending the conversation. "Doc! Give me good news."

Sharma looked up from where she was bent over some scar tissue on Ashlan's wrist, banishing some dark, unknowable emotion. She wiped her hands on a clean towel, which she tossed aside, as if she were still on a ship and there was some indenture haunting the wall nearby ready to catch it. "You're not going to like the good news, and there's plenty of the bad kind, too," she said.

The tension in the room tightened like a noose.

"Out with it," said Kate.

"She's extremely close to organ failure." Sharma rubbed the

back of her neck. "You were right to be concerned about her AST/ALT levels. She's going to need tissue regeneration to her lungs and a liver transplant to survive, so we need to get her off-planet to a proper medbay as soon as possible."

Kate took the news like a bolt to the face. She closed her mouth. Opened it again. Natalie recognized shock in the way her hands started to shake—or was that the celestium madness? It had been a year, after all.

"Natalie was talking about a treatment. Not major surgery."

Sharma stiffened. "Yes, but I can't do anything for the Vai tech in her blood until we stabilize her."

Kate's shoulders tightened. "Do it here. We can't go off-planet. It's impossible."

The doctor clasped her hands together in front of her abdomen, as if this were a normal consultation and a normal day. "You asked me to save her life. I need proper equipment to do that. Once she has a functioning liver and her lungs are drained of fluid, we can move on to the treatment."

"No." Kate's eyes focused on Ash's sleeping face.

"Well," Sharma said, giving her hands a last quick wipe on the front of her jacket, "if you don't want to save her—"

"Look at the two of you." Kate's voice broke. Natalie could feel her ex-captain's rage shivering underneath her own fingernails, tried to breathe in air salt-thick with her fear, and found she couldn't. "You're not here to save us. You're here to dangle *the cure,* the fucking nonexistent cure, just long enough to get us on a transport back to *Rio de Janeiro.* I'm never going to trust either of you ever again."

Sharma took two steps back, away from the surgical bed, lifting her hands, and when she spoke, her voice was careful and slow. "You asked me to be her doctor, and I agreed. I will not lie about a bond as sacred as that. There was no cure before the Battle of Tribulation because watching it happen—having access to

Heart-coma patients and memory devices afterward—gave me the last few pieces of information I needed to synthesize a cure. It's a very specific thing, customized for the patient's particular situation. I *cannot* do it here."

"Then what *can* you do?" Kate said, after a long, considering moment.

Sharma looked away, toward the ground, losing herself in a sudden thought. She tapped her fingers against the bedside. "I'm going to find some of my cloning equipment and grow her a functioning liver. I don't have the ability to do a full cell regen panel, so it won't be a good one, but it will last until we can get her to Europa Station."

Kate's shoulders slumped, like Sharma had shattered a bright and terrifying gem inside her heart. Natalie lingered in a conflicted silence, trapped between a lie and a truth, or perhaps two truths, or two lies. She'd seen dozens of indentures take out years of credit for medicine, for basic medical care, for splints and gunshots and the flu, and here Sharma was talking about growing an organ like an ear of corn. Talking about *borrowing it for a while,* like Ash had misplaced a shoe or a power tool. Is this why the executives lived so long?

"How long does that take?" Kate asked.

"Twelve hours."

"Not possible," Kate said. "The other companies will arrive way before that."

"InGen is already close," Natalie said.

"Liver structures are complicated, and need time to grow and resolve," Sharma said. "But they'd be *hers,* and rejection wouldn't be an issue during the transport to Europa."

"Which means there's an option where it would. Tell me about that one." Kate advanced and stared down the doctor. Natalie had only ever seen that look in fellow survivors of Cana. People who had been in the war from the very beginning, who had seen and done things so terrible they'd lost all sense. The old Kate Keller would have tossed off a joke at this point, lifted her chin, made you feel foolish and loved and accepted. *This* version—

This Keller made Natalie shiver.

Sharma pursed her lips and looked out toward the office complex. "Your coma boys outside. Odds are that you've been feeding them the proper intravenous solutions, they'll be healthy enough for surgery. We excise her liver and replace it with a lobe from one that still works. I inject some medicine that makes Ash's body think the liver is hers." She raised her hand to forestall Kate's immediate questions. "The surgery is risky to both parties, yes, but livers regenerate, and I can have her prepped for transport shortly afterward."

Kate looked aghast. "You can't do a liver transplant within the hour."

"Then you'll have to buy me time. If you'd brought the Heart to *Medellin* like I asked, we'd already have Ash treated and secured in a safe place, far away from anyone who would do her harm, and you would be with her. So, yes, we're doing this my way."

"All right. And the men? How do you propose to ask their permission?"

"Ask?" said Sharma. "We don't *ask*."

Kate's jaw worked for a second. "This isn't your fucking organ factory anymore, Reva. They can't consent to surgery."

"They are far past consent."

"They're breathing on their own—"

"It doesn't matter. The most important part, the bit that makes us human, is gone," Sharma said, tapping her memory device. "Who we are, what we make of our world, it's all knit together from the experiences we write on our brains and our bodies. Those poor young men were at the epicenter of the deployment of the Heart, and the Heart worked exactly the same both times it was triggered, and you know here—" She pressed against Kate's chest with one finger, and Natalie could see her former captain barely resisting some deep, aching anger at that. "You know that there's nothing left."

"Who are you to say that?" whispered Kate.

A new voice. Whisper-weak, crunching tight like booted feet on rolling gravel, but so familiar. "It's true. We've done everything we can. They're gone."

Three heads turned to watch Ash, her dull eyes open for the first time, her body almost entirely still. She shifted enough to raise her hand, then drop it to her lap and gather a part of the blanket into a rumpled ball. She was crying.

Natalie rushed to her side. "Hi," she said.

"You came back." Ash smiled through cracked lips.

"Don't get too excited. Doc wants to take you back to Europa, and I'm not at all convinced it isn't a good idea."

Ash laughed, a half-hacking horror show of a thing, and Natalie saw blood and spittle at her lips. "Oh, I'm fine with leaving, but not for Europa."

"Then where?" said Natalie, still hoping for an out.

"That's impossible, love," Kate said, sweeping in before Ash could answer.

"Not—impossible," Ash whispered, starting to shake. "It is the only necessary thing."

Sharma frowned. "What's she talking about?"

The comment had made Kate frown too, frown with a specific gray sadness that told Natalie she knew exactly what Ash was talking about. Instead of answering, Kate stood up. "Not that," she said, pushing back her hair, smoothing it against the side of her head.

"Put the evaporator away," Ash whispered, even though there was no way she could have known about the singing thing in

Natalie's jacket. Her eyes rolled back, and she slipped back to whatever quiet hell she'd been living in.

"Make a decision, Captain," Sharma said. "She doesn't have much time."

Kate turned away to hide her tears.

"Do it," she said, and then pulled away, running down the hallway. Her footsteps echoed in the blank hallway outside, and Natalie's eyes followed—she wasn't heading for the cavern, but the bugout bay. *That* bugout bay. Seconds later, she saw a sickeningly familiar violet-green splatter of light at the end of the hallway; suddenly, the memoria forced her back into the transport fleeing the battle, her breath hot in her throat, the blood thrumming in her ears, the memories that said *run, this is the Heart, run—*

"You don't need help, do you?" she managed, lost in the shimmer.

"Normally, I'd say yes," said Sharma, moving toward a case of bottled water in the corner. She rolled up her sleeves, removed the cap, and drenched her hands up to the elbows. "But, in this case, I think your skills could be better put to use elsewhere, say, prepping for our visitors, or . . ." Her eyes wandered to the light. "Making sure she isn't cooking up another rash decision, like using *it* on *us*."

—I'll be back for you, the memoria cried, as if Natalie were back on *London* with Ash, and she whacked the side of her head like she was attempting to dislodge water caught behind her eardrum. She was on the edge of panic, moving through a forest of could-have-beens, stretching sleek and delicious into the bloody sky careening over the ground above. She slammed her foot against the concrete to remind herself where she was, and then licked her lips, pointing at the doctor.

"Do not fuck it up," she said, quietly. "Do you understand?"

Sharma's mouth creased into an amused grin, and she picked up a white device with a pointed end, flipping open the lightning end of a cauterizing laser. "You're the one with the gun. Of course."

Natalie turned and walked off with the wide, angry strides of someone about to throw up. Sharma was right. She needed to check in on Kate, who was now in the one room in the entire complex Natalie didn't want to go. Couldn't go. Wouldn't go.

No.

She wanted to explain to Kate why she'd been right. Ash's claim of mass murder was insane, anyway, when anyone could see the alien had two hands and two feet and two eyes, that it was one creature, one breath, one heartbeat. Not thousands.

Kate would see. She would understand.

She could hardly breathe; everything seemed tight and callous and hot, like some dark executioner had a boltgun spinning hot just inches from her brain. The hangar itself was still nothing to write home about, meant to hide the Sacrament Society's stolen pods and shuttles in plain sight, kept at the ready in case they needed to leave in a hurry. There were no working shuttles here now, of course—just useless repair equipment, a burned-out Becker Ace, and half-empty boxes filled with picked-over engine parts, as well as piles of uniforms and smocks in the corner. Someone had made an aborted attempt to scrub away the bloodstains on the floor—brown and gray, human blood and alien.

The resulting smear glittered in the heliotrope light that remained. Natalie's eyes took a moment to adjust. Kate waited in the center of the room, her left hand hovering over an open quarantine locker.

"You remember this?" Kate asked. "The Heart?"

Natalie shivered. "Like I could forget."

"Ash told me that you left to run a perimeter check before the doctor turned it on, back at the admin center when everything began. You never saw it work. This is what you missed."

The room grew brighter—notes of pomegranate and sage, brighter than the sun—and Natalie felt suddenly breathless. The Heart sang in shades of purple and green, twisting inside a cage of black scrollwork that whined like vines shrinking and dying in the summer heat of her childhood, like blank arteries opening in the sun. The temperature dropped off a cliff, as if Sharma had shoved her in a cycling airlock without a suit, and Natalie felt cold panic in her throat. Her bones shook where they stood.

"Stop," she whispered.

"I think it understands what you did here," Kate said.

"I saved Ashlan. That's what I did." She used the palm of her hands to block the stabbing light.

"You have to stop telling yourself stories, Natalie. Justifying the horrors around you just to get through the day. If you don't, they'll eat you alive. You'll go straight into that maw, singing."

"That thing was killing her," Natalie said—*the blood,* the memoria showed her *the blood on the floor, red and silver mixing together, a Charybdis of it, the memoria making her remember how it swirled there, inhuman, only this time it was so cold in the room it froze in cells and crystals, glittering in the Heartlight*—"I did the right thing. Unless you think I should have let her bleed out."

"Excuses." Kate drew in on herself, shoulders hunching, and she turned so Natalie couldn't see the gun at her holster—not that Natalie was concerned. Kate had never held a gun any smaller than the railguns mounted on *Twenty-Five*'s prow when Natalie had known her, and she truly doubted she'd practiced enough to outshoot Natalie.

Natalie wondered if Kate was going to push this toward a fight, if she'd have to bloody this person she'd loved in Joseph

Solano's name. *You were a soldier,* she thought, *you chose that life, what did you expect?*

Not this.

"Turn it off," she said, shivering.

Kate didn't move. She didn't look affected by the plummeting temperature. "Not until you tell me what Solano has planned."

Natalie's jaw chattered. The air in the bugout bay felt like the aftermath of a nuke, like a black hull against midnight stars. "He didn't tell me. But they do want you back. And maybe for a little while, maybe, I thought about bringing you there. But, Captain—Kate—anywhere is better than this. The Vai are massing, Baywell won't back down, and the alliances aren't going to hold after today. I'm not saying Aurora is the best situation for you. I'm not even saying it's a *good* situation. But you'd live. You'd live."

Natalie heard yelling from down the hall. Sharma. *Keep that on if you want to kill her yourself, but I need the machines to work.*

Kate softened. She shoved the isolette back into the black quarantine box below and flipped the lid, sealing it shut. The last tendrils of light caressed her bent fingers, then surrendered to darkness. Heat rushed in like a wave, scrambling at Natalie's stiff muscles. She felt a scurrying gratitude.

"We didn't come here because we were running away, or because we *wanted* to die, Nat," Kate said, quietly. "It was the only way. It still is."

"Then explain it to me, because I don't understand."

Kate bit her lip. "She already told you on *London*. Nobody can have the Heart. Nobody."

Natalie nursed a note of frustration. "And when you die, what happens then? Someone's just going to walk in and take it."

"We've been doing our own research, trying to figure out what it will take to disarm it. We—" She swallowed. "We spent a long time with Sharma's notes. When she cut the Heart away from the Vai ship she discovered all those years ago, she cut the Heart from the Vai network in general. But if we could reconnect it, they might simply leave with it. But we couldn't do that because we didn't have a ship. Now that you're here—"

"Reconnect it, so they'll *know* their people are dead? I'm sorry, Kate, but that's the stupidest thing I've ever heard. This situation is far beyond solutions that sound like 'let's ignore it and hope it goes away.' We need to focus on active fixes."

Kate sighed. "We have." She drummed her fingers on the quarantine box, clearly nervous. "Neither Ash nor I will serve as a human trigger for Aurora or for any other corporation. That leaves us one option. We need to take ourselves out of the equation, and the Heart at the same time."

"You mean suicide."

"More than suicide."

Natalie blinked. "There's nothing past suicide."

"There is with the Heart." Kate cleared her throat. "The point is, no company gets the ability to use Vai tech."

"And if the Vai decide to attack again? Kate, do you want those millions of lives on your conscience?"

Kate opened her mouth to answer, but her words were drowned out by a rumbling from above. The bay doors clattered. Clumps of wet dirt fell from an unfinished section of the upper wall. Natalie placed her hands on the wall, feeling the reverberations— not Vai, she figured, but kinetic, human things, bullets and mortars and grenades. Most of it seemed to be coming from the north—*InGen, here early,* Natalie thought—but she also felt a violent answer from the east, a shaking, momentary blast that could only mean Baylor-Wellspring had brought the same kind of artillery that they'd been known to bring to decimate Auroran infantries over the past few months.

Her former captain's eyes closed, and her body bowed, exhausted.

"I don't have a better answer," she whispered.

"So we'll go find one," said Natalie. "Together. As soon as we're done with InGen."

"And Sharma?"

"Fuck Sharma."

A small smile danced across Kate's face, and she nodded. "All right. You're the tactician. What do we do from here?"

II

Natalie walked back to Sharma's surgery with her fingers dragging against the wall, feeling the thud of men and machines above. She reached out to the memoria and it responded, like spiders playing tiddlywinks with her vertebrae. Memories spun her back to basic tactics training, to when the execs still thought ordinary methods of warfare could win against the Vai. She tasted the glassy, recycled stink of the classroom, then the bright, clear air of the exercises on Bethel.

Bethel, only the second planet she'd ever visited, where she lost sixteen cit points and one whole credit-year gawking at the spindletrees instead of paying attention to her commanding officer. There were holes on that planet, too, moments of forgetfulness not even the memoria could salvage, faces she couldn't remember. It seemed unfair that she could remember the chorus to every stupid Smashboys song and not the friends from her very first unit.

"Natalie," Kate barked, behind her. "Focus."

The ghostly figures dissipated. "Do you have sensors? A comm system?"

"In the dorm. I have the ansible Len built. I wired it into some equipment the farmers used to measure crop yields and atmospheric percentages. It's not video, it's not holo or haptic, but it'll tell us where the assholes are. We tried to bring it all downstairs but didn't have the cable."

Len again. Was he another friend she'd forgotten in the Tribulation soup? She wanted to ask about him—*her? Who?*—but right now wasn't a good time. "That's good enough. Guns?"

"Two. In the kitchen with the comms."

"How much ammo?"

"Some." Kate took a breath. "The problem is, I can't aim. My hand-eye coordination, it's—"

"—just as bad as Ash's was last year. Okay," Natalie said. She remembered that, at least. A year into her illness, Ash had nearly piloted her salvage pod here and there into walls and debris, even a loose kinetic or two, although Natalie had figured it for exhaustion at the time. Fatigue was easy to entertain on long-haul assignments. "That's fine. Just because your aim is shot doesn't mean you can't tell *me* where to aim."

"It's not that easy. I have hallucinations."

"All you have to see is the enemy line. I'll take care of the rest. If we do this right, we won't even be doing most of the shooting ourselves." Natalie stopped in the hallway to squeeze Kate's shoulder. It was the kind of thing Kate might have done for her, once, and Natalie felt momentarily nervous, like she was going to insult this person she admired, but Kate didn't seem either embarrassed or grateful. Instead, she looked nervous.

"I really don't want to leave her," Kate said.

"You're not leaving her," Natalie said. "You're saving her."

Kate choked up. "What we've been through together, Nat, it changes you—"

"So use that feeling," Natalie said. "Do your best. Come back to her. It's not an option. Okay?"

"Okay."

They walked toward the cavern together. Natalie tossed a glance into the lab as she went; Sharma was bent over Ash's prone body, instruments flickering in the artificial light. Natalie saw bloody tools, spent syringes, the pale curve of Ash's chin. She saw the chain of jewel-red liquid scattering the floor, shining in the electric light, and followed it with her eyes all the way out into the cavern. Kate skidded to a halt behind her, breath hot on the back of Natalie's neck.

"No," Kate whispered, then took off.

"Wait," Natalie said, grabbing for her old captain's sleeve, but it passed through her fingers like water. She followed Kate into the cavern. One of the men on the mattresses was dead, his guts open to the ceiling, his forgotten body still too recent to enter rigor. From where Natalie was standing, she could recognize the shining red curve of the stomach, the empty bowl where the liver had been, and all the guts that had slurped in to take its place.

Kate turned back toward the lab, and Natalie's fingers finally found purchase in the other woman's ragged sleeve.

"Don't," Natalie said.

"She said she wouldn't kill him." Kate yanked her arm away.

Natalie's hand clamped around Kate's thinning, bony wrist. "She's in surgery. I don't know what'll happen to Ash if you interrupt her. And if we don't get everything set up, we're not getting out of here alive."

"*You* brought her here. You convinced me to—*you*—" She closed her eyes, unable to finish. "What happened to you, Natalie?" she asked. "You used to care."

But maybe I never did, she wanted to say, *or maybe I just can't take anything more,* but the words came too late. Kate stared at Natalie's silence with a disgusted twist of her lip, then turned back, walking quick and stiff toward the exit as Natalie had asked her to.

Outside, night was threatening, inky black and chattering, with only a whisper of moonrise at the tree line. It wasn't the most ideal time for rival companies to attempt a full-on assault of a facility where Vai weapons were known to be stored in spades, but Natalie had seen dumber orders given, and the plan coming together in her head, at least, felt more agile than anything In-Gen would pick up on.

Kate pointed across the plaza. "About a hundred feet," she whispered, and Natalie attempted to delineate the chunky line of the dorm from the obsidian darkness beyond. Failing, she picked up, running pell-mell with her former captain until the building was close, until the prefab plasteel wall was under her hand, until Kate pressed herself against the door, fiddling with the lock. It popped open just as they heard a whack-crackle from the tree line, like boots stepping on branches or a machete slicing through one of the hungry vines clogging the windows, and the two tumbled inside.

"Do you think they saw us?" Kate said.

Natalie wheezed, taking longer to catch her breath than she wanted. *Fucking Tribulation air.* "Always assume they did."

Kate nodded, pretending not to notice the crackling sound in Natalie's lungs. "It's all back here."

The air inside the dorm was slightly stale, tinged with the stink of blankets and linens left to rot in the humidity. Kate coughed, lighting a torch but keeping it low and dangling from her fingers. She pushed past a hanging knit blanket into what had once been the main dining hall.

"I don't remember all of those vines outside," Natalie said. "And the forest being so close."

"Weird, isn't it? I figure it has something to do with the return of the planetary atmosphere interacting with the food crops. They don't really belong in the biosphere, after all, and I have no idea what the biological implications are, which would be fascinating to think about if I had more time," she said, and pushed open a wooden door. "But there's never enough time."

Natalie tried to keep her disappointment from showing on her face. She failed. This had been the dorm cafeteria, a largely functional expanse populated by metal tables and twirling, fading homemade decorations from some lost festival, colorful paper cut into connected circles by the small, blunt hands of children. The shapes cast dark, whirling shadows on a set of west-facing windows meant to showcase the fields beyond.

It was the worst kind of room they could have picked for this kind of dark work.

Whatever. Ash and Kate had obviously picked the room for its ease of access and proximity to food as they grew weaker. Natalie shut her mouth on the criticism that threatened to spill out. This was what they had. They'd set up a bed and a closet. The settlement's ansible was here, propped up on a table that once functioned as a banquet server. Kate slaved a computer to it, one of the cit-consumer tablets left behind when the Vai turned the inhabitants of the ag-center into dust. Kate turned it on, sliding into the chair, then routed power to the terminal while Natalie hovered behind her.

Instead of the familiar blue of an Auroran machine, the terminal greeted Natalie with the simple black-and-white logo of the Sacrament Society before loading straight into the ansible data, displayed on an old, keyboard-directed interface. If Natalie had a few hours, she could have opened up the back end, matched the code with what little she knew from her Verdict days, and seen if Sharma had slipped her fingers into this machine as well. Unfortunately, she didn't have that kind of time.

"Wow. C-kalibre. That's a flashback," Natalie said.

"All of the Sacrament machines are built off C-kalibre," Kate said. "It still supports the best firewalling you can get."

"I didn't know you were a coder," Natalie said.

"I've had some time to learn this year." Kate smirked. "I'm surprised you recognized it."

The memoria blasted Natalie with one of the memories she would have liked very much to forget: the tang of smoke, rotten fear in her throat, watching the robot run by her classmate's program rip apart her own in the murk of the reflecting pool above the concourse. Her father, frowning. *Maybe we'll just give you a gun and put you on the wall. You're just not good at any of it. I don't know what else to do.*

"Learned it as a kid," Natalie said.

"Huh. Okay, I'm seeing three separate approach vectors. Three companies?"

"Yeah." Natalie narrowed her eyes in examination.

Keller nodded. "It's too bad we can't figure out which one is which."

"We absolutely can," Natalie said. "I'm going upstairs to look."

"Nope. Don't like that."

"I have to go there anyway. Guns?"

Kate hesitated. "In the kitchen fridge. Lock number 56278."

Natalie ducked into the kitchen—Kate and Ash had prepared meals here, messily and recently, from what she could tell. An empty package of carb-cubes lay sodden in the sink; nearby lay the remains of a desiccated onion. She moved to the refrigeration unit, flipped the lock, and opened it to reveal the armory, which consisted of precisely two boltrifles and absolutely nothing else.

Her stomach dropped. "Only two? Where's the stuff for the civvie police?"

"Elsewhere? We didn't think about the guns. We had blue screamers."

"Too bad you don't have any left." She removed the guns from their housing. "You could've just set them off and gone below."

"We already used them."

"On *what*?"

"Ourselves."

Natalie paused. *On ourselves.* Suddenly Kate's earlier explanations to Sharma made sense. *Practice. Oh, no.* Her blood ran cold, and the memoria blasted her again with images of Ash caught in the blast of the blue screamer, her bones rattling apart, her blood evaporating, and then her body falling to the ground, alive, alive, alive. Natalie's breath froze in her lungs.

You get time to practice, Kate had said.

They'd come out of it alive, every single time—

"Kate, you didn't," Natalie began, as she swung back into the dark cafeteria holding the guns. It was her imagination, not the memoria, that provided her with the gory details. She shivered. "You couldn't. You set them off? There were—there were *hundreds* of them. It would have been awful—why didn't you just defuse them?"

Kate looked up, the white light of the monitor underlining her bones. "Because *defusing* is not the same thing as destroying."

"But you—"

"Don't tell me what I already know."

"You can't be—" The words halted in her throat. "Are you all right?"

Her former captain looked back at the monitor. Motion reflected in her eyes. Letters, numbers. "You don't want that answer. Go."

Go. The word reverberated somewhere in the center of her bones, in the place where the Company had injected the messages that made her rush out onto battlefields to stare down the Vai mechs and their terrible promises. At the door, the rifles already heavy in her left arm, she stopped to take one last look at Kate. The other woman was already staring at the interface, bathed in white light, and Natalie watched the enemy swirling in whites and blues against Kate's face, closer and closer. There was something about it that made her want to say everything she hadn't, that made her think this was the last time she would see her, that all this was going to end badly.

"Kate," she managed, the name still so strange on her lips. "I just wanted to tell you that—"

"Don't be that person," Kate said. "You'll jinx it."

"Okay," Natalie whispered.

"I'll see you afterward and you can tell me then." The inter-face traced ghostly white lines on her face.

Natalie nodded, letting her muscles tense with unanswered energy before she moved again. Her fingers flickered against the wall as she counted off footsteps—one, two, three—to find her way in the pitch black to the building's staircase. She took two at a time, hauling all the way to the roof of the building, pushing open the hatch, and crawling through. Here, at the northeast corner, she could see an easy entrance to the plaza and most of the forest beyond.

There wasn't much of an overhang here—the dorm was built for basic use, to be slept in for a year and recycled when the in-dividual group homesteads were delivered. The wind had kicked up slightly, and Natalie was pelted by small buds carried through the air, little piles of dust and pollen swirling up from where they had collected below her on the roof. She dragged on the night vision goggles, then felt a tickle in her nose and clamped her thumb and index finger over it, tight, swallowing even the hint of a sneeze. Her lungs ached.

The goggles weren't military grade—these were meant for cit-sec rookies who were earning their way into command, so far under the quality she was used to. She adjusted the headset to fit her vision, then peeked over the lip of the building.

The headset's HUD chimed. Kate, sending her texts from below.

23R 14D 8G

That was *Twenty-Five* code, how Kate used to tell her about salvage items floating in the void, the Vai kinetics and moleculars she'd hauled in from the graveyard. She'd spent months opening and shifting her fingers into the slimy, bright innards, defusing and storing them for transport. The nostalgia hit hard as a bag of bricks swung at speed, much more vicious than she thought it could.

Not once during that time had she wondered why the Vai had chosen metal as the primary kinetic trigger instead of skin and bone, the soft curve of a cheek or a belly or a palm or a finger. Now it was obvious: they'd thought ships were human bodies and adjusted accordingly. The Vai had made all the same assumptions as the corporations. That *the aliens* were just like them.

Natalie nearly missed a bare hint of movement to her left, near the coordinates that Kate gave. She saw soldiers, at least eight, in black coldsuits that wouldn't have been visible to heat vision if it weren't for the way the rising moon caught the curve of their helmets. *Not InGen,* she thought, narrowing her eyes, *and not Baywell,* so not the source of the artillery she heard. *Someone new.*

She crawled on her belly to the northwest corner, to where the moon touched the treetops over the straight, shining line of the forgotten maglev. There, she caught the slightest flash of yellow behind the sharp-edged ruins of the train. The InGen team was using the old station as cover. Both teams were moderately within sight of one another, but it was hard to tell if they would be able to engage through the thick tree line. She'd need to lure them out.

And where was Baywell? There were too many questions, too many options—

"Come on, Kate," she whispered to herself.

48R 10G 12D, said her HUD.

Southwest, windward, past the maglev, a couple hundred feet back. *I'm getting some rattling. Artillery?* Kate texted.

Natalie had been planning on going back downstairs, moving behind the dorm, firing from InGen's corner position at the soldiers in the black coldsuits, but the artillery complicated everything, as did the knowledge that InGen had backpacks full of God knew what.

Natalie swung her gun around, pushing herself up on her

elbow with the grace built from years hiding from Vai mechs and angry bosses. She slid the boltgun's power level to the top, hugged the trigger, and fired. It was a gamble—a wager that the InGens wouldn't just drop one of their kinetics, slaughter everyone here, and have their execs scoop up Ash, Kate, and Sharma from the dusty leftovers.

She watched through the scope as the InGen leader's suit crackled and fried; she'd made a near-perfect hit. The leader capsized, her suited hands trying to grab onto a handhold that wasn't there. The InGens retreated back behind the wooden houses, ducking away from what they assumed was the line of fire. That was enough to make Natalie feel comfortable with bobbing back behind the overhang, crawling back over to the northeast corner. She waited for the retaliation, for InGen to recover and exact revenge on the unknown company that had slaughtered their leader—but nothing happened.

Cowards, she thought. *If InGen isn't going to start the crossfire, I'm going to have to do it for them.*

Up came the gun. Natalie leveled her gaze, took a deep breath, and pulled the trigger again. This time, her bolt hit one of the enemy's coldsuit helmets, and—*shit! Seriously?*—the suit slurped up the excess energy, cracking red and hot and blindingly cold for a moment. The target stumbled but did not fall. She'd never seen a coldsuit siphon and swallow, just protect and occasionally fry. She was making a mental note to toss Ascanio the idea of a siphoning suit when the black line responded by pulling back into the forest. The idiots were all being overly cautious for once.

Natalie chewed on the inside of her cheek. If she wanted immediate violence, she'd have to work harder.

She dragged herself to the hatch and clattered down the stairs, twirling around the cafeteria doorjamb to see Kate limned in the half-gray light from the monitor, She held a pair of headphones to her left ear. "Is broadcasting up? Can I talk on an open line?"

"Yeah," Kate said. "Why?"

Natalie jumped a chair on her way and scooped up the transmitter. "Hey, you coldsuit fuckers," she said, the words coming out angry and fast. "This is Citizen Sharma with the InGen vessel—" *Shit. What was it? What was their naming pattern?* She winced. Guessed. "*Martius.* We know why you're here. And if you think shooting our commander is going to stop us from getting what we were promised, if you think wearing those stupid magic suits of yours will keep us from killing you, well. We'll be down here and out with the package faster than you can say *goodbye, motherfuckers.*"

A few seconds passed, and then a voice returned. "If you had half a dick, InGen, we wouldn't still be here to continue this delightful conversation. You're not going to use your fun little toys, are you? Because you can't."

She exhaled. She met Kate's eyes, filled with warning in the bare, quiet darkness, then licked her lips before continuing. "If you're not gonna make the first move, let me propose an alliance. By the maglev, there's a third faction. I think they have artillery, and if we don't take 'em out—"

"We can hear you assholes, you know." A third voice: male, darker.

Jackpot. Kate looked slightly worried, but she kept her head focused toward the interface, monitoring the scraggly-fast, shivering atmospheric readouts from the fields. Natalie's breath came faster as she tried to figure out what to do next; she grinned, channeling the swagger from the adrenaline surge.

"Good," she said. "So we're all talking. We're all here for the same thing. Let's negotiate. Nobody has to die."

Silence.

Kate set the comm on mute, then took a breath. "It's not gonna work."

"It's gonna work," Natalie hissed. "Here, keep them talking."

"Keep them—*what*?"

Natalie's mind raced. "They're all within a half mile, aren't they?" she said.

"Why does that matter?"

"I still have the evaporator."

Kate's eyes widened. "No. *No*, Natalie."

The broadcaster hissed in answer, relieving Natalie of the responsibility of explaining her nascent plan to her former captain before she knit it together. "I don't know who you are, but you're not InGen." The voice was familiar, and Natalie placed it almost immediately as belonging to the team leader they'd encountered in the forest. "Whoever you are and whatever mess you're trying to spark here, you're not going to succeed."

Natalie unmuted the comm, her hand shaking. "My CEO sent me here for the exact same reason yours dropped you on this godforsaken planet. Let's be efficient. If you're not going to negotiate, why don't we just get started killing each other?"

Natalie fumbled with her jacket for a moment and brought out the evaporator, offering it to Kate, who stared daggers at her in return. Natalie heaved in a breath, told herself that she was doing the right thing, that the dread adrenaline crawling around her veins wasn't the last thing she was going to feel.

"Keep them talking. Once you hear gunfire, set it off," Natalie said.

"Set off—" Kate's face went from worried to angry in a heartbeat. She shoved herself to her feet, ignoring the interface. "No."

"I know you can set it off from a distance. You did before."

Kate's right hand made a fist. ". . . Goddamn it."

Natalie didn't tell Kate that her throat was closing. "I know what it's like to—"—*red dust in her mouth, and it felt like the evaporator was warming, death-hot against her heart*—"to be forced into this. But I'm fast enough to outrun a screamer. I did it once. Stands to reason I can do it again with this."

"I'm not making that wager."

"Yes. You are." Natalie leaned in. "This is what I do, Kate."

Kate's fist tightened, and her knuckles went ghost-pale. "If I do this—"

There were things Natalie *could* say: *I'm going anyway,* and *I understand,* and *we'll find a different way.* But she didn't. The words that came to her lips were like the knives she'd trained with, like a bolt slipping under someone's ribs. *She* could be a weapon too. That was one thing Ash had taught her, that Aurora had taught her. Her hands, her feet, her heart, her tongue. All of it was loaded ordnance.

And she knew how to use it.

"Do it for her," Natalie said.

Kate deflated. Her shoulders fell forward, and she took a ragged, soft breath, and in that terrible moment, Natalie knew she had won, and she shoved the evaporator back in her jacket.

"You're just as bad as Mr. Solano," Kate whispered.

"Got an extra comm?" Natalie said, ignoring the guilt shoving its way into her mind. She didn't have time for guilt. She wouldn't even have time for contrition.

Kate sighed and tossed her one. "Natalie, I need to say something—"

Natalie smiled. "Don't be that person," she whispered. And before her former captain could say anything else, could smile or throw a punch or react, Natalie grabbed the boltgun and turned so she wouldn't have to see Kate's face in angry rictus, engaged the nightviewer, and pushed out into the darkness outside.

The evening yawned in her throat like every chasm she'd ever faced. She tasted the faint metal of spun air and the crackling of promised crossfire, feeling terribly alive, like she had fire in her fingers and death in her heart, like she was where she belonged, her crackling-blood, strung-tight body the only investment she had left. She held the evaporator in her hand, still dull and gray, and looked out onto the plaza.

It was going to be a story to tell, if anyone was left to tell it. A death right out of an *Alien Attack Squad* season finale.

Alien Attack Squad. Adrenaline flooded her body, causing cold pins and needles on her hands and feet.

She'd thought the memoria had reconnected most of the days from *Twenty-Five* that remained, but here was a new one: an episode of the holo she'd seen five times (alone—it always bothered her, why she'd watch something that ridiculous *alone*), where the holographic sniper saved the day. It wasn't even her favorite. She didn't know why she was thinking about it right now. She'd forgotten it—

She felt a strange familiarity tickle at the back of her brain, a quiet brokenness standing behind her, but nobody was there, and the evaporator in her jacket was still quite cold. Instead, she stared down at the night vision goggles in her hand. The night vision goggles that received instructions from Kate's position as overwatch. With a little ingenuity, she could still have her little war.

She activated the comm.

"Kate. New plan," she said. "We're all getting out of here alive."

12

Natalie's shredded lungs nearly failed her on her four-story trip back to the dorm roof carrying the two boltguns and a crate of equipment. While she didn't fumble the initial setup of the larger boltgun on the courtyard side, the code that allowed the boltgun to interface with the comms was three years old, and wanted a number of impossible updates. By the time Natalie and Kate managed to wrangle a patch to get remote shooting up and running, Baywell had taken the maglev station.

Natalie crawled over to the other side of the building and did the same with the smaller gun. She made sure the courtyard side was ready for Kate's call, then programmed the first gun to work on a timer. She dithered for a few seconds, then entered a number ten minutes in the future and hoped for the best. The evaporator warmed in her jacket as she worked; Natalie knew Kate would never activate it without her permission, so she fished it out to make sure it was still cold and dead.

Must be my body heat, she said to herself, and stashed it in an inside pocket.

She fired up the gun on silent mode, then called Kate on her personal comm. "It's done. The big one'll go off nine minutes from now. The second needs your code when the enemy's in range. When you signal the positioning system on the goggles, you'll activate the firing solution. That should be it. Once both sides are engaged, get somewhere safe. *Not* downstairs."

Kate's voice was ice. "I told you I wouldn't leave her."

"They have no idea you exist. That's the kind of intel that wins wars, Kate. If you go to Ash, you'll put both existing human triggers directly in danger. You were talking about the sacrifices you were willing to make. Now's the time, Captain."

She imagined Kate's face darkening in familiar angry disbelief. "Fine. Fuck you."

Natalie grinned. "That's the kind of thing I want to hear."

"Just shut up."

Natalie pushed the door open and checked for enemies in the courtyard. "Let's go."

She tumbled out the door, her back slithering against the dorm wall, keeping to the shadows as she moved. She waited at the corner until she heard the sweet sound of boltfire from the fourth floor, and pained shouting as it hit the line of black coldsuits—proof that Kate was a better shot than she said she was. From her location, she could finally see the insignia on the unknown coldsuits: Ballard Solutions, one of Aurora's direct competitors. They started moving toward the plaza.

Ballard to the side, Baywell at the maglev station, and InGen still beyond the dorm, she thought, feeling like a fly at the center of some claustrophobic spiderweb.

It didn't feel like nine minutes when the second gun started up, startling her with quick, programmed bolts that weren't going to keep their targets fooled for very long. Natalie thumbed the charger on her personal weapon, peered around the side, aimed at the Ballard position, and fired, picking off some poor sod without a coldsuit who had popped up just long enough to die. The sound he made gave Natalie a stomachache, but offered her a better understanding of how far the enemy position extended, especially after someone started shouting to *take down the sniper, you nits, we're not losing this to a company of fucking toymakers.*

Hidden in the long shadows of the dorm, she looked to the other side of the battlefield, spying movement from the InGen camp. They'd taken the "sniper" as an opening as well, just as she'd hoped. They pushed forward in teams of four, moving quietly into the darkness of the plaza. Natalie ducked into the shadow of a doorframe, counting passing yellow-clad bodies, letting the adrenaline drive her exhausted limbs. She padded to the corner, toes before heels, casting her scope around the third corner of the building. She felt a tense thrill at the rattle of gunfire from Kate's gun above and the shouts that followed—the shadows of the coldsuits in the brush told her that they were having trouble mounting a grenade offensive.

Good, she thought, *we're pulling this off, just a few more seconds,* and pressed her eye to the scope and her finger to the trigger and waited.

She hated waiting, and the lack of decent intel burned at the back of her throat. It was a problem, this slippery adrenaline poking at her legs, the energy that kept her thinking in what-ifs, in *what if Kate doesn't leave like I told her to,* in *what if Ash doesn't survive,* in *what if Aurora hasn't checked in with* Beijing *yet and what if they throw that grenade and it hits the cafeteria—*

And then it was finally too late to wonder. InGen passed into the plaza, and Kate's gun stopped its rabid chatter.

Showtime.

Natalie aimed, cranked up her boltgun's damage rate, breathed out, squeezed the trigger, and painted an arc into the brush. InGen's back guard fell, one-two-three, in a crackling sizzle-splatter that might have been artistic in *Alien Attack Squad,* then let the gun charge, and let out another salvo to press the issue. InGen attacked the only visible culprit, Baywell at the maglev, and Baywell returned fire. This time, just barely in her scope, she could see the Ballard line, taking advantage of InGen's confusion, pushing forward toward the plaza themselves.

She swallowed a triumphal yelp, and pulled back into the shadows between the buildings.

Natalie moved around the second structure to the north of the battlefield, coming up behind the Ballard position. This would be trickier. She would have to be fast, and she didn't know how fast she could be with Tribulation-bruised lungs. She peeked around the corner, releasing fire on their back line. She got six rounds out before she had to pull back and make pell-mell for the forest line, her breath pushing out of her lungs, her feet making crackling noises, making her obvious, making her body a target—

—but everyone else was already engaged in the plaza, too busy to notice her.

Too busy with blood and guts and—

Catching her breath, Natalie stashed herself behind a stand of trees, warming her hands underneath her armpits, swallowing every cackle that threatened to expand from her heaving, oxygen-starved body. She lifted her gun again and pressed her eyes to the boltgun scope.

The results of her crazy little plan were almost too perfect.

Almost.

InGen was decimated, having taken significant crossfire from the other two companies. Bodies in mustard yellow shuddered on the plaza, half-dead, crawling for shelter. She shoved down her nausea, waiting for Baywell or Ballard to engage again.

Nothing happened.

Natalie adjusted her scope. Why were they hovering? Were they checking angles? Negotiating for peace? Realizing they'd both been had?

Fuck no. That couldn't happen. She needed to get closer. Find better cover. Try again. If Baywell had abandoned the maglev for their center position, that would be the best place to go.

She traced a tight arc around the wooden outbuildings. The forest's edge was unfamiliar ground, the vines skipping up and twisting, threatening to slip around her ankle and ruin everything with one swift tug. She ran hard until she was next to the maglev track. The one broken rail was a desperate, dark score in the alien ground, broken in places by plants she didn't recognize—woody, jagged things that didn't look like they belonged here on listing, burgundy Tribulation. Hauling herself bodily into the almost-empty maglev station, she found two soldiers guarding a few boxes of tools and a small, sector-only ansible. She shot both with a nauseous twist, feeling the thump of their bodies through the metal floor. Her stomach twisted but she pushed forward, grabbing the ansible handset and paging through the local frequencies until she found the Baywell-only chatter.

"Command, this is overwatch," she said. "Just spotted three figures fleeing into the underbrush below the south dorm. They seem to be wearing Auroran indenture suits. Recommend moving to intercept."

"Acknowledged, overwatch."

And for the first time since she'd landed on this stupid planet—for the first time since the war with Baywell began—she watched the giddy sight of the enemy actually breaking their line in the opposite direction of where she'd told Kate to go, sucking down her lies like candy. Three, four fireteams careening into the forest—

Wait, she thought. *I'm missing three more teams—where the fuck did they—*

A bolt hit her shoulder a millisecond before she registered the flash of the muzzle. Close range. The corner of her eye. She hadn't seen it coming. Pain sailed through her body, and she fell against the window behind her, her blood smearing the plasglas, dripping in a hot surge down her arm. She clutched at the bloody vacancy her shoulder had become.

"Don't kill her." It was the man who had acknowledged her feint.

"You really fucking should," she spat back.

Baywell cits grabbed her by her arms, took her gun, and

dragged her out of the maglev into the plaza. A wild screaming noise in her throat dragged her attention away from the pain. Distracted her captors. Made them think she was weak. This way she could count her living enemies, get a sitrep, and try not to die.

"On your knees," she heard.

Natalie went down hard, discomfort juddering through her pelvis and back, sending painful echoes to her shoulders. In the plaza, bloody survivors stared daggers at the ground, their hands knit behind their heads. She wanted to puke. All she'd done in the end was create a situation that put Baylor-Wellspring at an advantage and trapped her friends in the cavern below. *Some tactician I am.*

The leader pinched Natalie's chin between a tight, bony index finger and palm, wrenching it toward him like meat from a barbecue, pain-blue light shining in her eyes from a nearby torch.

"This the package?" said the commander.

Natalie started laughing, hiccupping little things that would piss him off, because *didn't they always get pissed off, these Baylor-Wellspring shits,* she thought. Ash had always told her they were big on *respect,* big on *knowing your place,* big on *cits-over-here* and *fuck-the-indentures.* She laughed so hard she didn't hear the answer.

"Can't be. She's too healthy. Where are the others?"

Natalie spat out blood. "I'm the only one here."

The butt of the gun came from the left, connecting with the side of her head, making the world spin. Her captor paused to eye the tags on her collar. "We can make you tell us."

Natalie smiled, her teeth slicked with blood. "You can try," she said.

"Where's the human trigger Aurora hid here?" he said.

"Dead."

She closed her eyes. Waited for them to slap her, or shoot her, or hit her again. She'd never been captured like this before, but she'd seen enough security theater to know how it went. The blow came again, as she'd expected, hot plasteel to the reach of her jaw, a hard crash of light exploding behind her eyelids. She sucked her teeth to keep herself from crying out.

"Where's the trigger?"

"*She's* a person. *She* has a name."

"Where is she?"

"Dead," Natalie spat. Focused on an imaginary vision of Ash's body breathing out for the last time. Winced. "I told you. She died this morning."

Crack. He struck her again, and she felt a rib give way, *crack*, like popcorn, like kindling.

"Give us her body and we'll let you walk."

She hurt, hurt all over, a starving, death's-head hurt, could barely catch a breath thanks to the burned-glass edges of her shoulder wound. "You think I can walk?"

"I think you want to live."

Natalie hunched over as much as she could, as if she was losing the last of her energy, as if the situation were too much for her to handle. The lie would come much easier if her body backed it up.

"Can't. I burned her." Natalie closed her eyes again.

She waited.

"What the hell do you mean?"

"I burned her. This morning. I told you." She let herself choke on the words. "I love her," she said. "Too much to let assholes like you lay one damned hand on her."

"You must be Kate Keller," the man said. His tone was almost reverent. "The one who killed *Phoenix*. You're supposed to be dead."

She huffed the ache in her chest like a drug. "You don't think that I would walk off your stupid Armour bucket with the Heart for anyone less than Ashlan Jackson, would I?"

"Check her blood," said the man. "Make sure."

Shadows moved around her. Women. Men. It was getting harder to breathe. She was dizzy, not getting enough oxygen, blood pooling in all the wrong places inside her body, the memoria struggling with upload overwhelm. A medic arrived, floating in front of her with a half-apologetic gaze. Natalie stared daggers at her as she flipped a case open to locate a syringe. Two others ripped her jacket away from her shoulders. The quiet evaporator dropped out of the inside pocket and hit the dirt with a muffled thump.

The world ground to a halt around her. The syringe hovered inches from her arm. The guards tightened their grip. The shadows just beyond her vision held their breath, and Natalie delighted in her sudden power, the control over the situation that this silver, half-cracked egg slicked with sweat and blood gave her. It was dead—*of course it was*, she thought, *Kate's gone*—and she looked around for something she could use to set it off, something plasteel—

The commander knelt to take a closer look. He had a typical birthright's build, slender-skinny like a flower, sculpted. Aesthetic. *Breakable*, Natalie thought, *if I could just get my arms free.* He snatched up the evaporator with his thin fingers, weighed it in his hand, and turned it toward the overhead light.

His men stepped back as if they were already burning, but he laughed. "Someone get an isolette. If you're going to threaten us, Keller, you'd best pick a thing that actually—"

The weapon whirled to life.

"—works," he whispered. "Wait, that can't—"

Natalie's entire body was wracked with sudden terror and joy, a cackle that shook her shoulders, anger and giddiness slamming into one another underneath her. She sucked down air, thinking *damn you, Kate, damn you for not leaving, damn you for doing this,* pulling at the grip of the guards holding her tight, feeling their fingers loosen with fear. She knew she should run, knew she needed to if she wanted to live through this, but a quiet and terrible rage had taken control.

It's not suicide if you're doing it to save them, she thought.

"Aurora's ahead of you," she whispered, the evaporator humming wild and alive in the air around her, humming thin, reedy songs through the commander's fingerbones. Inside this hellish music, the lies were easy. "We've always been ahead of you. We have the labs on Bittersweet now. We have your ships. We have your future. And you'd—"

"How?" the commander said. "This is a kinetic—"

Natalie coughed, blood spraying from her lips. The gambit was coming together underneath her tongue, whirling and whining there like the evaporator between them. *A good lie,* her father had said once, *always holds a grain of truth.*

"Is it?" she lied. "Or is it the best technology Aurora has ever developed? You have all of these soldiers, all of these guns, but I'm a human trigger. With one twist of my tongue, I could send you all to hell. Do you know what happens when an evaporator engages? It likes the skin, first, it goes layer by layer, and I'm going to watch—"

The leader breathed in, clearly considering this, but her screed seemed to be having the opposite effect to what she hoped.

He was actively *calming down.*

"Barnes," he said. "Explain."

The doctor shook her head. "She's lying, sir. Evaporators don't stall like that. If the weapon were going to engage, it would have already done so. I believe it's a fake."

Natalie kept talking. *Might as well.* "You know what I'm going to do? I'm going to watch from here when the timer goes off, and it's going to burn the skin off all your faces—"

"So do it," the commander said.

Why isn't it going off? Is Kate too far away? Is there not enough power? No, it doesn't make sense, she did it before—

"—and you'll be alive to watch your liver explode—"

"You can't, can you?"

"—and disintegrate, because the last thing it targets is the heart and the brain, and you're still alive when—"

The commander straightened and slapped his knees, letting out a brief, relieved laugh. "Let's get a move on, folks."

The guards fastened a gag around her mouth that tasted like blood and dirt and smelled like it had spent considerable time in a soldier's underwear. They dragged her toward the plaza as the evaporator spun and whined, thin and ineffective. Natalie spat invective, struggled, pushed against her captors even though she was in pain, even though she had no more moves left, even though this was it, she'd failed Ash and Aurora and even Kate, failed her for asking her bright heart to kill. They lined her up with the other prisoners, and she struggled, her feet and arms leaden and sharp. She couldn't move—

—so she tried to turn and spit and howl, but she couldn't move—

—but neither could anyone else.

It was like everything had *stopped*, like some unseen god had paused the holo and went to the cooler for a snack.

Stopped was the only word that felt comfortable, because *frozen* sounded like a rejected *Alien Attack Squad* script and *interrupted* was impossible. The still-whirling evaporator silvered the air with a single long note. Every single human in the plaza was motionless as stone: the commander with his skinny voice and his day-old beard, the guards behind her, the Ballard soldiers and the interrupted, bloody InGen kids. She couldn't even tell if anyone was breathing.

The plaza filled with light.

It tipped up from the chamber below the barn: violet-green, death-bright, hollering Heartlight, so strong it slammed into her eyelids like hot daggers. She could barely see the figures following behind it: Sharma walking, pushing Ash in a wheelchair, the black outline of her sickened hands clutching the alien device in her lap. Ash resembled nothing more than a skeleton with skin hanging in decorative strips, wearing loose blue scrubs that covered white autobandages, some saint drenched in wild violet heat.

Natalie tried to breathe, tried to say *it's me, help, please,* but her interrupted skin felt thick and hard, like she'd turned into a statue.

The survivors' eyes were all a glassy-edged green, as if the Heartlight had grown into their irises and taken root somewhere below. The last time Natalie had seen Heartlight this keen, it had been right before a rushing wave of *nothing* took her to death's waiting room. But the Heart couldn't be engaged, she thought. It swept, it slaughtered, it stopped—

—but not like *this.*

"I have what you came for," said Ash, scanning the crowd with a quiet smile. "The ultimate weapon. The ultimate source of power. You want it, and you *want* it, and you have no idea what it truly does. Perhaps you'd like a demonstration. I have no Vai hivemind to connect with, but I can see into yours." The sick woman paused, her hand tightening on the rail of the wheelchair, her voice brighter than it had any right to be. "In fact, I can do more than that. Let me show you how it works, and why we can never let you win. *Any* of you."

The light twisted behind Natalie's eyes. The air felt heavy in her mouth. She could only watch, hurting and helpless, as

Sharma pushed Ash and her chair toward the nearest Baywell fighter, a short young citizen with sweat-drenched black hair peeking out of her helmet. Ash rested her fingers against the inside of the woman's wrist, and a muddy stormcloud darkness rolled in over her pale face.

"You were his beneficiary and best friend—until you found out just how close he was to turning cit," Ash said. The soldier's eyes were alight with terror. "They called it a training accident, but you know better. And so does the coroner who chose to call the hole in your friend's head an *unfortunate occurrence* rather than what it really was."

Ash dropped her hand. "And the answer to your question is—no. No, you won't be able to live with it."

Ash moved to the next soldier in line—an older man with no helmet, blood matting his gray hair. Aurora would call him *too old for the infantry*, but Baywell had no such compunctions. Ash's fingers rose to rest like a blessing on his forehead, and she breathed out, letting out a quiet moan.

"Antje was kind to you, but you were not kind in return," she whispered. "She adored you, and you broke her. For what? To catch the eye of Citizen Eyler? Was that failed gambit worth breaking her heart?" She pushed him away, forehead-first, and he crumpled to the ground.

Natalie could only watch in horror as Sharma pushed Ash from soldier to soldier. She stopped before each of them, one by one, placing her fingers on their foreheads or wrists or hearts, dragging out their secrets. Some she spoke aloud. Some of them she kept for herself, her body softening as she read each of them like a human flimsy. And then, as if no time had passed, Sharma moved Ash in front of Natalie.

Ash hesitated.

No, Natalie thought, *don't you fucking dare.*

But Ash lifted her hand, pressing her cold fingers against Natalie's wrist. "What aren't you telling me?" she said.

We're on the same side, Natalie wanted to say, *I'm your ally, you don't have to do this—*

Are you? Ash's clear alto voice was a bell—

—a bell that tumbled her back to Bittersweet, to the puppet standing in front of the Baylor-Wellspring airfield, staring down the closed door, the pilots running for their ships, the little gusts of celestium dust picking up near the air vents. The Baywell team standing before her in their anonymous coldsuits. A name. Susan. One of them was named Susan.

Susan was dead.

I didn't plan this, she cried.

Looking down at her dreaming body, Natalie saw she was barefoot in the golden Bittersweet sand, wearing not the bulky puppet but her indenture's clothes, the blue jumpsuit with the patches at the knees, the one that had been washed so much it should have gone back to requisitions, but why get new clothes when you could save six days on the end of your indenture? And, oh, *oh,* someone she'd forgotten had once said she looked cute in it. *Why can't I remember?*

The evening wind kicked up around Natalie's ankles, snatching at her hands and her hair. Ash was trying to slip her fingers into memories that no longer existed, and she felt bereft, searching, and very angry. Her toes curled in the sand.

Stop, she thought.

Red dust filled her mouth. She heard Emerson somewhere. Ascanio. The words *they were just indentures* haunting the hollow notes of the wind.

Oh, Natalie. Ash's voice. *This, after everything.*

Don't judge me, Natalie thought. *I'm not your enemy.*

I had to make sure.

Natalie stared. *After what I did for you, you still wonder where I stand?*

Natalie felt anger, inchoate now, disconnected from her body, forced out toward Ash's disembodied voice. *The Heart took your memories. Nat, you might not even know how compromised you are. You might have forgotten.*

I'm fine without them. I'm better.

Ash's fingers left her wrist, and Natalie felt her fever-warm birdbone palm slide against hers. *You've forgotten who you are.*

The red dust kicked up now, dragging itself out of the Bittersweet earth in homicidal waves, and somewhere beyond the airfield were the keen eyes of Solano and the board staring at her with their info-implants shining and their diamonds on their fingers, their clean faces and their dirty hands, their hands full of the warm dreams of all the things she'd thought she wanted. The apartment. Ward. An entire department at her feet—

Look again, said Ash. *This is buried deeper than any of your other memories, which means you need to see it—*

Natalie was suddenly flat on her back, not on Bittersweet, but staring at the keening blue skies of Earth. She tasted the hot, sandy wind, saw the towers of the white plaza, the dark bridge, the doors to the concourse below, the tilting Egg. *Verdict.* She saw figures moving in and out of the old museum, where her mother sat strapped to all her interfaces—

—she is sitting at a desk on the fourteenth floor of Tower One, the city laid out below her, the mountains lost in smog. She is not yet a god, not yet a genocide. Her black hair runs loose, even in the heat. She is about to steal something important.

Her unknown mother turns. Her generic smile is too white. Too wide. Something is coming, something terrible—

Stop, Natalie cried.

What came next was a terrible scratching thing inside her mind, a clawed demon with the breath of Tribulation, scoring and scouring her memories with claws of silver Heartfire. She didn't want it. She hated her mother, *hated* every lost memory of her, or at least that was the story she'd told herself since she could walk—

This was love.

Not the kind she had for Ward, full of briars and bolts and fences, but open to the sky, full-throated and new, the unconditional love of a child for a parent who could never return it. The feeling was overwhelming, terrifying, and it threatened to destroy her, threatened to take the fortress that was her heart and dash it to dust. The kind of love that would hobble her, cast her off the cliff, drown everything she'd built in the river—

Get out, Natalie gasped.

I'm sorry. A shiver. *I'm so sorry.*

Get the fuck out—

—and gravity sucked Natalie back down into her own trapped body, leaving the experience shifting in her brain, receding like high tide in the bay. By the time she knit herself back together, Ash and Sharma had pushed on.

They stood in front of the Baywell commander now, and his green eyes were wide and streaked with red and washed in unblinking tears. She could feel his fear as Ash lifted four fingers to lay across his purpling mouth. Her head tilted back, as if she were some sort of oracle, and out of her lungs came a scarred breath.

"Baylor-Wellspring doesn't care about you," Ash said—loud, so everyone could hear. She let the implications swirl in the air, tightening like a ribbon around dozens of throats. "Your commander was given this assignment because he screwed the CEO's daughter without a contract. He brought his own yacht, and planned to have your lives cover his exit if things went south. I imagine you might have something to say about that. I know I do."

Natalie could see the shift in the Baywell ranks even as their bodies stayed frozen. Raw emotion crackled in their eyes. Ash pressed her fingers hard against the inside of the commander's wrist, and the skin whitened under her fingers. The man made a whining, desperate sound.

"The yacht is prepped for intersystem transport," she said. "We can use it to leave."

Sharma cleared her throat. "Are you quite done, then?"

At Ash's nod, the doctor pulled the wheelchair away from the crowd and pulled out a measure of quarantine fabric, wrapping the Heart in one economical gesture, staunching the light. A cold wind kicked up through the plaza like the planet catching its breath, and the soldiers began to move again, as slow and tentative as if their limbs had been encased in ice. Kate appeared behind Natalie, her fingers working the lock on the Baywell cuffs.

"Let's go," she hissed, expecting some kind of violent consequences, the three sides flowing back into the fight like a river bursting through a dam. But the desire for conflict had drained out of the plaza like a quick-punch breach. A redheaded woman fell to her knees, bawling. A few others wavered. One vomited.

The Baywell commander stumbled to his feet. He reached for his gun, but his fingers were still fumbling-cold, and he dropped it on the ground like a toy. He called out for the soldiers to *get her*, but none of them seemed interested in following the orders of a commander who would have left them behind, and they did nothing but stare and search for bandages.

The man scrambled for the gun and picked it up, but his grip seemed off. In the maglev, he'd been trained, vicious, sharp. Now, he held the gun like he didn't even know what to do with it. "W-what did you *do* to me? I can't—I'm too—"

Ash smiled. "I took it all away from you, all those bloody things you want so much. You'll never hurt anyone again."

His eyes darted toward his wavering platoon, clearly afraid.

He shoved the gun into the hands of his nearest subordinate like a too-hot cup of coffee. "I don't—I can't—who *are* you?"

Ash breathed out. She looked slightly disappointed. "After all that, you don't remember me? Of course you wouldn't. I was just another soot-streaked face to you. You might remember Christopher Durant, then. He was tall. Great sense of humor. Loved coffee. While you were stationed on Bittersweet, you took him from Dorm A to the admin wing three days a week for a year. For his *new job*, we all thought."

The man stopped fumbling. "You're *her*."

"I am. He died, you know."

"I had no control—"

Ash nodded. "I took some of your memories, yes. But I gave you a memory, too. I thought you might like to know how it feels to die. You were certainly very interested in giving that experience to others, after all," Ash said.

His jaw wavered, wordless.

Ash's eyes flickered toward the Baywell indentures, who were recovering quickly from their reverie. "Besides. You might need the practice. Ask your questions, friends."

His platoon pushed in like a wave, their anger kindling like a bonfire, and Sharma pulled Ash out of the tangle like they'd been forgotten by everyone else, and a quiet, insane thought nagged at Natalie, then—that, through whatever Ash had done, they had. She heard Kate's voice call a retreat, and Natalie gave herself over to the comforting balm of *someone else's orders*.

At the tree line, Kate muttered something about *the evacuation protocol,* and Ash said *no, Kate, the people,* and Kate pressed her palm against Ash's cheek, keeping her voice low. *We made this promise,* she said, *that nobody gets the Heart and nobody gets the research. All I'm going to do is kick off the charges we set. Don't leave without me.* She gave the woman a short kiss to the

forehead and was gone, sweeping up Natalie's boltgun and hauling back toward the city.

The wheelchair didn't last long—the road out of the ag-center
to the outbuildings was half-paved and cracked with crabgrass—
and before long the chattering, stinking normalcy of the forest
surrounded them, every step carrying them farther away from
Ash's hideous miracle.

What *had* Ash done? They'd *practiced*, Kate had said. Practiced with the screamers, practiced with the Heart. *Last year,
the thing had been a hammer, coming down hard and fast and
indiscriminate, because they weren't as sick and everything was
new. This year, they could use it as a scalpel. Who knows what
they could do with it next year, if they lived.*

Her blood ran cold.

"Ms. Chan," Sharma said. "You're going to walk into a tree."

Natalie looked up. She looked at Sharma in a completely different way, the nauseating pieces falling into place. The silver
she thought she'd seen in the doctor's blood after the transport
crash, the way Sharma had barked at her to leave the medkit
and find her own medicine. Natalie had lived through the Vai
war because of proximity, but Sharma had been on *Phoenix,* or
that, at least, is what the soldier on Bittersweet had said. *She
shouldn't have survived. Unless—*

"You'll need to support Ashlan," Sharma said. "The captain can
walk, but Ash is going to need assistance. I'll take the Heart—"

"—in your eternal generosity," Natalie snarled. "No."

Ash's face was a mask of bloodless exhaustion. "Let her take it."

"She's *infected*, Ash!" The words came out before she could
stop them. "I didn't think it could be possible, but it's the only
explanation. You give her the Heart, she pulls the trigger, and
hell, I'm like your friend the commander zombie."

Sharma crossed her arms. "That's it," she snapped. "I'm done.
You either believe I'm with you, or you don't. Draw your line in

the sand, Natalie, and hop over it, because that's the only way any of us are getting out of this alive."

Behind them, Natalie heard a familiar crackling sound, like fire against cellophane. She whirled, her animal brain saying *run*, her engineer's brain saying *you're far enough away*, her human heart saying *not again, not fucking again*—

Through the trees and spindly corn husks and jagged roofs she could see enemy transports landing, their lights being swallowed by a greater one on the ground, slippery-bright and greenish-gold. "Go," Sharma said, sweeping her arm under Ash's skeletal shoulder blades, "we'll be fine, but you—"

The metallic light twisted in the air, slammed up with a firework's breath to the sky, loosening the transports' grip on gravity, sucking up their hulls in one broken breath, leaving plasteel and bones and half-uttered screams. And she knew what that meant, had seen it before, had watched from a craggy cliff on Cana just four hundred feet away as the other teams disappeared in that crashing light. The evaporator.

And then: a second explosion. Fire.

Natalie wanted to feel something, anything at all, anger or relief or vomit in her throat, but all she had now was the run. That's all that ever remained, in the end: just the air in her lungs and the exhaustion coming up behind like truth come to take her down.

It was going to have to be enough for now.

13

When Kate swung into the transport fifteen minutes later, breathless and silent and blowing dust from underneath her fingernails, Natalie had patched herself up as best she could with a Baywell indenture-aid kit and was halfway through preflight.

Preflight was a mess—the ship ran an unfamiliar OS with haptics that didn't recognize Natalie's autonomic muscle movements and stalled when interfacing with her Auroran memoria. That difficulty alone kept her from immediately asking Kate the thousand questions dancing at the tip of her tongue. Those topics were taking up precious brain space, after all, cycles that should have been better devoted to figuring out how the piece-of-shit Baywell proprietary grav-drive engaged.

Sharma passed the Heart to Kate, who strapped her safety web across her shoulders and served as its human restraining bolt, fastening the lap web across isocloth, the edges loosening just long enough to prick the back of Natalie's neck with a thousand needles and that damned memory of her father at the Verdict gate.

"Let's go," Kate said, her face flushed, and it took a moment for Natalie to realize she wasn't making up the tension in the air. She turned to check if Kate was strapped in correctly, and her stomach dropped. Natalie would have recognized the death-pale look in her former captain's eye from a mile away.

"You set off the evaporator, didn't you?" Natalie said.

"Don't fucking judge me." Kate's voice was ice. She tightened the isocloth, and the nibbling pressure on Natalie's brainstem eased. "I set charges in the lab months ago so the assholes that inevitably found us wouldn't get any of the research. There were reinforcements coming. I was attacked."

"We saw the transports."

"I told them to run. I told them how far they would need to go, and how fast they needed to go. *You* of all people, to judge me, when you asked me to do it—"

"I'm not judging you." Natalie stabbed her assent to a release form, hoping Baywell was too lazy to cross-check her biometrics with an authorized-pilot list. *Fucking release forms, every single corporate entity and their fucking release forms.* "It looks like you're doing a good enough job of it yourself," Natalie said.

Kate rubbed her temples. "There wasn't any time."

"Stop thinking about it. Do whatever you need to do to get through the next few hours," Natalie said.

"I shouldn't have—"

Natalie whirled in her seat. "Fix your straps. Check Ash's safety web again. Recheck my preflight. Keep busy. Do whatever you need to do, but do *not* let the emotions win. There's nothing to regret."

Kate's eyes widened in surprise at the orders, but she didn't argue. Natalie knew what Kate was going through, entertaining those vicious, unhelpful human feelings in their soft meat-made bodies. She'd thought the Vai war had scrubbed hers clean.

She'd thought, at least, that the redshift star might have.

Kate simply nodded and turned back to check Ash's safety web. The transport's engines shuddered to life, and Natalie allowed it to calculate the escape vector on its own while she blatantly ignored the advice she'd just given to Kate and stewed in her feelings.

For the first time, she *didn't* really want command, didn't want the hot seat or the power to make all the decisions. Absolution was supposed to be the most comforting part of indenture: knowing that whatever morally gray things you did, you could push the guilt up the chain. You weren't really a human being, so you weren't liable for human emotions. You followed your director. You did what she asked you to, no matter what it was, because your human heart was legally in abeyance.

But she was the director here. She'd put herself in charge by giving absolution to Kate. She'd done it so easily that it made her nauseous. And maybe by doing it Kate could have the small measure of peace that was impossible for Natalie.

Maybe. Perhaps. The questions behind her teeth proliferated like bones on a battlefield, and there was so much else to consider: Kate's flinty, uncaring eyes, Ash's scary new abilities, the thousand new and terrible functions of the Heart. The implications had been bad enough when deploying the Heart meant the death of thought, a vacuum-sweep of all human memory. But Ash had learned to steal through the curls of the mind, sorting through their memories like citizens choosing diamonds for their hair.

Natalie thought about the innards of one of the kinetics she'd learned to defuse, looking at it through dusty old memories from Verdict: the Heart had to operate via some sort of organic learned access protocol, if Ash could use it to duck in and invade someone's brain. And if she brought the Heart back to *Solano*, and he learned how to do that too—

"I think that might be InGen approaching from the north," Kate called.

Natalie, shivering, slammed on the ignition.

"Check your straps," she called, like this day was anything close to normal. Normal was important at a time like this. When you were running unfamiliar haptics, *abnormal* got people killed.

She looked back. Sharma had fixed up a double safety net to keep a bloodied, half-awake Ash as still as possible during takeoff, but the doctor was still out of her seat, cracking open a medkit.

"I said strap in, Doc," Natalie called.

"Just five minutes, Ms. Chan. I need to make sure you don't have a concussion along with that shoulder wound. And your memoria—"

"—is fine," Natalie lied. "Focus on Ash."

"You're in pain."

"*Ash*," she said, turned, and brought down the HUD. She didn't wait to see if the doctor had complied, just adjusted the tiller with her stupid forgetting fingers and let the Wellspring autolaunch take them up and away from the cursed red world into an uncertain future.

The scene above the planet had changed significantly. Ballard had established three cruisers, weapons bristling, at the farthest Lagrange point on the far side of the planet. Armour was here, too, playing chicken with Penumbra, another newcomer. Farther out, she could see the needle-bright volleys of plasma lances and the bright confetti of Baywell railgun fire.

As the transport hurtled away from Tribulation and she brought up the long-range controls, her memoria went dark for a few seconds, and her fingers paused in white-blank terror. *I'm glitching*, she thought, *goddamn it*, and *Aurora, that's right, we're going back to Aurora. We're going home.*

Home.

The memoria kicked in again.

Home. With that keyword, she expected *Vancouver.* Her apartment. The white-bathed overhead light of Applied Kinetics. Solano's very particular rendezvous coordinates.

It gave her *Twenty-Five*. Gave her gin rummy and burnt coffee and glossy after-dinner laughter over the howl of the Baywell engines, so familiar and delightful and lost that her heart ached to stop—

"Nat! Incoming!" Kate called.

She blinked. *Glitching again.* The interface threw up fighters approaching from 40 degrees port-south, backed up by a large cruiser. Baywell colors. They already knew the shuttle was stolen. They'd been tracking the shuttle, she guessed, using the transport's IFF protocols. *A stupid mistake*, she thought, *I should have seen that coming*—

She hollered for the others to hang on, then threw her head back to gun the engines, tilting the rudder toward the closest escape vector. The ship sped up fast enough that the antigrav almost didn't matter. She could feel the accel in her bones, screaming up her marrow. She could almost feel her ribs cracking, her planet-scoured breath being yanked away and replaced by vacuum. Ash let out a grinding scream.

Natalie, distracted, fumbled for the weapons and lost focus on the vector. "Shit! I'm sorry, I'm sorry!"

Ash let out a wordless sob.

"I got targeting," yelled Kate.

"You said you can't shoot—"

"I just need to find an exit." She'd risen from her chair, given the Heart to Sharma, then strapped herself into the copilot's seat. She called up the weapons display. "You just get us out of here."

Natalie nodded, keeping the ship stapled to the escape vector, the transport obeying her Aurora-trained motions in angry shudders. Kate fired the railguns wide and scattershot, painting the transport's wake with fire, making it possible for Natalie to put enough distance behind them to safely fire up the long-distance engines.

Even then she hesitated.

Home, she told the transport, but it again caught not on *Vancouver* but on gin rummy and laughter and stars. The transport rumbled in response and the engines attempted to engage, but Natalie's glitching memories of *Twenty-Five* weren't workable coordinates, and the hesitation lasted just long enough for the fighters to catch up and fire. The enemy guns found purchase in the transport's clean underside, wheeled around, and came around for a second sortie.

Kate was suddenly next to her, slamming the copilot's neural net on Natalie's head.

"*These* coordinates, Nat! Now!"

—and new coordinates appeared, coordinates that were *somewhere else anywhere else*. She seized on them with all of the fear and guile and forward motion she could muster, swinging the nose of the vessel around to face interstellar space. The engines engaged below her, and the ship shuddered forward, leaving Tribulation and its secrets behind in the whir of fulldrive.

Kate ripped off her haptics, letting out an unchained, bright laugh. "We're free of it," she said.

With her senses returning and the long-range autopilot engaged, Natalie's muscles unclenched, leaving her in aching agony. Kate unhooked herself from the safety web of the copilot's seat and rushed over to Ash, leaving Natalie to bring up the coordinates again, to see them full and bright on the galaxy plot.

She'd expected a quick waypoint, perhaps a fueling station or a transfer ansible—not a well-considered route to the most dangerous nebula in the universe, one that would take them away from most commercial shipping lanes.

The White Line, she thought. *We're going to the White Line.*

She looked back to see if Sharma had noticed. The doctor hovered over Ash's torn stitches, her face turned away from the screen. Natalie wiped the interface as fast as she could, thinking of the bomb in the doctor's head. She thought about switching the coordinates back to *Vancouver*.

Thought about *home*.

A cold metal table in a tiny mess hall. A salvage pod.

Again.

When it came down to truth and bones, what she was being asked to do here was simple salvage work: dragging Auroran assets back to Auroran space, no different than bodies or weapons or computer parts or cable. Easy. This decision should have been just as easy.

Her hand tightened, hovered over the coordinate entry interface, then withdrew.

Home wasn't a small white compartment with an in-wall storage space, or Emerson Ward's jagged hipbones in her bunk, or even her chair in Applied Kinetics, as much as she wanted to be. It wasn't the tall white towers of Verdict. *Home* was just out of her reach, in the way Ash and Kate looked at each other, at the sacred space between their fingers. *Home* was so far out of Natalie's grasp she might as well be sucking down vacuum somewhere near Betelgeuse.

It *was* an easy decision.

There was one last problem to address: whether or not Reva's cortical bomb would handle the change in destination. Whether Reva herself could, even if she wanted to.

Well, Natalie thought. *She'll have to deal with it. We're going.*

"Reva," she said, using the doctor's citizen's name for the first time. It felt like a tiny poisonous victory. "We're settled on a vector back to *Vancouver*. Why don't you bunk down first? This, ah—might give you a headache."

"A headache."

"A *bad* one."

Sharma understood immediately. She made a small, wordless nod, then pushed against her knees to stand. She hovered there for a moment, her conflict clear, then lay her fingers against Ash's wrist to check her pulse, then tangled for a moment in the isocloth around the Heart, settled in next to the dying pilot like a swaddled child. And then, careful to avoid looking toward the front interfaces, Sharma disappeared into the bunkroom.

She was in.

For whatever that would get them.

14

In theory, the White Line was a treaty agreement, not that any treaty had been formally negotiated. Not that any treaty with the Vai *could* be formally negotiated in anything but blood and oblivion.

In practice, the Line was the edge of a great roiling nebula, dust and gas and guttering light from the new stars within, the edges twisting into a bright silvery white, tracing a twisting, rope-like pattern across a vast expanse. Humans had gone farther, elsewhere, but until the Vai emerged in their dreamlike cruisers, nobody had given that area of space much of a spare thought. There were no colony worlds nearby, no celestium-rich moons to strip, and far more interesting nebulae elsewhere.

So when the Vai emerged from the other side in their twisting teardrop starships, no individual company had ever made a legal claim to the space. The only ships wanting to spend time here were the underfunded, ignored research departments interested in the inner workings of stellar nurseries—people like the Auroran science crew where Sharma had spent time as the staff medic, Natalie had learned.

These days, a virtual city wall of ansibles decorated a cobbled-together monitoring station within spitting distance of the nebula, a scattering of sparkling human metal against an alien sky. They were still networked and supporting one another, a shining testament to the wartime alliance that was currently in the middle of falling apart like a box of broken toys.

Natalie had hoped to see the station in person one day. The

array was a feat of spectacular reverse-engineering the Verdict coders would have appreciated, a house of cards made from sixteen different proprietary coding languages and machines not meant to work together, and her wayward hacker's heart thought all of it an absolute delight. The thought of finally seeing it kept her centered on the four days of the trip—four days that Natalie knew Aurora was expecting to hear from her, four days in which the other companies would be attempting to track them. She'd already made a list of reasons justifying this to corporate if she needed to, mostly laying the blame straight on Sharma's shoulders.

The Baywell midrange shuttle had much more space than the yacht. Kate spent a lot of the journey with the ghosts rattling around in her head, playing solitaire with a deck made from the backs of ripped-up, forgotten flimsies. Natalie let her be—she recognized the cold, haunted look on her former captain's face as the same one Natalie'd seen in the mirror after Grenadier, although instead of the solitaire cards she'd chosen far too many bottles of Second Company's toilet liquor. Ash rested most of the time, limbs and shoulders and hips tied to a bunk with the safety net to keep her bandages from malfunctioning.

Sharma stayed in the bunkroom, where her purposeful lack of knowledge kept her cortical bomb from exploding. When not checking the progress of Ash's autobandages, she coded programs in a language Natalie didn't recognize on a borrowed Baywell tablet, or read text—*old diaries,* she said when Natalie asked, downloaded quickly from a backup drive while on-planet.

"Anything interesting?" Natalie said, regretting the words as soon as she said them.

"Very," Sharma said, and heaved a sigh. "I think I've lost more than I realized."

"Research-wise?"

"No." The doctor paused. She swallowed, switched off the tablet, and knit her fingers together, composing herself before continuing. "Somehow, I thought that Robert—he's my son with the Horton contract—had been listed in the Sharma line. I registered him that way when he was born. But I wrote here that he re-registered as a Horton three years ago. Before he died. It makes no sense."

Does to me, Natalie thought, thinking of Xie on the bridge over the Verdict concourse, watching her take the long walk down the hill toward the corporate skyscrapers for the very last time, both of them ready to live the rest of their lives in anger and shame and guilt rather than admit they might have been wrong. "Are the Hortons a problem?"

"No. I mean, yes." Sharma frowned. "The Hortons are middling at best, even if Davin was running personnel at the time. It's like being able to choose between a pod and a yacht and choosing the pod."

"*You* took a contract with someone middling?"

"I'm a Sharma. Most lines are middling. I suppose I can't fault Robert for hamstringing himself to spite me, but to do that to my granddaughter—he must have been under pressure from Solano. That's the only reason that makes sense. When I get back, I'll—" She let the thought drop and looked back at the tablet. Then back up again. "We should have linked up with *Vancouver* by now."

I doubt it's the only reason. Maybe Robert Horton is the smartest shithead in the room, Natalie wanted to say, but she bit her tongue. "I'm sure we'll hear from them soon," she said instead.

From the bed, Ash groaned. "Nobody told her?"

Sharma set down the tablet. "Don't tell me, please. The cortical bomb—" she began.

"We're not going to *Vancouver*," Ash said. "We're not going back. Ever."

The bunkroom went silent, save for the humming of the engine. For a moment, Natalie's hand slipped toward a boltgun that wasn't there, until Sharma's fingers stretched over the tablet, her face curiously blank, her voice curiously flat. "Ah. It's too bad I am a prisoner. Help. I am being kidnapped."

"What?"

"It's too bad I'm stuck in the airlock, tied up, and can't quite hear what they're all plotting. Oh dear," Sharma said, matter-of-fact, rising from her seat and heading for the cargo compartment.

Ash blinked, confused.

Natalie sighed, then explained the bomb in Sharma's head and how it worked.

"So whatever she *really* feels about this—she's not going to tell us. Because if she does, she explodes."

Natalie hadn't thought of it that way. She got up and went to the front, sinking into the pilot's chair and checking her vectors as they moved in toward the Alliance comm station. Sharma had to know by now that they weren't going back to *Vancouver*. She was quite sanguine about the whole situation. Was she simply trying to stay alive? Or was she counting on *Vancouver* coming to find them?

Natalie put on the HUD and switched to the bunkroom camera. Ash's eyes were closed again, and she'd started to fall away into one of the fitful, uncomfortable catnaps that ruled most of her days. Ash's tracking device would kick in when they were within range of the Auroran ansible at the comm station. That might be what she was waiting for.

Sharma had certainly been careful. Careful to only talk of her desire to help Ash, careful to avoid entanglements with what might happen next. Even the recruiting talk had been circumspect. But *Natalie* hadn't—and she'd been in the doctor's eye the entire time. As soon as they arrived back on *Vancouver*, the neurotechs would make a download of the doctor's memories. Sharma might be able to get around implicating herself, but

Natalie? Sharma had her on the record agreeing to help Ash and Kate. It would be damning.

She flushed, angry—but before she could figure out what to do next, the ship's proximity alarms sounded, and she slammed the haptic gloves back on her hands, yanking the shuttle out of fulldrive with an economical jolt. The stars slipped into place around her in sparkling, foreign gatherings, and she muttered a soft *oh, shit* under her breath.

The Vai massed at the White Line in numbers Natalie had only imagined in her nightmares. She saw dozens of ships of all shapes and sizes, lit from the back by the constant glow of the stellar nursery. Their mother-of-pearl hulls roiled in patterns she'd never seen before, resembling tendrils and teardrops and the root systems of alien trees. The uniform variation made a quiet sort of sense to Natalie: if the Vai truly were what Ash said they were, if shape was a *choice* rather than a constant, she was staring down both individuals and colonies at the same time. Not a hivemind, not an insect's view, but something completely alien. Wrapping her brain around that thought was like trying to make Len be serious for five seconds. She couldn't do it.

(*That name,* she thought, again. *I'm glitching.*)

Natalie gulped down her fear. There was no way around the line of ships, no way to hide from it, nothing to do but hang here in space, a little black bug facing down a thundering silver river, taking its last breath before being swept away.

"Now what?" she whispered.

"Wait," whispered Kate, looking up from her game of solitaire. "We just wait."

And Natalie did, even though the anticipation made her bones ache. Any moment now, the Vai ships would realize the human transport was present and break formation. She knew it. That's what had happened in the war. She tightened her hands and put the haptics into standby. Waited for the adrenaline to squeal into action. Waited for the inevitable.

Back in the war, the most important quality in a gunner hadn't been the traditional measures of effectiveness and accuracy; that was a bonus. The most important quality was reaction time, the ability to transfer a sitrep to a trigger finger. Reaction time meant the difference between allowing a Vai mech to drop a kinetic on her squad and being far enough away to give them a good middle finger. The Vai were always more accurate, and they were fast. But a good gunner could buy time, and she'd blown dozens of Vai mechs this way, splattered their silver blood on her gunsuit as they turned suicide before the ordnance crew got close. By breathing. By waiting. By being ready.

I'm ready, she breathed, if saying it could make it so—and still jumped when the sound came over the speakers, a sound darker and deeper than anything she'd ever heard, rolling through the haptics, a sound that rattled her bones and brought her straight back to Cana, a marrow-clattering *vvvvvaaiiiiiiii—*

She ripped off the haptics, searching for silence, only to hear Ashlan whispering in unknown sibilants from the back of the compartment.

"Move us closer," Kate said, helping Ash back into one of the passenger seats.

Natalie's hands shook. "No way."

"They won't hurt us."

"How the fuck do you know that?"

But Natalie didn't get an answer before the line of ships shuddered into motion, like they'd all dropped into the same thought at once.

Natalie wanted to turn back, wanted to run anywhere and elsewhere, but it was too late; the transport listed to the side.

Her hands snapped for the haptics and their shattering communication, and she shoved them back on her head and her fingers, letting the chatter of ship operations fritter its way into the back of her brain. She wanted to drown out the sudden panic, the tight feeling in her chest that had been there since bouncing into the airspace above bloody Cana, that had *always* been there. She fumbled for the coordinates to Aurora, because, *God, she'd made a mistake—*

"They're not talking to me," Ash whispered.

Kate kissed her shoulder. "Give it time."

Ash shuddered. "I don't think being out here is enough. I need to go aboard with the Heart."

—vvvvvaaiiiiiii, whined the comms, and Natalie's hands went white-knuckled on the console—

"No," Kate said. "You can't even walk."

"I just need to get inside."

"The pressure differential alone, after surgery—it's too dangerous."

Ash lay her hand on Kate's. "I love you, but you're not going to tell me what I can and can't do."

Sharma knelt next to Ash, checking her bandages. "The captain's right. Not to be rude, but autobandages only do so much. I don't think any of us wants to clean up the mess if your intestines rupture all over the floor. Which they *will*, if you move from this chair. And then my head will explode, because I didn't keep you safe."

Kate shot the doctor a disgusted look. "I'll go."

Sharma laughed. "You're barely in better condition."

"But I *am* in better condition."

"You're exhausted, Ms. Keller. If this were *Twenty-Five*, and any of the crew were in this position, you wouldn't allow them to proceed."

"You're right. *I* would go in their place." Kate took to her feet, wobbling like a broken doll. Her hands pinwheeled, and she fell back into the seat next to Ash.

"You're exhausted," Sharma repeated. "You're light-headed, dealing with end-stage symptoms of your own. You're not going to be able to operate a heavy coldsuit, let alone deal with the hatch and slogging through the rib cage room. I'm the only one of us who has been aboard a Vai ship and lived to tell the tale. I know exactly where to put the Heart, because I was the one who took it away. I know what to say and how. I'm going."

Sharma had the narrow look in her eyes Natalie had seen a dozen times before: the doctor had been sitting on her thoughts for entirely too long, her mouth moving in occasional spasms, ready to speak as soon as she found an opening. It was the look the birthrights in her department shoveled in her direction whenever Natalie had a new idea, and sitting in the pilot's seat, the song of *vvvvvaaiiiiiii* making mincemeat of her composure, she finally realized what that was.

Contempt.

Ash laughed, a broken, half-carved thing, then used her fingers to claw herself upright. "The last time you went aboard a Vai ship, you started a war and doomed me to *this*, so no. You're not going. Kate, help me stand."

Sharma's frown deepened. "You can't possibly think you understand the Vai."

Ash breathed. Fought for the breath. "More than you. You'll go over my dead body."

The doctor looked hurt. "That transplant was a masterpiece, Ash. Death is the last thing I want for you."

"Then tell us why you're so desperate to get aboard."

Sharma's tone thinned. "I can save you if I do. I can save all of you."

"I thought you had a *treatment* if I went back to Aurora," Ash said.

The doctor blinked. "I do. But—"

"Another lie!"

Natalie felt the standby haptics cold against her fingers, a new idea congealing like old blood, and her mind divorced from operating the shuttle. The argument behind her went fuzzy as she concentrated on the shivering sound of the white fleet. Sharma was right: Ash and Kate couldn't go. But neither could Sharma.

There was only one person left who could.

"I'm the captain," Kate said, "and I will go—"

"Sit down, please, Ms. Keller," Natalie snapped.

Kate cast her a disparaging glance. "Natalie—"

"This isn't *Twenty-Five*. You're not the captain."

"Oh, and I suppose Doc *Cannibal* here—"

"*I* am the captain here," Natalie said, feeling the safety web release cold and ready under the pads of her fingers. "This is my mission. So I'm going."

The other three stared.

Sharma blinked after a very long moment filled with beeping machinery. "I'm the executive present."

"No. You've been taking my orders for the past four days. You're listed as my *medic*. Solano made sure of that. Plus, I'm the only one here who can make unbiased decisions. The *only* one who is invested in all *three* sides of this story." She stared at Sharma. "So I'm the only one who can do it."

Kate snorted. "Unbiased my *ass*."

Ash shook her head. "You aren't infected."

"You can fix that. There's a syringe in that medkit."

It was like Natalie had dropped a bomb.

Ash was the first to speak. "And what? You go back to Aurora afterward? Give them what they want? Because if that's your play—"

Natalie snorted. "There are other options. I can't even *use* the

Heart for six months, right? That's how long it took Ash to manifest on *Twenty-Five*—"

"Six minutes," Kate snapped. "It took me *minutes* to get some sort of hold on the Heart when I was on the Baywell ship, and that was with Ash *much* less ill that she is now. I took down a fire team in *eight*."

Natalie kicked her safety webbing aside. "Kate. Do you trust me?"

"You know I do." Kate looked away.

"Then you know I don't want this."

"Everybody wants this," whispered Ash.

"I don't," Natalie said. "Ash, you know what I want."

It was Ash's turn to look away. "And you're one of them now. You're going to *want* until it kills you, Nat."

Natalie thought of Ward, of her father in his new Auroran assignment of her citizenship, of all the clawing things she *wanted*, and all the things she'd thought she wanted. Of Joseph Solano with his fingers splayed on the wooden table in the boardroom, the other executives watching her with the magpie eyes of Verdict codelords just waiting for her to fail.

Earth. The Hudson. Verdict. The blazing summers, the humid winters that settled wet and angry in her throat, the river creeping slowly up the hill every year. The corporate skyscrapers. The stony concourse. The plaza. The comm outpost up in Tower One, arcing gray against the blue sky. Verdict's leader, whoever it was by now, would take her back. They'd strip all the corporate secrets from her mind, and she'd give them gladly.

No, not gladly. But she'd give them.

The secrets would buy her a place. A place could buy her influence. Influence could buy her power. And power—

Maybe you were right, Doc, she wanted to say. *Maybe we are more alike than I think.*

Natalie swallowed, then grabbed Ash's hand. "Then *trust* me. I won't go back to Aurora. I'll bail back to Earth so hard they won't even know where to look. It's really the only solution, and you know it."

"The infection is a death sentence," Ash said.

"Sharma has a cure."

"I'm never going to believe that."

"It's a *treatment*," Sharma said.

Natalie shrugged off the difference. "And this isn't the first time I've been told to grab a weapon and walk straight into the line of fire on bad intel. It's what I do."

"But—"

"It's what I do," she said again, and forced a smile. "Hell, I'm surprised I got this many years in first."

Sharma stood. Sighed. "It's settled, then?"

"Go get the syringe," Natalie said.

Kate fumbled in the medkit, then removed the syringe in question. She pushed the needle into her own arm and filled it, a scramble of water-thin liquid that was darker than blood and swirled with silver light. All Natalie could feel was an unexplainable sense of loss and an immediate pang of regret.

"Stop," Sharma said. "Just stop. You don't need it, Ms. Chan."

Natalie rolled up her sleeve. "How else am I going to get onboard?"

"You don't need it because—" She looked away for a moment. Cleared her throat. "You're already infected."

15

Natalie heard nothing but the rush of blood in her ears. *Infected.* The word was blood-thick, needle-sharp in her mouth. She tasted iron.

"What?" she said.

"You're already infected," Sharma repeated, heaving a sigh.

Bullshit, Natalie wanted to say.

"No," began Kate. "I can't even believe you, I can't—"

Sharma huffed, cutting Kate off. "I had to *try.*"

And that was true; the truest thing Sharma had said for a very long time. The truth settled like a fast-acting poison into Natalie's belly, and she felt the smack of vertigo, the compartment spinning like she was a bird that had suddenly forgotten how to fly. The survivor on Bittersweet had been a celestium hallucination. The evaporator hadn't gone off when Baywell took it from her, because she didn't believe she could trigger it. The weapon never got whatever it needed out of her thought process. "When were you going to tell me?"

"I wasn't going to tell you at all." The doctor crossed her arms. "And before you twist the knife again, please know that I'm *very* surprised that the bomb in my head didn't just go off."

"Whine, whine, whine. When? How?"

Ash cleared her throat. "It happened on *London.* It must have. We were on the bridge. We were talking. We shared that canteen, remember?"

Natalie felt numb, like she was skating around the edge of rage. "You can get this shit with *backwash?*"

"I didn't *know*."

"I shared a bunch of drinks at a lounge party last week. Why the hell isn't Aurora *full* of hidden triggers, then?"

Sharma wasn't even looking at her. She was looking at her toes. "Maybe it is. But none of them would be as powerful as you. Bog-standard celestium sickness requires constant exposure to unrefined celestium over the space of years. It kills in a little over a decade, shorter if you keep yourself exposed via indenture. The modified weaponized version Wellspring created in the war multiplies on its own, enters the bloodstream through the brain, and needs only a few molecules to begin. The Wellspring scientists on Bittersweet didn't get far enough to realize how it happened. I couldn't get the answers from my own history. I only figured it out myself when I studied Ash's progress on *Twenty-Five*. So, yes. There are probably others."

And there it was again—the anger, same as it always was, tight and strong and strangling. Times like this, Natalie missed dirt under her boots. Being able to solve arguments with her fists. "When I get back, we're gonna talk about how you know that. And then we're going to sit down and make a plan," she said. "In this plan, I am going to explain, in *graphic* detail, how we are all going to walk out of this alive. Because—"

Behind Sharma, Ash had gone cherry-red. "I'm sorry, Nat, I—I didn't know."

Natalie choked down something hot and tight and completely unhelpful, then turned back to the interface, her haptic devices, the vectors that would bring her closer to the Vai line. "Because I'm not a fucking martyr. Not like the rest of you."

The others were silent as she flew closer to the Vai line, then docked the Baywell shuttle alongside the largest ship in the line—the *flagship*, she would have called it, if she thought for a second the alien minds who built these ships sorted their hierarchies like humans did. She knew now that it was folly to ascribe human motivations to alien constructs, which is why it had been so easy to slip straight from sitting in a Verdict sniper aerie to scattering fire at Vai mechs.

Sharma called it a heartship instead—a ship big enough to store the bodies and mechs they needed when dealing with planets and people and the rest of the universe, a ship that stored the devices that connected Vai to and from their central civilization. Heartships had airlocks, Sharma said, even though human instruments wouldn't recognize the space inside as *air*. Natalie pulled alongside the first one she found, a perfect circle surrounded by a dark line that seemed to be the only real joint in the flagship's too-smooth hull.

The Baywell coldsuit went on slack and glistening—almost as easily as an Auroran one, which meant Natalie didn't trust it as far as she could throw it. Natalie checked four times that the seals on the wrists were drawn tight, that the oxygen was connected to her lungs and the rest of the air to the engine, and that the comm connection to the transport was working. She didn't expect much more than that. The suit had a vector accelerator—not a proper propulsion system, but good enough if something happened to the tether.

Sharma latched a go-bag containing the Heart to her left leg and then a standard tool set to her right. She instructed Natalie in how to talk to the Vai: how many seconds she could leave her suit open once she broke the seal on her glove to make contact before she died, what she should say (not that she'd be *talking*, which was nuts), and what to do when she was done. Natalie nodded, keeping her fear to herself. Her lungs were already compromised, and every breath felt like someone had tipped a glass of needles down her throat; if she didn't time it right, there wouldn't be enough air left to get back.

And when Natalie was ready to go, she tried to think of something to say, something other than *I can't believe I'm doing this*, but found herself without words. Sharma haunted the door. Ash sat on her bunk, leaning on Kate's shoulder, with Kate pressing her palm against Ash's forehead, her eyes pooling with liquid. Natalie felt a pang of something between sadness and jealousy; she managed a final, solid smile, though, as if she were just going off to *London* to pick up some cable.

"Don't be so fucking *serious,*" Natalie said. She coughed up a counterfeit laugh. "I'm coming back."

"I honestly didn't know," Ash said. "I didn't know I could spread it to you like that, Natalie. If I'd known, I—"

Sharma rolled her eyes and ducked into the front compartment. "I'll be on the comms."

"It's fine," Natalie lied. She wanted to vomit. Instead, she smiled. With teeth.

"Everything's fine, Ash. I'll be fine. I'm always fine."

"Remember," Kate said. "Space plus bullshit—"

"—equals death, yes."

"Except for the hallucinations," Ash said, closing her eyes and trying to hide the pain she was in. "Listen to them. They can be useful. They're your own brain processing the information you're receiving."

Natalie nodded. The Heart hummed little silver notes against her leg, and she closed the airlock, turning away from the window. She didn't want any more goodbyes. She didn't even want the chatter she usually relied on to keep herself calm and focused during an EVA. She heard the clattering of the oxygen injection system, felt the loosening gravity of the back airlock, drew her gloved hands around the still-slack safety of her tether, and surrendered to the bright, lifting feeling of weightlessness.

Then: the airlock door opened, revealing the slippery edge of the alien vessel wringing all of the memories of the war from her stomach, and the slow yet sudden knowledge of the celestium cooling in her veins like a promise.

She took deep breaths. Focused. Space was cold and Wellspring-era suits were leaky. Natalie counted to ten, and then counted again, then reached for her tether.

Behind her were the rest of the Vai vessels, hundreds of them, shuddering and spinning and unworried as Natalie crossed the space between the shuttle and the heartship. She kept expecting the aliens to open fire and the world to go dead in a riot of color and song, but the Vai line remained tight and unbroken and devoid of any formation Natalie would understand as useful for battle. Ash proposed that the Heart's presence on the transport had kept them from identifying it as anything other than another Vai ship, which was a good enough explanation as any.

Natalie's memoria likened the oscillation of the ship-skins to the disorienting shiver in her stomach as she crested the high ground at Cana—the moment just after she realized the twisting silver bones on the scoured rocks below used to be human.

"Ms. Chan, can you hear me?" Sharma said.

"Affirmative."

Static. "All right. What you're going to have to do is—"

But Natalie didn't have to do anything at the airlock. While still tethered to the transport, her hand brushed the skin of the ship and something dark and terrible beyond the door sang to her, sweet silver voices of *glory* and *home* and *welcome home sweet sister*—

She froze.

"They're singing to you," Sharma said. "They know you're coming. Don't get distracted. Keep on going."

Natalie caught her breath. "That's not the memoria glitching?"

The Heart warmed against her coldsuit, sang in harmony, and it was insane—beyond insane—that a Vai construct could suddenly be so beautiful, could twist into her spine with a song called *glory* and convince every nerve in her body of the *rightness* of it.

She wanted to vomit.

Nothing's right, she said, *they tried to exterminate us,* glory *is just blood and shit,* but her mouth wasn't working. She repeated the question, but Sharma still didn't answer. Perhaps she couldn't hear human voices behind this wretched cacophony. Was this the silver speaking? The Vai themselves? Echoes made from the celestium in her blood? Did she have months to live, weeks, or just days?

Hours?

She wanted to split her skin in two, dump her blood into the river, anything to reverse this nauseous ache.

Instead, she pressed her gloved hands against the airlock and the covering shivered aside. It felt strange to Natalie that *hands* could make an alien construct work, but *of course, the Vai had hands sometimes,* she thought, remembering the long, spindling fingers on the hands of the aliens on Tribulation. *Hands are a pretty decent tool.* And with one last, lingering gaze on the wheeling darkness of space, she pulled herself inside. The covering slid shut behind her, and everything went dark.

She slapped the helmet light on. Swallowed an immediate, wild panic.

There was no door on the other side.

She shoved the panic where it belonged—in her gut, near her diaphragm, where it couldn't mess with clear battlefield thinking—then placed her fingers against the smooth, silver wall, looking for another seam. The wall moved like water, like she'd shattered the surface tension of a bead of mercury, then reformed, crawling up her arm, gobbling her up like a marble in an ocean, wrapping her in a symphony of skin and blood and intestines.

Terror took over. *Sick. Unprofessional.* She held her breath until it spoiled, until the knifing, rotten dregs of it forced the air out. She tried to breathe. It hurt. The bulkhead of the alien ship burned around her, so tight and tough she thought the face-plate might crack, that the ship itself would pour into her suit and drown her and slick up to her skin and her bones. She'd suffocate with only her shipmates to hear—

—and then the ship released her, slipping away from her body like the tide going out, and she found herself standing on the other side of the wall.

Natalie stood in a wide, dark bay lit in reds and purples, the aching, breathing walls decorated with oscillating colors that had no human names, so massive that the ceiling was lost in darkness. The helmet light wouldn't be enough, and she fumbled for her torch.

Sharma's voice came over the suit's comm. "—Chan. Ms. Chan. Respond, please. Your heart rate just spiked."

"Yeah, that happens. Were you going to tell me about the fuck-ing door?"

"Breathe in through the nose, out through the mouth. If it makes you feel any better, *we* blasted through."

"How?"

"We thought the ship was in distress at the time."

"You are so full of bullshit," Natalie said. "*Space* plus bullshit."

"We don't have time for bad language," said Sharma. "What do you see?"

"I'm in some sort of"—she searched for a word to properly describe it and failed—"belly."

"The rib cage room?"

No, she wanted to say as her torch finally came on, drenching the bay in light. *Worse.*

She could understand why Sharma described it that way. Soar-ing above and below was what Natalie thought might be the structure of the ship: wide white pillars in high gothic arches, resembling nothing less than a rib cage, stripped and striated with the slightest of gray lines. It was like being inside a massive, dreamlike leviathan, like she was Jonah and she'd just shoved herself gleefully into the whale. It resembled the experiments in Sharma's underground lab writ large, or a thousand childhood nightmares. The walls pulsed with organic energy, thick and twitching, reacting like she was a tiny invader inside a massive set of intestines. She felt the thrum of the ship like an insomniac heart.

The floor—she couldn't call it a floor, because it met the walls at the oddest angle, pockmarked and breathing, and she wasn't sure gravity was the reason she was attached to the surface— was just another facet of this flesh-coated diamond. Her boots squelched where they held fast to the surface. All around, she could see veins of rushing silver, tightening and stretching like blood vessels headed for a stroke.

This is someone's body, she remembered. *Thousands of some-ones.*

"Okay, Doc," she breathed, keeping her voice low. Low like church. Low like an ambush. "I don't see the obvious interface you're talking about. How far do I have to go?"

There was no answer.

She thumbed the comm. Silence. Not even static.

She would not panic.

She was beyond panic.

With the comm down, she could hear the ship, muffled by the coldsuit. The walls seemed to be breathing, long straight ex-halations that the memoria told her were actually the breaths of her first boyfriend, the one she'd met in the ordnance-training barracks where names didn't matter. It swore in golden certainty that she was right back there in her thin bunk, her ear pressed against his chest, listening to the wheezing of his lungs and the echoing thump of his heart, like he was some ancient chamber of secrets.

"Where the hell are you, Reva?" she said. "Ash? Kate?"

Nothing.

It was too late to go back. Natalie traced her next few steps according to where bone met bone, then scurried carefully across the pulpy floor. The room narrowed slightly toward the apex, where the flesh shifted to a much brighter red. Her muscles felt tight, tighter than they had any right to be, and she ached down to her teeth.

Finally, Natalie's torchlight found her destination. Natalie was tempted to call it a slaughter—*but no,* she thought, because it was clear to her now that these bodies had not yet been alive. They lay in front of her like cadavers in state, silver-white skin thinly arranged over sensible bone, connected with arteries, tubules, and flaps of the skin to the floor and the walls like they'd grown there. *Maybe they had,* she thought, her stomach doing a backflip. She inched closer, to see their eyes, but was distracted almost immediately by the Heart, trilling excitement and bliss under her skin.

Something was answering, singing a song that wasn't quite a tune, using notes formed by a throat that did not exist. The closer Natalie came to the apex of the room, the louder it got, and her eyes started to pick up a violet turbulence that by now was as familiar as the taste of blood on her tongue. She knew what she had to do as if she'd always known, as if her heart beat not with leukocytes and plasma but with Vai silver. Moving toward the apex of the room felt exactly like coming home. Her arms moved as if she weren't in control, removing the Heart from the sling and placing it at her feet. She heard a *click* that was also a *slurp.*

One of the bodies moved.

Sat up, slowly.

Opened its eyes.

Sharma had said *blood contact,* and Ash had said *wrist to wrist,* but the voices in her blood told her *anywhere would do.* The knife was in her hand before she knew it, and all thoughts

of being careful evaporated into the too-thick air. She heard the
aching rip of her suit fabric, the arctic laceration of the knife
going into her vein, and the hot regret that rushed in right after.
She offered it to the alien, who slipped its long, knife-vine fingers
around her wrist.

And she fell.

Natalie struggled through it: a thousand feet, a million, until she couldn't stop falling, until her body went limp with exhaustion, until she became the fall itself, until she was no longer
Natalie and existed only as a moment between moments, as a
cold wind in a canyon. The cliff was too far away, the ground
a yawning lie. And the silver was on her tongue, drenching her
with *presence*, with the murmuring breath of a consciousness
that stretched across the nonexistent sky, that wrapped around
her mind, hot and alien beyond the whisper of her functioning
air filter.

She felt like she was on fire, every nerve jangling, the silver a
waterfall in her mind. She was drowning, her mouth full of viscous liquid, her mind being rewritten. The memoria couldn't handle the input; it gave her people she didn't know, faces she didn't
recognize, places she'd never been, *things* that were absurd, *feelings* that were impossible—

Hello, she heard—

Are you here, she said.

We,
said the thousand,
and sang in roses,
in the song of morning light on metal,
in the smell of a thousand seasides
Natalie had never seen.

She heard a wild clattering. Bathed in violet light, her body far behind, the only metaphor Natalie could think of for what was going on was *upload*. She didn't need to speak, didn't need to think, because the silver knew her, was inside her, *was* her.

Natalie bled into the poison air, too overwhelmed to move. This was not the choir Ash had described in the transport. This was an ocean, a desert, a crashing sibilance that went down to the atom. They were voices, but only because that was the nearest thing her memoria could give her; she imagined the thing smoking and sparking on her head from the effort to make sense of this impossible song.

Of course, she said, clawing herself back from the brink. *Ash only met a colony. This is the civilization. This is the whole fucking thing.*

Natalie tried to push forward with the script Ash gave her, but her mouth was full of hot blood, red and silver. She gulped it back down, trying to make room for language. The room became brighter, slippery, *wrong,* and she could see the silver rolling through the walls like blood careening back to a beating heart, just like the thin, squelching insides of a Vai weapon. She knew that pattern, the motherboard-jagged movement of viscous liquid against the gaunt layers inside. The ship *itself* was a molecular.

Ash had been wrong.

They didn't know we could die, she'd said. She'd turned the war into a *misunderstanding,* and desired to make peace. But how could she make peace, when the very existence of the aliens was death itself?

She choked down a scream. Did Ash know? Did she care? Natalie wanted to say *fuck it* to the plan, to spit out every atrocity she'd seen at Cana against every prospective offer of friendship, to let them know how they'd woven themselves into the horror that was her life. How was she supposed to negotiate a truce when she hated, hated, *hated*—

Natalie felt a hand on her shoulder and whirled.

Her father stood behind her. A hallucination. He was bearded, older—wearing the old sweater he'd given her three days before she left, his hair rustling in the alien atmosphere like it had in the winter wind that kicked up as she walked away from Verdict for the last time. She knew the two days' worth of stubble curling around his chin. She knew the sad light in his eyes. He stood just a foot away from her, edges lost in mist, as if Ingest had paused halfway through a render.

You wish to talk to this iteration. The sound of a human voice, although no lips moved.

No. Not him. The words echoed around her like bells.

Speak, she heard. *You know where they are.*

Natalie felt a tickle at the back of her throat, wrapping her cerebellum, an ice pick behind her temples. The Vai was not wrong. *Let us be,* she said. *Go home.*

He had a galaxy behind his eyes. *You know where they are.* The words were difficult, were tied around her tongue and stuck in her teeth.

They're dead. It was a mistake.

Bring them home.

I can't, she whispered.

The script was dust in her mouth.
You know what death means.
You have to know.

The word had come from her, but it was new to her
alien hallucination.
He tested it, tried it, rolled it on his tongue,
swayed where he stood.
Death, he said. *Unfamiliar.*

She moved back to the script.
I am returning the Heart so we can end the war.
So nobody else dies.
Vai or human.
Do you understand?
The words felt wrong on her tongue,
and the air shivered around her.

We must find them.
He was shaking now, and behind him an
orchestra—

Don't you understand?
They're not coming back,
Just like our millions aren't coming back,
And if you don't leave, if we don't leave—
she said, suddenly desperate,
the words pushing out
like a spurt of blood from an open jugular.
My people, we're not the forgiving kind.

Go back behind the White Line. Get out of here.
They're gone.

We must find them.
His words were lost in a sudden orchestral discordance.

I get it. You don't understand.
You've never lost someone before.
They're gone.
They're fucking gone
and there's nothing anyone can do about it.
The truth of it caused the rehearsed words
to stop on her tongue.

Impossible.
Everything comes home.

His words hurt in the folds of her brain where her team still lived, where they played cards and dreamed and breathed and their blood thrummed under their skin. His words hurt in the space he'd carved out.

You're in my head, she whispered.
Can you see the memoria?
Let it show you the bugout bay—

And he did—

Together,
they saw Natalie,
the bullet, the spray of silver,
the dead alien—

Impossible, she heard.
They are alone
—dead
—how, impossible

The dreamworld shook in desperate convulsions around her, and she felt for a moment like her body filled again with blood, her lungs with hell. She heard a wail, louder than any gov-raid siren over the concourse, louder than any blue screamer. *We didn't know,* she said, suddenly desperate,

the rehearsed words pushing out like impatient waterfalls, like
a spurt of blood from an open jugular.
We know now.
—well, some of us—
We were just so—
—So afraid, she whispered.

The alien didn't respond. All Natalie felt was a silence so deep and dark that she couldn't even hear herself breathing.

Dad—
she said—

And then—

Her puppet-father animated, just for a moment.

These words. Some. Death. Fear.
This is what you want for us.
I did not know until now. I did not understand until now.
Did you come here so we would understand what was happening

to us when you took it all away?
                                A pause.
You do not want peace. You never did.
      Know this: I will not be alone.

Wait, no, we do want peace—

                                Jagged screaming—

—her own screaming, a month of it, a year—

—a wild violet light behind her eyes—

—and she came out of the trance seconds later, years later, gasping, clawing at her throat, feeling like a too-full water balloon. She was enveloped in blue light, running above and under her skin, burning in her veins. She felt a violent whisper somewhere at the back of her skull, and scalding in her lungs.

The alien flagship shuddered around her in great seizing gulps. She yanked back her poisoned, peeling hand and the silver slurped back into the portal, leaving her bereft of the carnival noise. She felt alone again, gasping for breath in her suit, devoid of a single clue about what to do next. If she'd succeeded. If the Vai would leave.

It hadn't felt like a win.

"Autobandage," said a man's voice. "Bleeding."

Autobandage. Right. She was bleeding and everything hurt and the poison atmosphere was pouring into her suit. The sitrep could wait. Her hand moved like she was trained to do it, right into the tool bag on her left leg, flipped it from its housing, slapped it on the hole. The oxy-mix flooded in, and the suit's environmentals began properly cycling, and she tried to steady herself on the floor as the alien ship shuddered again, and she—

—she looked up into the brown eyes of the Bittersweet survivor.

She knew him now. His name was on the tip of her tongue, just behind the memoria's graying curtain. He was *Twenty-Five*'s indentured mechanic—but they'd never had an indentured mechanic on *Twenty-Five*, had they? The ship left Europa without a mechanic—and even as she had the thought, she realized how nonsensical it sounded. The memoria spun hot against her forehead, and she reached back to her recollections of that year, running the faces of her fellow crewmembers through her mind, over and over: Ashlan. Kate, in the captain's chair. The traitor Ramsay. Reva goddamn Sharma.

Staring at the hallucination, the memoria provided a jangling, black-and-white sketch: the mess hall, a stack of cards, a broken spanner, the feeling of a warm, one-handed hug from a person who didn't exist.

One of the lost memories, then.

Here. In the rib cage room.

It made no sense.

Her mind didn't remember him, but her gut did. She could see every detail of the time they last met: the smudges of week-old dirt on his pants, the scabs on his fingers from working on an ansible without his gloves, his indenture's haircut going curly-wild around the sweat-crushed shirt collar three months in.

His name poured into her mouth from somewhere forgotten, sweet like sugar water, like plain sunlight, as if engaging with the Vai through the Heart had pieced together her shattered drive core and restored her entire heart, and flowed out again, forgotten.

It was fine.

She didn't need his name to know who he was.

The forgotten engineer crouched next to her, whole and smiling, as if she'd never lost him. The memories of his smile flowed back like a spring downpour. He filled a space inside her mind that she'd never known was empty, his brown skin bright against the alien backdrop, his crooked front teeth whiter than they'd ever been and his eyes laden with stars.

He felt like nothing less than a fucking miracle.

Except, she thought, *except he died.* She knew that even though she knew nothing else—and now she was the one dying, swinging straight from the diagnosis of the infection to a full-on hallucination in a grand total of forty-five minutes. Or maybe she'd been aboard the Vai ship for hours. Days. She'd lost time after the battle, so it made sense that she might have lost time here—

"Outside," he said, pointing to the airlock. "Now. Emergency."

"I *forgot* you," she whispered, taking in an uncontrolled gulp of air, feeling knives in her esophagus.

"This was deleted," he explained.

What? Her breath came in shorter gasps—*save it, save it, calm down, you're still alive, you still have choices*—and, as she calmed down, she checked the timer on the suit, to see how long she had left.

She'd lost twenty-six minutes.

Just like before, just like every single damned time the Heart was used, and hopefully not long enough for the transport to give up on her and bail. Not that Ash or Kate would give up, but she'd left them on board with Reva Sharma, hadn't she? And Sharma had plan after plan after plan—

"Emergency," he said.

"Yeah. You're telling me." Natalie's temples rang with a sudden headache. *Twenty-six minutes,* she thought, *the Heart takes twenty-six minutes to fuck you up, oh God—anything could have happened in that time.*

She turned and ran, as fast as she could, across the rib cage room, throwing herself bodily into the shaking, shivering wall near where she thought the airlock might be; it took her in, wrapped her up in the whisper of *sister*, of *child*, of *we*.

He came with her, his limbs wrong and close in the darkness. "We—" he said, then stopped. "We—"

"You're dead," she whispered. "When I saw her on *London*, Ash told me you died. I remember now. You died for her, not for me, and—and—there's really only one way to tell if this is really happening."

There was no tether here, simply the motion of *pushing out*, and the skin of the hull twisted aside. Natalie expected to see the tether, her transport, the clean, straight lines that meant safety. What she saw instead was a twinkling black nothingness, as deep and as dark as death itself, as eternity. She turned to grab the alien ship, but physics was the same everywhere; she was punted out into the vacuum with a bang, and she went head over heels into the black shiver.

The transport was gone.

16

As she went head over heels, Natalie tried not to panic. Instead, she fumbled for the vector accelerator on the back of her suit, using it to propel herself back toward the Vai ship, slamming her coldsuit against the wild oscillation of its hull. She scrambled at the thin, dark line of the alien airlock, but nothing happened this time. Physics bounced her back into space—slower this time, like that was any help. Natalie's lungs stopped functioning and refused to push oxygen through her system. Dread spiked near her heart. *Calm down don't panic don't panic don't panic—*

"Emergency," said the hallucination.

She pawed aside the useless tether. The hallucination hung nearby, knees bent, eyes glimmering, as if he could breathe in vacuum. He looked confused. She was somehow sure her nameless friend had never looked confused before—not at work, not EVA, not with his elbows deep in engine guts. Not even when he'd been holding a gun in the shadow of the ag-center barn, unable to remember he worked for Aurora (is *that* where they'd met?).

"If you're going to fuck with my brain, at least be helpful about it," she said. "Ash said you could be useful. So be useful. Help me find the ship."

"The *ship*," he said, slowly, as if the word were new.

"The green one. The Baywell transport." She drew in another precious breath. Canned oxygen, the bright hint of metal on the back of her tongue. Limited, now. "The description is right there in my memoria. I should recognize it—"

"There are too many to tell."

"Too many *what*?"

"Green ships."

She fumbled for the accel controls, trying to swallow the edge of annoyance building up at the back of her throat. She plotted a vector that took her around the curve of the heartship, aiming to get a slightly better view of the Line. Her vision was caught by slivers of light too bright to be this far away from a star. Weapons, starships—

"Oh, come *on*," she whispered.

Of course they'd been followed. Of course Baywell had arrived with their forest-dark, interchangeable cruisers, and of course Ballard had followed them, and Armour, and—goddamn, Aurora too, flanking the rest with that familiar, stomach-twisting boxy blue.

She wasn't really trained in space vector analysis, wasn't meant to work without her feet in the dirt or on a deck, but she could tell enough from the tight, defensive bubble formations to know that this was no united force, no common-cause Corporate Alliance, despite the fact that they'd all arrived with their noses turned against the Vai.

Teasing out the ties within would have to wait; her hallucination had told her to *survive*, and survival meant maximizing her leftover oxygen, figuring out who was going to shoot first, and finding the transport, because railguns or not, her coldsuit and her angry breathing human skin and bones weren't going to last long out here. She'd been yammering on about peace, while the Vai had already discovered the only truth about humanity that mattered: the hot, wordless truth of the plasma lance.

"Death," he whined.

"You're not helping," she said, seeing bright explosions in the corner of her eye.

Natalie couldn't tell who started the fight, and in this petri dish of corporate suspicion, it almost didn't matter. There would be captains on vessels listening to executives on planets who weren't even present; anxious, warsick gunners with bellies full of nightmares; board members with inchoate memories of quarterly losses. Human greed was a sick fucker, and fear—

Well.

Fear was a psychopath.

She didn't need to be afraid. All she needed to do was activate the suit's homing beacon. The polite alarms inside clanged, giving her the transport's location on the helmet HUD: far, almost too far, twirling in the staggered light of plasma lances, limping away from the battle. It was hard to calculate the distance between them, as the relative sizes of the ships and the vastness of space meant anything she decided by sight would be dead wrong. She hesitated, imagining what it would be like to die in her suit, how far decomposition would get before the chill of space found its way in to harden her body to ice.

"You're not helping," the man said.

"Fuck you," she replied, bringing up the suit HUD. For a moment, she doubted herself—and then thought *fuck that, if I wait I'm Natalie-flavored soup,* plotted a vector that would hopefully not kill her too quickly, and slammed her thumb on the accelerator.

Natalie was swept up in fire. The pressure in her ears built as she lurched forward, reaching into her eyeballs, the sudden acceleration heavy against her head and shoulders. Using the suit to fly had one advantage: her power signature was small enough that cruiser haptics might not differentiate her from space dust. She tested that theory immediately by tilting herself to the side as she approached the first cruiser—yellow, with InGen markings—making a close enough approach to slip into the ship's blind spot. The cruiser was firing, but she was too close to see the target.

Natalie skated close enough to see the hull dancing by her nose, then kicked up thirty degrees to use the ship's exhaust to punt her up and away. The suit cackled its temperature alarms, and she broke into an immediate sweat, sucking down hot air at top volume. She lost control—which was fine, just fine, she'd get to the transport faster—and found herself heading straight toward a Baywell cruiser cutting a tangent toward the Vai heartship, which had started to move in formation with some of the smaller ships. Light brighter than her corneas could process erupted above her—the familiar brilliance of an Auroran spinal lance—and she closed her eyes, hearing Ash's breathing advice for being EVA, *sip don't gulp*—

—and she nearly clipped the thing as it passed beneath her like some dark leviathan, curling into a ball, twisting around, making one more course correction—

The transport was right behind, damaged, spitting air—

She flicked the switch to decel, feeling pins and needles flood the aching bruises on her shoulders and trunk, swinging her boots hullwards. It was the worst way to land, coming this fast and this hard with only boots and bones and bad lungs to catch her. She slapped the boot magnets with her left hand and a breath to spare, then hit the hull with a devastating crunch from her left foot.

Pain rocketed up her leg. Natalie hollered, her fingers fumbling for the clamp on the airlock door and slamming the entrance code. The airlock opened without a sound—or maybe she couldn't hear it for the sound of her own voice. She threw herself inside, waiting for the air pressure to equalize, swearing at the way her ankle rested, screaming and wrong, against the inside of her suit.

She hit the inside comm. "I think I broke a bone, Doc," she said. "I'm gonna need one of your magic splints."

Nothing.

"Ash?" She hit the comm again, just to be sure. "Kate?"

The transport chimed, letting her know the atmosphere was safe. She ripped off her helmet and chestplate, then released the boot magnets.

Her feet lifted from the ground; she ran her hand through her sweat-soaked hair, watching droplets loosen and pull away. The antigrav was off. *What the hell—*

—and this time she skipped ingress protocol entirely, stowing the suit and decontamination and the rest of it, forcing herself through the door, tearing through the empty bunks using her hands and upper body until she reached the main cabin, where their names died on her lips.

Ash's thin body lay buckled and unbreathing in her seat, blood streaming into the air from a nasty new head wound. Sharma's memoria was hacked into her skull, like the doctor had followed up the hasty liver transplant with some last-minute brain surgery. Ash's eyes were filmy in death, fixed on somewhere beyond the ceiling, her lips parted halfway between terror and hope.

Natalie felt her stomach lurch.

Sharma was dead, too, her head open and bloody where someone had yanked out the entire memoria, interior storage and all—but that wasn't what killed her, Natalie realized, as the woman's head floated to the side with the juddering of the cockpit and she saw a broken, bloody, grayish mush that was, no doubt, the result of a cortical bomb. *Installing her memoria on Ash would definitely not be on the approved list,* she thought.

And Kate was in the pilot's seat, her fingers twitching on the haptics—

Kate was alive.

First aid kit, Natalie thought, then, *where do these Baywell bastards keep it—*

Alarms clanged. The transport hadn't figured out its pilot was unconscious. No first aid kit would help them if a spinal lance sliced them through, so Natalie muttered a reluctant apology, yanked the haptics from Kate's fingers, and hooked her elbow through dead Sharma's safety web, thinking a dislocated shoulder would be better than a railgun breach. A wild yellow plasma bolt came within inches of the transport, singeing the hull, and the bodies waved and thumped behind her in their seats. She winced. Every moment she wasn't focused on saving Kate and figuring out what had gone wrong was wasted time.

And what *had* gone wrong? Boltfire bad enough to kill three people at once would have done far more than just fuck up the gravity. And it didn't explain why Ash was wearing Sharma's memoria.

And it didn't explain why the Vai seemed to be having a hard time fighting back.

She dodged another Ballard bolt, then set the transport's vector to drop below the battle, away from danger. "Go," she whispered, and the transport shuddered its compliance. Natalie felt the curve of the safety net digging into her shoulders with its agoraphobic fingers. She didn't realize she was holding her breath until the transport slowed down.

Natalie had some leeway. Some. Not a lot. Definitely not *enough*.

She cast off the safety web and turned back to the carnage, pushing across the room to yank a first aid kit from the wall. At least with the antigrav off, she wouldn't have to put any weight on her broken ankle. She could keep Ash alive, she could call for help, she could—no, she *couldn't* call for help—

None of this made *sense*.

"*Alien Attack Squad*," the man whispered; Natalie whirled to find him floating by the bunkroom hatch. A second later, she realized what he—what *her brain*—was trying to say. *There's a recording—*

She slid the haptics back on and the ship roared into compliance seconds later—Baywell holorecording software and renderbot technology was remarkably similar to the Auroran kind, so ubiquitously present that she'd nearly forgot to check if they existed. Natalie ripped into the first aid kit as the renderbots spat out bright violet versions of Sharma's long fingers, Ash's half-lost limbs, and the wisp-soft streamers of hair lining Kate's face.

"We need to call her back," said Ash. "We're not going to be alone for long."

Reflected in the HUD, Natalie could see **Kate lit from behind by faraway railgun fire, the kind of crazy Baywell shooting they'd all hated, her eyes glassy. Ash shook,** or was it that the bawling afterburn of a plasma lance hard to port? The breath in Natalie's lungs? The ghosts riding shotgun? Natalie tried to focus. She slammed autobandages on Kate's lacerations, stemming the bleeding, then brought up the local situation map.

It was worse than she'd hoped. Baywell had found them, and they were in the process of pulling the battle down around her ears.

Kate's fingers made small, comforting circles against Ashlan's left shoulder. The woman moaned, closed her eyes, and her head listed to the side. "We'll hear from Natalie any minute now," Kate whispered. "Then we can bail, and—"

A slow blink from Kate, a shudder of realization that something under Ash's skin had simply *stopped*.

"Doc. Something's wrong. Reva!"

But Sharma didn't respond right away. She was concentrating on something else entirely: silent in the rumble seat, she'd been removing her memory device from her head, fiddling with the insides with a spanner, exactly like she'd been doing in front of Natalie ever since they left *Vancouver,* **railgun fire alight on her skin like freezing rain,** causing Natalie to pull hard to shotgun, ninety degrees up and out, *keep moving, keep moving,* her old CO's voice telling her that *when there's nowhere to go you make a hole,* her skin slithering against the playback like there was some alien thing still inside her, some rotten radiation—

"Doc," Kate spat, violent. "Now."

The doctor looked up from her work. "I'm sorry, Ms.

Keller. There's nothing I can do. Her body is rejecting the liver. I matched the phenotype as best I could, but her body is recognizing it as foreign."

"Get the fuck up and fix it, then."

"Kate," Ash whispered, waking. "Stop."

Kate was a wildfire. "You said it would work."

Sharma nodded. "I said it *could* work. I said it would get her off the planet and that's what you chose to listen to. You knew there was just enough fuel to get here and not enough to get anywhere else. We all make sacrifices to get what we want. You wanted this. It's not my fault you didn't think about what would happen next."

"You absolute—"

Sharma stood. "See, the problem with this memory device—I *knew* I needed to come to the White Line. I thought I had to get on board. That's all I allowed myself to know. But I think I might have been wrong."

She stared at the memory device, made a few final twists to the innards. Watched it blink. Pushed it back against her forehead.

"Ah." Barely a whisper. "That makes sense."

—and *damn it*, Natalie thought, *that was railfire*, she was losing the engine, she was losing in general, and Sharma's body clattered behind her like a bag of rocks drenched in clots of gray and Natalie wanted to be sick, *extremely* sick, everything was sick, her whole life was *sick*, and behind her **the doctor was in motion, slammed with new purpose, chased by a demon Natalie can't see. She rose up, out of her chair, moved away to the front of the transport to where Natalie was sitting right now, her purple outline settling in over Natalie's space-wan skin and bones.**

"I told Natalie. I should have been telling *myself* the same thing. You have to control how it delivers the memory," she

said, like a hymn, like a psalm, and dropped into the chair, pulling the transport back and away from the shuddering Vai ship. If Natalie could just get to Aurora, just let them know somehow that she was here—

Exhausted, Natalie leaned to port. She thought of Ash and it nearly got her killed, lighting up the cockpit and the bodies and the death with another near-miss, some Vai weapon, because they were truly engaged now, the silver Vai monstrosities and their clambering human counterparts. The transport followed her motion. The plan—*fuck it, there was no plan but react, twist, react*—became pulling out, pulling down, swinging around and swinging away. It was the next thing. The thing after that. It was always like that, had always been like that, back in Verdict and defusing kinetics on a battlefield and kissing Emerson Ward. The next thing. And the next thing was—

—Sharma launching a wide-band distress beacon, a wail every company within three sectors could hear. She worked with intention, with a slight and thinning mouth, with the steady hand of a tech working on a kinetic meant to activate against human skin.

"Natalie never told you why she chose to trust me. It was this." She tapped the memory device. "The cortical bomb our delightful CEO put in my brain so I'd behave. He paired it with the memoria so he could trigger it whenever he saw a thought he didn't like."

"That's sick," whispered Ash.

"It was a last-ditch effort on his part, a method that he doesn't normally approve, and that was largely my fault, you see. I defeated every measure they used to keep me cowed. Every single one. Until this." She tapped it with her still-lacquered fingernail and *shit shit shit,* she had to get out of the crossfire—

"You're going to set it off," Kate said. "Stop."

"That's the point," Sharma said, her eyes bright. "I programmed this to deliver instructions to myself the next time I was near the Heart, instructions I didn't want Solano to see, at least not until it was too late. And, thank God, everything actually fell into place. I'm far ahead of him. I'm so far ahead of him now, there's no way he's going to see any of it coming."

"You *wanted* to come here."

"I don't even need to go aboard. All I have to do is—"

"Reva, please—"

—and the recording was cut off by a power surge. *The cortical bomb*, Natalie guessed. The violet recordings ceased. Outside, space had gone dark again; behind the interface, she saw the darkening squat hulk of *Vancouver*, then a few last bright lights blossoming and blinking out. The battle was petering to a close, but she couldn't for the life of her figure out who had won.

Natalie knit her haptic-laden hands behind her head and tried to calm down. It was impossible. The exhaustion weighed on her eyes, her head, her shoulders. Her guts were blank, her throat and tongue a barren desert, and everything hurt.

She checked the fuel level. Not enough.

There would be no going back to Earth.

"Kate?" she whispered.

Natalie knew the truth of it now, every sickening alarm bell she'd pushed aside to make herself feel better, every crying shame that called for her attention, every wrong decision she'd gleefully made. The kick of her broken ankle was just the beginning. She'd traded everything for this defeat: her self-respect, her desire, her body, her love, her mind. There was no way up. There was no way out.

Kate stirred. "Is that you?"

"It used to be," Natalie managed.

She wanted to say more. She had so many questions. But her

former captain had already drifted off again, lost in a haze of painkillers. Natalie's mind wandered to her boltgun. She'd forgotten where she'd put it, like a complete fucking idiot. She could go find it. A flick of her fingers and it would all be over. Her body would fit easily next to Ash's. Everything would end: the Vai war, the secret of the silver, all of it.

Natalie would see *him* again.

"No," said the hallucination, as if she'd conjured him up by just thinking of his face. He smelled of vanilla and sweat, and slid into the rumble seat nearby, knitting his fingers together. Too real. Far too real.

"You're dead."

"*No*," he repeated. "It hurts."

Natalie bit her bottom lip. "It hurts like a star going nova. God, it's so stupid. I just—why me? Why the fuck am I still alive?"

"No." A statement.

She shoved her broken foot against the wall. The purposeful pain shocked her system. Kept her awake. Breathing. "That's right. I can't leave Kate. She needs me now. And that's just fucking arrogance, isn't it? To think she even wants to see me now? To think that I have a right to be here, to say that I can just walk out from here and—and *breathe*, when Ash isn't here, when—" She descended into a painful coughing fit, covering her mouth. When she removed her lips from her balled hand, she was slick with blood. "That makes me a bigger fucking coward than ever before. Doesn't it?"

But the man said nothing more.

There was, of course, a good ten minutes between when the transport was authorized a slot inside *Vancouver*'s expansive shuttle level and when the bay doors opened. The ingress protocol for boarding a captured enemy ship, even an enemy ship broadcasting an Auroran IFF, required infantry teams. Probably some App-K support, just in case. She wondered, idly, if her teams had finished upgrading the puppet drone for superhaptics.

Gravity embraced the transport, gently snatching her comrades' limbs out of the air. Ash's body lay bruised on the back bench, crusted red blood darkening her mouth, her eyes blank and open. Sharma stared toward the ceiling, missing her info-implant, the gold traceries leading back to her cortical bomb dull and dead with the loss of brain activity. Natalie would never know what she was trying to do when Aurora killed her.

Sharma hadn't even seen it coming. An ironic end for a woman who had spent her entire life working a *plan*.

Natalie heard the clatter of boots, the familiar arrangement of infantry teams and their guns, the whir of the machines meant to crack plasteel hulls like eggs hauling into motion. She curled up on the ground, vomiting up blood, and with a sense of sick shame, she flipped the codes to keep the airlock open. *I surrender*, it said. *Don't shoot me.*

Auroran soldiers came through the airlock in force, blue cold-suits clattering, their hands holding guns and torches. Smoke blew in from the shuttle, distending above her. Natalie closed her eyes, the light flickering red and brilliant beyond her eyelids. She heard someone coughing. Was it Kate? Why did her chest hurt so much? Why was she so tired?

"It's our people," someone called.

A deep voice called for medic. A coroner.

"I'm not dead," she managed, as if she had a choice in the matter. "Kate's not dead." Her pronunciation slurred. Voices were telling her that she'd be okay—like they knew anything about *being okay*. Nothing would be *okay* ever again.

The last thing she saw as she dropped into black exhaustion was her bright new silver hallucination, watching her from the corner, as if he'd never seen anything so beautiful in his life.

17

Natalie came awake to a blur of frantic voices. She was in a private room in an Auroran medbay, surrounded by people in white coats whirring around her body like they actually cared about saving it. Someone was shouting for *anesthesia;* someone else, *the pulmonologist.* She caught disorienting sparks of light like hornets in her cornea, laid over flashes from the memoria—the transport, the recording, Ash's fragile corpse, her own smiling hallucination. Thankfully, the scratching fabric clutched in her hand was a hospital blanket, not the thick lining of a coldsuit glove.

She sucked down oxygen into overscarred lungs that had forgotten what it was like to be full, coughing so hard she curled into herself, spattering blood and mucus down her hospital gown.

"Where's—" She coughed. "Where's Ms. Keller?"

Blue-gloved hands wiped eggy gunk from the corner of her mouth and told her *everything was going to be all right,* a theory Natalie very much doubted from the way her recalcitrant body was ignoring nearly every request her brain made. The hands belonged to a middle-aged doctor with shockingly tame silver hair. He held her down as politely as he could while barking orders at other people in blue jumpsuits, all of it junk like *surgery* and *yes, Dr. Coriolis* and *send more samples to the lab.*

Natalie struggled against the doctor's grasp, pushing herself up to her elbows. She opened her mouth to speak and felt her lungs burning.

"Lie back. Don't try to talk," said the doctor. He was wearing a white coat with the name *Arturo Coriolis* stitched over the heart, and he wore an info-implant that looked a lot like a memoria. "And, please. Stop fighting the medical personnel. If you don't, we'll have to sedate you again."

A Coriolis. A fucking Coriolis. I'm important now. Natalie coughed out a chuckle, then watched as a nurse picked up a nearby tray of tissue laid out in chunky gray strips like rotten sushi—hers? Gross—and ushered it out of the room. She'd ended up in medbays often enough to understand that once a Company doc dragged out *that* particular chestnut, some functionary nearby was already prepping a syringe whether or not you had cit tags or cared, so she spat out a mouthful of blood and grinned at him. "How's a kick to the face sound instead?"

Coriolis's cheeks flushed. "Listen," he said, grabbing her hand. He pressed a thumb against the inside of her wrist, searching for a pulse—redundant, of course, in a citizen's medbay full of bells and whistles and expensive equipment. It was just an excuse to lean in, lower his voice and address her directly. "You need to stop screaming about *Len*, whoever he is."

"I don't know who—"

"It's making them suspicious," Coriolis hissed, cutting her off. "They won't trust you, and we need them to trust you. They're going to require you to get the superhaptic upgrade. It's important that you refuse. In fact, it's crucial. You see all those zombies walking around outside? I've managed to keep most of them away from our work, but it's difficult, especially when Ingest is listening. You need to—"

"Pulmonologist's here," said someone by the door.

The doctor closed his eyes for an exhausted moment, then let go of her wrist. "Stay in the medbay until you receive further instructions. Be *careful* what you tell them."

He straightened and flipped the long-awaited soporifics into her main line, switching back to medical jargon she couldn't quite understand. A drug-strong, inevitable darkness took her words away seconds later.

Her body ached like she'd been dropped from a skyscraper and left to rot in the sun. She took a hard breath, muttering at the needle-bright pain occupying her lungs; a moment's clawing at her hospital gown found a collection of six tiny new autoban-dages denoting some sort of robotic surgery. A nurse flickered by, adjusting the blanket near her feet, and the fact that she even did that was insane, wasn't it—hospitality was the kind of billing con-job bullshit they pulled on unconscious indentures.

But she couldn't pay for a nurse, for surgery or soporifics or quiet or the blanket. She had to leave. Now. She pushed herself up, feeling the cold deck through the thin socks, the entire room listing to the side as she *remembered*.

She was a citizen now. The nurse, the medicine, all the blink-ing equipment that existed to keep her alive, even the interface silently playing the Company news channel in the corner—she'd paid for it in effort and sacrifice and seven long bloody years. She was a citizen. This was earned. This was *hers*.

Then why did she still want to panic?

"Help me." A too-familiar whisper from the back wall.

Natalie didn't want to look, but she eventually turned her head. The hallucination—her Bittersweet survivor—leaned against the back wall in an Auroran indenture's jumpsuit, striped with thick Tribulation dirt. Worry creased the wrinkles near her hallucination's eyes, and his hands dangled useless by his sides, as if he did not know how to use them. Stitched onto his breast pocket was the number 25.

She didn't reply. She flushed with embarrassed about talking to him in the transport. She'd been sicker than she thought. What was the use in replying to herself? She was less concerned with what coughing, confused part of her needed that kind of whiny *help* than the fact that the memoria hadn't yet connected him to any of the other memories in her broken brain. There were holes in her six months on *Twenty-Five*, as there were holes in everything, but an entire *person*?

Could she really have forgotten a whole *person*?

The answer was yes, of course. A resounding yes. Sharma had literally blocked out whatever memory had been keeping her brain from blowing up. Natalie's memoria had helped her wrap her mind quite well around a father she could hardly remember.

She ran through her memories again. Her mind fed her dependable Kate, a straight-faced Sharma, that bitch Ramsay, and Ash, the lead salvager—but no ship's mechanic or cargo mate. Which was the mind-boggling thing—that she just understood it as the truth that she'd left for a year's salvage mission *without a mechanic*. It hadn't occurred to her until this very moment how *wrong* that seemed. There were other holes—she could have sworn someone had been there with her to watch that entire second season of *Alien Attack Squad*—but she'd always brushed that off as being standard human brain nonsense, like forgetting a crucial piece of information while under pressure.

"You are just my stress response," she told the hallucination in the corner, sucking down her sudden anxiety. "That's all you are. You're not a ghost. You're not my disease. It's too *early* for symptoms."

He extended his hand. "No."

"Get out," she whispered. Dizziness clawed at the corners of her vision. "I refuse to see this. You're not real—"

She realized her mistake in seconds: she was still standing. She shouldn't have been standing. Acid twisted in her trachea, closing her off from speech, and she grabbed at the corner of the medibed. Her chest constricted with the effort of keeping herself upright, and instead of sucking down air, her lungs seized, throwing her into another blackout coughing fit. The floor hurtled toward her, and her head cracked on the floor.

Darkness followed.

When Natalie awoke, the hallucination was gone and she was once again lying on her medibed. New bruises purpled her bare left arm. Her head ached. She probed a loose tooth. The doctor was missing, having been replaced by the board's personnel director, of all people—slim, perfect Cora Aulander, looking svelte in an impeccably tailored suit, a matte-gold info-implant that seemed different from the one before, and a thin, quiet smile. She held out a glass of water, as if she could be trusted.

"Don't try to get up," she said.

"They keep on telling me that."

The executive pressed the cup to Natalie's mouth and tilted it for a second or two; the water stopped her questions, tasted like *ship,* like *metal,* like familiar memories, and she felt a grateful anger alongside a ridiculous discomfort. Natalie slid her cold fingers around the cup, brushing Aulander's warm ones, worrying it from the executive's hands and polishing off the contents herself.

"Perhaps you should listen, Ms. Chan," the executive said. "You've had a trauma. Take it slow."

"I'm not good at *slow.*"

"It's a learned skill." Aulander paused. "How are you feeling?"

Natalie exhaled. Each breath she took resembled a hot, double-bladed knife under her breastbone. The sheer pain of it stopped her from speaking long enough to consider and load in the old, familiar indenture's lie, the brush-and-switch that kept doctors from poking around in their cit accounts with costly tests. "I'm fine," she replied. "Can you tell me where Ms. Keller is?"

"I wouldn't use the word *fine* to describe your condition," said Aulander, following it up with a muted chuckle.

"I've had worse." Natalie shook her head. "Now, if possible, I need to see Ms. Keller. I need to know she made it off the transport alive."

Aulander paused. "I have no idea who you're talking about."

"Kate Keller. The captain of *Twenty-Five*. I found her alive on Tribulation. She was with us on the transport," Natalie said. She put the cup aside; she fumbled the landing, and it rolled onto the nearby table, trailing droplets of water. "I need to see her. Now."

Confusion creased the corners of the executive's eyes. "I'm sorry. You were the only survivor, Ms. Chan."

"That's ludicrous. You must be lying."

"That's quite the rude accusation."

"There were four of us. You'll see three of them on the cockpit recording—Dr. Sharma, Ashlan Jackson, Kate Keller—"

Aulander pursed her lips, lost in thought for a moment, then flickered her fingers to access her personal comm. "Dr. Coriolis, can you join us, please?"

"Don't call that asshole."

"You might be hallucinating. It's possible your memoria took damage in the firefight, and your infection is quite advanced. The nanotech is everywhere in your bloodstream. It's possible that—"

"I'm—" *Definitely hallucinating.* Natalie swallowed. "I'm having problems, but there's no way I hallucinated the captain. *Someone* set off those guns I put on the roof of the dorm, and I had entire conversations with all three of them at once."

"But there's nobody who can confirm that." Aulander looked worried.

Natalie opened her mouth to say *Reva Sharma*, but the name turned to stone behind her lips. She asked the memoria for a memory that had Kate doing something she hadn't been there for, and—*No*, she thought. *I could have programmed the gun. I could have threatened the InGens without knowing it. I could have activated the Heart in the bugout bay. But there was a mattress in Sharma's old lab, meals—*

—only eight of them, she countered. *Not enough for two.*

A cold doubt ate at the corners of her warm certainty, and she wanted to throw up. Ash couldn't have lived all of those months alone. Lived all those *deaths* alone.

"The answer's on the recording," she said.

"There's no recording," Aulander said, her voice kind. "Ms. Chan, dozens of salvage and health workers gave sworn statements telling us that only three of you came off the transport, and that you were the only survivor."

Natalie's hands twisted in the blanket. "I know what I saw."

"We've been doing research on the nanotech infection for some time now. Dr. Sharma spent some time with us after she was rescued, and we learned quite a lot. The brain is a marvelous machine, capable of many things, and we're only now figuring out how the memoria really works with the messages sent to and from the hippocampus."

"This sounds like Sharma's research."

The executive's thin fingers extended to pluck the cup from the nearby table, to hold it between her thumb and forefinger. "Which is why we think she was manipulating you the entire time. To explain: You think I'm holding this cup because your senses tell you I am. But your senses are run by your brain, and your nerves tell your brain what you see and hear, and your nerves, Natalie, are being attacked by an alien nanotechnology we're only beginning to understand."

I saw her, Natalie wanted to say. *I touched her. You're lying. Executives lie. And you have every reason to lie to me. You threatened to take away my citizenship.* The words were just on the tip of her tongue, full of red dust and pain and the memories she couldn't erase. She'd seen the hallucination on Bittersweet, so she'd had symptoms for a long time. What else about her life was counterfeit?

She looked away from Aulander, finding the room's interface, focusing on that instead. Like many of the public interfaces on *Vancouver,* this one defaulted to the Company news channels when unused. She waved on the sound and caught her least favorite announcer—the perky, cream-haired morning-shifter, a longtime cit who wore the gaudiest and largest info-implant Natalie had ever seen—in the middle of describing the recent battle with the Vai.

At a ceremony on Watcher Station, Mr. Solano gave credit for the stunning victory—humanity's first against the Vai—to the captain of the heavy cruiser Vancouver, *Lucia Varela, honoring the Varela line with elevation to the board . . .*

"Oh, my God," Natalie whispered. "I'm going nuts."

"No. That was quite real, actually. You did everything we wanted and more," Aulander said, her voice warming. "You brought back Ashlan's body and your own, ensuring Aurora has access to the alien nanotechnology—the advancement that will push Aurora to the front of the market. In fact—"

But Natalie wasn't listening to the executive spin out her bullshit praise. She didn't even feel like she was in the room. Her head was lost in the rush-rumble of disbelief. Everything was wrong. Everything was *off*. This room, the hallucination haunting the shadows next to the cabinets, Aulander talking to her, this entire world. It had been that way for so long.

She'd known for a long time that there was a dishonest edge to the official feeds; the week she'd spent getting her bones knit back together after the rout at Cana was riddled with interface announcers yammering about *victory* this and *a great Auroran advance* that, when she'd been there, she'd seen it, and she knew how little reality was in it.

They'd stretched the truth after Tribulation, too, calling the Heart a *Baylor-Wellspring superweapon,* using it to justify the continuing war in front of the Corporate Alliance. Ash had come from Bittersweet–Wellspring space. They'd had a word for this kind of truth-twisting over there. *Propaganda,* Ash called it, an old, extinct phrase like *injustice* or *slavery,* one of those old hurts from the history books.

She didn't know how something could be propaganda when everyone knew *the truth* was something companies owned outright. Maybe *the truth* had meant something different when she was growing up, but she'd signed over those rights in the pursuit of her Auroran future.

But this—

She expected to hear the Company line—a good citizen always expected that kind of bullshit—but the channel was displaying the actual, honest-to-God truth, aside from the announcer droning on about Varela's heroism in the face of *bloody whatever*. She wasn't seeing quick edits and explosions interspersed with the faces of the dead. There were no bright and bombastic emotional appeals masquerading as facts. This was a direct, uncut feed from *Vancouver's* gun-level cameras, a plain record of ordinary railfire finding purchase in the white bellies of the line of slippery alien ships beyond—and then, impossibly, *impossibly,* those ships exploding, one by one, like pearls crushed beneath an executive's heel.

She hadn't noticed any of that in the thick of everything, when she was just another mote of dust spinning out below the Alliance plasma lances. She'd been too focused on keeping herself alive.

"That's impossible," she whispered. "You're right. I'm seeing things. I—" She gulped. *"How?"* she said.

She'd been expecting the same kind of bullshit explanation from Aulander, too, but the executive relaxed slightly, her tone going almost friendly. "We were hoping you knew."

"You were just explaining to me why I can't be trusted."

Aulander blinked. "I think after what you've done for Aurora we can at least take your story and verify it."

Natalie nodded, then rubbed her eyes, trying to sort through her memories and buy some time. She remembered the doctor from earlier, his words, his warning to be careful. She fought some nausea. This was absolutely some sort of test—Aulander's friendly voice was probably for show, and their ostensibly private conversation was taking place under the eyes of Ingest's renderbots. She had to assume they'd seen everything: her absence from the shuttle's records, the silver nanotech in her veins. They'd have discovered the liver transplant in the autopsy. She closed her eyes, searching her memoria for the last few moments of the recording, then exhaled and chose something relatively close to the truth.

"I don't know," Natalie said, finally. "I'd gone outside to make some repairs to the hull. I think they waited for me to leave."

"Did you?"

"It was a Baywell bucket. It had *problems*."

The executive nodded. "You were drenched in their blood."

"*After* they'd died."

"Was that before or after you came back inside?"

Natalie's mouth opened, closed, opened again in disbelief. "*After*. God. You can check the door access log, if Wellspring was smart enough to put one in. There was no gravity. They'd been bleeding. I got *splattered* trying to get away from all the railfire. Basic fucking physics. Wait, are you asking if I *killed* them?"

"I'm asking for the full story, Ms. Chan."

"So this *is* a test."

Aulander's lips thinned alongside her patience. "When we meet the Vai fleet again, we need to know how to defeat them. And we need *trustworthy* people to help us. I'm sure you've always wanted a place on the bridge."

"Now I know you're fucking with me."

"I would never do that. Not to another birthright. All you have to do is explain why you were at the White Line and not on a direct vector back to *Vancouver* and we can talk about that."

Natalie felt her blood thrumming. Her heart kicked, a wild hope rattling around in her broken head. *A place on the bridge,* she thought. *Birthright status. This isn't a test. It's* the *test.*

"I'm not a traitor, if that's what you're asking. They wanted to go to the White Line," Natalie stammered, scrambling for a lie they'd believe. "Sharma—" Was dead. Natalie could throw her into the gears with absolutely no guilt. "She was a member of the Sacrament Society this whole time. I knew you could track Ash, and I knew you'd be watching. Frankly, I thought I could bring home more than just the nanotech. It was a chance I had to take. *You* would take that chance. I even sent you a ping, so you would know. I did everything I could to make sure *Vancouver* knew exactly what was happening."

"I see," said Aulander. "Of course, the offer is contingent on the fact that you're telling the truth."

Natalie's lungs ached. Everything hinged on this conversation. Aulander was the only one besides Solano with the authority to raise anyone to birthright status. "What are you expecting? For me to say that I sold out to the Sacrament Society? I don't want to hear any of this *contingent* bullshit. I went to Tribulation. I found Ash." *And Kate,* she thought, although doubt had started to slip through the cracks in her faulty, broken mind. "Give me the promotion, or let me go back to work, or whatever. It's not my fault you sent the doctor along with a bomb in her head. I have no idea what you want to hear. Whoever recorded her bomb records will."

Aulander blinked, clearly confused. "Bomb? What bomb?"

"The one she said R&D put in her head."

The executive's eyes widened, and she looked genuinely horrified. "In her *what*? Who do you think we are?"

Natalie was about to answer—something cheeky, something inadvised, something related to *so this is how you keep me from birthright status, by making me look like a drama hound*—and was saved at the last minute by a violent coughing fit. The doctor handed her a towel; Natalie spit salty blood into it, folded it and placed at the bottom of her bed. "That's how she died. She told me Aurora had installed the bomb, that it was recording what she spoke, and that if she wandered off script it would explode. I'm done playing games. I'll only take this offer if it isn't contingent on *anything*."

Aulander's forehead creased with worry. She placed her warm hand over Natalie's chilly one. "No wonder you're not cooperating. Ms. Chan, I told you from the beginning of this conversation that you have done everything we wanted you to do, and more besides. And I understand you believed the deal we offered at our last meeting to be unfair."

"It was—"

"Unfair, yes." The executive breathed out. She seemed rattled, and her voice had lost its previous guarded accord. "I came to tell you that you can write your own future with Aurora, and that remains true. Why don't you wait here, focus on your recovery for a few days, get your superhaptics installed, and then we'll do the official paperwork at the end of the week? No contingencies."

And without an answer, she patted Natalie's hand three quick times, turned, and moved out the door.

The room was relatively quiet for a moment, with some nursing assistants moving in the background, checking equipment and writing on tablets. Natalie felt dazed, drunk, like her head was filled with cotton. The doctor from earlier—the Coriolis, the one with the cryptic comments about the superhaptics, which still bothered her—walked in and filled a glass of water. The news announcer droned on about *changes at the Corporate Alliance,* about Solano and *the shareholders* and *a radical shift in power,* and as soon as the doctor arrived near her bed, Natalie yanked the glass from his grasp, using a long sip and the curve of her hand to give her a few moments of privacy.

Natalie imagined that Aulander's conciliatory behavior was meant to make her feel more comfortable, but there was one thing the executive was getting wrong—Natalie thought on her feet, not in a boardroom, and sitting around made her feel *more* uncomfortable, not less. On top of that, she didn't want to make any decisions until she confirmed that Kate Keller had been killed at Tribulation last year, and she needed to do that independently, on her own. Perhaps the support staff had sworn Kate was absent because they were sent in after the captain was removed. Natalie had been hallucinating. In pain. She didn't remember.

If Kate was on *Vancouver*, Natalie would find her.

Her first idea was to check the company directory, which had been partially automated by Ingest six months ago. She thought about waiting until she was alone and using the interface to do that—this was allegedly a private room—but Coriolis and his people moved in and out with the choreography of people instructed to never actually leave her unsupervised for very long. She thought about signing out and making her inquiries on the computer in her quarters, but she was still sure Ingest monitored citizens' queries, and simply remembering certain masking tricks from her Verdict childhood didn't make her a good enough hacker to get around that.

A *birthright's* private systems, though, were robust, specific, and, as far as she knew, hadn't been upgraded for superhaptics. Ingest might get suspicious, but the department needed a warrant from the personnel office to check, so she might be able to get the answers Aulander was clearly unwilling to give her. She needed a private room. At this point, there was no way she *wasn't* going to check for a bomb in her head after a few days in the Company medbay. Too bad she wasn't close enough to any current birthright to use their private interface.

No. She *was*.

Natalie pushed the empty cup back in the doctor's direction, then pushed the blankets aside to place her feet on the cold floor. *The cup exists*, she thought. *The blankets exist. The floor exists. I exist.*

Kate exists.

"Thank you," she said to Coriolis, waving him down. "I quite appreciate the hospitality, but I'm going home. I want my own bed."

That was not the reaction the doctor expected. He looked down at the cup, confused, then back up at her. "That's really not a good idea," he said. "You're still recovering."

Natalie smiled. "You and I have just met, so let me fill you in. I'm not known for my reliance on *good ideas*. Or executives."

"Your lungs experienced significant interior trauma. We've rebuilt much of your capacity, but you're in absolutely no condition to leave. The executives aren't just being *nice* to you. They're acting on my express advice."

Natalie felt fuzzy. "Rebuilt? How long does that take?"

"About a month. You—"

"A *month*? I've been awake for an *hour*." She felt a twist of dizzy nausea and tried to stand again. The doctor slipped in right in front of her, sliding a hand underneath her forearm. She tried to twist away, then stumbled back onto the medibed.

"We had to put you in a coma."

"Give me my jacket. A month! *Fuck*."

"You're not authorized to leave."

She frowned and tried to stand again. "I'm a citizen. That's enough authorization. And I don't trust you. You said some really weird things back there about the superhaptics, and I'm too tired for games."

His voice lowered. "I can explain."

"I'm just interested in going."

"Hear me out. Please." Coriolis's voice lowered, and he moved in close. Too close. It was only then that she saw the necklace dislodged by his motion, swinging out from behind his unbuttoned collar—a saint, an oval, an arrow, hidden from the renderbots in the shadow of his chin.

This was the sigil of the Sacrament Society, Sharma's shadow company, the organization she'd founded to figure out how to use the Heart. The organization responsible for the sick experiments under Tribulation, for pushing forward the crushing wheel that was this new life of hers, the weight of which had taken Ash and Kate and *Twenty-Five* and God knows what else.

Natalie pushed against his breastbone, harder this time. "No."

He stumbled back. "Ms. Chan—"

"I'd rather lick Solano's *butthole* than trust the lot of *you*."

"You have to trust us."

"Shit, is Aulander part of this too?"

"No," he said. The doctor reached up with his left hand, tucking the necklace back underneath his collar. His voice remained quiet, measured, and his body calm, as if he knew exactly how much Ingest would take in before it figured he wasn't behaving as expected. "Dr. Sharma told me you might feel this way. She also told me that you'd come around."

"Sharma's *dead*."

He paused. "Her work continues. If you knew what I sacrificed to be in this room right now, to talk to you directly—"

Natalie was standing now, feeling a little steadier than before. "I don't care. I'm a citizen and I want my pants. I've spent thousands of hours dreaming of this moment, this delightful moment, when I can do whatever I fucking want in my very own pants."

He sighed. "But—"

"*My* pants, from my compartment. Not new pants. Not someone else's pants. *My* pants."

The doctor wavered. This was a citizen's basic right: he had no grounds to hold her or control what she chose to do with her body. His jaw worked, to one side and then the other; his hand flickered up to his chest, a few inches short of touching the Sacrament emblem she knew was there. For a moment, she expected the indenture's treatment—a brush-off, a non-explanation, a cuff to the bed *for her own good,* or some other bullshit. He finally sighed, slipping one glove off his hand to rub his temples. "I'll get your pants," he said, and walked out.

She wavered where she stood, and grabbed the edge of the bed to steady herself. The interface had flashed back to the news channel—to the *victory,* they were saying, *the incredible triumph of Auroran ingenuity,* to *Auroran engineering—*

A month, she thought, *a fucking month.*

She needed to find Kate *yesterday.*

"I don't understand," said her ghost.

She whirled dizzily. The nanotech hallucination was sitting cross-legged on the floor nearby, his back straight against the wall, his body preternaturally still. His eyes were red, and his cheeks skin-scrubbed, as if he had been crying and trying to hide it.

"I do," she muttered.

"Explain," said the man.

"Aurora wants what any company wants," Natalie said. "Profit, market share, expansion. To be at the top, to be unassailable. The Sacrament Society, well—we know they wanted Vai weapons, and a corpse is a corpse, no matter what story the executives are telling. The only move we have right now is to make sure we're not standing in the middle."

"They are lying," he said, as if it were some mad new realization.

"Someone is. We need to find out which one. Or both."

The hallucination frowned, and then rocked himself against the wall, over and over, his eyes filmy, his shoulders shaking. For a sliver of her disintegrating brain, Natalie thought, he was remarkably upset about a basic truth of the universe, something Natalie had known since she was a very small child. "Humans lie," he said.

Humans lie, she thought. "All of them," she said. "Every single one."

"Even you."

She thought of the doctor, of Aulander, of all the things she planned to do. *"Especially* me."

And now she was starting to see the details on her body she'd been missing earlier. No pants, no jacket, no underwear, no jumpsuit, just a hospital gown—they didn't want her to leave. The interesting, useful tools were stuffed in cabinets sealed with fingerprint locks—not a common practice for a citizen's space. Her fingers brushed at her throat, at her lack of a collar, of tags. *Humans lie,* she thought, and she felt a desperate ache at the thought of Aulander's offer, of the possibilities that lay there, of the possibility that that, too, had been a lie.

Natalie had built so much of herself on the prospect of citizenship—of becoming something more than hungry spinning Earth could ever offer—but now she just felt shaky and small, just as alone as she'd been on the last day of her life in Verdict. Part of Natalie had thought that Ash would come back to Aurora after the battle, because that part of Natalie that wanted so much to belong—the part that threw herself into the war, into her platoon, into that *feeling*—still believed. She'd believed, even though Ash stood in *London*'s dead engine room and said *no,* said that *over my dead body will I be a weapon.* She'd believed even until Ash wasted away for it, until Natalie saw her use the Heart to dip into those Baywell soldiers' minds in the plaza, until she'd died for it.

Natalie hadn't gone so far. She'd sold herself to be a weapon, of course, because that was the price she could get for her life—that was the game and the bargain, and the only way off Earth was pushing through the indenture shit sandwich to get the citizenship that would make it all worthwhile. It was depressing to discover that she was still in the game, and that the only way to win was to be born into victory in the first place.

"Humans lie," the ghost repeated.

And maybe that's the truth Ash knew, she thought. *Maybe that's why she decided not to play. Until I forced her to.*

Truth. Lies. Propaganda. Truth had to be more than just orders to be followed. It had to be more than *belief.* She remembered Solano in the boardroom, telling her what was right, what was *true,* and he knew that truth, knew it with every straightened nerve in his body. Sharma had certainly believed in a truth beyond any corporate reach or order. And there had been a truth in the way Kate and Ash held each other during their rattling escape from Tribulation, more truth than anyone offered here. *Kate is real,* she reminded herself.

Natalie grabbed the blanket and dragged it around her body. She adjusted the socks. She knew a month was long enough for R&D to put a bomb in her brain, and maybe that's why they were so sanguine about giving her a chance at a promotion.

She couldn't wait for her own pants.

She dug around in the bottom drawers near the back corner of the room and came out with a too-big pair of maternity underwear, pulled them on, and went to leave. For a moment, she thought the door might lock against her fingers, but it, at least, lined up with whatever game they were playing, and opened for her. Not that it mattered. It was going to be easy to track an oil-haired, sick-mouthed, hospital-gown-wearing soldier when there were renderbots every three feet in the ceiling.

The game is on, she thought. *May the best liar win.*

18

Emerging from her room wearing only the hospital gown, a blanket, and her borrowed underwear, Natalie felt better than ever.

The medical section was like the rest of *Vancouver*: blue, sterile, perfect. No weapon-bright heat choking the doorways, no enemy shadows, no pervasive planetbound dirt or ragged edges or weapons or enemies wearing mechsuits. With her bare feet on the floor and the fabric in a flail at her exposed back, she was the one radically different element in the Aurora-standard spectrum of variegated blue and gray, of clothes made for management and similar cit jobs, where you could be elegant and delicate, where you didn't have to wade through people or engines or the dead corpses of broken cruisers.

She watched cits pass by, going this way and that, most of them attempting executive style—twists in their hair, short heels, skirts that hugged their thighs, and gaudy info-implants that she would have called memorias, if she hadn't known she and Sharma had the only prototypes. Quite a few sported the new superhaptic tattoos she'd seen in the medbay, golden and twisting, like wires or chains or vines winding around their arms. Some walked in a funny sort of lockstep with each other, arms and legs swinging at exactly the same pace, faces gray and bored.

She nearly laughed at herself, at the months of fussing with the fit of her jacket, wondering how fast her hair would grow out. No—to be noticed, all she had to do was be the child that had left Earth once more, saying *fuck it* to every convention she was taught to be good, going from ambitious director to hallway curiosity. This felt like power, even though it shouldn't have. She reveled in the way she caught each of their gazes, the way they snapped their chins toward her, the slight widening of their eyes at her bare legs and her sour mouth and her balls-to-the-wall ambition. She bet Cora Aulander never felt like this, but Aulander had never sat quietly in a Baywell shuttle alongside the corpses of the last people that really knew her as a human being.

Ash would have told her she was being ridiculous. But Ash was dead, and Kate was missing, and Sharma—

Fuck Sharma, she'd said, but *damn,* had the woman really deserved to die like that? A gory vision of Sharma's cracked skull splayed in front of her eyes, scorched and spilled and twirling in the transport's loss of gravity. She stumbled, nearly crashing into a crowd of people waiting for the spine lift.

Most were citizens in heels and miniskirts—involved in checking their social credit rating on their tablet or watching the news channel on the wall and definitely trying not to stare at anyone else, especially Natalie. Natalie felt frustrated that she had to wait in the crowd, that it allowed Aulander or Coriolis that much more time to catch up, and that she couldn't just head for the indenture ladder to the left. But she tapped her index finger against her thigh like all the others, enjoyed the staring, took the lift, and got off at Ward's deck.

Aulander didn't really need to chase her here. Ingest would see her path and figure out she was going to Ward's place, but since she'd gone so many times before, the algorithm wouldn't flag it as suspicious. Ward might not, either. After their last conversation, the last thing he'd think when she showed up at his door in her underwear was that she wanted an airgapped place to do brain surgery.

As she walked, she entertained the woolly feeling that always rose to the surface whenever she thought of Ward. His slanted smile, the twist of his hand on her hip when they slipped into close proximity in the lab. It had been fun until the proposal. It had been perfect. He'd made her feel warm again. He'd made her laugh again. And now—

Natalie paused in front of his drab blue hatch.

She should leave.

Instead, she pressed the ringer. A few seconds passed, and the door slipped open to reveal Emerson Ward, half-dressed in lab pants and shirtsleeves, a grav-comb dangling from his hand, his cit jacket tossed over the couch behind him. His hair was half-curled, the long lines of his yellow locks still slightly matted from sleep. Golden tattooed lines twinkled from his fingers to his ulnar vein, then up his arms, to disappear under the fabric; like everyone else she'd seen on the walk here, he'd obtained the superhaptic upgrade.

"Hey," she said.

"Hey," he said, blinking.

"Hey," said the hallucination, waving from a seat on Ward's couch.

She waited for him to move aside, shuffling her feet, trying to keep her eyes on him rather than the breathing lie behind him. "Can I come in?"

He pressed his lips together; there was something uncomfortable and gray there, a startling weight she'd never seen on his face. "I have a shift, Chan."

"I come back from the dead and walk all the way from medbay in someone else's underwear to see you, and all you have to say is 'I have a shift, Chan'?"

He sighed. Rubbed his face. "You said no. I've spent the last month coming to terms with that."

"I said *later.*"

"You said *later,* and then swanned off on some mission—"

"—which was not my idea—"

"—and didn't get back in touch with me. That hurt."

She pursed her lips, trying to fight off the sudden annoyance she felt. Natalie expected him to be uptight after the refusal, but he'd gone full dumbass on this one. She was suddenly reminded why she had a hard time connecting to him on any other level than the physical. "Yeah, a medically induced coma and full lung rehabilitation makes it kind of difficult for a person to make calls."

He tried to hide the surprise he felt at hearing that, but Natalie caught his raised eyebrows, his deepening frown, the slight dip of his shoulders.

"You didn't know?"

His face flooded with regret. "I didn't think to ask."

"You never do." Her fists balled with a growing annoyance. "You're a Ward, you know. You have friends on the bridge and some connections in pretty high places, as you told me a bunch of times. You could have cared about me enough to make a few friendly inquiries."

He crossed his arms. "I'm not that kind of Ward. And you could have cared about *me* enough to not make me jump through hoops for you. But that's your thing, isn't it? You get off on it."

"Look. I wasn't ready to say yes." She wrestled down a sudden anger. "If you'd have asked me the next day, or when I calmed down—you *knew* I was upset about what had happened on Bittersweet. You had shit timing."

"You said later," he said. "In cit talk, that means *no.*"

"It means *later.*"

"Chan, I—"

"It's later now." She placed her hand on the doorjamb and stepped closer. The guilt she felt about using him like this had dropped out sometime during the conversation; now, she just wanted him to move aside.

He let out an embattled sigh. "Fine," he said, and took a step back into his quarters.

Like the rest of *Vancouver,* Ward's compartment hadn't changed much. It was significantly bigger than her own—not that he'd done anything with the extra space. She hadn't realized until now how much his blue, blank surroundings bothered her. The guy had the chance to exercise his personality since the day he was born, to do anything he wanted within the confines of his social credit, and yet he'd chosen to be indifferently Auroran: blue Company blankets on his bunk, the blank, smiling faces of Company advertisements on his walls, Company sweatpants to relax in, preferring to keep his jumble of possessions inside the drawers of his bathroom and kitchenette.

The only personal effects he exhibited were the pictures hanging on the mirror just by the door: parents, siblings, line-mates. No boardschool friends, but then, from what she'd heard about boardschool politics, friends were few and far between. His picture of Natalie, the one taken at the App-K party where they'd met, was gone. She blinked, feeling a lump in her throat, then reminded herself that she should have expected it.

She turned away, anyway, toward the kitchenette at the back of the room, balling the blanket in front of her belly, letting him see the curves of her body, her exposed collarbones. She knew the effect it would have, and she watched it with some disobedient pleasure. Ward swallowed and crossed the room, standing in front of her—close. Too close. He put the comb aside, and she responded by turning away. *Hell if I'm gonna make it easy on you,* she thought.

"Where's your info-implant?" she asked.

His hand flew up to touch the blank cover just over his left eyebrow. "Oh. The old one started glitching when I got the su-perhaptics, so I was going to head to the neurotechs after my shift. I'm . . . having a really weird afternoon. You want some food?" he said.

She snorted. "I'm not eating your garlic noodles."

"I like the garlic noodles."

"That's the only thing you like."

"Not the only thing," he said, and moved up behind her. She felt his body hover behind hers, his hands light on her hips, the tips of his fingers moving slowly toward her belly. A quiet, forgotten greed curled under her skin, and she let out a breathy sigh. He took this as permission to go further, and she felt his fingers find her waistband and slide beneath, his breath hot in her ear, his lips—

—and she slapped him away.

"This isn't talking," she said.

"I'm sorry," he said. "You're still recovering."

"It's not that," she said, turning, immediately regretting it. One hand went to press lightly against his chest, and underneath, she felt the thrum of his heart and the heat of his body. She felt something else, too, a quiet whispering, the kind of alien shiver she'd only recognized after her experience in the rib cage room.

The realization was slow and inexorable, a molecular darkness stepping over into her skin and destroying it from the inside. Her breath hitched, and she was unable to speak; she just leaned forward, her forehead against his chest, hiding the guilt on her face. Ward was *infected*.

Of course he was. How many times had they kissed? How many times had they—

—did he *know*?

She blanched and turned her face away to hide her nausea; he took that as demure invitation and tugged at the edge of her gown, sliding his hand up her thigh. There was usually no talking when he did that kind of thing, and she didn't want to talk, didn't want to tell him, not now when there was so much else on the line—

"I thought you had a shift," she managed.

He leaned forward, drew his lips up her neck. She felt the tug

of his teeth in the sensitive space under her ear, and she shivered. "I'm the director. My meeting isn't for another two hours.
It'll be fine."

Natalie felt a painful itch at the back of her throat and brought
her fist to her mouth to cover her cough; when she removed
it, she saw flecks of ruby-bright blood on the skin. She wiped
it hastily on the gown behind her leg, where he wouldn't see it.
"The director. A *promotion*. That's good. They're finally seeing
your potential. Where'd they put you?"

"Applied Kinetics."

The reaction was nearly visceral; she pushed him away, palm
of the hand to blue-shirted breastbone. "What the hell, Ward?"

"You went on a mission. They told me you knew." His eyes
widened in surprise. "I've been the director since the day you
left. I supervised the entire superhaptic switchover. We've made
a ton of revisions to your proxy rig project. And we couldn't have
done it without you."

Anger flared. "I didn't leave! I was forced on that mission."

"Nobody's *forced* on a mission, Nat." He paused. "Cits, at least."

"You are such a dumbass." She stopped, wavering where she
stood, rubbing her temples. *No*, she thought, she couldn't be mad
at him. Not for this, at least. Walking off her proxy assault of Bittersweet, she hadn't even been sure she'd wanted to continue as
director. She hadn't even had time to think about it before Aulander arrived to upend her life. There'd been no space to consider
what the red dust meant for how Aurora was going to proceed
against Wellspring and the Vai and the other companies—she'd
expected some bad behavior and occasional skullduggery, but a
redshift star? A fucking *war crime*?

Of course she doubted.

And in a department as crucial to the war effort as Applied
Kinetics, there was no room for doubt. The director needed to
support the CEO with every mad scratch of his heart. And that

was the decision Ward had made. She was not safe here. She crossed her arms in front of her thin gown, feeling nauseous that she'd spent any of her time at all on this bullshit relationship.

"I need to use your shower," she said, swallowing a shameful lump in her throat. "And maybe borrow some of your cit-wear."

"Right," he said with a frown, shoving his hands in his pockets. "You came to talk. So now you don't want to."

"Congratulations on the promotion," she muttered, gathering the hospital gown over her shoulders and tearing it off. "You worked hard for it."

"I don't have any control over Aulander's personnel decisions," he said.

"But you do have control over how you react to them." She yanked the grav-comb from his counter, crossed the room, then opened the thin door to the tiny shower compartment, dialing it to opaque.

"That's unfair. You know if you say no to something like App-K, you're never given another chance. You wither away and die in—in recycling, or bookkeeping."

"There it is," she said, smiling. "Ward is worried about Ward again."

Without waiting for an answer, she shut the door like she had a dozen times, then went through the other grooming tools lined up in front of the spigot. None of them would do. Instead of grabbing Ward's rinseless soap and getting to work over the collection of scars that covered her skin, she turned on the scraper, set it on the ledge to whine and whir and cover her tracks, then sat on the bathroom floor.

Outside, Ward switched on a shaver. "Nobody else will understand. I thought you might."

That caught her where it counted. She had to pause to fight the sudden jolt of anger, her hand halfway up to the faceplate. "Understanding goes both ways, asshole," she said. "You saw what happened with your own eyes. Don't you care about what they made me do?"

"They didn't *make* you do anything. It's not my fault you didn't follow instructions."

"We had cleared another plan. A plan that would have *worked*. You were in all the meetings. You voted for it. You're okay that they made me a mass murderer because this is how things are, this is the law, these are the rules?"

He snorted. "You're a soldier. Don't you care that we won? Don't you care that there were no Auroran casualties?"

"Yeah, I am a soldier," she snapped. "And soldiers aren't robots. We're not computer programs or murder machines or—or Vai. We have morals and we have feelings and we're doing a job, and that job includes *not following immoral orders* like that one. That's why they had to lie to me. Did you ever think that Mr. Solano could be lying to you? How are you fine with this?"

And she could hear, in the silence, in the quiet way he was holding his shaver without moving it, that he had not.

"I'm not—I'm not fine with it," he finally said. "But things are how they are. You're overreacting."

She slammed her mouth closed, biting her bottom lip, and focused on the task ahead of her to keep from yelling at him.

"Aurora comes first, huh."

"It has to."

"I guess that's your answer."

He paused. "I guess it is."

She tightened her grip on the grav-comb, raised it to her temple, and called up the recollections of Reva Sharma poking at the innards of her memoria in the Tribulation forest, as well as the work she'd been doing on the transport recording. She found that the motions were quite similar—and that the memory was also reassuringly full of an angry Kate Keller. Which made sense: *if*

Sharma could hide memories from herself and from Aurora, she could certainly do the same for me, Natalie thought.

Natalie lay the comb against the bottom of the faceplate, then used the comb's tiny gravity-field generator—usually used to finesse the reality-defying hairstyles found on executive climbers—to loosen it. The comb felt like a low-powered civilian version of a similar tool to defuse Vai kinetics in the field, and Natalie relaxed, allowing herself a little more confidence. This was her Auroran career, wasn't it? Teasing apart the insides of things she couldn't possibly understand? Opening the memoria was no different than defusing a screamer. She tried to put aside the thought of making a mistake and ruining Ward's precious face pomade with bloody Natalie bits.

Although the first thing he'd probably think about was how I ruined his day again, she snorted.

Natalie slipped the comb under the hinges, and the memoria's faceplate came off with a metallic shiver. She felt the connection between the front and the back snap tight in her head like a fishing line. It was the only sign that her brain didn't function like everyone else's, that Natalie's neurons were knit together less like a proper human anatomy diagram and more like a bad sweater. She turned it over, not seeing anything new or different in the skull implant—no corners cut, even if Sharma had told her so in the forest.

But the bomb would be *in* her head. She needed to go further.

Ward cleared his throat. "Are you okay in there? You're taking forever."

She sighed, then shoved her face as close to the shower mirror as possible. "I'm not overreacting."

"Mr. Solano says—"

"Right. Mr. Solano. Go fuck *him* if you love him so much."

He sounded exasperated. "Natalie—"

"Get to your meeting."

"Not with you acting like this."

She nearly laughed. "You're not at all afraid it's going to happen to you? I'm not the first to get screwed like this, Ward, and I'm not going to be the last, but, hey, it's okay, Emerson Ward is playing by the rules, Emerson Ward gets to be a comfortable asshole doing what he's told, and that's what matters. Nothing's wrong in Ward's world. Bad shit happens to other people. He doesn't see the bad shit, so he doesn't feel the bad shit. He looks away."

This time, Ward didn't respond. The shaver went quiet, and she heard the slither of clothing against skin—Ward putting on his jacket, no doubt.

She used the gravity fields to pull the housing of the implant section of the memoria away from her skull, staring for the first time at the intricate interior of the memoria under her skull. She saw transistors and resistors, newfangled haptic cards, the detritus of human industry, familiar metal twisted into the technological alchemy that made space travel possible. No sign of a bomb, she thought. She was about to breathe easily, to close the housing, when she saw the light.

It was hidden behind the warren of wires, deeper in the recesses of her mind, so deep it was buried behind the other side of the implant, so deep it was almost an ache. Light, familiar, purple and blue and sickening gold, *silver, silver,* the song of silver *right fucking there.*

There was something exquisitely Vai in it, a roiling on the back of her tongue like the canned aftertaste of rotgut vodka. Everything went bright and fuzzy, lighting her nerves on fire like a blowtorch. She heard a chorus, atonal, wrong, music that disappeared into blue light, a song taking her apart from the inside. She disappeared into herself like a camera down an artery—

—and no. *No.* It had only been a year since Tribulation. A

year in which Aurora hadn't even discovered the nanotech in her body, a year in which they didn't even control the Bittersweet labs. Now that they did, she could imagine the Auroran R&D machine roaring into gear, ripping apart every single piece of Baywell research to find the secret that became Ashlan Jackson. Still, though, she imagined the only person who knew enough about Vai technology to incorporate it into a memoria would be Reva Sharma.

Was that why she'd gone along with Solano's requests? The bomb in her head? To make sure she'd be in a position to put this Vai thing in Natalie's head and check to see if it was still there on Tribulation? What was it for? For that matter—

—was *this* the bomb?

"Can't be," she whispered. "No, that's stupid. She wouldn't have put a bomb in her own head."

"Why not? She's done worse."

And then he was there—him, the hallucination, occupying the rest of the space in the shower, all wide shoulders and ship-smell and kind brown eyes. Adrenaline kicked in and she shrieked, cracking her head against the bulkhead.

"You okay?" said Ward.

"Fine," she lied, thinking *not fine not fine not fine*—

—and *fine* came forward like an overwhelming intoxication, thanks to the memoria, like it was made bespoke for her pain and her fear, with the scent of a memory and the consistency of a dream. *Twenty-Five* was long dead, but the caustic instant coffee served in its mess was burning the inside of her mouth like gasoline. She felt the heat of his body. He hummed the *Alien Attack Squad* theme. She remembered a time when they sat like that, a long time ago, when her cheek had pressed promises into the hollow of his neck.

She placed her fingers to his pulse point. No heartbeat shivered there, no matter how she prayed for it.

A moment passed as she considered the situation. She'd been here before. This was obviously the memoria trying to process her current situation, making connections between the things she couldn't remember and the things she could. Is this confusion why they wanted authorized neurotechs? *I don't even like* Alien Attack Squad, she thought. He had been the one who'd brought those holos on board, and she watched it because of him, because it made him smile—

—*Len,* that was his name, *Leonard Downey*—

"There." A whisper in the black. "Full organic integration was difficult in substandard organic equipment, but I suppose I've made it work."

The hallucination took a deck of cards from his back pocket, slipped off a rubber band, and started shuffling them near her cold bare feet.

"What the hell," she whispered, half-hoarse.

"This is familiar to you," Downey said. "You like this."

"Yes, but—"

The last time she'd played cards with Leonard Downey—and she remembered it now, remembered it all—had been in the mess hall on *Twenty-Five* three days before Ash had discovered the Heart. Len looked exactly how she'd last remembered him, down to the white crescents of his nails and the notch in the collar of his favorite jacket, his fingers tap-tap-tapping against the cards in his hand, the warm sound of his humming running just under the mumble of the engine.

She swallowed something tough and hard in her throat, then looked down at the blank playing cards in her hand. *Of course they're blank,* she thought, *I didn't play to win. I didn't even care about winning. I'd lose any day just to see him smile.*

"Oh," Natalie said, losing her breath. "I loved you, didn't I?"

Sitting on the floor of the shower, Natalie stared at the memory she'd lost and felt the tearing in her heart all over again.

He looked up, the ghost of a smile on his lips. "I died, and I left you alone," he whispered, as if all of it were some wild revelation. "How do you stand it?"

"I—" She felt lost for a moment. Cold. "People die. They die every fucking day."

"Impossible," he whispered.

"You're—" She rubbed her temples, trying to push aside the burgeoning headache right behind her eyes. She'd expected a smile from him. A joke. Len had been the kind of sardonic asshole who dealt with tough situations with black humor learned over too many years of indenture. He deflected. Swerved. Ricocheted. It was why they'd gotten along in the beginning, and partially why they'd come apart at the end.

But this wasn't Len. It was just her memory of him.

"Right," she said, "I'm talking to myself. That's why you have no sense of humor."

"What is humor?"

"For *fuck's* sake," she repeated. "Ash told me this was going to be weird, but I didn't expect it to be this weird."

The Len-thing blinked at her and templed his fingers over his stack of blank playing cards. "We need to find them."

Grief sucked her down into herself like a heat wave, and she bit down hard on her bottom lip to keep the renderbots from seeing that she was close to tears. "There's nobody left to find," she said. "Everybody who really knew me is gone."

He folded his hands. "We need to find them," he repeated.

She looked at him—*really* looked, took in the texture of his skin and the curves of his fingers; after the Battle of Tribulation, Natalie was never quite sure if she was remembering anything the way it had actually been, or if her mind was just filling in the blanks with dreams and expectations. She had no way to be sure.

"This isn't the first time you've lost someone, Natalie," she whispered. "You got over it. Get over this."

He looked shocked. "That's not possible."

She snorted.

"Death is shit and life is worse, but at least you're still breathing. At least you're here. At least you still have a chance. Because you're right, Natalie. All you have to do is get the fuck out of here."

The Downey-thing nodded. His fingers hovered, reverent, over the blank cards spread out on the floor, as if he were afraid to touch them.

"Nat, who the fuck are you talking to?"

Ward.

She looked away, and Downey disappeared.

"Nobody. Implant glitch. It doesn't matter."

He knocked on the shower door. "Can I come in? Aulander called. They want you in Applied Kinetics along with the rest of us."

She was still half-naked and shivering and dirty. She looked back in the mirror, pushing the housing back against her forehead and fastening it on her skull, then clicked the rest of the memoria into place. No bomb. Vai tech, instead. That was much worse. She yanked the rinseless soap off the shelf and scrubbed her face and underarms, made a face at her scummy hair, then opened the door.

"I need more time," she said.

He looked perfect. "I know. Your hair's still way too short. Ascanio will talk."

She stared. "I can't believe you think I'm worried about my hair."

His mouth formed an unhappy line. "That was a joke."

"I have a shitty sense of humor."

He sighed. "Do you? I don't *know,* because you don't let me in. You never have. You don't talk about what worries you. I just have to—" He waved his hand in her direction. "Guess. And after you left, I assumed you never would. Chan's out for—"

"Don't you dare use that one on me, asshole—"

"Chan's out for Chan, I told myself." He smiled briefly, showing white teeth. "But I'd still rather be with you than without you, though, so I guess I'm just screwed."

It was Natalie's turn to look away. Her stomach soured. "Guess you are. Asshole."

He shrugged.

"I keep on calling you an asshole," she said.

"Yeah, well." He shrugged. Squeezed her hand. "Takes one to know one."

It was the kind of thing someone in her old platoon would have said, someone she couldn't *quite* remember, and the jibe felt familiar, even coming from Ward's too-earnest face. She didn't want to laugh, but she did. "Tell me the truth. Was I just something you had to do to get ahead?"

He flushed. "I could ask you the same question. And it's complicated."

"Then why can't you admit that the rest of it is complicated too?"

"I think I'm about to."

"Ha. I ought to go away more often."

He laughed. The corners of his eyes creased, and his hand dangled on the small of her back. "Don't."

Natalie put the grav-comb back on the shelf and lifted her chin, daring him to go further. He swallowed, wordless, for a moment, and his fingernails dug into the tight muscle near her spine. She hooked her fingers around his belt loop and drew him closer.

"Fine," she said. Then: "I'm not sorry."

"You don't have anything to be sorry about," he said, and met her lips with his, and after a while she was too lost in his bedclothes and his body to say *this, this, this.*

19

Afterward, her naked back curled against the cold curve of the bulkhead, Natalie traced the winding gold tattoo on Ward's arm to where it met the rig port in his neck, feeling exhausted and satisfied and incredibly guilty. This port looked like a permanent part of his body—installed by a neurotech, with a metal rim and a proper hygienic seal. It made Natalie think he was going to be using the proxy rig on a daily basis. *We didn't make a rig that would handle a daily load,* she thought.

"Can we talk?" he said. "About why you said no?"

"Didn't we have to be in App-K ten minutes ago?"

"Come on." He drew his hand up her thigh, making a quiet circle there with his thumb. "I'm not going to let you brush me off this time. That's the problem—I ask, you say *later.*"

"I'd have to explain Verdict to you." The memoria flashed: the scent of trash in the harbor, wind whipping up State Street, the five white towers that dominated the view from the swollen Hudson.

"Explain, then."

"You never cared before."

He pushed up on an elbow. "You never let me care. You wanted space. I gave you too much of it."

There's never too much space, she thought, the memoria pummeling her with *blood in her mouth,* with *code under her fingers,* with *her first gun.* The dust-choked summers, the hot winters, the twinge of uncitizen rations on her tongue, the warren of streets that was old, broken Albany. The world they'd built on dying Earth under the thumb of the companies.

"It's nothing like here," she said. "And nothing like what you see in the holos. There's no way up, so you build *out*. Street by street, if you have to. There are a lot of dead suburbs. It's different out by the mountains—more cooperatives, fewer orgs, moisture farms and shit, more people just living their lives. Most of that's all Armour territory. But Verdict—"

"It's a hacker cult, right?"

She managed a laugh. "You know about it?"

"Half the infosec team on Europa's recruited from hacker cults. Why not you?"

She snorted, then pushed him away, tossing the blanket on his body and dropping to the floor. "Because I was shit at coding, that's why. I couldn't keep up with the other kids. Couldn't bring in the resources. I was a big disappointment to my father. I think." She paused. The memoria gave her Xie's face at the windswept gate. His frown. She always thought he'd been disappointed, but now that she was older Natalie only saw worry. "I *was* good at guns, though."

He lay back. "So your parents were uncitizens."

"Just a dad. And a bunch of teachers." She went to his drawer and started pushing through piles of very similar skirts. "He was a programmer. A really good one. Could have aced an Auroran skills test, been one of your Europa infoseccers. He was pretty disappointed in me."

"Why didn't he join? An office indenture's a cakewalk."

Natalie pulled on a set of tight blue leggings. "He hated the companies. Something to do with my mom, I think. Hated *space*." She paused. "He told me that if I listed up with Aurora to fight the Vai he'd never talk to me again."

"But you did."

She chose a shirt and dragged it over her head, trying to block out *her father, watching by the gate. Worried.* "He got over it." *I hope.* "When I got my tags, I went to look for him, but he'd already indentured into Armour. They'd bought out Aurora's investment in the rest of the city, see, and the war—" She shrugged on one of his jackets. "The war changed everything."

Ward watched her for a moment, as if at a distance; he then got up and started fishing his clothes off the floor. "And your mom?"

"I don't have any memories of my mom."

"She left when you were little?"

One last dive into the drawer netted her a second grav-comb, which she used to smooth out the wider fit of his shirt. She ran the device over his jacket, and the wrinkles fell out like water; pulled the jacket snug at the shoulders and waist and the wrists. She looked at herself in the mirror, then ran the grav-comb so her hair slipped back into a peak at the top. A faint try at cit style.

"That's the story. My dad doesn't remember."

"So he won't tell you."

"Maybe." She sighed. "He said he doesn't remember her at all."

Ward blinked, clearly flummoxed. "How do you not remember someone you had a baby with?"

She tapped her info-implant. "Maybe he chose to. I used to wonder if that was possible, and then—I came out the other end of Tribulation with swaths of my past just *gone.* That's one of the reasons I got back in touch with him. I don't know what happened, but brain damage can fuck you up."

He blinked. "Doesn't it bother you that neither of you knows?"

"Why would it bother me?" She shrugged. "I remember *not knowing,* and that's enough. I used to think that as soon as I entered indenture, she'd get in touch. Help out. That she just didn't like uncitizen life—and, yeah, I mean, it's not for everyone. But she never did. She didn't want to make me a part of her life, so

I'm not going to spend any more than a few seconds making her a part of mine."

He looked uncomfortable. "Ah." He paused. "So that's why you don't trust people."

"I—" She bit her bottom lip. "I suppose that's part of it. I mean, my dad wasn't a killer parent, either."

Ward paused. "You know, I still think we'd be good together."

"Because this would ensure our line's eventual stranglehold on Applied Kinetics and all of the daughter departments?"

He smirked, and didn't deny it, throwing a pillow in her direction. "Are you going to actually take a shower?"

"You go ahead," she said. "I'll go eat your garlic noodles."

He nodded, and went into the shower.

Humans lie, she heard. *You're not going to eat the garlic noodles.*

Natalie opened the fridge and removed the dish in question— brown protein noodles, plainly dressed like everything else in Ward's world, twisted by some sort of culinary grav-comb into whitecapped ocean waves. Her stomach hollered; she hadn't realized just how hungry she was. She grabbed a fork and dove in, shoving in a too-big bite, then another.

"Oh, no," she said, through a tangy mouthful, "I am. I'm starving. That's just not the only thing I'm going to do."

She ate the noodles like she was still back in training and had five minutes to go from the distribution line to her bunk, tossed the dish into the recycler, then crossed to Ward's interface. It was off—*off*, of course, which never really meant *off* unless you had the credits to purchase such a privilege. And now that she thought about it, *off* in her cupboard of an apartment meant *still on*, or how had Aulander found her after the massacre at Bittersweet when she was supposed to be in the medbay? Had Ingest followed her from App-K and watched her enter? The optikal surveillance was passive, everyone knew that—

—so how long had they been actively watching her?

She thought of her father. *At least we're free,* he'd said at the gate. *At least we can do what we want.* She hadn't understood what that really meant at the time. She'd been too angry.

I understand now, Dad. I do.

The scraper whirred in Ward's bathroom, and she turned on the interface, swiping over from an episode of *Corporate Idol* past the news channels to Ward's work interface. It looked so much like hers—messages from Ascanio, schematics, meeting reminders—that she entertained a momentary pang of jealousy. She then paged past that and went to the Company directories.

Auroran directories were more than just lists of who worked where. They were a social invitation system, a historical record, a matter of pride—and because of such, the code was rarely updated, and Verdict had introduced a hack a long time ago that allowed them to see the back end, to see personnel moves on a macro level and respond in kind. It was possible that if Kate was alive, her movements could be seen here.

She went straight to Kate's entry. *Citizen Katherine Keller,* it said, *former indenture,* the picture plucked from the moments before *Twenty-Five* left Europa Station. She grumbled. *Twenty-Five, captain,* it continued, with her cabin number and credit rating. *On Abeyance.* Not dead. Not missing in action. *Abeyance,* the most bullshit of statuses.

She chose the credit rating and paged back, then chose *file a grievance.*

These old systems were the places where you could find your way in, her father had taught her: the far edges, the places that didn't get updated, the forgotten directories. And with enough Verdict folk in infosec, she hoped—she *prayed*—that they'd left some of the old doors propped open. She wrote a familiar, almost-forgotten line of code, then sent a request to Ingest to see the video from the last time Kate was aboard.

<<Request not allowed.>>

Huh, she thought, and then did the action again.

<<Request not allowed.>>

She paused for a moment, then reworded the request. Maybe they'd finally figured out a proper firewall protocol—

<<Check directly with Central Ingest for updates about this listing.>>

She drew her hands back as if scalded. "That's what I'm *doing.*"

The scraper had stopped behind her, and the door slid open. "Are you okay?"

"I'm—" She paused, made something up. "I'm trying to access my mail from your console, and—yeah, uh, I can't."

Ward crossed to his mirror, grav-comb in hand. A flick of his wrist smoothed and locked another curl of yellow hair into place, then another. *Some new style,* she thought. It was impossible to keep up with birthright styles, although if Aulander had actually been dangling that birthright status, she'd have to figure it out faster than she thought, or it wouldn't just be Ascanio tittering at her.

"Yeah, it's a new security protocol that came in with updates to Ingest. You'll have to use your own tablet."

She rose. "Then I'll go by my place."

"No time."

"Of course there's—"

He adjusted his collar. "We're late."

"Cover for me."

"I have *Ascanio,*" he said, eyeing her in the mirror. "And Vanelder. You know the Vanelders. If I'm a *second* late, she'll trash me to their family council, and—"

Natalie snorted. "And you think it bothers me that I don't have a line. And you think I want to join *yours,* if this is the kind of bullshit Wards have to put up with—"

He sighed, and his hand paused in its work. "I thought we figured this out."

"We had sex," she said. "It doesn't mean we figured anything out. You're still an asshole. And I'm still—" She hesitated. Thought of the secret under his skin, under hers, the borrowed silver that whispered and took and *became*. There was no way she could explain what was happening to him now, and no way he'd believe it.

But she still needed to tell him.

"I'm still feeling like shit," she decided to say instead.

"Look," he said, heaving a sigh. "You're probably going to 'feel like shit' until the end of time, aren't you?"

"It's a distinct possibility," she said.

Curl. Flip. Curl. He was silent for a moment as he finished his hair, then lay the grav-comb on the lip of the mirror, tilted his head to catch the waves he'd created in the light, nodded, and reached for his eyeliner. Slipped it against his lids, then shoved it in his pocket. He looked like some bright ancient god, and it made her uncomfortable. All of a sudden, Natalie became extremely conscious of the dirt and dried sweat still colonizing her body, despite the clothing, the hair, the sure future. She grabbed a few hairpins from his top drawer and used them to paste down her one wild cowlick. There was no time for anything else.

"We'll figure it out," he said. "You ready?"

She nodded and followed him out.

20

Like the rest of *Vancouver*, Applied Kinetics looked both nothing and everything like it had when Natalie left it.

The lab kept the same sort of soft, even light and curved white walls. Six tidy workstations gathered around the rig in the center, with the director's desk to the side, connected to the large wall interface that looked dead but probably was only feeding back information to workers with superhaptics. The workstations were covered with the remains of defused Vai kinetics in safety isolettes, pored over for parts by techs with mask-obscured faces and medical machines appropriated from operating rooms. She'd helped build this. She'd seen what had been done under Tribulation, pitched it to the board, was given directorship. Orders were in her throat as soon as she walked in, orders that she had to choke down.

But the rig—

—she hadn't built *this* rig.

This machine was no longer the tidy mess of straps and cables she'd developed with Ward and Ascanio. It had metastasized— invading every corner of the room, hissing and breathing like a living thing, all knives and tentacles and smoke. She thought she heard a voice wailing at the sight of it, something unfamiliar and wild and misled, and she couldn't look away.

The specs she'd signed off on back when she was director were for well-ordered, properly constructed work, the kind of reliable engineering she never got while out in the field—

not whatever *this* was, this wild mayhem of ill-soldered cables and wires. Some of the old connections had been hacked off and reconnected to the extra equipment she'd seen in the medbay: a ventilator, two heart regulation machines, a dialysis device. Discerning the purpose of any of it was like trying to read poetry written by a drugged-up child with a half-melted crayon.

Ascanio stood in ramrod-straight surprise as Natalie walked in, trailing Ward, vertebrae crackling and lips smoothing out from a frown. She'd been slouching. Her polished heels flashed as she stepped out from behind the desk. She removed an unfamiliar, slim new interface from her fingers; the finger-caps retracted to a golden wristband. Her trendy golden tattoos seemed to flicker in the soft white light.

"Mr. Ward! You're almost late," she said.

"I was held up by business."

"I see." Her eyes, almost accusatory, flickered toward Natalie.

"Is it ready?" he said.

Ascanio cleared her throat, and Natalie caught the leading edge of her smirk, the knife's-edge regard of her eyes, and if the screaming in Natalie's head hadn't been mounting, building, drowning everything else out, she would have wanted to punch the younger woman. Sometimes she really missed the dorms, where nobody cared about that sort of thing. "The executives will arrive in less than ten minutes. If the test goes well, we can have the rig moved to the bridge by—"

Pain flared behind Natalie's eyes. The hallucination appeared in a sudden screaming lurch, shocked and stumbling; the noise belonged to him, the howling like metal on bone, his eyes wide and his arms pinwheeling like he'd been ejected from a burning transport.

"Deletion," he wailed, "death—"

And then the Downey-voiced ghost was no longer just

something dangling from her consciousness, frightening and unhelpful—he was the *entirety* of it. He held her vision on the tables and slabs and their half-blank, dismembered corpses, watched him shudder to his knees, screaming *alone, alone, they died alone—*

She saw App-K for what it was now, thanks to the *thing* in her head. Ward and Ascanio presided over a slaughter: over the weapons laid out on a table with their insides open like corpses in a morgue, over the isolettes blinking with disassembled screamers. Some of them were still occupied by fallen, tortured Vai. The room, the rig, its straps and tentacles: this wasn't repurposed technology, but an impossible necromancy.

She hadn't made the connection until now—and she'd seen it before, heard it on the Vai ship, when she inserted her human intention into the massively inhuman structure of the Vai *civilization*. She held her own body, her blood, her flesh, her one chance, her unfolding future writ in the gray slush of her brain, the only one she owned and could ever own, even with the grosgrain shambling of the memoria patching it all together.

But the Vai slipped in and out of bodies in cascades of shimmering silver, uploaded and downloaded into long-fingered walkers and immutable mechs—why not into a fragile human body connected to the alien mainframe in the middle of a battle they could not win?

She had been right from the very beginning.

Downey wasn't a hallucination.

"No," she whispered. "Not possible."

"Excuse me?" said Ascanio.

She blinked away pain, saw her former tech staring. "I'm fine," she lied, like *humans lied—*

—and turned away toward Downey and the rig.

If you had not come,
Downey said,
standing over the dead,
I would have been lost forever.
He was still. Inhumanly so.
I would no longer be alive.
What an amazing thought.

She whispered. *How—*

The Downey-thing stepped forward.
Placed a warm finger on her forehead.
Empty, he said. *Empty space. Your file structure.*

I'm not a computer. I'm alive.

His eyes still brimmed with tears.
Acetylcholine is code. Norepinephrine is code. Serotonin.
Dopamine.
Glutamate. GABA. The nanotech that holds it
together.
This is your code.
You allow me to read it.
I am the master node.

The scent of celestium dragged Natalie's tongue, and swirled up in her brain like a shot of barracks rotgut. *Oh,* she thought, *I'm not the only one in my brain.*

The light in my head, it's—

A rush of nausea came from nowhere; her stomach loosened, and acid rocketed up her empty throat, swirling at the back of her mouth. She scrambled for the door, thought better of it, then sailed over to the trash chute, where she vomited until there was nothing left and she tasted rot and garlic between her teeth. Some of the workers hovered nearby, clearly repelled.

We're not done, said the node.

We are for now, she replied.
But—
Unless you want them to find you.

"I—" *I need to get out of here,* Natalie wanted to say, the words barely forming in the midst of her sudden dark panic, like getting out of here would rid her of the Downey-thing, the light in her mind. "Um. I need the medbay."

"Ingest says *he's* ten seconds out," a tech said.

"No time. *Wipe your face,*" Ascanio whispered.

She looked around for something to do that with, found nothing, and raised her sleeve, making quick work of the last few rotten noodle bits clinging to the corner of her mouth. The doors opened, drenching the lab in light from the corridor, and the age-old corporate dance began.

She knew who it was going to be from the way the air choked in the throats of her former colleagues, from the way Ascanio snapped her body straight like a marionette's, from the way Ward's eyes filled with a quiet, excited dread. As the Downey-thing—the *alien,* the *thing*—howled in her head, she threw everything she had left into staying upright as Joseph Solano entered the room, ignored Ward and his deputies, walked straight to Natalie, and picked up her vomit-streaked sleeve, like he'd seen her throw up. He frowned.

"Ingest," he pronounced, "tells me you left medbay, Chan. I'm not happy."

Natalie's tongue stumbled still. "I-I wanted to get back to work, sir."

"Indeed. But we have to talk about what *getting back to work* means for a person who is hallucinating about having her pants on."

"Sir, I wanted to show you—"

Solano's jowled face softened. "Listen. You don't need to prove anything to us, Ms. Chan. You did everything we asked of you."

She wanted to relax, wanted relief, but behind her the master node was still sobbing, still whiling in her head, still stealing her breath. She hauled in oxygen, felt the now-familiar ache of her healing lungs, let that pain ground her in reality. "Of course, sir."

"I'm not entirely happy about having to chase you all the way to the White Line, but you came through in the end, and that's the point." He shrugged, then sat back on the edge of Ward's desk, crossing his arms. "It's understandable that you're nervous. The birthright examination is tough. It's different for everyone. Yours was harder than most. But we had to be sure you were loyal enough to bring Ash home."

Behind her, Solano's team parted to encircle the rig—Aulander and another executive leading a team of white-coated bumble-bees dipping and bowing around a monstrous flower. She was wearing a new info-implant, as were the others. Larger. More like Natalie's.

Solano cleared his throat, annoyed that Natalie seemed to be drifting. "We'd like to offer you a position on the bridge. You'll be a ship's gunner—a Defender, a new rank qualified only on the superhaptic rig. It's a position of trust, so you must be a birthright to take it. You'll be the originator of a new line, if you want that. A witness to history."

Words rushed to her throat and died there.

He waited a moment, and his eyebrows knit together. "Are you willing?"

Was she?

It was everything she'd ever wanted. Beyond what she'd wanted, actually, when she'd placed her signature on the indenture contract and was whisked off Earth for the very first time, away from Verdict and its petty pyrrhic victories. This was *freedom*.

She felt nothing but the master node pinballing in her head.

And she had her father's words in her mind—*this isn't freedom,* he would say when she finally got the guts to leave him a message a decade later. Her blood in a machine, powering the death-dreams of the most powerful corporation in known space—how could she really call that *freedom*?

A black dread built, and she slammed her hands into fists at her side to prevent herself from clawing at her head, screaming *get out,* from ruining this farce for good. Was she willing? No. Did she want to be a birthright? More than anything. Could she be both willing and not, like Reva Sharma? Could she do better than Sharma? Ash, of course, said *no* outright, had been violent in her refusal, and Solano had changed the game in response. Natalie could say she was *willing,* if she wanted to turn her back on Ash, on the captain, but hadn't that been what she'd done all along? And didn't she deserve the right to have what she wanted? She loved her friends, missed them—but she'd always wanted different things.

Natalie knew she would have to commit. Sharma's fate showed her there was no way for one person to go up against a juggernaut like Aurora. No way to tear away from an Ingest that indexed the twitch of her mouth, the shiver in her step. Ash and Kate had tried and failed. Sharma had tried and failed. Natalie could choose a different path. Work from the inside. A contract marriage to another bridge officer could be played straight onto the board.

And then she could change *everything.*

Solano waited for her answer with an impatient twist to his mouth, Downey wailing somewhere in the corner. *Downey.* Shit. She hadn't figured out where Downey fit. The proxy rig would allow Aurora access to Natalie's mind, her broken body, her memories, and that included the alien now. There was no way she could allow the Vai in her head access to Auroran systems, just as there was no way she could allow Solano access to the Vai.

It didn't matter what Natalie wanted.

Like always.

Solano translated the panic on her face as excitement. He clapped his hands together once more, then stood.

"Good," he said. "We'll get you set up."

No. She needed to buy some time. "Why me, sir?"

"You're an excellent soldier."

"I'm not a gunner, though," she said. "I *had* a gun. I had a platoon. But they trained me as an ordnance tech. I'm more qualified to build and detonate."

He examined her hands, her face. "A gunner's skills can be taught. What you have—cannot."

"You mean the nanotech I contracted on *Twenty-Five.*"

"I do."

She thought of Ashlan. "You have the nanotech, sir. You can inject someone who is an *actual gunner.*"

"I said that what you have cannot be taught," Solano said, his brow creasing in growing annoyance. "Chan, the propagation of your nanotech can't be fabricated or counterfeited. Someday, you'll be able to step down when the other Defenders are ready. We'll give you the cure then. One month's exposure is not one year's exposure."

"There's no cure. Just a treatment."

"There will be." Natalie examined his face, trying to weed out the truth from the lie, and Solano sighed. "But we have to survive first. *Vancouver* is being chased by the Vai fleet right now—and nobody's here to honor their mutual defense treaties, not Ballard, not Penumbra, not fucking Baylor-Wellspring. It'll be *us*, Chan, *here*, on the thin fucking red line between the Vai and the rest of human space. Do you want to die?"

Ascanio made a strangled noise and disappeared behind the rig.

"I'm dying anyway. Apparently."

Solano's eyes gleamed. "So go out screaming."

She turned toward his words like a tree ached for acid rain, knowing it was poison, wanting it anyway. everything she'd ever worked for. And the Vai in her head—

The Vai *in her head*—

She was dumb. She was an idiot. She was just catching up right now. Natalie searched the room to find him; he shook, hunched, in the corner, his face haggard, pleading, like he knew *that face* was the one she'd respond to—

If the Vai master node is in my *head,* she thought, *then what is controlling the Vai fleet?*

"I—" she began, letting the vowel ride for a moment, just to fill the space. "Yes, sir. Yes. Screaming."

He brought his hands together into a loud, unexpected clap that scared a tech across the room. "Fantastic. Ms. Aulander, why don't you take Ms. Chan to get her moved up? We'll need the tattooist here, and a couple proper—"

He nattered on about all the things Natalie would need to access the bridge, like she hadn't just axed her way in to a half-dozen Auroran bridges while she worked on *Twenty-Five*. She felt outwitted, outplayed, like Solano had woven a trap in her path and waited for her to step into it, like she'd prepared for years to avoid getting hit by a train only to step into the river and drown.

Solano finished talking and moved over to the rig, and Ascanio rubbernecked her way to the front of the crowd, intent on being the one to present the new machinery. The white-coated bees were moving around Natalie now, handing her a tablet where blue letters on a white background signified a legal contract written in the way they'd been written for centuries; twenty-two pages flickered by in a half-breath. One thin finger flicked to the end, told her to sign, moved off to do something else.

"This is a contract," Natalie said.

"Yes." Aulander had taken Solano's spot at her side. "Delineating your responsibilities as a birthright citizen. What you own, and what you do not own."

The words seemed almost lost in the haze that was the master node's grief. Natalie's finger hovered over the signature box. "But I thought there was no contract. I thought—"

Aulander clutched a different jacket in her hand; the dark-as-heaven, gold-trimmed formal coat of a birthright. "Oh, lord, you thought we were free," she said, then laughed. "That's just in the holostories, Ms. Chan. It's contracts all the way down until we die. Well, go on. Read it, if you must. I don't have all day."

Natalie paged through, her headache roaring. A good chunk of the contract was ensuring the rights of the company versus the rights of the birthright, what they owned on elevation and what they could accrue and what positions they could take. She scanned most of it, not quite understanding the economics of it all, but stopped when she came to a clause that sounded like it might affect her directly. *Any technology owned by the Birthright at the time of elevation will remain the property of the Birthright; any technology owned by Aurora will remain the property of Aurora, unless purchased by the Birthright or their Line.*

"This," she asked. "The memory device. I can buy it?"

"Let me check," Aulander said. Her fingers twisted in the jacket's collar, wrinkling it, and she used her other hand to fire off a question to some unseen eye. She received a response back almost immediately. "No," she said. "It's still considered proprietary technology."

Natalie's hand flashed up to touch it, felt its warmth where it was soldered into her skull, heard the master node crying somewhere nearby. "But it's in my head. It runs my *body*."

Aulander nodded. "And as a birthright citizen, you have the right to make purchases and sell items, but only consumer tech. You can't sell proprietary data storage secrets, Natalie."

"I'm sorry?" Natalie shoved the tablet aside. She choked down something tight and sharp in her throat. "The memoria is data *recovery*, not storage."

"No, it's storage," she said. "Or didn't they tell you?"

"There's a difference?"

"A big difference." Aulander's face changed, ever so slightly adopting a quiet sheen of confusion, almost as if she'd understood she'd said something wrong, but couldn't figure out what. "You don't need to be worried. As long as the info-implant is updated correctly, it won't matter who owns it. And you'll get updates without having to collect credit."

But it will, she said, watching as Downey slowly picked himself up from where he'd been shaking. *It matters. And you know it matters, because why else would you have tried to con me with a birthright position that isn't?* It was such a simple difference. Such a tiny thing, a shift from flesh to tech. They'd been able to save her because she'd been infected, but they hadn't been able to put her back in her body.

Of course they hadn't. For all of their medical technology, the autobandages and cloned organs and lung reconstructions, the brain was still such an uncharted territory. She wasn't *in* her body, occupying the tissues and gray matter and veins and arms. She was *in* the device.

And the device was owned by Aurora.

And so was the Vai.

"I—" It took every inch of her composure not to claw at her memory device, to rip it off her head, to slam her heel into it and watch the machine go to glitter, to go to glitter herself. Instead, she put aside the tablet and tried to stand straight. "I don't feel well, Ms. Aulander. I'll sign this when I get back from the bathroom."

"Don't take long," Aulander said. She yanked the birthright's jacket back, tossed it over her shoulder. "You can wear the jacket for the big test."

Natalie stalked into the corridor, leaving Aulander and Ward and the Vai *master thing* behind, kicking up her pace until she was in the bathroom nestled close to the spine. She shut herself in the little toilet cubby away from the optikals, trying to breathe through the overpowering, incredibly human scent of urine and bleach, holding her rapidly souring stomach and trying to figure out how she could take apart the toilet to kill herself. *Really* kill herself, this time, not just her mind and memories, leaving her a useless breathing husk they couldn't shove in a puppet rig.

She wasn't even sure that death would solve the problem. If she wasn't in her own head—if everything she was resided in the memoria—what if the master node just slid into her fingers when they were free? Then the Vai could just walk around in her rotting body, and who knows what next—

This time, she vomited.

She couldn't stand the noise of two of her rattling around underneath one skull, a ghost inside a zombie like some sort of queasy nesting doll. She wanted to rip out her eyes, her tongue, her belly, anything that the alien in her brain had touched. The alien swam in her fingers, through every shuddering beat of her heart. Maybe if she set herself on fire—she looked around for a knife, a boltgun, hell, even someone's soldering wand. She could put one of those straight through her eye, ripping open the squishy framework that ran her used-to-be-human operating system.

She'd thought they'd wanted her because of the celestium. Turns out *that* was as easy to accomplish as a couple of swigs of water, and what they'd really been doing was taking apart Sharma's device, seeing how it ran her body, putting it back together again, figuring out how to make a puppet rig of a human being. Natalie was always one to tease out the implications, and these implications made Bittersweet seem like boot camp.

No. She couldn't possibly go back.

She tossed herself against the cold wall, taking fistfuls of too-long hair, tugging until it hurt, digging her fingers into her scalp, whatever hurt the most—was there a knife, she thought, was there a comb, could she gore a hole in her skull with her spanner and let the cursed thing out? Could she do it now?

I won't allow you to kill yourself,
he said, appearing—

—and oh, it came rushing back,

with him so close—

—Len's stupid beautiful face, the way he leaned back in his chair when Kate was talking, the way every one of his smiles tilted from the left side of his mouth. Len talking endlessly about *Alien Attack Squad,* the way he'd decorated his room with little toy figurines he'd dragged out of wrecks from here to Omega Colony. His warm, patient hands on hers.

It hadn't started as love. They hadn't wanted it to be love.

Love on a vessel as small as *Twenty-Five* was difficult and messy and wrong and inevitable, as inevitable as hate. So she'd shoved it down, wrapped it in a coat of the everyday, until it was far too late.

And then he'd died, and she nearly drowned in the thick anger of it, so tight and so tough in her chest that she barely spoke, she just pushed it all into Applied Kinetics, into her promotion, into whatever it was with Emerson, and placed an iron staple around her heart.

Until now.

Now it was all ruined for good.

"Why him?" she managed.

> You needed to trust me.
> It was the only way to survive.
> I need your help.
> If there had been any other option—

You want me to help you? she thought, dizzy. *You came for us. World after world, you sent down your weapons. You fried entire cities. You took everything I loved. And now you're wearing* him *like a coat.* She closed her eyes, but he remained there, she clawed at her eyes—

> He hovered. Warm.
> You're the one who taught me it could be done.
> Your secondary node came for me.
> Took my world.
> My people.
> Help me.

No fucking way. It's war. We have to protect ourselves. She squeezed her eyes shut and he was still there. *And she's not a sec-*

ondary node. It doesn't work like that. We're on our own. You're on your own now.

So are they. Alone.

And it's not my fault, she said, almost desperate. *I was doing what I was told.* Her throat closed with the hypocrisy.

We are not different.
You'll help me.

Never, she said. *You can rot in there. They'll find some way to shut you up if I can't.* He sounded like Len, so much like him, down to the cadence of his words, but that was just the master node fucking with her head, wasn't it?

The thing paused.
Then you'll give me to them?
Of course. You are human.
Weapons are evil.
You called them evil, so you felt justified in taking them apart.
Killing them.
He was close enough for Natalie to feel the warmth of his skin.
Your daily bread.
Just a job.
Then: a joy. His hand tightened.

"Not joy," she gasped, "never joy." She stared at the Downey-thing, searching behind his work-lined face, his too-human eyes, and discovered his hand warm against hers. When had it learned that trick, to be warm?

That's a lie, he said. Humans lie.

She exhaled. "You're lying too."

> No. I tell the truth.
> I can do no other thing.
> I am alone, she heard.
> Alone—

"It's not so bad, being alone," she said, through the angry wire closed around her throat.

The master node's grief was a seismic rattle at the center of her rib cage. He showed her his memories: his people, silver and streaming through the expanse of the heartship, the great shining expanse that had once been his body. He showed her what he would do to hear them sing again: anything, *anything*. Even take Natalie's broken body for his own—

"You wouldn't," she snarled, and imagined the entire terrible war with the Vai, negotiated down to a single set of unimportant skin and bones—

> It would be wrong to take that from you, it finally said.
> And I'm not sure I could.
> Two master nodes cannot exist in one network.

And now it has morals. She nearly laughed.

> What are morals? He weighed heavy in her mind, tight and cramped around her heart.

"It means that I can't sign the contract. Even if I wanted to. I can sign for myself, but not for you. Not for *all of you*. I'm going to have to think of something else."

She heard a rapping noise on the door—hollow, blank, knuckles on bulkhead. "Chan? You didn't want to sign?"

It was Ward. Shit. Natalie wiped her eyes, and removed the foot from where she'd wedged it against the door, then grabbed the bottom with her toes, pulling it open. Somewhere in her borrowed, aching head, she heard the master node settling in, searching, mourning.

"I'm thinking about it."

His voice was lined with worry. "You all right?"

"Fine," she said, biting off the word.

He paused. "You don't sound fine."

"I'm taking a shit."

Ward's voice grew tight, and he took in her fully clothed form, right down to the vestigial buttons on her borrowed pants. "Right. This is the second time today I've had to come rescue you from a bathroom. This is becoming a pattern."

"You aren't here for a rescue. You're here for a hijacking."

He blinked. "You're making them nervous, Chan. Aulander's worried that you might need a second visit to the medbay. She asked me to take you."

Natalie shook her head. "That's not what Aulander is worried about."

He canted a hip, blocking her way out. "To be honest, I'm worried too."

She stood. "You're not. Move it."

"So you're going back?"

She sighed, the master node with her. "I can't."

"So where are you going?"

"Up your—"

He raised his hand. "Hey. I'm not here for them. I'm here for you. I told you I wanted to work it out, but I can't possibly do that unless you let me in. And you have to make that decision, not me."

She worked her jaw. "You're being too fucking nice to me."

"Not *nice*," he said, shrugging. "I've . . . just been thinking about Bittersweet."

The words came out acid-edged. "Only now?"

"Since it happened." He looked down. Away. His shoulders shuddered. "Look. My head's full of things I shouldn't be thinking. I don't even know where to start."

She considered this, pushing away several dark thoughts—then hoisted herself up to the countertop.

"Okay. Start here," she said. "There's a problem with my contract and I'm not sure what to do about it. I think it might have something to do with some lies they're telling me about an old shipmate of mine. And I'm worried."

"Tell me more," said Ward, and she did.

21

To his credit, Ward listened to most of her story about needing to find Kate and the red flags in the contract—leaving out the aliens, of course, because there were certain lines that she was sure Ward wouldn't cross. He folded his arms and frowned, his back going taut, his baffled body language saying everything Natalie needed to know about his reaction. She stopped midsentence, heaving out a sigh.

"Right," she said, brushing past Ward. "If you're not listening to me, I'm going to the medbay myself."

He blocked her, palm against shoulder. "I've heard that one before."

"Yes, well, this time—"

"*They've* heard that one before. If you're going, I have to walk you."

"Yeah," she spat. "*Freedom,* huh."

In the bright white bathroom, she could see the signs of nanoscale sickness encroaching on Ward's face in a way the quiet of his apartment hadn't afforded. He was too pale, and he'd thinned slightly; he'd consider both a personal achievement, not a problem to be addressed. She herself had thought her early illness an effect of stress from citizenship onboarding. She wondered if he was seeing things yet. Hallucinating dead ex-girlfriends. Hearing hijacker aliens. Maybe they'd convince him someday that he'd hallucinated *her.*

She didn't know why she'd even tried to get him to understand. He wasn't like Ash. She couldn't trust him. He'd probably never thought to interrogate the terms of his contract before to-day. After all, he'd been born into those terms, and he'd never yet run into a situation where he found those terms unacceptable. Frustration fired behind already-exposed nerves, and she moved to knock his hand away.

"You don't believe me," she said.

"I don't believe they'd *enforce* it."

"The company that tacked on three weeks to my time because I needed a bandage for bashing my knee in the mess hall off-shift wouldn't enforce it?"

He sighed. "Natalie—"

"The company that dropped a Vai nuke on a mining planet instead of sticking to the limited-casualty plan the war committee voted for? Look," she said. "I don't have time for this. I'll explain, you'll keep on arguing with me, you'll do the frowny thing with your eyebrows—"

"I just don't understand how you got to be so paranoid." His brow furrowed.

"You're doing the thing."

He clapped his left hand to his forehead. "For fuck's sake."

She took the moment to make another attempt to push by, but he stood in her way. This time, she responded by grabbing his wrist and twisting it toward the sink, using a little more force than she probably should have. "Okay, asshole. Tell me what I should do about finding Ms. Keller if you're so smart."

Ward winced. "I'd ask the board directly."

"Only if you think they never lie, and I'd never date anyone that stupid. I already asked Aulander about it, and she told me I was *seeing things*."

"I'd—" His brow furrowed further, like he might actually agree with her. She tapped the sink in frustration; she could almost see the gears grinding in his head. "I'd get independent verification."

"Tell me how to do that, Director."

"I'd—" His eyes narrowed. "*You're* doing the thing, now. Trying to make me come up with the answer you've already had for twenty minutes so *I* think I came up with it."

Natalie raised her eyebrows. "I plead innocence."

"Just be out with it." He rolled his eyes.

In the corner of the room, Downey shook his head. "This is fascinating," he said. "The concept of disagreement laid so plain—our best philosophers never quite understood—"

"Shut up," Natalie told the alien ghost, but it was Ward who winced. Whatever. She didn't care what he thought right now. She did one more scan for the renderbots that supposedly weren't present in citizen bathrooms. "Okay, *Emerson*. You keep on wondering why I didn't say *yes*, and it's this. It's all of this. I have to *manage* you whenever our relationship moves out of bed. It's not that you don't care about me. It's that you don't care about anything."

Ward's eyes steeled, and he shuffled his arms, settling in against the sink. "I just don't understand why they would even try to hide your old captain."

She paused. Considered how much to tell him. "She's dying. Everyone who gets it dies. They're probably concerned about mass panic."

Ward clutched his crossed arms closer, stiffening slightly. "*Dying* of it. It kills you." He wanted to say more—Natalie could see the words fighting in the back of his throat.

"Two years and you get liver failure. On the way, you hallucinate. Are you okay?"

He licked his lips. "And you have it."

"Yeah."

"You're dying."

Her stomach twisted. "I suppose."

"*Shit.*"

"It looks like *you're* the one that needs the medbay."

His fingers clamped down on the edge of the sink. His knuckles went white. "I'm fine. Everything's fine."

He has to know. Natalie nursed her suspicion but didn't press. She didn't want him to know it might have been *her* who caused his illness. Not yet. She was being a coward, but she could do that for Kate. "I can't go back and sign the contract until I have more information. And they're hiding it from me."

"I bet Central Ingest would know."

"I know they would."

"So, you're . . . not just going to wander into Central Ingest and *ask* them?"

Natalie breathed in. Her lungs ached, a slow, needling crescendo. "That's not the worst idea, actually." *I can use salvage tricks on the direct interface to find Kate. Then I could take her and Ward and the thing in my head and we can—go somewhere. Anywhere. Back to Verdict. Beyond the White Line. We could make our own damned company.* "Yeah, that would work. If I went, would you stop me?"

He considered it—she could tell he did, the way his lips twisted to one side, the way he shuffled his hands back into his jacket pockets. His commlink trilled, and he fished it out of his pocket, giving it an annoyed little snort. "They want us back. Look. Do you think you could actually get the answers you need without any of *them* figuring out what you're doing?"

Natalie was already putting together the plan in her head, her mind slipping through the maintenance tunnels of *Vancouver* like she was back on *London,* stripping power cables to store in *Twenty-Five*'s massive cargo bay. The memoria provided her a quick memory of Solano picking at her vomit-streaked sleeve, like he'd been watching her moments before entering App-K. She shivered.

"It would be difficult. Ingest can find us—"

He blinked. "So no."

But she was already on to the next thought. "So *maybe*. Ingest can only find me if I'm *inside* the ship," she said, and then stuck out her palm. "Gimme your eyeliner."

His eyes widened a little. "Don't you think there are more important things to deal with right now?"

"I know you have it. Just give me the fucking eyeliner."

He fumbled in his pocket, coming out with the black vial. She twisted off the cap, then switched off the autodraw. It was black—not perfect, but better than nothing. She pushed herself up against the sink, staring at her face in the mirror, at the shape of her eyes, at the turn of her lips.

The basic steps to getting around facial recognition hadn't changed in four decades. Maybe they would now that Ingest existed. Variable holomasks were preferable, of course, but you could still get pretty far with markers and paint. She made a few lines to lift her cheekbones, triangles to disrupt her fore-head, opaque geometrics to change the way a renderbot might understand the curvature of her nose. Circles around her mouth, arcane circles on her cheeks, triangles and lines like some kind of nightmare clown.

"It's really fucking obvious," he said.

She snorted. "Nobody stopped me in the corridor when I walked to your place with no pants on."

Ward closed his eyes, rubbing his thumbs against his eyelids, drawing blood to the bleached-sugar skin. "Give it here when you're done."

"You can't come."

"Oh, I can."

"No," she said. "You have to cover for me."

"If I cover for you, I might never find out what I want to know."

Her hand stumbled a little, squiggled a line. "I can find out for you."

He paused. Waited for her to finish with the tube of eyeliner. There was something reticent in the way Ward scratched at the back of his neck. "Or I can go."

> *He doesn't trust you*, said the master node.
> He slipped in like an alarm on a groundcar
> screaming in from the edge of town.
> *You are alone.*
> *I don't know how you stand it.*

The ache tied a knot in her chest.

You just do, she said. You get up in the morning and go on. No matter who's screwed you over. Because the other option's worse.

Deletion.

"Got it in one," Natalie said. She breathed out, nodded, and then turned back to the mirror. Finishing her work, she capped the eyeliner and turned her chin to the side. *Perfect.*

"Fine," she said, quickly. "Now shut up and come here."

She made dark swirls on his face—exaggerating his cheekbones, expanding his eyes, making mincemeat of his nose. A few minutes later, the eyeliner stowed, the two of them pushed open the cramped maintenance tunnel at the back of the bathroom.

Natalie had a salvager's basic knowledge of the systems—where to find them and how to rip them out. The cramped maintenance tunnels on *Vancouver* ran between decks, above and beneath the corridors on citizen and executive-level floors. They allowed secluded access to environmental systems like plumbing, air circulation, and trash evacuation—systems too smelly and messy to be dealt with in front of people who had bought their way into something better.

Twenty-Five had maintenance tunnels around the engine and computer core, but the reasoning for that was the maximization of limited space, not creature comforts. Lower floors on the newer, post-Tribulation cruisers—inhabited primarily by indentures and citizen bosses—had slightly wider hallways to accommodate the larger number of workers, with all maintenance running behind the main walls, actual corridors and locked-away compartments to keep more people alive in case of a hull breach. Here, hiding the tunnels meant that citizens and executives didn't have to witness the mess. It also meant that she could get pretty far without triggering Ingest.

She didn't like enclosed spaces. They reminded her too much of the trenches on Cana, where so many of her teammates died. As if prompted, the memoria sent nightmares following behind: zombie-slow Vai mechs, slim-fingered Vai bodies dragging light into substance behind her, and the alien with her old friend's face haunting every remaining shadow like a vid emcee, muttering about *being alone*.

She'd just about despaired of ever leaving the tunnels when she came across a thin hatch in the wall. Nothing special. Nothing interesting.

Except she'd done salvage work.

"Wonderful," she whispered to nobody in particular. She pushed it open, revealing a noxious stench. "Take a deep breath before you go in," she said. "Breathe through your mouth."

"What?" said Ward.

"It's a trash room."

"A *what*?" he said.

He ducked inside, Natalie following after a moment of exhausted annoyance. "A trash room. Where the trash goes."

"I thought it—" Ward started. He flushed cherry red. "Right." About the size of a birthright's closet, the recycling room was an organized archaeology of daily life on *Vancouver*, full of human detritus cast aside and aged over weeks: plasteel bins full of used meal boxes, sealed disposal bags, and broken tools. The room itself was compact, no bigger than four toilet stalls wide, with walls meticulously scrubbed with bleach solution—possibly to counter the stench.

The rest of it was broken tech: tablets, pre-haptic innards, and stacks of flimsies too old for recycling. She saw an old purpose-slaved terminal on the wall—most likely used to access janitorial logs from a time before most Auroran ships allowed indentures to have even restricted access to the central computer.

"Can you find a spanner?" she said. "A laser scalpel would be helpful, and a couple screwdrivers. They don't have to be perfectly functional."

Ward nodded and turned to an upended bucket of tools, holding his nose. Natalie turned to the pile of old tablets, choosing one that seemed to still have a decent amount of battery left. Like most of the tablets headed to recycling, it had been stripped of any personal data. She stuffed it into her waistband.

"How'd all this end up here?" Ward said.

"It's just tossed."

"Like trash?"

"Well, to you, it *is* trash," Natalie said. "Cits and birthrights don't even think about it. They just bundle all their old tech into recycling and move on. Along with some stuff that isn't supposed to be here, because you're lazy."

Ward snorted. She was hallucinating now—black filigree turning at the edges of her vision and the alien slouching among them. She swallowed, and picked through the tablets, operating boards, and crystalline data matrices. She hadn't seen this much tech in one place since some of the storage rooms at Verdict. The coder kids she grew up with would have killed each other for access to a room like this.

A faraway alarm began to howl: the stomach-bottoming,

three-elevated-horn pattern she'd heard first over Grenadier and hoped never to hear again.

She'd hoped to go to her *death* before hearing it again.

"That's not standard stations," Natalie whispered. "That's—"

Ward gulped. "Battle GQ, yeah."

She paused. "We can still use that to our advantage," Natalie said, cutting him off before he could drop off an emotional cliff. "While they panic about the Vai approach, we'll keep going toward the next level."

Not the Vai, whined the master node. *Not my people.*

"Does it fucking matter at this point?" said Natalie.

"I didn't say anything," Ward said, slowly.

Natalie waved off his sudden concern. "We can't move up through the ship itself. The maintenance tunnels don't go there—just the spine. And at battle GQ, Ingest will be especially concerned with spinal movement. So we just need to take the outside route," she said. "That'll reduce the amount of time we're in the corridors. We'll hop up to Deck 3 on the gunside, and from there we should have a clear shot to Central Ingest. The flimsies will open the door, and we'll be inside before Ingest gives a shit."

"Out—what?" gulped Ward. He stuffed another tool in his pocket. "You don't mean *outside* outside?"

"That's exactly what I mean," Natalie said.

He shook his head. "I've never been in a coldsuit, let alone EVA."

"It's easy," Natalie lied. "Keep three points of contact at all times and go slow. Keep your eyes on the surface of the ship. Don't look behind you."

He gulped. "It's all well and good when you're sitting inside with some snacks."

"You *will* be inside," said Natalie. "Granted, think of the suit as a ship barely bigger than you are, but it's still a ship. It's there to take you from one place to another, to keep you alive." She opened the hatch.

The corridor was full of cits hollering and running from place to place. She couldn't imagine what *London* would have been like at a time like this, just linked compartments and hatches with no corridors, people having to work amid all this *clattering*. Natalie caught the black eyes of the renderbots above as she climbed out, felt the weight of the crusting black eyeliner still smeared on her cheeks, then helped Ward out and replaced the hatch. From here, they had only a short time—minutes, if they were lucky—to disappear outside before Ingest noted there was no original access matching that open hatch and started investigating.

As she walked quickly toward the cruiser's gunside, in unfamiliar corridors she'd never had to traverse, Natalie marveled at how small her world had become. Applied Kinetics, the puppet drone, the smattering of citizens' lounges where they kept the lights low and the drinks strong. Her rooms. The gunside armories. The flight deck. She hadn't needed to know any of the rest, not like she'd known *London*. Where were the coldsuits?

The memoria dangled a thought: an afternoon sitting in a pod, learning the ropes, watching Ash cut through doorway after doorway, descending into the outer shuttle deck, noting the various life-sustaining system cabinets along the way: life support, engineering, hull repair. *Hull repair,* she thought. The master node muttered about *so much space, so much wasted space,* and she tried to ignore him. Instead, she superimposed *Vancouver* over the memory of *London,* allowed for the new flagship's bigger bones and corridors, and made a snap judgment.

"Down three, over five," she whispered. "We should find suits there."

Ward kept pace alongside; not too fast, not too slow, just the quick-swept motion of a citizen on his way to work. The closet in question was twenty feet from where Natalie had expected it to be, and she fumbled it open with too much force, stuck between the countdown in her head and the need to be careful. She reached in and found two suits; engineer and spotter. She disengaged the second from the wall and handed it to Ward.

"Here you go, cit boy."

Ward snatched the suit from Natalie's grasp. "I don't know how to put this on."

"Legs first."

"You're judging me."

She fumbled with the waist fasteners. "I'm not judging you."

"Then why do you look like you've just eaten an entire lemon?"

Natalie flipped open the seals on her suit with more force than she probably should have, settled her feet inside, then helped Ward to do the same. "I said I wasn't judging you. I'm just . . . kind of flummoxed that you don't know how to EVA and you've been living on ships for your entire adult life."

Ward gave her a sour look, then helped Natalie snap her seals closed as Natalie did the same for him. "You *are* judging me."

"Absolutely not," she lied.

"Sure."

Natalie's passenger ducked into existence right behind Ward's shoulder, staring out of the darkness of the suit locker, his eyes oddly accusing. She felt the same quiet draw to his hands, the same soft pang under her breastbone. "Stop distracting me," she whispered.

You don't trust him either, said the master node.
Of course you don't.
You have no idea what he is thinking.
How did your species ever learn spaceflight?

We did science.

If you did science, you could properly expect and predict behaviors. You could communicate properly.

Maybe that works for a hivemind, she thought. *But humans aren't predictable.*

How do you stand it? said the master node.

Natalie thought about it. *Orders. Societal norms. Expectation. Ranks.*

The opposite of trust. Of together. There must be so much violence—

Like a million humans dead?

He paused.
His mouth opened, like a fish.
You don't trust me, he said.
What a feeling, what a delightful feeling—

She tried to ignore the master node. Ward's pathetic attempt at fastening his suit was a much easier target of her derision.

"You don't know me, not really," she said, fixing Ward with an icy stare. "You think you trust me, but you don't know what trust is, not until you're facing down the enemy and your teammates are the only thing keeping you alive. I'm not going to coddle your feelings. Because on the other side of the hatch? Is death. Death feeds on *feelings* out there, and sucking vacuum is a *shitty* way to die."

He looked hurt for a moment, then flashed a nervous smile.

"Oh, come on, now. Would you throw yourself out an airlock with someone you didn't trust?"

He tapped the final seal to his helmet like he'd been doing it his entire life, the smile disappearing behind the treated plasglas. Natalie stayed silent as the two of them climbed into the airlock, sealed the hatch behind them, and felt the airlock cycle out to vacuum with a meditative hiss.

With a final click, the outside hatch rolled open, revealing endless, wheeling black.

The master node was waiting for her outside, exactly where she thought he'd be, nearly lost in the shadows against the hull. He seemed silent for now, thoughtful, regarding her with a new, contemplative intelligence. Behind him, as she reached for her tether, Natalie saw the reason for the alarms, bright and shimmering in the white light of the unknown nearby star: the bright Vai fleet, settling around *Vancouver* like snow on shattered stone.

Ward's face turned toward the black. "Holy shit," he breathed. "That's—that's—oh, my God—"

"Look away." Natalie widened her fingers, palming Ward's helmet, directing his faceplate back down to where she was attaching his tether. She knew very well the hell Ward had just introduced to his brain: the formless black forever, the stars spinward, crowding out his common sense. Space-sickness, her old team had called it, or "the reality bends." It might even have been the first time Ward had seen space the way it really was, instead of behind the perspective-inducing assistance of a porthole or window. *Human brains aren't meant to understand that kind of depth*, Sharma had said, before.

"Don't think about it. Don't look. None of that exists. Your feet exist. Your breath exists. All you have to do is breathe and move and follow me," Natalie said.

Ward's breath moved in quick, ragged spats. "My feet exist."

"Just breathe. Keep three points of contact at all times. We're going to stay close to the hull, just beginner moves, none of this walking straight up like you see in *Alien Attack Squad,*" she said, going into instruction mode, trying to remember how Ash had acted when she'd been teaching Natalie how to use the salvage pod. She didn't like sounding like somebody's whiny CO.

Ward made spider-like, tenuous movements, his shoes making the sucking-quick transition of movement to seal against the plasglas. "I've never seen *Alien Attack Squad.*"

"Why not? It's great. It's full of assholes doing karate when they should actually be shitting their pants."

"Sounds funny," said Ward, following.

"I think so. Or, at least, I think I do." The pressure and give of the suit calmed Natalie with all of the grace of a weighted blanket. This was familiar: the movement, the weight, the meditative slowness. *Don't look up. Don't look out.*

"You *think* you do?"

"I—" She paused. "I used to know a guy who liked it. I watched it with him, but all of those memories got nuked at Tribulation."

"A *guy.*"

"Fuck you."

He snorted. "That guy why you said no?"

"I said *later,*" she hissed.

She tugged on her tether one last time, engaged her own magboots, reached for a handhold, and promptly went against her own advice, turning her face toward the bright, spindling Vai ships cornering *Vancouver* against the asteroid field.

Cornering *Vancouver,* she thought, or *Vancouver* using the asteroids as a sensor-blocking tactic? It mattered, and she didn't know, and that dragged like an itch in her backbrain. Assuming the Vai used sensors was assuming they thought like humans did, which Natalie knew by now to be dead wrong. But *hiding* was an awfully human thing to do, and the Vai had never *hid* before. Which choice would she take?

What is a choice?

She paused, her hand hovering in space. *You know. You can do one thing, or you can do another, and you pick.*

Ah. She felt a quiet, rumbling acknowledgment. *Yes. We make choices to ensure the longevity of every node. It must be so difficult to live when someone else can make a diametrical choice to your own.*

You have no fucking idea. Natalie pulled herself up again, trading handholds for footholds in the slow, methodical fashion all salvagers were taught. *What if I choose to do something that you don't want?*

You will not, he said.

I'm an alien to you. I don't think like you at all. We are not in any way similar. There's no way you're going to approve of everything I do from here. I'm going to make choices that you hate, and you're going to have to make a choice to support me or not. I need to know what happens when you object.

The master node sounded serene. You are my master node right now. We are together. I cannot object.

You're in a human body. All we do is object.

We are together now.
You can't object.

She snorted. *Watch me.*

You didn't object to Leonard Downey.

Don't you fucking say his name.

The master node was right, as much as she hated to admit it; she didn't mind taking orders when it calmed the chaotic sea that was the rest of her life. An order made sense of the nonsensical. It explained the next step. Adapting to giving the orders had been a little more difficult, but it made committing to a task much easier, knowing that you had a force of smart, knowledgeable people covering your exit.

But she now understood that living to take orders messed with your very sense of reality. Because of that, it had been so easy for Sharma to undermine her on the mission. She'd almost fallen for the *I care about you* shit, the *there's a treatment for the death* shit, when what she'd really meant was slotting Natalie into one more step in her master plan, which was—what? To install Vai tech in both their heads after the battle, and then blow herself up, leaving Natalie to puzzle things out alone? It made no sense.

And then she'd done the same damned thing with Joseph Solano. She'd followed his orders, given her own, perpetuated the entire cycle, ensuring Kate's disappearance and the kind of culture that ended up in Ash's death and Sharma's brains spread all over a borrowed transport.

She didn't want anyone to give her an order ever again.

I can help you with that,
said the master node.

All you do is give orders. You're a master node. It's what you are.

He hovered there, far enough to avoid triggering her defenses.
Not if you're a master node too.
But two in one place is impossible.
So we're impossible—

Her hand went automatically toward her memory device; her glove bounced off the faceplate, and she stopped dead. Something about how the battlefield was set up looked *wrong*. Behind her, shaded in the light of the Vai starships, the master node cleared his throat.

I thought that was impossible too, he said.

She focused, narrowed her eyes—instead of the long line, the vein, the inexorable waves that would come, the ships were gathered in clumps, deadly outparcels flanking a killer center. *Human tactics,* she thought. *Human arrangements. We never saw that in the war. We lost because we couldn't even understand what you were doing.*

This is different.

This we can win.

The comm shivered into action at her throat, the sound of a stranger's concerned lilt buzzing there, silencing Natalie's own answer.

"Engineer 6–324, Engineer 6–324, you are not authorized to be EVA at this moment. Please return to your home airlock."

She could hear Ward's sudden, panicked breathing in her ear, and raised her free hand to silence him. Before answering, she made sure her feet were magnet-flat against the hull.

"Home base, home base," she repeated, waving for Ward to stay quiet—she knew these patterns, knew how to respond with the right accent to the other's citizen's patter, knew how to get them out of this, or, at least, knew how to keep deluding herself long enough to keep Ward from a well-deserved panic spree that might kill him. "I received an emergency notification of a small hull breach at coordinates—" *Shit. Where were they?* "—just outside Deck 3."

"Engineer 6–324, we aren't reading a hull breach."

"I understand, control, but the situation being what it is—"

"—which is at battle stations, so you need to return inside."

Natalie rolled her eyes, grateful that her grimace was hidden behind the radiation faceplate, and engaged the comm again. "I might as well get eyes on it while I'm out here, control."

"Engineer 6–324, it's not safe. We'll have Ingest take a look."

Natalie could hear Ward's ragged breathing hot in her ears, or maybe that was her own—

"Acknowledged. Heading in." She managed to spit the words out before shutting down the comm, pulling at the next hand-hold. She and Ward were still too far away, still entirely too vulnerable, and she should have realized that Ingest could see them here, too, that the renderbots had found their way outside, in the same exact way they'd crawled into every damned cubbyhole in each overwatched Auroran life. In the corner of her eye, the Vai ships loomed in their incomprehensible mass, and her breath felt hot, too hot, sweat beading her upper lip.

Ward cleared his throat. "Damn."

"Let's go," Natalie said, catching her breath. "As fast as we can."

"You told me not to rush!"

"Fuck what I told you. Ingest will probably check with the duty engineers and discover that they're not actually outside, so we need to be *inside*. Yesterday." Natalie was hauling, now, skipping handholds and trying to keep her heart rate down so it wouldn't twig the suit controller's suspicions. She felt the hum of the ship through her boots, imagined Ingest as a disruptive shiver emerging from the black beyond. Shivered herself.

"They might not see us," Ward said, following her. As he reached for his next handhold, the silver connectors of his gloves caught and returned the bright white lights that illuminated the hull.

"Where did you grow up that you're still so *fucking* naïve?" she responded.

"You're *such* a bitch."

Natalie bristled, pulling herself along. "You don't know me."

"Oh, I think I do."

She could tell he was angry from the way he was breathing, even in the bulk of the suit, and he reached for the next handhold at a weird angle, coming too close to a jagged edge of his vestigial toolkit. She opened her mouth to tell him to *be careful,* but it was too late. Natalie heard a tearing and a warm, hissing hum.

"Shit," Ward said, his voice jumping a register. "What do I do?"

Natalie's annoyance spiked, and she made sure her mag-boots engaged against the footholds before turning to check. A small amount of smoky air slithered into existence just below Ward's left knee, disappearing into the vacuum just as quickly.

"Just stay still. Suits like this have an automesh that takes care of microbreaches."

His voice tightened. "Like a bandage."

"Exactly."

She heard a slurping noise, and then the hiss subsided, and what was left was Ward's hyperventilation, tough little spikes in her ear.

"Breathe, Ward."

"Fuck," he said, gulping down air. "You could have *warned* me."

"That's in at least six training holos. I can't believe they don't teach you this shit on station boardschool."

She didn't want to tell him that things were *worse* now, that suits like these also had medical monitors that set off alarm bells in control rooms, that if the fuckers in Central Ingest weren't paying attention before, the algorithm had certainly alerted them that something was wrong and they were still outside. She tightened her jaw; there was no reason to make Ward any more freaked out than he already was.

"I didn't grow up on a station," he said.

"Don't all birthrights?"

"I've never told anyone this," Ward said. He straightened after another too-long moment, then checked his mag-boot seal. "Right. I'm not *naïve,* you know. In fact, I—" He sighed. His breath evened out. "You asked where I was from. Technically, the Wards own half of Los Angeles. I would be there if they considered me a full Ward. They don't."

Natalie pulled herself up to the next handhold. "I thought—"

"That's why I asked you to contract with me. Because one look at the directory and all the other guys and girls have a laugh and move on to my cousins."

She continued moving up the hill, *hand-foot-hand-foot,* muttering it to herself like a mantra. "You're not exactly making your case, here."

"My mom was a Ward. My father was an indenture. That's why it fucks me up when you think I've had everything so easy."

She fought her surprise. "I didn't know that was possible."

"Failed reprocontrol? Apparently it happens." Ward still sounded slightly out of breath. "It was a massive scandal. When I came along, my mom decided she'd rather enter a contract with a Mejia on Los Angeles than pay off two indentures, so she only paid off mine. The family board wasn't interested in having me on Los Angeles, so I was shipped off to Dauntless Colony. My dad's been a celestium miner ever since. I was put in the boardschool there, all paid up as a Ward, but everyone knew the whole story."

Hand. Foot. Hand. Keep moving. Keep him distracted. "So that's why you can only marry someone straight out of indenture. I get it. What was Dauntless like?"

"Cold."

"Space is colder."

"Natalie, do you think this is important right now?" She heard the edge of panic in his voice. He pointed; the Vai line was moving.

"Keep talking. Distract yourself. So you finally found your way to *Vancouver*?"

In his voice was the shrug she couldn't see. "A couple years ago, the Ward occupying the Los Angeles seat on the Auroran executive board died, and the family gave it up to the Aulanders. I wasn't privy to why. Politics, maybe. Without the scrutiny, Mom could use her influence to get me on a ship. I did the rest. Turns out that some of the shit you learn in school on a celestium depot are skills that come in handy years later on the flagship."

"And your dad?"

"I dunno. I can't get letters out there reliably enough to see how he's doing."

Natalie thought of Ash. Of her own father. "You're just going to leave him behind?"

"I can't possibly pay off his debt. *Joseph Solano* couldn't pay off his debt now."

"I'm sorry."

"Well," he breathed, reaching for another handhold, "I don't intend on being like him."

She laughed. "That's why you're so obsessed with your looks. You feel you have to be perfect because he wasn't."

"I'm not obs—The *point* is," he said, hauling himself up, his hands and feet almost as fast as Natalie's, "that the deck is stacked, and you need to be on top."

Natalie snorted, then came to a stop over the airlock, her hand hovering over the latch, and she imagined the two of them as they actually were: two tiny motes of dust, barely recognizable against the grand machine that was Aurora, lost brackets in a code that no longer needed them. Just extra characters occupying one sad fucking story.

She wondered what it would be like to simply let go. To float backward, open her helmet, do what should have been done when she was an indenture—

> *That's not what a master node does.*
> Downey hovered nearby, his face serious.

But I'm just me, she wanted to say, *a nobody-nothing who can't even see when she's being used,* but the words clogged in her throat, wrapping around the year in App-K. The embarrassment of having everything she ever wanted and hating it, the inexplicable loneliness, staring at the ceiling, listening to the blood rush in her head, feeling lost and wild, even with Ward, even when she should have been close to being perfectly happy.

She grasped at the latch to the airlock like it would save her from drowning. Leaving now wouldn't do a damned thing, and Natalie Chan was no deserter.

Not anymore.

"You okay?" Ward said, as if he'd sensed something was wrong.

She hauled the seal open as an answer and dropped directly after him into the bright womb of the airlock. She heard the echoing slurp of sweet, ship-conditioned air beginning to cycle back in. She imagined she felt the pressure of wind against her suit, equalizing the atmosphere against her skin like the truth, neutralizing all of the lies she'd told and been told.

The truth will set you free, went the old Verdict phrase. *That's for people on planets,* she thought. *For people who were free.* For indentures, for spacers, for people like her trying to come in from the cold, it was more like: *the truth will give you the bends.*

What came next was just the inevitable.

"Yeah," she said, grabbing the interior latch. Beyond was Aurora, Ingest, the truth. The future. The light next to the interior door snapped to green, and she pushed through the last of her hesitation, opening the door to whatever consequences came next.

22

During Natalie's first days on *Twenty-Five*—during the long week's ramble to the Tribulation star system, after the enforced Company icebreakers but before she'd navigated a space for herself between Kate's brash optimism, Ramsay's smirking wit, and Downey's easy confidence—the captain had planted her in the mess with Ash and a sickening number of salvage training holos to wade through.

With the grav-drive engaged, training on actual equipment was too dangerous—so she and Ash drank bad coffee and answered interactive tests on their tablets, bonding over the stupidity of it all. They poked fun at the announcer, whose voice sounded like he'd spent years guzzling quarts of macadam. They criticized the terrible animations. They had races using the holographic pod controls. Salvage training was pathetic compared to the grueling months of ordnance disarmament training and the constant threat of shivering oblivion—it had been *easy*.

But now—

Now, hovering outside the narrow gray door to Central Ingest's main watchroom, her fingers cold on the unresponsive passpad, she couldn't remember any of it. The memoria was blank. She swore, drawing her fingers back like the thing had burned her.

"I don't remember how to beat this," she whispered, if she'd ever known—forgetting for a moment that Ingest would hear that, too, that her anonymous steps wouldn't matter if the damn thing had her voice on record. People walked by behind them, trudging in lockstep, their eyes blankly staring ahead, new info-implants on their heads. They looked tired. *Me too,* she wanted to say.

She waved on the tablet and typed: *Superhaptic locks. DNA-based. You're going to have to go through the office.*

Ward's eyebrows furrowed, and he stole the tablet from her. *I'm going with you.*

But her mind was already on another plan, already folding out beneath her like the Auroran computer core, spiraling out from behind these doors like a willow tree from its central complex on the citizen mid-deck. She grabbed his wrist, then tugged him down the corridor, kneeling in front of a maintenance hatch. He tilted his head—a clear *what?* as a group of fighter pilots jogged by in bulky exo-suits, and he turned to watch them. *Lockstep,* she thought. *Again. Weird.* She grabbed his chin, moving to hide their faces from the passersby with the hiked shoulders of someone angling for a kiss. As soon as the pilots rounded the corner, she ducked into the maintenance tunnel.

Ward tumbled in behind her, his face set like flint. "I'm going with you."

"No," she hissed. "This isn't a holo. We're not going to get a second chance at this—"

"So I need to come with you."

She flushed. "Tell me what you want to know. I'll find out for you."

"I didn't just fuck myself over with App-K to be your decoy."

"Then you're not here to spy on me?"

It was his turn for his face to go red. "For fuck's sake—"

"Then do as I say." She picked her way down the tunnel until she found an unlabeled maintenance hatch—and, if she remembered her deck plans correctly, the access point for indentured techs whom the cits didn't want accessing feeds in the watchroom.

She found the proper door—but it wasn't the standard dual authentication of number and access token she'd expected. This, too, had been converted to a superhaptic.

She stared at it for a moment, feeling dumb. Of course they'd slapped a superhaptic on the door. *You can't fool a superhaptic.*

Her father would have shrugged. Picked up his tablet. *Someone has to try,* he would have said.

"You can open this?" she asked.

He recoiled visibly. "Probably. But my name would come up in Ingest immediately."

"So you'll go in and complain that the back door isn't working, and ask to be let in the front," she said. "Ingest is new, right? You don't really know where to go. And, besides, you need your new info-implant. Central Ingest has neurotechs. You're the big, fancy App-K director. Go ask them."

Ward stared. "Someone'll get suspicious. They don't send directors to do scut work like this."

"*Mr. Solano* does. He sent me to Tribulation. He's *in your department* right now. Ingest can see that." She breathed in. Pain seemed to be buried deep in the lining of her lungs, and she wondered if it would ever withdraw. "He sends people like Aulander on *fetch missions.* It makes perfect sense that he'd send you to Ingest. You need that info-implant to work on the rig, and you need it installed by the best."

His face darkened. "You have all the answers, don't you?"

"I do." She tossed him a jaunty smile.

"You're using me. Like always."

"And you aren't?"

He barked out a disbelieving laugh. "Apparently, I'm learning from the best."

Downey pricked the edges of her vision, lost and breathing somewhere behind her in the tight quarters of the maintenance tunnels. She focused on Ward: on the hollowing of his cheek, the anger in his jaw, the breath that smelled like stale coffee. The graying of his skin. In this light, his illness was hard to deny.

The pain was evident on his face, something bright with anger, and she almost felt sorry for him. She touched his smooth cheek with two light fingers, and he turned away, the anger settling quickly into resignation. "You need to do this for me. For us," she whispered. "This is the only way."

"Is it really." A statement, hollow-voiced, hurt.

"Yeah."

"There's nothing else you need to tell me?"

She breathed out. *Everything*, maybe. *It's my fault. They're already using you. Which is why you can't come with me.*

Maybe: *I did this to you.*

"Nothing," she said. "What do you need to know?"

It wasn't the answer he wanted. Natalie saw a nasty, slippery echo in his eyes, some sort of uncontrolled anger that she couldn't quite understand. He took off his jacket and turned it inside-out, using the lining to wipe his face. A few moments later, he slid it back on, the last of the eyeliner tracing gray streaks under his left eye.

"I wish I'd never met you," Ward said, then placed his fingers on the superhaptic interface, and the entire thing went gold. She felt the shiver of the ship preparing for battle under her feet, and saw the hurt in his eyes harden into something else, into the thing she needed him to be. Seconds later, he was back in the corridor.

She watched the space where he was.

"They always leave," Downey said.

"I made him leave," she responded, hoarse. "It's not the same."

"If there's one thing I'm learning," he said, "it's that you can't ever *make* a human do anything."

She snorted. "That's extremely fucking true."

"Keep going," he said, hiding right behind her shoulder, his nonexistent breath in her ear.

She shuddered back into motion. Beyond the now-open hatch to the computer core, alarms wailed in varying shades of *attack* and *general quarters,* alarms that accessed her shivering animal brain, the place where the war had dug in and scrambled it, and she had to keep herself from that Pavlovian response to find the nearest jumpsuit or strapdown.

No. She had work to do. That first week on *Twenty-Five,* she'd learned the basics of how Auroran ships were built. Most of them kept the cylinder-and-spine design of the earliest colony ships, the huge spinning vessels that had gone out before antigrav was common. She still knew enough—how to access maintenance tunnels, how to remove walls, how to cut cabling while preserving function. How to find the useful items, the reusable stuff, the expensive shit. How to blow past standard locks. Natalie thought it was incredible that more salvagers didn't just go pirate.

It was only on *Mumbai* and *London,* moving carefully through the cruisers' dead veins, that the blueprints became real. She'd learned how citizens and birthrights lived, saw the massive chunks of ship owned by the different family lineages, saw the obscene open space occupied by executives and board members. But those living dead so rarely remembered the smaller details, the tinier spaces, never smelled the acrid, metal-bright scent of warm cabling close to a core vent.

"You're wrong about that," she said to Downey, who was following her like a sad puppy. "You can make people do whatever you want. All you have to do is be an executive."

"Nobody ever made you do anything," Downey said. "Isn't that true?"

"I—" Her hand paused. Was it? "I don't know. I'm starting to wonder if that's just a story I've been telling myself to justify acting like *him.*"

Downey pursed his lips in thought. "So you can choose to hide the truth from yourself. I thought you couldn't simply choose to believe something antithetical to truth. Truth is—"

"Fungible," she said, stepping through the door.

"That's impossible," he said.

"You're human now. Everything's impossible. Keep up."

Inside was the computer core. *Twenty-Five*'s core had been smaller, accessible from the front and the back. A cruiser's was five levels deep, with a labyrinth of progressively larger data centers clustered around the main logic towers, with passages between for techs to run repairs, replacements, and updates. There were no techs here today—just the great rainbow bulk of it, the blinking lights, the hum of almost-intelligence, the breeze from the vent, the places on the first logic tower, where she saw vein-slippery Vai tech hacked into the rest of the technological nonsense.

She stopped. "You seeing this?"

Downey was barely breathing. "*Together*," he whispered.

"I'll take that as a yes."

It was hot in the core, almost unbearably so. She came around the last arc to see the second logic tower, and stopped in her tracks, sweating. The tower had become an arachnophobic nightmare of cables and legs and dripping oil or water or golden blood. It had probably been a proxy rig once, maybe even built off the plans for *her* team's proxy rigs, from the way the struts leaned against one another. She wondered, seeing the familiar way the Vai weapons parts were so carefully soldered in place.

And she recognized the rest of it, machine on top of machine, the Sacrament tech Solano's teams had loaded up on Tribulation while she'd been watching Downey walk away instead. It was paired with medical equipment—ventilators, life-support systems.

Beyond it, she saw the body.

A woman's corpse was buried in the computer. Cabling wrapped around her matchstick legs, ran into veins at the neck, wrists, and ankles. Her eyes were gold-rheumed, mouth hanging slightly open. Someone had started replacing the woman's skin with superhaptic circuitry, with boards and braiding that had become arms and fingers and skin, slipping up from the extremities like a river slurping up a valley. And the face—

She knew that face.

Beside her, the master node gave a sob and dropped to his knees, and Natalie felt a sudden, grinding headache, the purpling feeling of the alien in her brain trying to understand what he was seeing.

"Captain," she whispered, unable to move.

I'm too late.

The body stirred. Its eyes flickered open. Kate's voice, left unused, was a wondering croak. "Natalie?"

Natalie's limbs moved almost under someone else's control, taking her to the rig connections, fumbling in her back pocket for the drill. "Captain! I—I'll get you out of there," she stammered, taking inventory of the parts, understanding how thoroughly she had just lied: superhaptic connections at the fingers and the belly, drug delivery to the brainstem, the way the neural crown sat against Kate's pale forehead.

She didn't have to call for the node to help; didn't have to even ask him what she was looking at. He was in her thoughts, he *was* her thoughts, and his half-life hands danced over cables and circuits like a master magician. *I know this,* he said, his eyes widening. *It breathes like I do. I'll show you what to do.*

Kate shivered in her tomb. Pain and a quiet disgust slipped across her face, and her gold-rheumed eyes closed. "No. I'm all right. Live your life. Go back to Aulander and get your nice fucking jacket."

The master node was a crescendo in Natalie's ear, and she tried to wave him off. "Tell me Solano made you do this. Tell me you didn't volunteer."

Words formed around Kate's mouth, but nothing came out. "He promised," she managed. "That I could see Ash. He promised."

"Ash is dead."

"No."

Natalie's fingers closed on the cables. "She died at the White Line. I saw her body."

Kate's cracked lips parted. She fought her own breath, lungs filling and emptying of air, cables tightening around her body. Her wire-crusted hand curled around Natalie's cold fingers, and underneath the metal, Natalie could still feel sinew. "No. She wouldn't be captured. I wouldn't let her die. You have to understand. I see it all. This is the way it has to be."

"Make me understand. What have they done to you?"

Bony fingers brushed against the inside of Natalie's palm like a twisted benediction. "It's the treatment they promised. It's not what we thought, but . . . it was the only way Ash would live. She went inside, Natalie. Sharma showed her how to do it. I was supposed to go in too, but I was knocked out before I could install the memoria. And Solano—"

"*He* did this to you."

"When I'm done, I can go to her." Her voice cracked. "It's the only way."

I know this, said Downey, grabbing the cables.
I know this. This sings.

"Go," Kate said. "They already know you're here. Your stupid boyfriend—"

Home, Downey breathed,
and lay himself against the cables,
twisted them in his fingers—

"No way," Natalie said. "I'm not leaving you now." She dropped Kate's hand, put her attention back to the rig itself. *"Go to her,"* she thought. *How? Ash is dead. You can't just go somewhere and leave your body behind.* She followed Downey, touching the things he touched, trying to figure out what he was trying to say to her. The rig helped its user *go* places by broadcasting information from a proxy into the brain; the actions of the user on the ship would drive the proxy elsewhere. Hadn't she left her body behind when she took the redshift star to Bittersweet, in a way? She knew enough from her days in Verdict and her chats with the R&D legates that the puppet wasn't a *true* upload, just a fancy wireless rig, that the mind contained too much information for a real upload. And that was *impossible*—

—but she was watching Downey, a real creature wrapped in a hallucination, his eyes turning against the light at the center of the rig, and she *knew*.

Vai tech can handle that level of information. It has to.

Her hand snapped up to touch the memoria, and it hummed under her fingers. She didn't need to find evidence that consciousness transfer was possible. She'd been living it this entire time.

Natalie's chest tightened. The memoria. The device that Sharma had spent time adjusting on Tribulation. The device she'd installed on Natalie's head, the Vai technology inside. Was that it? Was that why Sharma had wanted to go aboard the heartship? And when that became impossible, she sent Ash instead?

Sent herself?

And what had happened to Natalie on the Vai ship? If she had the same sort of technology in her brain as Sharma, why was she still living in her own skin? Had that grand, silvering rush at the end been some gate in her mind swinging open—and instead of tentative steps taken toward some unwanted heaven, the master node came through the other way instead?

I had to live, the master node said.
I had to survive.

I know, she whispered.
That's how I know you're alive.

She turned to follow the master node's gaze, and caught the edge of a familiar, violent light. Her breath hitched. She tugged his borrowed hand aside, and slipped her own through the tangle of cables, pulling them back to see the center of the rig keeping Kate alive.

No, she thought. *No, no, no. They have the Heart—*

But she could also immediately see that she was wrong, that this roiling ball was not the Heart but a haphazard construction of human make, fashioned from the innards of Vai weapons, surrounded by a slapdash housing inspired by the utilitarian motives of the board. It only *looked* like the Heart. Natalie traced its connections—cables attached to the ship's main computer, tiny arteries running in and out and through Kate's body—but its purpose remained opaque.

This is my fault, she thought. *They built it. But I pointed to photographs and records and Sharma's old lab logs.* And almost immediately afterward, she recoiled. *No. I was doing my job. Taking orders. I'm not responsible.*

The more she looked at the strange machine, though, the more she felt the responsibility weighing on her body, tugging at her faulty lungs. She could not deny that the housing was pure Applied Kinetics. The Heart as built by the Vai was both power draw and power source for a race that was power; this wild screaming ball, then, was the power source, and she traced the connectors with her cold fingers back to the power draw—

—of course.

Kate.

Natalie almost trembled. She could see the whole system now, through Downey's dead eyes, through the master node's living ones. She could feel the energy exchange pulsing beneath her fingers. In the real Heart, Vai bodies were both input and output. How had that been changed here? This—Solano's Heart, Solano's computer, Solano's world, Solano's entrance to the Vai universe, all of it controlled by *life* running through it like a river—*Kate's life*—

Her head snapped back to look at Kate. "You're *Ingest*," Natalie breathed.

Kate coughed again. "Not for very much longer."

"You're still dying," Natalie whispered. "And you don't want me to leave. You called me through the directory."

"I knew you'd be smart enough to pick up on it. I need to warn you."

Natalie found herself at Kate's side again, her hand pressing against the older woman's forehead. "Solano is going to let me see her," Kate said again.

"Don't tell me you believe that," Natalie whispered.

"I have to."

"And what is he going to do when you're gone?" She smoothed back Kate's hair; it came out in thin, broken clumps.

"He needs someone who's been infected for over a year, Natalie," Kate said; the effort to speak an entire sentence was palpable, and she closed her eyes, trying to manage her breath. "Who do you *think* is next?"

Natalie didn't need to respond. She pressed her forehead against Kate's, breathed out, letting her anger boil.

There had been a hundred moments like this: simple, incremental choices that meant nothing by themselves, just chips in the dam holding together the world she'd constructed for herself. *Keep on trying, keep on making progress, and eventually, one chip breaks the dam,* she heard her father say, somewhere in the memoria tying her living mind to her dead body. *The river runs free and drowns everything.*

"I can go home." Somewhere bouncing around in her spleen, the master node was pulling apart the revelation too. She felt his cascading joy so deep and wild that she couldn't help but smile. His mouth moved for the first time. "We can use this to go home."

"I don't know," she whispered. "I'm not entirely sure of that."

"*Home,*" the node sang. "It's right behind the door, it's right there—please—"

Natalie's fingers found and closed on the rig's neck jack, wound up and hung exactly where she'd expected it to be. Downey ignored the hand, sliding into a Len-like hug, all arms and fingers around her shoulders, smelling of sweat and cheap Company soap. "And if you go home," she said, "you'll keep your promise? To go beyond the White Line?"

"Yes," he whispered. "To go, and never return. Keeping promises is what you would do."

A knot formed in her throat as she felt the tight warmth of his biceps, his torso, his body, and her senses told her that this was Downey in every way that mattered, and it was difficult not to feel like this was the goodbye they'd never had.

She swallowed that feeling, biting her bottom lip, using the resultant pain to drag herself back to some semblance of reality. The hellthing hugging her was not Leonard Downey. It was the hellthing that killed millions of humans in the war, and the more she forgot that, the less human she became herself.

No, she wanted to say, entertaining a desolate, angry darkness. *I would follow and salt your fields and blow up your matrix.*

Or I would have.

Before.

"We have a deal, then," she whispered.

"Who are you—" A wheezing sound, breath pushed through cables. "You're not talking to me."

"There's an alien in my head." The words felt foolish on her lips, so she barrelled forward. "The Vai control node. I'm taking him home. Kate, this works like the puppet rig, right? Neck jack, immersion drugs, haptics?"

Natalie didn't wait for a response. She scrambled for the familiar parts of the rig, the things she needed to slip into the proxy world: a second drug infusion cable, haptics for her fingers, the neck jack. Without anesthetic, without hooking her into the strap-induced antigrav, it was going to *hurt*.

Kate coughed in a breath, taking the announcement in stride. "He'll control you."

Natalie knelt on the floor, slid the haptics on, raised the neck jack, made sure the end would work with her own hardware. *Barely.* "I know how he thinks. I'll be fine."

"No. You *can't*. Natalie—" Her chest fluttered, struggling for breath. "This connects to the Vai world, yes, but it's not the Vai-controlled network. He's made himself the master node of his own connected network. That way, he can get around—"

"—the fact that you can't have two master nodes. Okay. *Shit*." Natalie felt a wail inside, something breaking in two. It felt like the master node losing the grip on hope. It felt like she was losing her own hope, too, a wild winding sadness building in her tired shoulders. She slapped herself to make it stop. "So we fight."

"No," Kate wheezed. "Fuck, Natalie, you can't *fight* him. You'll have no power in there, no power at all."

"Then we'll find Ash. Sharma uploaded her for a reason. She didn't do it out of the kindness of her heart, and you know it—"

Kate sounded desperate. "Please. You need to run while you still can. She would want you to live your life. Steal a transport, go anywhere else—"

And then Natalie heard voices approaching the door. Laughter.

Ward's voice. The noise meant only one thing: that she had to make a decision. Now.

"What do you want to do?" she asked the master node.

"Fight," he whispered, crawling to his feet.

So we fight.

"No network is inviolable, Kate," Natalie said, then slammed the cable into the opening at the back of her neck, felt the stabbing pinch of the needle—

Nothing happened.

—fuck, I forgot about the permissions, she thought, *the gold tattoos are permissions.* She'd suspected, but it was entirely clear now what they were—the changed, adulterated silver of her Bittersweet-born nanotech, turned to Solano's needs, the one thing she needed to connect to this sick Heart.

She exhaled.

Stared at Kate.

"Oh, fuck no," said Kate.

Natalie fumbled for the drill she'd brought. "I need to."

"He'll *control* you."

"He won't even be able to find me. He might have access, but it's the master node's world. We'll be fine." Natalie hefted the drill, tugged the trigger, stared at the shining, twirling bit.

Kate's chest caught in a wheezing, defeated laugh. "You should be lucky I'm not writing your monthly evaluation right now."

"I'm fucking killing it, Captain," she said, and moved before she could really understand the insanity of what she was about to do, before she could stop herself. She brought the twisting drill bit to her scarred wrist, then grit her teeth against the pain as she pushed the bit against the skin. The skin peeled aside with a bloody pop.

Kate didn't even close her eyes when Natalie applied the drill to her wrist, as if she weren't in pain—or in so much pain one more gaping hole wouldn't even matter. Natalie squatted in front of Kate, applied wrist to wrist, and the golden nanoprobes sputtered into her body, mixing with the original silver—

—the master node screamed, crawling to his feet, swaying—

"Stay strong, Len," she said.

This time she lay down on the floor. This time there would be no support for her arms and legs, no chest harness buckled tight to keep her safe. She'd come out broken. Bruised.

Worse than bruised.

But she'd been broken before.

The lock turned. She wasn't ready. She had to stop it. She reached for the commlink as the drugs began to flow. "Ward," she said.

His voice crackled through, and the lock stopped cycling. "I thought we were meeting at the lounge," he said, carefully. *Not out of hearing, then.*

"Go private."

"Done."

The words stuck in her throat. "What you wanted me to tell you. You already know, yeah? That I gave you the nanotech illness?"

A pause. "Mr. Solano told me. You—" She could tell he was swallowing. "You should have been honest before."

"Why?"

The world swirled around her.

"It's nothing," he whispered—cheery, like someone was watching. "I'm fine."

"You're going to have to be more than fine," she said. The dizziness clawed at her mind. "Everything changes, when you have something they want. You have to stay two steps ahead. You have to read every contract, you have to figure out what they want—don't be me."

"You're scaring me."

"Read your fucking contract, Ward," she said.

She closed her eyes. The memoria gave her the long walk from the Bittersweet crash site, with Ward's voice then and Ward's voice now, with yellow stones crunching underneath her feet. Everything was exactly the same and yet completely different, the visuals more immediate, the scents twice as slippery, the sound a bitter pinball in her skull. *Upload,* she thought. *I thought I had built a fancy holorig. But was I already out of my body? Was I really there, in the puppet?*

She felt a presence at the edge of the airfield.

Here was her memory; here was the airstrip, glinting in the sun, and here was the sobbing in her belly and the doubt and the dry mouth and it was shit that a travel drive wasn't big enough for all of it, or maybe it was. She heard a faraway heartbeat, a squelching, aching cannonade, and a shivering, thin wail sailing above it all. She'd thought that had been some sort of broken gadget, when she'd been hearing the Vai the entire time.

A slurping hiss wound in her ears as the cables engaged. Without painkillers this process was nausea and fever and fire, electricity scurrying across her nerve endings, and even if she wanted to stop it all, even if she could at this point, *upload* was the pull of a hull breach, as violent under her skin as a screamer. There was no denying it.

She felt herself separating from her skin, growing numb, compressing, slipping away from her eyes and her throat and her fingers. Someone had told her once that she would see her life flash before her eyes as she died, that in the split-second before the electricity in her brain sputtered to black, she'd know any truths she'd hid from herself. Natalie never believed it—those thoughts were the woebegone lies of a dead society, left behind in the rinds of broken religions, and she was glad that it wasn't true. She expected one long, black shudder. Nothing to relive. No war, no regrets, no long walk to the river.

The installed combat HUD unfolded in front of her, looking

like a thousand capillaries layered one upon another, each one a crying possibility. She was inside her mind now. It was too much information, so much her heart sped like an overtaxed engine as a migraine tied itself around her eyes.

Go deeper, she thought. *Upload.*

This was what it was like to be a machine, to move as fast as numbers and code and a silicon brain, roiling in the delicious bodiless thick of it. Her body twisted—violent and hypnagogic, as far out of her control as the movement of the planets and the streaming of the stars. The world became a thousand colors that her brain couldn't process, a thousand voices wrapped in shards of glass, an entire silvering world hovered there, suspended in her throat, close enough to kiss.

And then: light keen enough to kill.

23

Natalie's experience in the rib cage room had been oceanic—a sibilant trance, a careening seduction, an entire civilization pouring into her skin and settling straight into her bones. There hadn't been enough space left in her brain for wonder, much less room to figure out how wonder was *coded*.

There was even less time now. Natalie's new world came together with all the comfortable excitement of thick needles lancing through her eyes. She'd peeled her consciousness from her body as easily as the rind from an orange. Putting it somewhere else felt paralyzing and vast and brilliant. Loading in, her connected brain got to work on making sense of it, turning impossible feedback to patterns she could see but never understand: jagged alien shapes in streams of synesthesiac light, unforgivable rivers tasting of citrus and blood and infrared.

But this connection wasn't anything like the intoxicating, inexplicable warmth of *together* she'd experienced on the cruiser. This connection was a hangover: bare, echoing, *alone*. The light that had been so total instead flickered in stabbing blasts, illuminating a space as large as a cathedral and as bare as Bittersweet. And the silence—

It was a silence so deep, so beyond space, that it was like the Vai were no longer even there.

She told herself to *be quiet,* to not *jump to conclusions*, but she could feel the difference keenly enough that fooling herself wasn't easy. She was already too late. It had been *too late* for weeks.

Natalie felt smooth stone under her knees. Silence. The prick of air-conditioning on bare arms. The light beyond her eyelids reminded her of coming awake after a night of drinking, and the sound that accompanied it not the Vaisong she'd hoped for, but the hum of human machinery.

She fought vertigo as she picked herself up from the marble floor—hard and cool, like the white stone of the plaza, but fashioned instead from expensive dark blue marble, intricately worked with golden constellations. The floor was drenched in moonlight pouring through wide, crystalline windows with velvet curtains tied back with skeins of golden silk. Human, all human—nothing Vai, nothing remotely alien, and what was worse, it was all birthright bullshit.

She recognized the colors and constellations: they were on the banners displayed behind the talking heads on the talk holos. The open arms of the Galilee farming colonies, the square of Cana's four moons, the delicate filigree of the Gethsemane acropolis, carefully polished for any number of high-heeled shoes to stand on, stretching down a hall that seemed to go forever, for people who planned to rule forever.

The whole place was so beautiful, so excessive, so *real*, that it made her want to puke.

"Len," she whispered. "Node? Len?" Then, quietly: "Ash?"

She didn't know how to act in a place like this. Didn't know the rules, or how not to get caught by the system.

So you figure out the rules, dumbass, she thought, *just like you figure out how to defuse a new kinetic right on the battlefield. Don the Vai-thick safesuit, pop open the casing of whatever this is, and look inside. Follow the connections, whisper a prayer, slice those that lead to the center, the nerves and ligaments and veins. Silence the Heartsong. Kill the light. Watch it flicker out, fizzle like a match in the rain, spark like a computer tossed on a bonfire. Keep it quiet.*

She caught the barest hint of ghostly music from beyond a set of ornate glass doors on the other side of the hallway, open to darkness. Just outside was a stone courtyard, a long expanse of green grass, a great cliff nearby, and a gray cityscape against the skyline, flanked with tables and chairs dressed in thin, wispy fabric. A party. *Shit.* She moved down the hallway away from the approaching voices, choosing instead to duck into a much darker, larger room.

During her time as an indenture, she'd posted flimsy-printed pictures to a dozen different Auroran walls and hung jumpsuits from a dozen different Auroran bedframes. Not even Ward's chamber, decorated in tasteful navy blues, with its walled-off bedroom and dedicated laundry chute, looked like this. This was *money*—a massive ballroom, empty as bone, lit as for a party, all swirling lights and walls made of nebula-scented satin.

"You came." Light spilled from a door opening behind her, and with it came a familiar voice. Natalie whirled. She saw the bare outline of skin, of human curves formed from the song-soaked smoke of the Vai world. She thought, almost reflexive: *Ash.*

But it wasn't. She barely recognized this person sweeping into the center of the cavernous hall, wearing an old-style, flaring suit like she might wear an atomic bomb: flames at her fingers, silver behind her eyes. The tight collar was closed at the hollow of her throat by a sapphire that shone as loud as a molecular, and on her thin fingers were rings laden with the same terrifying blue ache.

"Finally," breathed Reva Sharma. She rushed across the room, the light dying as she walked, smelling of daisies and jacaranda—and frowned. "Damn it. You came through *Ingest*. I bend over backward to leave you a proper door in your memoria, and you use *his*." She paused. "This makes everything much more complicated."

Natalie felt numb and wrong. Her eyes stole to the shining

rings, the necklace, the song that felt closer than ever somehow. "Where's Ash?"

"She's fine. You *remembered*, didn't you? Ash helped me remember you at the plaza, and since then I just wanted to make sure you were all right—"

"Can I see her?"

Sharma ignored the question. "Have you remembered?"

Natalie's tongue was ready with an insult, but the doctor's eyes were so earnest in the whirling party lights that it made her pause. The *no, bitch* fell away, replaced by something more calculating.

"Of course I remembered," she lied.

"Then we have a lot to talk about. I—" Her voice caught. "I'm not going to apologize, Natalie. Let's just get that straight from the beginning. It would be false, and it would be wrong, and you deserve better from me. But we can't honestly get to any of that until you're here as one of my secondaries, not his. You'll have to alter some code on your end. In meatspace. I'll write a program." She paused. Looked up and around at the ballroom. "Let me make things more comfortable for you while I do that."

Sharma made a quiet little twist of her wrist, and familiar things began to form around her feet, erupting like tree trunks or veins of newly opened oil: chairs, a table, the cheap, bent-metal things they'd had on *Twenty-Five,* slithering into existence as quickly as she could remember them. She'd never created a holonovel, but imagined the process rendered like this—

"Holy shit," she said. "Are you getting this from my memories?"

"From mine. We think we've come so far, we stitched-up suitcases of carbon and hydrogen and water. We have not." Sharma smiled.

"Is this . . . what the Vai do?"

"In their own way. Imagine them as *space* explorers, Natalie, in the purest form of the word," Sharma said. She walked slowly around the table, golden shards falling in her wake, her long, loose hair coarse and jagged from too long spent tied above the nape of her neck. "What we are born understanding in our very blood and skin, they needed to learn. The very concept of *up;* the reality of down. Sight and touch. Sound. *Distance.* Weight. They've learned to manipulate it over the years and incorporate it into their natural state."

Natalie slid slowly into one of the chairs. It hit the bony parts of her hips in exactly the way she remembered, the cold of the metal seeping through her jumpsuit. "Where are they?"

"Does it matter?"

"I think it very much does. Especially if you killed them."

"Really?" She looked surprised. "That was never a problem for you before."

"It was war. Not genocide. And not my goddamn fault."

Sharma looked slightly ruffled. Her tone adopted a cutting edge and her fingers danced at the gem at her throat. "They're safe. Out of the way."

"So all you did was *run a coup* against an *alien government*?"

The doctor's jaw set, and she took her eyes off Natalie, turning instead to something she couldn't see, her fingers moving as if touching haptics or twisting magic. *Coding,* she realized, *or whatever that looked like in this world.* "I found a way to win the unwinnable war. I thought, out of all of them, you'd at least understand."

"I do understand, which makes it worse."

"And what do you *think* you understand?"

The words tumbled out before she could stop them. "You want power," she said. "Just like Solano."

Sharma's fingers stopped mid-air, and then came down on the

314 K A R E N   O S B O R N E

back of the chair that had once belonged to Kate, a swift strike, a clanging noise. "I am nothing like him," she said. "The war wouldn't have ended without me. Without my work. I figured out how to fight them. I did what the corporations could not. Would not." She brought her fingers back to sweeping and slipping.

"But he got what he wanted anyway."

"Corporations always will, in the end, and Joseph is not stupid. What did you think was going to happen? I thought we'd have years to prepare, but he's just gone so far, too fast. Gold, oil, celestium, *progress*—all of it led to lives lost, countries destroyed, civilizations broken and destitute and ground to dirt, and the corporations—" Sharma's voice cracked. "Ah, they're the worst of it, war and money and greed distilled into its purest form. I didn't give my life to this work to allow the corporations to continue to hurt people."

"The *Vai* are people," Natalie said.

The overhead lights glinted on Sharma's dark hair as she nodded. "Yes. And they're hotboxed. Partitioned. They're fine. They don't even know anything is wrong. Natalie, I'm concerned about you. You said you remembered—"

"I do."

"Then imagine the possibilities." Whatever she was doing, she finished, and clapped her hands together to push away the interface. She began to walk around the table. "Look past a simple application of zero-point energy to colonization and spaceflight. The upload is freedom. Nobody will shiver in the cold or the rain. Nobody will suffocate when their oxygen runs out. Nobody will need to work themselves to death just to see a doctor and then find out it's too late."

It took Natalie a moment to register what the doctor was really saying, and when she did, she felt nausea stabbing deep in her belly, a feeling that expanded straight down to her toes. "Because they'll be *dead*," she said.

"It's not death," she said. "It's the only logical next move if we want to continue to live in space. The Vai are *made* for it. We need to be made for it too. Unless you want people to continue dying from preventable diseases and hull breaches."

"You really believe that, don't you?" Natalie said, shaking. "You haven't thought for a second about helping people as they are. You haven't thought of actually *curing the preventable diseases*."

"There's never enough funding—"

"So it's better to *upload people*? What, is oxygen too expensive? Ration bars not a good investment this quarter? Sacrament execs need more diamonds for their hair clips?"

"You sound like your father," Sharma barked.

"Well, maybe he had a fucking *point*," Natalie spat. The nausea had turned to anger, and she was overwhelmed with memories detailing all the terrible things men and women with power had asked her to do for them with her body, and the hunger and sickness and privation she'd been given in return. She rose, pushing aside the chair with a metallic clatter, moving toward the cabinets. "You want to be a master node? You say it wouldn't have happened without you? That's what people like you have said from the beginning of time. Birthrights. Rich fuckers. They take your labor, then your dreams, and then *everything* you are."

Sharma's eyes narrowed. "Then why did you use the memoria, if not for us to be together again?"

"*Together* again? We worked together for *six months*. You're crazy."

And as soon as the words were out of her mouth, Natalie knew she'd said the wrong thing, although she had no idea why. She felt a shudder in the world around her, malignant and sad. "You *don't* remember," Sharma said.

"I don't need to," Natalie said, rounding on Sharma. "There's nothing you can tell me that would change what you've done—to Ash, to us—" *To the Vai*, she wanted to say, but couldn't quite force the words out. "I was there, Reva. I saw what happened in your lab on Tribulation. And you can try to justify that, but I can't. Trust me, I've tried."

She sighed. "Nati—"

"I'm talking," she spat. "And then you used *Twenty-Five* to get back there later and pick up what you left behind. Only we're not that stupid, and we didn't do what you wanted. You don't deserve to even walk this deck. Get rid of it. Stand in the ballroom where you belong."

This caused the doctor to sway where she was, if she could be called a doctor now, wearing the sun and the moon and stars, wearing an entire civilization, the silver chorus of the Vai in their partition swirling around her fingers, bouncing against the walls. "No," she said, quietly. "We're all being used. Sitting in our cesspools of profit and loss, fighting each other, figuring out new ways to destroy each other, when the solution was obvious. My Society reaching out, helping them discover their own power. You know what it's like to be indentured—do you know what it's like to be free?"

For a single, bizarre moment, Natalie did imagine herself as the person she'd wanted to be once upon a time: in heels, in silver tattoos, her chin aloft. The person she might have been, if the dice rolled differently, if she'd been born into Sharma's world. A dragon in a golden cage, handcuffed to a life as strict as an indenture's, thinking she was free.

She breathed out, banishing the thought.

"That's a real nice sales pitch, Sharma. But you don't understand them, and you sure as hell can't make decisions for them."

"And you do?" Her mouth was a sneer.

"Me? I don't need to understand. I'm just a grunt. I get gut feelings. And mine tells me—" She hauled in a breath. Here, at least, her lungs were clear. "That even if I could remember whatever you want me to remember, I wouldn't *want* to."

But Sharma didn't hear that last portion; the doctor-god's attention was already somewhere else, her eyes checking the rafters, her body suddenly straight. *Twenty-Five* flickered out around her in shards of light. And then Natalie heard what the doctor was hearing—a faraway, frighteningly familiar voice whispering in her ear, a rushing that took her head and twisted it back into a slurping—

—I will find you—

She felt like she couldn't breathe. There was a cacophony in her head, a whirling, whistling song that reminded her of night sirens in Albany, of the scent of salt and river garbage, of the geometry of trauma.

"It's Solano, isn't it?"

She nodded. "I've been waiting for him to arrive. Two master nodes cannot occupy the same space. I'll take care of it," Sharma said, and met Natalie's eyes. Natalie heaved out a final, hot breath and shoved herself to her feet, feeling awash with cracking violence.

"I'll help."

"You're on his system. You can't."

"Doc—"

"All you can do is die, and I'm not done with your recode. *Stay.*"

She swept out, toward the party; the massive room felt suddenly claustrophobic, like she were folded in a dollhouse under a massive unblinking eye. It had the tenor of an expectation, an order. But Natalie was on Solano's network, not Sharma's, and Sharma had no power over her.

And she was never one to *stay*, never one to *wait*, not when her life was in danger, so she followed her out, into the blue hallway, watched Sharma's atomic sleeves disappear into the garden, heard the exhalations of people talking. She lay her fingers lightly on the old-fashioned doorknob. Before she could open it herself, the thing swung open.

She saw a gaunt man in a uniform Natalie had never seen before—a frillier, less dirty version of the heavy engineer's apron Len had used on a daily basis. He looked peaked, transparent, wispy at the edges, like he couldn't decide if he existed or not.

"Ms. Sharma," he said. "Congratulations on your elevation. The Solano boy is waiting for you by the ice sculpture."

"I'm not her."

"Enjoy your evening," he said.

Natalie stopped. "Right. This is *her* world, so it's her memory. I get it."

The man simply extended his hand toward the gathering, toward the twinkling lights and the sparkling stars above.

She had no idea what an *elevation* was, or why Sharma would throw a party for it, but as long as the permissions recognized her as valid, she wasn't going to complain. A quick cast of her eyes to the vast, imaginary sky, and the barely there, familiar constellations above, confirmed an initial theory.

"This is what," she said, "Earth?"

"Enjoy your evening," he repeated.

The air outside the building smelled sweet and bright, like she imagined it might in the northern mountains far away from the oily, rising river. Nearby, she saw tables laden with ice sculptures and food—pastries, meat, iced cakes larger than her head. Just beyond the corner, lost to mist, she heard skeins of live music and the rush of feet dancing underneath a gossamer tent. Auroran birthrights loved their expensive affectations, their old-style parties, the sheer wasteful tradition of *crystal* and *metal* and other things that could be used to cut into flesh as easily as mushrooms and vat-meat, the trappings of an Earth that had long since ceased to exist. The ground felt spongy, wet from a recent rain— *God,* Natalie thought, *the* details *of this place.* It must have been a formative memory for Sharma.

The only thing she had to compare to this was an episode of

Alien Attack Squad she'd watched with Len—it had been set at a party like this, actresses dripping with metal and crystal and inlaid diamonds, high heels twirling, skirts swirling, and even that had been less interesting than the pair of engineer's hands that lingered near hers, so close. Too close.

Bells rang somewhere on the breeze. Alarm bells. She stumbled, then saw flashes of her body on the floor of the computer core, seizing, doctors surrounding it—

Stop fucking with my immersion, she wanted to whisper, like this was any normal mission, like she wasn't shaking, like she wasn't scared, like—

—like Solano wasn't sitting *right there.*

She ducked behind a table.

Solano and Sharma sat together in garden chairs at the edge of the party near the sheer white cliffside, an old-style cigarette hanging loose between his fingers. He took a drag and handed it to Sharma. The smoke mingled over their heads in an amiable cloud, like they were friends, like they were—

—*Allies?*

Both of them were wearing vintage clothing that fit in with the scene, gold-trimmed finery that even Natalie's ill-trained eye knew to be years out of date. She imagined that this version of Solano was the man he wanted everyone to see, the man that even a birthright's resources struggled to maintain: a set of chiseled cheekbones over a flat belly and bones that hadn't yet been filled out by the beautiful life. His hair was drawn by a gravcomb in absurd triangular whorls, and his heels shone bright with encrusted diamonds.

Sharma hadn't changed so much as shifted; she looked every inch her age, wrinkles carved into familiar places, and every glistening star on her dress was crammed with Vaisong.

"It makes sense you'd think of this place," Solano said, after a moment's drag on the cigarette. "Our last dance. Our last hurrah."

Sharma frowned. "I conjured this place for my Society. *You* weren't invited."

"But I'm here," Solano said.

"Alas."

He leaned forward. "Did you think I'd just bury your body without looking at it? That was your fatal mistake. Underestimating Auroran R&D."

Sharma dropped the cigarette on the ground, not even bothering to put it out. "If you're pushing for détente by putting on your peacock hat, you've come to the wrong person."

He shrugged. "You have *Vancouver* pinned. It looks like you intend to force Aurora's decision in the matter by trapping its board and suborning its computer core with your operatives. Meanwhile, my Company is adapting faster to the new way than your Society ever could. It's uncouth."

"*Uncouth* is forcing your way into someone else's world."

His eyes flickered to the gem at her throat, rested there, pushed into a dark little grin. "That makes two of us, then."

She tossed her chin back, staring at the fraudulent stars above. She slowly sat up, slowly slid one leg underneath. "This better not be about *me*."

"Just as, for you, it's always been about *me*."

Sharma choked out an incredulous laugh. "That's rich."

"Why else would you pick our elevation party for this little chat?"

Her eyes widened. "Our elevation was thirty years ago. Do you honestly expect me to remember why you're so goddamn prickly about it?"

The CEO sounded incredulous. "You *walked away from me*, Reva. Right over there by the ice sculpture. I offered the best contract you were going to get, and you turned me down, like I was nobody. Like I was worse than nobody. This was the worst night of my life."

Sharma rolled her eyes. "I had bigger dreams than fucking *you*."

"Bigger dreams? Your line was seconded for CEO after mine. What bigger dreams could you get? Our dynasty could have held on to power in Aurora for decades. Instead, you disappear for years and then you come back and contract with that fucker Davin—"

She stared. "Do *not* talk about Davin. Or the boys."

"They're dead. I can say what I like."

"There are more important things than your fucking *ego, Joseph.*"

"No, I understand now. I get it," he said. He rose from his chair, slow and deliberate, then fished a cigarette from his pocket. He flipped it, lighting the filter from inside, and raised it to his lips. "You used them, too. It's all one big game."

"A game." Her voice was angry now. "I don't play games."

Click. Click. Natalie heard the advance of high heels on stone, and she watched him dip his hand, offer the cigarette to Sharma. When she didn't take it, when she touched the sapphire at her neck instead, he grabbed her wrist and hauled her to her feet. Natalie's throat caught in a silenced gasp, and from Sharma's stunned eyes, the way she swayed on her feet, she wasn't the only one so surprised he could do it.

"No games? Let's dance, then."

"You can't," Sharma mumbled. "You can't *touch* me here, not unless I allow it—"

He spun her, stopping her wavering in her steps. His eyes seemed lit from within, and for the first time, Sharma's own light sputtered. "You just don't get it. You think you've been leading the dance this entire time. But in our long dance, I lead. I *always* led."

"You can't touch me," Sharma whispered.

"But I am. I have saved you so many times, Reva. Your lab on Tribulation; who do you think turned a blind eye, when the board would have reported you to the Corporate Alliance? I lost three of my best cruisers to make sure you were saved, and testified that the Vai killed them, when I knew it was *you*."

"Come, now, you earned a tidy profit from that."

He dragged her closer, close enough for his breath to touch Sharma's cheek, and his lips nestled there for a second, and Sharma winced—

"What about the year you infiltrated Bittersweet on the Society's behalf, when you were supposed to be working on *Medellin*? The results that you hid from me—"

"Don't think I didn't find your spy codes, your bugs, your listening ears—did you think that would convince me to come home? That's abuse, Joseph, not love."

"It's self-interest against a corporate enemy. You played a pretty incredible game of chicken, Reva, but it's over now."

Sharma laughed, like broken glass, like cut, razor's-edge glitter, and worked her wrist free, snapping her outstretched fingers protectively over the singing sapphire. "This is *my* world. It's poetry. It's perfect. You have a broken, hacked-together Heart and a bunch of stooges. You can't win."

Natalie tightened, her estimation of the situation turning over on its side. This *was* Sharma's world, wasn't it? Sharma was the Vai master node, its center, its commander? She'd integrated as the Vai master node after tossing out the real one, she'd chased Solano's small fleet to this quiet place in the universe, she had control over the millions of Vai souls and whatever other Sacrament Society reps were uploading, this *was* the doctor's memory—

"You've forgotten," he said. His voice dipped. Became almost kind—an executive's kindness, veiled in lies and chains and expectations. "We've known who you are for a very long time. We've been preparing for this moment."

Her voice dropped. "You stole my life's work."

"We perfected your research." Solano frowned. "That's how it's done, Reva. You taught me that. I gave up a *lot* to get here."

"How dare you. I have given up more than you'll ever *have*," she spat.

"That's true. And I'm sorry."

"How?" spat Sharma.

A shark-like smile spread over Solano's lips. "I really wonder how you've done it, all these years, taking to your own head with a melon baller, dumping it out, shoving it all in again afterward like a puzzle with missing pieces. You're still *you*, Reva, still so recognizably yourself, and it's amazing you didn't drop the ball years ago."

She narrowed her eyes. "And I still haven't."

He paced. "You remember all of this—first-contract night, right down to the flavor of the *amasijos*—but you don't remember that you put a data drive in your pocket before the Heart ruined Tribulation, when you knew you were going to live through Ash Jackson's bloody feint. A doctor found it when she rescued you. You never even thought to look, because your own damned weapon took that memory from you. You got sloppy."

Natalie's fist tightened through this exchange, had made red, smarting half-moons in her palm, had crafted rubber bands of her legs. She tasted a strange electricity in the air, a tangible tang of anticipation, as tart as the too-quick, dragged-out moment before a fistfight. *This is what adrenaline tastes like,* she thought. *I'm going to have to choose,* she thought, *I'm going to have to pick one over the other. Aurora. The Society.*

Cliffside, Reva started to shake, and she raised her hands, turning them over and over again, staring at her nails, her fingers, her palms. "There are no blanks. I am the master node."

He took two small steps toward her, his face smug. "Certainly you know how memory *works*, Reva. How it fills in the blanks with fiction to make your universe make sense. Details. Entire days. The space inside the blink of your eyelids."

Natalie felt a cold wind behind her, blowing in from the building behind her, and she took her eyes off the altercation long enough to see that they had company. People—*no,* she thought, *not people, ghosts, almost people*—pouring into the hallway, passing behind the windows, filing past.

Some were people she knew, people from Europa and *Vancouver.* They had the short hair of indentures, the same skinny exhaustion Natalie had seen on her own frame. But the men were drawn wrong, the women sketched off-kilter; their eyes were too big in some cases, or their waists were twisted, or their feet dragged, like physics no longer mattered—people rendered by an alien engine that couldn't quite understand them, adulterated, degraded, walking down a large staircase leading to the city below.

And the city—

—it had looked normal before, like Earth, like Albany and the Hudson basin, all jagged and ragged and flooded and dead. But she could now see buildings that could only be real in the imagination, or perhaps, in the imagination of a Vai: a thousand stories tall, wild with protrusions, with tentacles, with bridges and bindings and fantastical twisted towers winding through needless streets, reaching up to the sky, dancing out into endless silver forests, proliferating like algae on a broken ocean: the Vai aesthetic, the Vai framework, forced into human restrictions.

For the first time Natalie had ever seen, Sharma looked scared. She clutched at the sapphire. It glowed, and silver light began to pour through it, through her fingers, though they struggled to prevent it, struggled to cover it—

"You didn't even *ask,* did you?" she hissed. "At least with the Sacrament Society, they consented."

"They have contracts. As for your Society—"

"We worked for it—but look at them, Joseph. They don't know where they are. They're lost, they'll be of no use to you—"

"I don't need their *souls*."

Reva breathed in, shuddering. "That's sick."

"But that's the problem with ascending to alien godhood, Reva," Solano said. "Makes it a bit hard to sweat the details back home, doesn't it, when you're off piloting an alien fleet or whatever. *My* alien fleet."

"I won't let you do this," Sharma said.

"You already have."

Natalie's hand was wrapped against the table leg, and for a moment she wondered if the pain she felt was *expectation*, was *memory*. How had she not seen that there was more to this than the proxy rig, that *Vancouver* had been working on small puzzle pieces to fit into a larger picture? Oh, she'd been covering up her complicated feelings, trying to stay drunk enough or at work enough to forget about Ash and what she'd done in the bugout bay.

And she should have realized what the proxy rig was doing when she'd been on Bittersweet, that it wasn't just cameras and controls—that her *mind* had been on the planet, that she'd triggered that weapon—and all the while, Solano had been sewing up indentures' minds through Ingest and delivering them straight to hell, tattoos only, no memory device needed.

He'd just needed nanotech to move his own Heart from a dream to reality, to upload human mind after human mind. He'd needed Kate. When Kate was gone, used up, they'd exercise their right on the memory device, they'd stick her in. And then—who? Ward? Others? A grand corporate machine, gobbling up bodies and brains—

Ingest, she thought. *It was right there. Right there in the damn word.*

"I'll fight you," Sharma whispered.

"Oh, fight. Fight all you want, darling." He lifted his index finger and curled it around the sapphire. "I think this is going to look good on me."

Sharma tried to punch him.

From her hiding spot, wincing, Natalie saw Sharma's arm twitch, saw her cast it violently toward him, saw it catch an inch from his face—and then saw her go still, as if she could not move. Natalie felt the following tectonic howl in her bones; the people on the staircase paused, looked up with their scared clearwater eyes. And Sharma had enslaved the Vai, made them into a bauble for her own unknown task, but this—

—*Sharma* had the code she needed to stop this. She couldn't let the doctor die. But Sharma wasn't a soldier. She couldn't protect herself.

Natalie *was*.

Each step toward Sharma and Solano felt like fire, like thick oil at her ankles and fingers. They both saw her immediately—it made sense, if they were all code.

"Remind me to ask Aulander to chain you to the medbay," he said.

Sharma stared at her, and Natalie had never seen anything like it, never seen that kind of fear. "Natalie, *no, run*—"

Natalie tried to move her feet, but she couldn't, she couldn't even wiggle her toes, but the same affliction that kept Sharma a statue held on to her as well. Her eyes flickered over to Reva. Frying pan or fire, devil or demon, the indenture's choice. She cleared her throat, going for the confidence she did not feel.

"Step back," she said.

Solano considered her for a moment. "You're in the direct-jack rig near Ingest. You think you're breathing. You think you're breathing in here because you think all of this"—he gulped in a long, heaving breath, then started laughing—"is air. It's not."

Fluid filled her lungs, and this time, it felt worse than Tribulation, than a desert, than acid. She was drowning. Seconds later it felt like there hadn't even been any *air* around to begin with. She wanted to fight it, but her body couldn't move. She couldn't even claw at her throat, couldn't even cry out, and as quickly as it began, what was left of the fight was over. Even now, her surroundings were changing in small, almost imperceptible ways, from Sharma's memories to Solano's—the night darkened around them, the murals on the stone walls grew brighter, the golden constellations in the halls bloomed and branched like metal flowers and chains. Even the air smelled different, like burned coffee, like the bruised petals of broken flowers.

A light flickered in Solano's eyes. "Stop *trying*. It's over."

"The Society will come for you. It will never be over." Sharma's chest forced breath in and out. "And if you ever knew anything about me, you would know that."

"A few scientists? I'm not worried."

"You have no idea."

"Goodbye, Reva," Solano said.

"Natalie, you need to know something, you need to know—" Sharma said, gasping, but she wasn't able to finish; Solano's fingers twisted in the air, and she clawed at her throat. Her hair had started to go brilliant with golden light, and her hands started to glow with an incandescent purple Heartlight so bright and heavy that even Natalie could feel its power.

And she felt its intention in the air, clear as a kinetic whining into kill mode; her body was subject to it, like gravity, like the wind, like love. Solano's own hands slipped razor-sharp into the wind, his own intentions clear.

"You *forgot me,* Reva," he said.

Solano closed his fist.

It wasn't even a fight. It was over in seconds like any effective fight, swirling in sheer light, in blacks and purples and silvers. Sharma fell to the floor like a wadded tissue, and Solano squatted next to her body, his hands searching, a hunter's knowledge of the liver, the carotid, the heart. He popped off her rings, one by one, loosened the gems, each beautiful singing treasure on her god's gown, and devoured them, the soft silver song, *death-brother*, gulped into silence in his stomach.

Natalie struggled, her heart beating so hard she thought it might burst; he noticed, walked over, slid his large, blood-silvered hand around her wrist, and pulled her closer. She felt hot breath in her ear, and then she was in so much pain she couldn't even wince.

"Are you going to kill me, too?" she said.

"Of course not," he responded, and the words came out like light, scrambled around her wrists and feet, tied her like stone to the ground upon which she lay, tilted her own body to face the sky, the stars, the amber sunset, the midnight-blue sky, the trac- eries of home. "You have a contract to sign."

She felt sick. "You can't expect me to be your Defender now. To be a *birthright*."

"My dear," the CEO said, "you don't really have any other choice."

Solano looked back at Sharma—an engineer checking his work—then turned, sweeping out of the party with the gravitas of a chief executive who had places to be, of a master node who knew his secondaries could make no moves without his express authorization. His boots rang against the stones as the ghosts walked endlessly to the city below.

She stared at Sharma's body. It was like so many other bod- ies she'd seen, the face relaxed beyond relaxation, less a husk than a stone. She stared at it long enough that she expected it to evaporate, to slip away like the ghosts into the city below. But this was Solano's world now, and in Solano's world, dead meant dead.

Remember like the Vai remember.

She wasn't exactly sure what kind of code made up a Vai memory, what kind of brilliant wild magic, but she knew exactly how Vai consciousness was passed between Vai and human in any world. She grabbed a knife off the buffet table and crawled toward Sharma's body. She was getting the practice of this—the flip of the hilt into her hand, the quick painful parting of skin on living soldier and dead scientist. The place might be almost entirely a metaphor, but she doubted Solano knew about *this*.

The older woman was fading at the edges. She grabbed the dead arm, pumped it for blood, gasped as Sharma's cooling blood crossed the border of her own skin. It was almost completely silver, almost completely gone to the nanotech, and full of slivering mysteries, full of whispering ghosts, and a memory that hit her in the face like a brick in the hand of a terrible god.

She could see herself from the outside: her silver capillaries, her beating heart, her machine at work, her *system*. There was a vine at her heart, growing dark and dismal around her spine, its roots in her heart and her mind. It glistened, too, almost as if it were an experiment in Tribulation's dark cathedral, some sick experiment wired into the heart of humanity.

At the same time, Natalie could see Ashlan Jackson in a small, quiet room on *Twenty-Five,* tied in golden chains, goose bumps on bare arms. She could see a small child running up State Street on a too-bright, choking-hot Albany afternoon. She could see a memory stored within a memory, could see the half-finished code Sharma had promised her, the code to open the gate for her to walk through.

She reached out to touch it—and the world shook inside her like a parting of lips and took a very long breath. She felt her heartbeat loud in her ears, echoing in her chest, her immersion skipping for a moment, hearing Ward's voice, smelling an acrid and smoky somnolence—

—and she tumbled back onto half-drowned State Street.

24

Natalie was no longer in her own body.

She'd become a small child for some reason, all limbs and legs and arms and skinny wild energy, fed on vat rations and code. She barely remembered what it had been like to be this person, this wild creature who wasn't aware of the vast internecine battles over which faction was responsible for the decomposing post-oligarchic coast and its desperate hangers-on, for whom the heat of the winter had always been normal and the northern mountains almost completely brown.

None of that was as real as the summer outside, as the rattle of shoes on the road, of games on the plaza, of shooting lessons with her father from the top of the old Tower One, staring down on the grand white plaza Verdict held by its fingernails at the center of the city. On the Egg that held the leader that kept them safe, the ancient rowhouses ripped open like broken teeth, and the spindly new towers rising from the drowned downtown.

She wondered why she wasn't seeing Sharma's memory.

Why she was seeing *her own*.

The memory had the juddering shiver of dream-logic, moving from one important moment to the next, crushing the unnecessary lagniappes between. This particular remembrance was certainly one of the many forgotten afternoons, with the child playing with the coding toys in the corner of her family's fourteenth-floor lab and living space, the stink of allspice and rot slipping through a cracked window. One moment her father Xie was standing at the door, and the next he stood, fingering the grip of his holstered gun, in front of her mother's desk.

Her mother's desk—

A woman sat behind the white expanse. Natalie may not have known her smooth, young face, but she knew it was her mother with the barrelling certainty of the very young. Her mother was bathed in the light of old interfaces, wires loose and twisted at her feet, surrounded by pieces of glass and light and eviscerated machinery. At work, like she always was.

The air between her parents had decayed to poison, even now, and even a child as innocent as Natalie could taste it.

Natalie *remembered*.

"You're really going to do it," he said.

"I told you from the very beginning that I wasn't going to stay with Verdict for more than five years. I told you the night we met." Her mother bent over a set of half-finished server cards, holding a soldering gun. Sparks flew, illuminating her face. She was young, with only the hint of a crease at the corner of her mouth.

"I thought, after the baby—"

Her mother lifted her eyes from her work, lifting the goggles slightly. "The reprocontrol failed. I *told* you the deal when you pressed me to go forward with this."

"And I told you where I stand."

She flipped down her protective goggles again. "Then it's settled."

Xie's body tightened like a bomb about to explode. "You won't stay even for her? You're really going to do it? The long walk to the harbor? Stealing our life's work for a fucking *contract*, Iris? What's so important on the other side of *five fucking years* that you'd miss her grow up?"

Her mother's eyes flickered over to where the child sat, controller in hand. "For one, my name isn't Iris."

The world crackled. Re-rendered. Shock, as only a child could feel it. "What?" Xie whispers.

"It's Reva," she said.

Natalie went numb all at once; it exploded in her chest and blasted like a rocket to her fingers. Her ears rang, and for a moment she lost track of the conversation.

No, she thought. *It can't be*.

But the memory jumped forward again, until the memory-mother finished whatever it was she had come to do. She lifted the finished chip in the air, letting it catch the light, then folded it in a cloth, which she put in a bag by the window. Natalie could see her surgeon's control, the tilt of her refined fingers, even two decades younger, as familiar as Len's smile. "Don't be sad. I'm still leaving you the plans."

Xie moved to block the door. The gun was in his hand. It gleamed like the crescent moon. "How much have you stolen from us?"

Reva sighed. "You'd understand, if I could take you with me. If I could show you why."

"I wouldn't go for all the money in the world." His hand made a fist, then released it. "And if you think you're taking Nati—"

"I'm not taking Nati. I can't explain her. It puts everything I've done up to this point in jeopardy." Sharma yanked up the bag and moved toward the door.

He flashed the gun again. "Iris, I told you a long time ago that I'd never let a Verdict secret fall into corporate hands."

"You're not going to *shoot* me in front of Nati."

The gun shook in her father's hand. "She's young enough that she won't remember."

"Verdict's memory technology will help people, Xie."

"It's not meant for you!"

Reva frowned. "You're not doing anything with it!"

"We're perfecting it!" He spat the words like nails. "You

corpses, you don't understand that sometimes you do something just because it's beautiful! Because it's kind! Because it helps other people! For you, everything's exploitable, everything's on sale, even me, even *her*—"

And with those words, Natalie-the-child realized that this fight wasn't the same as the others, that something jagged and inevitable was coming over the horizon to gobble up her entire world. Her folded, gangly legs clambered up in a frightened second, and the dread made her entire little body shake with fear. She rushed across the room, tumbled into her mother's unwilling, clammy hands. Everything was wrong. Her mother's back was too straight. Her smile was made of tight, tilted lips and hidden teeth. She held the hug, shaky and strong, then pushed the child away with a soft palm to her sternum.

"Don't go," the child wailed.

"I have to, baby," her mother said. "I can't take you back with me. You're not a part of the line. You'll be better off here. You'll understand, someday. When you're older."

"Don't want to be older."

The child struggled for another hug, and the mother's hands clamped on her shoulders, keeping her from moving. She made a sad half attempt at a smile. "Yes, you do. And someday, you'll realize what *really* matters and take the long walk, just like me."

"Jesus," Xie whispered, barely holding himself up in the doorjamb. He folded. Stepped aside. It was only now, seeing all of this as an adult, that Natalie heard the anguish in it. "All right. Just stop. Just *go.*"

Was this what ruined him, Natalie wondered, *this, Reva's receding back and the secrets she stole?*

Mama doesn't love me, the child thought, and her world tilted to the side and shattered. The young Sharma rose, hoisted her bag, and headed for the staircase outside. Natalie wanted to tell her to *stop,* that *everything from here will be death and violence and terror,* but this was just a memory, a record of old wounds, unchangeable as drought. The child tried to pass her father and run, but he grabbed her wrist and dragged her back. "Don't, baby," he said. "Forget her."

Sharma stopped where she was. "Stop crying, Nati," she snapped, staring straight ahead. Her eyes filled with water, but she blinked it away. "Where I'm from, people don't cry."

And then she was gone, and Xie was dragging the child back into the room and Natalie could do nothing but watch from inside that flailing, feeling body, her little animal heart pounding, fighting her lockjaw brain. Like the logic of a dream, Natalie found herself in her adult body, the door clicked closed, and she was standing in the stairwell. She understood now, in some sort of stabbing, inchoate way, the blank space inside her body.

This time, she followed Sharma.

The two of them clattered down the stairs of the old white tower out into the plaza, past the ancient statues and white marble to State Street and the crumbling remains of a cathedral made of red sandstone. Only this time it was midnight and dark and gleaming, the moon bright on the pavement, the air full of ozone, the road a river. Sharma walked down the hill, wearing her *Twenty-Five* outfit now, a blue shirt and pants and a white jacket. Blue-feathered birds wheeled overhead, *birds,* not that Natalie had ever seen a *real bird.*

She caught up, breathing heavy—

"You didn't remember me," Natalie said. "On *Twenty-Five.* Over six months, at *least* two meals a day, and not even once—"

The dream-Sharma closed her fist on the bag she stole from Tower One. Tight. Her heels echoed against the plasteel and brick edges of the grand walls of the plaza and the crumbling sandstone cathedral to her right. Natalie hadn't realized until now how much the ancient, broken space reminded her of the lab under Tribulation. "When she realized her experiments with

the Heart were erasing her memories, she wrote code to stop
it. It might have been too late by then. She only remembered a
month ago—through the memories Ash unearthed in your mind
during the end of the battle."

"How the fuck did she think I would be up for reconciliation,
knowing what she did to my father and me?"

Sharma shrugged. "I don't know. She is dead. I can only interact with *your* memory now. With you."

"So she honestly didn't know."

"I am unsure. The code she wrote in the last moments of
her life has no answer to that question. Instead, it was meant to
give you a defense against Joseph Solano. Whatever you saw up
there"—the Sharma-thing's eyes flickered up to the tower, the
dark sky above—"was your memoria's response to that request."

"That doesn't make any sense. I don't understand how remembering this would do anything more than—" She didn't finish
the sentence, instead using the moment to shove down a lump in
her throat. *Crying. Crying was shameful.* "And her other family?
The real one, the one in the Sharma line? There were pictures
on Tribulation. They existed, right?"

"They did. They were on Gethsemane when the Vai arrived."

Natalie felt a tight little curl of ghastly satisfaction. "Where
they died."

"Except for the granddaughter, who was at boardschool. She
perished in a completely unrelated accident. Reva mourned, I
suppose. In her way. I know she often blamed Solano for many
things. She believed that if he hadn't reacted that badly to her
request to pursue her own dreams, she would have become
CEO. She had a lot of regrets." The Sharma-thing turned away
from her, staring down the long, laboring hill to the water below,
the improvised, guttering harbor that rose around the spires of
crumbling office buildings.

"Are you her ghost?"

The shade shrugged. It had begun to rain again, misting slightly against her cheek. "Her unsorted notes, mostly."

"I—" Natalie rubbed her eyes. "She left us, she left them, and she reaches out to me? What changed?"

"We can't explain the darkest parts of the human connection," said the ghost. "It's possible that people can change."

"Fuck that."

"*She* thought so."

Natalie's tone was acid. "Was it in her notes?"

"She certainly tried to change. She was different from the others in her class at medical school—she expressed her discomfort with the practice of using indentures for experimentation many times—"

"Which is rich, considering that her Society was so into human sacrifice—"

The doctor tipped her chin toward the sky, then reached inside her jacket, removing a cigarette, of all things. She turned the front and it lit; Natalie recognized the old, unbelievable scent of tobacco. *What a world,* she thought, remembering the searing pain of her own lung reconstruction, *where people can afford to just fuck up their lungs like that because they can just get it fixed.*

"That would come later," the ghost said, exhaling again. Her heels *click clacked* against the asphalt. "After Gethsemane. After things got bad. It's funny, really. She couldn't crack the secret of immortality until she got her hands on Vai bodies and discovered how they lived, but by then, everything she loved was dead. Tragic."

"I'm so sad," spat Natalie.

The ghost stopped where the shops ceded to skyscrapers, where the river was slowly rising into the broken streets. The smell of rot and mold was strong here, of dead fish and garbage in the water. She looked wistful. "I don't think so."

Natalie stopped. The wind kicked up around her, bringing in stinging sand from the uplands deserts. "You agree—God, of course you agree, you're her fucking *notes*." She breathed out, rubbing her temples. "I'm not going to argue with a fucking notepad."

"That's probably wise. It's almost morning. You probably have time for one or two more questions before they wake you."

And Natalie *had* questions—so many, about the braingear Sharma had stolen, about how the nanotech was developed in the first place, about how the tattoos worked, about how Sharma linked the Vai weaponry into her memoria, about how she discovered she could upload and supplant the master node, about all her years of quiet, heads-down labor in the service of her secrets. She could have, but her mouth was stuffed with a far more important mystery.

"How did *I* not remember, if it wasn't actually taken by the Heart?"

The ghost took one more long drag and exhaled a gray cloud of smoke that spun in the streetlights. "The human brain is a marvelous organ. Sharma studied it intently. Some people live their trauma in remarkable detail every day until they die. Others block it out so completely they might have had it ripped out by a molecular." She offered Natalie the cigarette. "But it's always waiting for you. Always there. She knew that intimately."

Natalie took the cigarette. Spun it in her fingers. She'd never held something so expensive. She lifted it to her lips and took a small huff. Her mind filled with thoughts of dead forests and dried farms. The bright, peaceful songs of undead birds.

"I was happy before I forgot," she said.

"Were you? Really?"

She eyed the ghost. "Oh, great, now the notepad's a therapist."

"I'm only saying that she went ahead despite it all."

"Is that your advice?"

"Heavens, no. I'm not coded to give you *advice*. I'm coded to

give you *this*." The ghost reached into her jacket, and then offered an old-style red access card, the kind that used to be used
in the Verdict building. It had been scrawled over with black
marker in C-kalibre, the coding language used by most Auroran
systems.

"What's this?"

"Partition access," she said. "It's what Sharma wanted you to
have. You'll be able to use it to get back into the Vaispace through
Solano's device when you're ready, then back out without him being able to control you. You'll get one shot, because his secondaries will lock up the exits when they figure out what you've done.
This access will lead you to Ashlan. Sharma meant to save her,
not lock her up. She was going to use it herself, but you can't help
her now. *You* need a body to return to."

Natalie licked her lips. "And when I wake up, it'll still be
with me?"

"It's lodged in your memoria. It'll auto-activate the next time
you go in. You'll know it when you see it."

"Like the trauma. Ha."

"Pretty much."

Natalie caught the morning chill with one last, long breath,
then tossed the cigarette into a puddle. Had this end always
been waiting for her? Her mother took the long walk not once
but twice—away from Verdict, then away from *Twenty-Five*.
Natalie had taken the same two walks, and neither of them had
escaped the pain that held them down. Natalie was more like
Sharma than she thought she was, more like her than she wanted
to be. And she'd spent her life running away—

—yet everything had just led her back here, to her past, as the
sun slowly crept over the horizon.

Maybe there's a long walk back.

"I know what I'm up against now," she said, watching the aching edge of the morning light up her ghost-mother's chin. "It'll

be different this time. Solano's no alien. He's no god. He's just a man." She tipped her chin toward the sky, and took one long, last drag of the dead world. "And you can kill a man."

Natalie shivered in the cold, feeling reborn.

The doctor smiled, with teeth too straight and white to have ever lived on Earth. "That's my girl," she said, and—

—and Natalie felt the pop of instruments being removed from her body, the crashing ocean of the reintegration drugs, and the flickering of the lights of the logic tower, and the dragging scream of reality as someone brought her back to *Vancouver.*

25

Natalie emerged from Ingest with a tearing, ripstop headache, famished and shaking. Her body ached. She felt overwhelmed with grief over a tower and the click of a shut door and a figure receding down a staircase, and hidden anger hit her like an avalanche. She tasted blood and smoke, followed by a caustic black stink she recognized from the last time she'd been in the same room as melting plasteel. *Burning plasteel* meant *bulkheads melting,* or the computer core frying—whatever it was, she had to *get out.*

But she couldn't move. Her limbs felt bruised and leaden, and her skin hung loose and wrong on her bones. She smelled something base and organic, something just around the corner from dirt and sweat and rot. She didn't have time to wonder what it was before the intravenous line was pulled from her skull with a bloody pop.

Ward appeared nearby, ripping the haptics from her fingers and toes. His jacket lay akimbo on his shoulders, the gravving on his hair unspooling, sweat slicking his temples. She felt her heart constrict.

"There's something I have to tell you," she said. "You have to disconnect the captain, get her out of here—"

He cut her off. "Stop writhing. Unless you want brain spatter on the floor."

"And then I need to get to a shuttle," she said. Her throat felt sliced by glass, and she grasped at her neck with one newly freed hand. There was something she needed to do *right fucking now,* a thought that was evaporating like a dream after waking. "I can beat him, Ward. I—I have an idea. I forgot. We can make him forget. Them. We can—"

Words were too slow. She needed to be up and moving fifteen seconds ago, but she was half-blind, and the master node still hadn't shown up, and had she lost him in the upload? Panic spiked. *Where are you?* she thought. *I think I can do it—I can get you back to your ship, we can use the Heart, you can leave with your people—*

And she felt the master node's sudden hot breath in her ear. *And what would happen to you?*

I'd—She paused. *I'd forget, of course.*

Would you forget me?

She opened her mouth to answer, and the only thing that came out was an overwhelmed howl.

Ward fumbled at the last few proxy connections with the technique of a frightened raccoon. "You're overclocking. Calm down."

"I thought you left," she whispered.

"I did leave. You need to *calm down.* You can't beat him. Nobody can beat him now."

"I tell you, I can."

His shoulders tightened, and he grabbed her wrist. She felt his perfect crescent nails skimming the clotting wound there, and winced. "I'm not doing anything for you. Not anymore. I'm in a stupid place right now with Mr. Solano, and it is literally *your entire fault.* You *knew* the whole time that I was dying. You knew he had a cure. You could have told me that back in my room, before you fucked me, before you sent me away, but you needed something out of me. I should have kept my boundaries exactly where they were and not let you in."

"Emerson—"

But he was already pulling away, looking up at someone else, hiding her open eyes with his skinny torso. "She's overclocking for sure."

The realization came too late: there had been more than one pair of hands.

Ward wasn't alone.

She went limp, hoping it wasn't too late to salvage the situation. She'd never heard overclocking applied to a brain before, but knowing what she knew now about what had brought her to this moment, it made a sick sort of sense. Of course her brain was doing too much. She'd been uploaded to an alien world through a piece of technology that, by all rights, shouldn't exist, and forced to remember a trauma that she'd voluntarily forgotten. Her brain was so slow, so slow, like a starship burning itself blind to escape the accretion disk of a black hole.

She felt the master node nearby and the warmth of his not-body kneeling close. *You can get me back in.*

To a partition.

An imperceptible nod. *The long walk. A lie.*

Natalie ached. *What?* She hauled in a breath, and the pain, the *pain. I'm not lying about this.*

The long walk never ends.

She couldn't see him—couldn't see anything, really—through her blurred vision, through the heat bath of the computer core, a sudden and soiled midsummer afternoon.

It did. A long time ago. Fuck. Tears. *It's the last walk you take in the city when you're heading to list up with the corporations, and the indenture afterward. It ends.*

It hasn't for you, the master node said, retreating slightly. *And it does not matter. If I take my fleet and my people and I leave, you'll pursue us to the end of time. The long walk never ends.*

There are people who want peace, she said. *I'm one of them now. You see that people can change.*

Yes, said the master node.

His fingers danced against her cheek.

But humans lie.

Someone else was talking now, someone bombastic and familiar. The figure was too round to be Ward, the hair too intricately piled in curls too delicate to accomplish on one's own. His ring-laden fingers twirled a bloody rag. "Just give me the needle, Mr. Ward. We don't have time to call the tattooist. She'll get a couple ragged lines and be happy with it."

"Yes, sir," said another voice. Ascanio, hanging around somewhere out of sight, like she always did.

The man with the rag tossed it at her, grazing her open mouth. She smelled iron and perfume before it slipped off her face and fell to the floor. She kept silent, her eyes closed. No need to let the others know she was awake before she knew more about the situation.

"I thought this rig was ready to go," he said.

"It is, sir," Ward said, faint and uncertain.

The man spoke with a disappointed, sour edge. "She's unresponsive."

"Sir, she's just—"

"I do not wish to be *unresponsive,* Mr. Ward."

She slit her eyes. Golden tattoos climbed his neck, shimmering in the keen lab light like they were alive. In his right hand was the Company key, embedded in the large ring he was always wearing. *Ah,* she thought, *yes.*

"I'll show you *responsive* when I get out of here," she said, when her tongue returned to her. "*Joseph.*"

His first name. Like he was an indenture.

Just to watch him squirm.

It was as if she could truly see Solano for the first time. All of the things that had made Joseph Solano imposing—the historical function of his hairstyle, the thick lines of his eyeshadow, the dramatic way he was lit for announcements, his thick vein-blue manicure—melted away at her disrespectful address, leaving only the shine of greed in his brown eyes.

"Mr. Ward," he said, and turned toward the younger man. Her ex shifted from his left foot to his right like a walking prevarication. "Suggestions?"

Ward stammered. "We can—ah, we can run some cables to the bridge and hook her body in directly, if you're really concerned about having both her and Ingest in the same room."

"Make it happen," he said, wringing the rag around his silver-flecked fingers. Natalie noticed some movement at the back of the room; a group of stone-still indentures moved immediately toward the door. "Damn. We were doing it all wrong before."

Natalie stared at Ward, trying to communicate her true feelings through eyes gone blade-hard. *You asshole. You heel-licker. You total fucking sociopath.* It made her feel better to go through the entire library of creative invectives in her head as she forced her fingers back into her skin, as she recovered her strength. And even those felt wrong, stretched and bruised, like her body wasn't even hers. Like it hadn't been for some time.

"Ah, um. To a point, sir," Ward said. "If you want to keep the wetworks functioning, it seems to me that we should install an advanced life-support system. More than just the improvised versions we have now. The Vai don't honestly *care* about their wetworks, and obviously, neither did Dr. Sharma or the Society, so one example isn't enough. If we want to preserve that aspect of, um—*us*—we need better aftercare ideas. Which won't happen in the twenty minutes you've given us."

"Twenty minutes is what you have. The ships are on their way."

Ward shifted from foot to foot. "I think it would be to Aurora's disadvantage to lose you permanently because of shoddy implementation."

Solano stared at him. "Are you saying you're going to do a subpar job, Mr. Ward?"

"N-no, sir—"

"There you go, then." With that, the CEO had switched his gaze to Natalie, crossing his arms as if he weren't even listening to Ward. Natalie felt increasingly filthy as he *looked* at her, as he *examined* her, like a doll or a broken pod. She tried to pick herself up, but her limbs were sloughed and leaden. She was no longer tied down, but without luck and a shot of adrenaline, she wasn't going anywhere. *Fuckers,* she thought. *Where the hell is the master node?*

"So, what did you think of the party?" Solano asked. "The city?"

"Trash," she croaked.

"It wasn't quite like I remembered."

"Nothing ever is."

He chuckled. "They never tell you the truth," he said. "They never tell you that's as good as it gets." He picked up a squat syringe of a sort that Natalie barely recognized, needle-sharp and golden. He slipped out a canister, turned to Kate—unconscious now, her head lolling as far as the cords wrapped around it would let her—and, like filling water from a spigot, squeezed out a mouthful of red-gold blood, slipping it back into the device like a magazine into a gun grip.

"You can't," she said. "I'm a citizen. I can refuse medical treatment—"

He laughed. "This isn't medical treatment. It's proprietary technology needed to fly Auroran ships. You'll find that the only people able to refuse are those of us who have truly earned it." He tipped the syringe down to her arm.

She squirmed. "You gonna tell me how you recoded Sharma's nanotech?"

Solano turned away from her, his golden tattoos catching in the light, at his neck, at his fingers, shimmering underneath his fingernails. His aides moved around him like pale crows. "How does anyone do anything in this world? Spies, a shitload of resources, and a bunch of really smart scientists."

"Oh, my God, you think the superhaptics you built in a month on a dead woman's blood are—are going to stand against her work of *twenty years*?"

"Aurora builds to win," he said, and snapped his fingers.

Cit seccers stepped forward, taking the syringe out of Solano's hand. The contents glittered cash-gold, and the heat of the room pressed in on her bare arms. She sucked air into her lungs, seeking out Ward. He stood in the back, his chest stirring shallowly, his entire body saying *don't move, don't move, they can't notice you if you don't move.*

"Em," she said, feeling the prick of the needle, the warmth of the silent gold, the sob of the master node hidden somewhere— *how would this affect him? Is he dying? Shit*—"You know what this is, Em. Ingest. The superhaptics. He's never going to give you a cure. He's going to line you up for *this* as soon as I die. You're next up. Em—he's going to control everything—"

Ward looked away.

Solano stepped forward. Seemed to consider this. The smell of blood soaked the air between them. "You're not going to die. I'm not a monster, Natalie."

"No. You're an *executive*."

"You say that like it's the same thing."

"Isn't it?"

The silver had felt like an invader, the master node like a thief in the night. Solano had stolen from her, then tossed in the match to burn the house down. "You need us," he said, watching her, as if he could see the gold rush through her body, pump through her heart, convert the walls of her capillaries.

"People need freedom."

"Freedom is starvation. Freedom is constant war. I know this *intimately*. I haven't made a single decision for myself since I walked out of that garden party." He snapped at someone in the background. "There are so many ways to starve."

"You always looked happy from where I stood."

"So did you." His mouth curved into a smile. "You liked your compartment. You liked our praise. You worked hard for that praise. You cleaned the toilet, puffed the pillows, stocked drinks in the cooler for when Mr. Ward came over. You were proud and happy."

Happy. Had she been happy? Didn't she love the white walls, the schedule, the booth in the lounge, the way she'd open her arms against the leather back, opening her chest to the thrill of alcohol in the air, the feeling of a citizen's clothing on her skin? Hadn't she been happy? Hadn't she been—

—*so fucking happy* she'd cry, that her sheets would be drenched in sweat every morning, that she'd vomit from the stress of going from taking orders from genial Kate Keller to running a department of people who'd rather stab her in the back than listen. So fucking happy that she'd walked straight into an enemy camp and vaporized people just like her, citizens and indentures who had the fucking temerity to have signed with another company in their search for comfort, and a better life. *So fucking happy* that she'd built the framework that made it happen, hadn't even questioned it.

Not your fault, she wanted to remind herself.

Even though it was.

"I was happy," she lied.

He swept his arm to the right. "Mining. *Janitorial.* It's all such a terrible waste. So the indentured body will work in the world, doing exactly what we need it to do, while the mind lives in the city, messing around or doing crafts or whatever you'd like to do. There'll be computational work, of course—"

"And I suppose we're supposed to be eternally grateful."

"But isn't this what your sort wanted, back in Verdict?" He peered at her. "An equal world, where everyone can live as beautifully, as grand as any executive? You can have that now." He paused. Raised his voice. "You can all have it. All of you."

"It won't be real."

He turned, adjusting his coat as he walked out of the room. "After a few days, my dear, you won't care. Have her up on the bridge in ten minutes, please."

She cast a glance around at the room as the door shivered closed. He'd left behind four guards, burly men she could probably take in a fight one-on-one, but not all four at once, and certainly not with boltguns. Ward looked away, down at his drawer. Ascanio motored away toward storage, as if she could remove herself from her complicity in this bullshit simply by looking elsewhere.

Kate unconscious—

Her brain threw out plans. This wasn't over. If she could get a boltgun from one of the guards, she could get out of here—

Node, she whispered. *Get the fuck up. Make yourself useful for once. I'm about to punch some assholes in the face and I need you to watch out for me so we don't die.*

I'm running simulations.
The master node's shoulders shuddered.
For when we get back inside.

When I figure out how to beat him.
How much time it'll take to reintegrate.
If I can reintegrate.

Well, *that's just stupid of you to say. Of course you can.*

I've been alone, he said.
I would be coming back from the dead.
I would not be the same person.

She made a fist, stared at the roaming cords in the ceiling, at the familiar breadth of server and interface and the unfamiliar curve of Vai cord. *Of course it's possible. I'm doing it.*

I'm not the same. I have limits.

Don't tell Solano that. You know, she said, after a long moment. *I really doubt they'd use their boltguns in here. These assholes are cits, but this equipment isn't easily replaceable. As long as I keep them away from Kate . . .*

She heard a deep sigh.
I'll do what I can.

Natalie groaned. Tightened every part of the body that could—arms, legs, cold heart—and grabbed the sides of the gurney, swinging her feet around to the floor with what little control was left to her. The guards approached immediately. The master node fed her an attack plan, and Natalie made short work of the first two. The remaining man had the advantage of height but, by then, Natalie had the advantage of pure rage. Her fist came into contact with the man's jaw, and he staggered back.

She pushed forward through the jagged stiffness that was left, advancing—

And then she felt the rattle of a boltgun, took the discharge of a stun-shot impact under her right shoulder, heard the crack of her lowest rib. She stumbled back against the gurney, her muscles bowing out, her breath seizing, dragging herself up to turn and face the shooter. A guard neither she nor the master node had seen emerged from behind a logic tower, and she swept up the first guard's lost boltgun with her left hand, shooting him in the head. He sagged back, still breathing. *Low setting. Probably some brain damage.*

He deserved it.

She waved the boltgun and stumbled back into the logic tower where Kate resided, using it to keep her more upright than she felt she could be. She hadn't expected Ward to help her, or Ascanio, but they were *cowering* behind an interface, and somehow that made it worse.

"Come on, you two," she screamed. "Help."

Ascanio pushed up with two hands. She was wearing a dark blue suit with different cit tags. *Yet another promotion for those who kiss ass.* "You don't know," she said. "They—they are. You—you don't know. Any damage you do to yourself right now is permanent. You won't heal. You're too far gone. Just stop. S-stop."

"Too far what—"

"Look at yourself."

And she did. The gray pallor, the failing eyesight, she was just tired—"I'm fine."

"No," she said, quietly. "Really look."

Ward turned away.

And she knew she shouldn't, but the aching discomfiture, the feeling that something was terribly wrong, just increased, and this time she took it all in for what it truly was—the slight stinking edge, the tightness in her joints, the graying in her hands. *The wetworks,* Ward had said. *Her* wetworks. She'd seen this before, at the end of the battlefield, in the bodies that lay there—

"This isn't possible," she whispered.

It was Ward's turn to emerge from his hiding spot, and his hands grabbed at the interface as if for support. "That's what I was trying to tell Mr. Solano," he said, and his voice was infinitely kinder than it had ever been, and she hated him for it. "You—tested this for him, in a way, when you connected. Now we know what happens. That is—ah, that you die, and that you come back, ah. Different. Mx. Ascanio, we'll need a ventilator sent to the bridge—two, if you can get them—"

Natalie knew the blank feeling that rolled in was shock—if that was a feeling at all, and not old feedback from the memoria. She was just inhabiting her body, just pasted to her heart and her nerves, a walking thing that used to be a woman. She'd been dead for an *hour,* her consciousness severed by the Ingest upload, her mind stapled to her body by the memory device. She'd been dead, but her body and mind *remembered,* and perhaps that's why the memory device was keeping her *here.* She almost couldn't speak. She stared at her hands, and the room spun around her, a wild anger building from—*God,* she thought, is this anger real or is this all just a memory—

—what would happen if I took off the memoria now?

Is that all I am now? Coded memories?

Shock turned to anger, and she snarled at Ward. "Fuck your *I didn't know.* Is that all you are? Some shit that shuffles around and does what they say and thinks they have a choice. You're okay with this? Ward—"

He shuffled his feet. His jaw wavered. "I'm not okay."

"Ward. What did they ask of you?"

"Don't tell her anything, Mr. Ward," said Ascanio.

"I have to be okay with it. I have to be okay. I have to."

The words had the forced cadence of a mantra. He shuddered; his hand hovered in front of his face for a moment, and then he stopped resisting the habit and drew it through his gravved-up hair. The overhead lights caught the edge of something long and bright and silver-gold just under his hairline, of broken, burnt skin, bloody around the edges, an expanse she hadn't seen until now. It had the look of the info-implants she'd seen on nearly everyone else, except this time she could get closer, and see the light peeking at the edges—

"Ward," she whispered. "When did you get a memory device?"

"What does that have to do with anything?"

Natalie grabbed at his hand, leaned forward, alarmed, repeated the question as if it were lined with daggers, with poison, with murderous intent. "When did you get a memoria?"

He blinked and pulled back. "It's not a memoria, it's the info-implant for interacting with the superhaptics. The one you *asked* me to get—"

"Show me," whispered Natalie.

"You're scaring me."

Natalie's breath came in nervous little spurts. She stared— the install was haphazard, of course, performed by some neurocit who couldn't have known what they were doing, someone who had perverted Reva Sharma's Sacramental intentions; his skin puckered patchy and dark around the circle where someone had fit the memory device over his normal info-implant. He took it off, turned it over, handed it to her.

"It's for the superhaptics," he said. "Isn't it?"

"That's definitely a memoria," whispered Natalie, weighing it in her hand. "Next-gen. But why would they do that? You're not dead, or in a coma—"

The ship shivered around them, as if it were laughing—

—*laughing at her*—

"I, uh," said Ascanio. "I had mine installed last week. You can check that one, too." She'd pulled herself out from behind the interface. Her face was lined with nervous energy; her body thrummed with it. And Natalie was about to turn to accept her help when she saw it: the quiet little click from *Ascanio* to *something else*. One millisecond, she saw Ascanio's bright eyes; the second, something broken and cartoonish.

"If you're going to do this," Ascanio said in a cadence that wasn't her own, "pick somewhere farther away from Ingest, mm?"

> *She's going to—*
> *Natalie!*
> screamed the master node.

Ascanio launched at Natalie, and without the master node's warning it would have been the last thing she'd expected her former tech to do. Ascanio was not a fighter, but this was not Ascanio. The gait was wrong. The fight was short and violent, and ended with Natalie's fist breaking Ascanio's nose, a spray of blood, and a cracking noise as Natalie pushed her into a table, insensate.

Ward was nearby in seconds, sweeping up the gun she'd used. "What the fuck was that?"

Natalie saw the master node in the corner of her eye and sent him a grateful nod. "Not Ascanio. Give me the gun." She leaned over to check Ascanio's fluttering pulse, but Ward didn't move. "Ward, give me the boltgun."

"I—I—" Ward's face looked chalk-white, and his jaw wavered, wordless, a few times. His eyes watered and his knees shook, like he was fighting something with every muscle he had. His hand was sweaty and unpracticed where it held the boltgun, and he raised it, slowly, examining it with a sudden horror in his eyes, like it was some kind of hot coal or his own beating heart. "I don't think I can," he said.

"Give me the gun," she whispered. "Switch it off, or whatever, just—"

"I think—"

"The gun, Ward!"

She could tell he had figured it out when he turned the barrel toward his own body, his face, looked down the darkness like it was some sort of beacon. "I should have read the contract, right?" he said.

She stumbled toward him, her fingers desperate to grab the weapon, to pull it away, but she was too late. She saw the *switch* in his eyes, too, a beat where anguish ceded to anger, and the motion of someone else sweeping in to occupy the space behind his eyes. She saw the silent petition of his finger pulling the trigger, and he fell to the ground, a half-breathing insensate sack of meat—

For a moment, she was too shocked to move.

And then she was on her knees, grabbing at his clothing, shoving her fingers against his neck in search of a pulse. He was alive—and before she could reach for a first aid kit, Ascanio was pulling herself up, wiping at her nose. "Ms. Chan, we've dispatched cit sec. Please stop making problems for everyone around you."

"Sorry," she said, hovering there, staring at the bleeding Ward. She recognized the cadence of Ascanio's borrowed voice now. Knew who it was. "I—I'm just doing what you told me to do."

"Oh?"

"I'm going down screaming."

The doors opened with a curt *swish,* divesting six more members of citizen security, new men smelling of uniform soap, their arms and legs in eerie sync, each of them now wearing a memoria and a jack at the back of their neck. She scrambled away, grabbing Ward's gun, until she was next to Kate Keller slumbering blank-faced in her rig, tied to her ventilator and her pacemaker and the machines that controlled her mind. Before she knew it, Natalie had her bloody fingers wrapped around the cords and wires of the ventilator, feeling them thrumming somewhere beyond like a heart, like life, like Vaisong. She pointed the gun at their connection to the computer.

I'm sorry, Kate, she thought.

"Stay away. Or I'll fire," she said, her voice gone gravel-soft with effort, with lungs too damaged to save. *My lungs*, she reminded herself, *the dead broken things rotting in my chest, every savage thing I am yet proud to be. Mine.*

Ascanio pulled herself up from the ground with the help of the others, brushing the blood from her face. She pursed her lips and surveyed the scene, just like Solano had done earlier. It was the creepiest thing she'd ever seen. "Come now, Ms. Chan. A *tantrum* every time I leave the room."

"Fuck off, Joseph," Natalie spat.

Ascanio smiled. "If you wanted to stop this, you needed to start last year. As it is, Aurora builds—"

"—to win," she finished. "I've heard that one before."

She tried to fight, to raise the gun toward the approaching guards—but even she couldn't handle seven on one, not in this heat, not with her scarred lungs, not with her beaten body, not even with the willing, whining gun. Not when she noticed each of them was in lockstep with Ascanio, all dancing to the same twisted music, all of them uploaded to Ingest, guiltless of their crime. There was no way Natalie could pull the trigger. No.

The zombies took her gun away, hauled her up, and dangled her by the armpits, moving toward the door.

I can help you fight,
the master node said.
Like before. I can help—

But he couldn't, she thought.
Nobody could.

26

Outside the computer core, alarms howled. Natalie's escorts joined "Ascanio" in heading straight for the ship's spine, dragging her along like a recalcitrant sack of trash. She saw the blank bodies marching in tandem—and now it wasn't just something strange she'd half noticed while doing something else. No. The indentures in the hallway pulled themselves out of the way even before Natalie and her lockstep guards turned the corner.

Compared to this, Sharma's vision of a bodiless paradise had been positively utopian.

To be honest, turning humans into nodes made a sick sort of sense to Natalie, who'd watched wartime decisions be made not from tactical necessity but profit/loss margins. A node would be efficiency embodied, the closest to a perfect profit-bearing system the corporate model could provide. Nodes would support a company running at full throttle, able to produce faster, fight faster, close logistical holes—everything that made the human experiment messy and independent and beautiful excised and thrown aside. Orders could be accepted almost before they were given. Margins could be guaranteed. It was the final iteration of an ancient system that had spun into being long before the companies left Earth.

She examined blank face after blank face as she passed for people possibly running their own minds. Certainly not everyone could function as a secondary or tertiary node; Solano was human still, and not Vai. He was no master node, evolved over millions of years for his specific purpose. He needed people for

their skills or their knowledge, people like Ascanio and Ward.
People like Natalie.

People who weren't here in the corridor.

Every so often, Natalie would catch a sidelong smirk, or some
shoulders held at a certain cant, like the black optikals in the
ceiling weren't enough of a reminder that he was watching, that
he was master, that he was a god with his many black eyes.

And she would have despaired had it not been for the master
node walking alongside, reaching for her hand.

Goddamn it. You're still here, she whispered.

> *I could "fuck off," as you like to say.*
> *But then we'd both be alone.*

I've been alone my entire life.

> *Which is why you should not be alone now.*
> He smiled, lines creasing the corners of his eyes.
> *You think there is power in loneliness.*
> *And perhaps there is.*
> *I have learned this from you.*
> *But there is far more power in—*

If you say love I'm throwing up.

> *You'll throw up anyway.*
> He laughed.

She stumbled forward, grief tugging her down, the guards
catching her with quick, forceful hands. And she laughed, too, a
wave of it, angry and bitter—

Stop trying to make me feel better. Love. Whatever it is you think you mean when you say it. I left it behind, I let the sky-scrapers infect me, I let them tell me what mattered, and I gave it all up. Everything that Ash and Kate died to protect. I just tossed it. Sold it. Like a good citizen.

And then he was there, holding her hand.
Finally.
Truth enough for together.

Willowy, thin-mouthed Cora Aulander met them at the door to *Vancouver*'s central spine, dressed in a dark blue suit cut thick around her shoulders and silver heels strapped to her feet. She looked sour, like she'd just realized that it wasn't going to be a fun time having her boss literally everywhere she went.

Aulander touched Ascanio—*Solano*—on the wrist, keeping her voice low. "We don't have to do this. You have control over the next body right now," the board member said. "Emerson Ward has been infected for six months—"

Solano's borrowed eyes flickered over toward Natalie. "Ward doesn't have enough juice, and he just shot himself. Besides, I need him to run the direct jack to the bridge."

"You can't trust her, sir."

"We can't wait for another one of the infected to get strong enough to handle it. We need her *now*. We have leverage enough to keep her in line until I can enact upload protocol. And besides: are *you* going to do it?"

Aulander's mouth turned into a polite frown. Solano's words were acid-edged, poison covered in sweetness, and Aulander's shoulders slammed forward, her body language going on the defensive. "Of course, sir," she said, hitting the lift button with more force than necessary.

And Natalie smiled at that, smiled through the nausea and the overclocking and the brain stuck permanently on guest mode, running too fast, too hot, the memoria a hot coal against her forehead. She smiled, because she finally understood. It didn't matter how high she climbed. Everyone was tied down. The only difference between Aulander and Natalie was that Natalie no longer held any delusion that she'd been anything but *a body* the entire time.

She cleared her throat, ignoring Solano.

"Ms. Aulander. Ward suspected he was infected, but I'm not sure he actually knew that he was dying," she said. "Do you know? Did they tell you that you're dying?"

"Excuse me?" Aulander blinked.

Laughter bubbled up. "Sharma never gave anyone the cure but herself. Or were you going to reverse-engineer that, too? And even if she did—was she really going to give it to you?"

Solano and Aulander shared a dark, dangerous look as the party loaded the car. The doors swished shut, and the lift whirred underneath her feet as it pushed up through *Vancouver*'s bloated midsection.

"I see what you're doing," Aulander drawled.

"Seriously, though. You need to be educated. Celestium madness is a shitty way to die. If you like your original liver, at least."

Aulander rolled her eyes. "God, you can talk."

This isn't working either, Natalie thought, but by now the words were coming in tiny tsunamis like they always did, too fast to stop. "I'm pretty sure Ash was vomiting up her intestines at the end. You have to know you haven't got long, when your blood goes silver—or are you just choosing to ignore what's happening because he *lied* to you?"

"I'm a secondary node." Aulander's fist balled; something in her delicate neck fluttered in swallowed anger, and Natalie thrilled to the sight of it. "Not tertiary. Not like *you*. He trusts me."

"Cora," Ascanio warned.

"We might be able to win with our own firepower, sir," she said. "We just need to wait for *Cartagena* and the others. We don't need the Vai ships."

Is he really in all of these bodies? Natalie asked the master node while the two executives sniped at one another.

*The master node stirred at her side.
His presence, walking next to her, was strangely calming.
Direct control? No. If his brain is anything like yours,
he probably couldn't handle it.
That's why they're all moving the same way.
You probably remember that from the war.
There were times I didn't understand what was
going on, and I had to pull back—*

The memoria gave her a flash of mechs approaching across a dark battlefield. *I can't talk about this.*

*The good news is that he'll designate secondaries to run the
various departments, to colonize a planet, to operate ships. You'll
need to take them down before you can deal
with him.*

Natalie nodded. *I'll do that while you escape into the partition.*

*He snorted.
I'm not going there.
That is a trap.*

Do you want to die? I'm too weak to fight again—

You? You're never too weak.

That's something Len *would say.*

The ghost of a smile. *It's true.*

The doors opened onto the bridge. Ascanio stepped back with a thin smile, gesturing for the others to go first. Natalie responded with a smile of her own: a wide, tactical, shit-eating grin. She got a painful prod in the back for it as they stumbled together onto the bridge. The doors closed with Ascanio still in the lift car, and with that any chance of going anywhere else.

An Auroran bridge was supposed to be a lively place, or at least it was in the holos: loud, bright with readouts, alight with muttered chatter, with hollered reports and orders and the all-too-human scent of sweat and coffee and someone wearing too much perfume. People working in concert, getting in each other's personal space, making mistakes.

Instead, the *Vancouver* bridge was utterly silent and crammed with superhaptics: black boxes and proxy rigs, wires and blood-silver connections to hands and fingers and necks and even the corners of bloodshot eyes, the indentures inside twitching and moving like marionettes, their eyes open to everything and nothing at the same time, the scattered board members standing in silent supervision.

And not just one or two of them, either, but the *entire* board, she realized: Aulander, yes, but also Coriolis and Stephenson and Amberworth, McCarthy and Li and Buchanan and Issa.

We might be able to win with our own firepower, Natalie remembered Aulander saying minutes before.

She looked over to the main interface to figure out who had the advantage. The superhaptic displays were migraine-bright and different for everyone; since Natalie wasn't yet connected to a bridge station with the right permissions, her view was of a

basic set of weapon-tied exterior vector cameras returning ordinary, old-style sensor data. She saw *Vancouver, Rio de Janeiro,*
and *Athens,* all heavy cruisers, all flanked by the silver-wild Vai
fleet that Solano had stolen from Sharma's control. Across the
black expanse, riled up and in attack formation, a smattering of
colors from the Corporate Alliance, or what was left of it, that
mishmash of old enemies that barely spared a ragged word for
one another if not for the Vai. Dozens of ships. More than dozens.
Thousands and thousands of lives.

But we're a part of the Alliance, she thought, *we're a leader,*
and as soon as the thought was in her mind so was a memory of
the master node whispering *humans lie—*

Because she hadn't been paying attention, had she? She'd been
on Tribulation and unconscious for a month and avoiding the
news as best as she could. The Alliance had come together against
the Vai. They *were still together against the Vai.* The Vai were the
only massive threat that would make them cooperate, and gather
up an expeditionary force with railguns thick as a forest.

"All pre-battle reports to the chair, please, and load ordnance,"
said Aulander, sweeping to the right and then down toward the
commander's chair, which was occupied by a rig and a silent corpse
she couldn't quite see wearing fancy boots and ring-rounded fingers. *Solano,* she guessed. She took up a place right beside it. The
guards pushed her forward toward an open rig, toward the *gunner's rig,* a complicated riff on the proxy rig she'd designed for
Applied Kinetics—to take the blood out of warfighting, she'd
thought. She'd *hoped.* The HUD designed by R&D operated
like a puppet, just below the level of consciousness, placing the
gunner directly in the center of the battle.

It took her two seconds too long to realize that *she* was the
ordnance.

"Wait," she called to Aulander. "You're not really doing this.

You're not going up against the Corporate Alliance. You're not—"
And the realizations came faster than her mouth could handle
and the ship shuddered underneath her, the kind of terrible wail
that presaged some of her worst memories of the war. She nearly
lost her balance, and they used the moment to shove her into the
chair.

Last year, she'd thought that the war with Baylor-Wellspring
was just necessary fallout from the debacle at Tribulation, but
that had just been the Auroran message. Aurora had only always
wanted what any company desired—full control of the market.
Hegemony. Monopoly. The Wellspring war had been a pregame,
the debacle on Bittersweet not a misunderstanding or mistake,
but a weapons test.

He doesn't want to stop at Aurora, she realized. *He's going
for the whole fucking Alliance. The Vai aren't the enemy. That's
been us—it's us, it's always been us. All these years, all these
wasted years, building towers for people who deserved only
graves.*

Natalie was too exhausted to fight. The install was sweaty and
too fast, the jack going in like a knife and the drugs like a tsunami. From here, she could see the commander's rig and the
changes they'd made; the CEO was barely recognizable in his
mess of cables and life-support devices. It looked like he was
sleeping, his skin shining with a faint golden glow. His mouth
was covered with a breathing apparatus that fed air into his
lungs, inflating and deflating. She'd seen soldiers like this as
she'd left the hospital after Tribulation, men and women in the
coma ward who had escaped death to slip instead into death's
waiting room, their consciousness locked inside a brain that no
longer made any connections.

So this is what you have to give up, Natalie thought, *your
very own body,* and looked at her own graying hands, her own

blackening exhaustion. She was a prototype in more ways than one. She wondered how many minds they'd already severed—just the ones in hallway lockstep, just Ascanio and Ward, or was the entire ship in the process of being changed? Had Solano found a way to reverse-engineer the cure and save his nodes from the facts of death, or were they all just going to go the way of scrollwork and rot?

The shiver of *Vancouver*'s spinal lance preparation echoed in her jellied legs, and she felt the slight kick of the railguns in her useless fingers as they shuddered online. The interfaces came online too, jumping in front of her vision, clamoring for her full attention—weapons manifests, targeting, vector analysis, all of it so familiar she flashed back to Bittersweet. For a second, the adrenaline almost convinced her that she was back in the shuttle coming up from Tribulation with Ash, with Alison Ramsay attempting to convince them that *everything was fine.*

Everything was not fine.

"I'm not doing this for you," she said. She heard the whir of targeting readiness in her ear. "You put me in there and I won't do a damned thing. I'll let this whole fleet turn to rubble before I pull the trigger, I'll sit there and watch my *fingers fall off*—"

"It's all right, Natalie. You don't have to do anything at all."

"Then turn off the drugs," Natalie said, scrambling to hold on to the edges of her consciousness for as long as possible. She set her teeth on edge, and then the master node was nearby too, holding her hand, whispering *hold on* like he was actually Leonard Downey—but even he couldn't hold her recalcitrant body against the tide, and she was dragged down, down—

Aulander patted her corpse, and looked to the captain's chair. "The body's ready, sir. You can take it at any point."

And Natalie couldn't scream—

—and the world twisted around her, re-forming in shades of black and silver.

She stood at the center of the circular, three-dimensional HUD that she'd designed for the puppet to make proxy combat more efficient. This time, instead of looking at a 360-degree view of golden Bittersweet, she was hanging in the middle of black space, her body in place of *Vancouver* in the center. She was able to see in a hundred directions, her bare skin a beacon of light against sheer vacuum. The Auroran side was thick with stolen silver Vai ships, shimmering teardrops and seeds and tentacle-twirling lengths glowing in the deep black. Farther off, corporate ships of every shape and size hovered just outside of firing distance.

Nearby, the master node had manifested like Len, all scrubby beard and dirty pants and *Alien Attack Squad* tee. He ducked away immediately, moving into a darker area where no ships flew and no lights shone.

The HUD popped up with a battery of sick choices—the entire Auroran Christmas list, more kinetics and moleculars than she'd ever imagined could be in one place. *Green screamer. Edison spiral. Catherine wheel. Expirant. Black gloriana.* Beyond it, the tac-HUD fed her information on possible vectors. She reached for it, greedy—

—but her hand did not move—

Solano appeared in front of her, loading in like a tornado made of glass. Natalie felt him slide straight into her skin, wearing it like a coat. He pushed her aside, taking her place at the center of the battlespace. She stumbled back, out of the area of effect, unable to touch the weaponry or the gunspace or Solano himself. It made sense. Applied Kinetics had only ever expected one mind per puppet.

We weren't thinking big enough, Natalie thought, and opened her mouth to drop a sentenceful of swear words in the CEO's direction.

"Cora," he said, sighing. "She's still here."

"Working on it, sir." Aulander's voice echoed from every direction. "If you want the wetworks working, the drug mixture has to be absolutely correct."

"I don't want you to work on it. I want her gone."

I'll fight you, she thought, *I'll fight for every cell, every nerve ending—*

She felt his sneer more than saw it, weighing heavy against her borrowed mouth. Solano flexed her borrowed fingers. *Fight me, then.*

But he didn't throw a punch, or even wait for her to respond, because the Corporate Alliance ships had taken his few distracted seconds to fire off the first volleys of the battle. He slipped into her fingers and toes and legs, taking every breath, firing every neuron. All she could do was retreat, fall backward toward the master node, not even a welcome visitor to her own DNA.

Natalie felt a crashing wave of despair, for how *could* she fight? What did she think she was doing, going up against the technology that had turned an entire alien race into just another *corporate asset?*

"Cora," snapped Solano.

Natalie laughed. "What, am I being annoying?"

"Cora!"

"Oh," she whispered. "I *am.*"

And she could not fight him, but she could speak. And if she could speak, she could sing—and oh, when he was alive Len would make such a show of clapping his hands over his ears when she started singing. The *Alien Attack Squad* theme was the first song that appeared behind her teeth, and she threw it in Solano's direction, full-throated and rowdy, like she wanted to fill a beach or a battlefield. *When aliens come to ruin your day, the Attack Squad's just a second away—*

It worked almost immediately. Solano plucked a K-7 screamer from the menu. Flesh-bright, acid-edged, it hollered toward a gathering of Alliance gunboats and missed. A second popped an Estrinbel fighter like a can.

"When aliens come to ruin your week, the Attack Squad has a killer technique—"

He threw a rattler; it hit a Wellspring corvette, stripping the thing of its plasteel hull, and she saw people blinking in the light, poison spangles working on their bones, *and god*, she thought, *I'm sorry—*

"When aliens come to ruin your month—"

"Shut *up*," Solano said. "Cora!"

Natalie laughed; the words hiccupped in her parched throat. *When aliens come to ruin your year, something something persevere—*

Solano roared. He cast a black gloriana at her, straight through her nonexistent throat—and it made contact not with an enemy vessel, but with one of his own gunboats. The gloriana gobbled the ship's engine in seconds, and the escape pods glittered among what was left, all of them twisting in the black wind neither of them could see.

"Cora," he whispered.

From far away, Aulander's voice: "Sir, you fired on—"

Solano snarled. "Do you *see* those Baywell cruisers at seven o'clock? You should be worried about your *own* goddamn wetworks out there, because unless this body is fully mine, I'm going to lose my immersion—"

"Getting it done, sir."

Natalie scrambled back. No more singing. But she wasn't done yet. She refused to be done. She had the master node, and a working knowledge of his entire repertoire of Vai moleculars, still had her pants on, and that meant she was still doing better than she had been earlier in the morning. She would not lose this in front of the fucking Vai master node, oh no, she was going down screaming.

She plunged her hand into her pocket, fishing around for the code dead Sharma had given her. She felt ice against the pads of her fingertips, pulling out not a card, but a jewel as bright as a curse on a dead god's forehead, whispering heat and light and welcome. The partition. All she had to do was speak the right words and they'd be gone.

What are you waiting for?
The master node, his throat closed in wonder—

I get one chance to do this,
she said.
I don't even know where this goes.
She said it was Ashlan, but—
But humans lie, she wanted to say.
But Reva lies.
Something else instead.
I wanted you to have a chance to go home.

This is home.
And we will fight for it.
The master node was quiet. Serious.

A brilliant ache at that sound.
Natalie didn't want to care, but she did.

We.
You and I.

Is this how humans make peace?
They just find other humans to attack instead?

The master node exhaled.
He was laughing with wide, white teeth.

And she laughed, too. Her fingers closed around the gem. It burned. It brightened. She held it close to her nonexistent heart.

I think that's your first joke, she whispered.

When aliens come to ruin your life, howled the node. *Something something—*

Route to partition, Natalie screamed.

Her vision tunneled. Dragged to black.

Upload, she thought.

Natalie hadn't expected to wake up, but she did.

She lay in a cabin on *Twenty-Five,* on the floor in a nest of dirty blue jumpsuits that smelled of sweat and tomato sauce. She picked herself up, hearing the muffled hum of the engines in her ears like an earthquake wrapped in cotton. This wasn't *her* room—the only photograph was tacked to the mirror by the door, a faded printout of a young man, exhausted, holding a coffee and grimacing. This was *Ash's room—*

"Holy shit," she heard, and was half-tackled by a dead woman.

"Reva wasn't lying," Natalie whispered, reveling in Ash's staggering hug. She grabbed for Ash's shoulder, thinking *impossible, impossible,* and felt tight, strong muscle where she expected waste and cartilage. This was not the dead woman she'd left in the transport over the White Line, her blanched skin stretched over rattling bone, her hands full of torn miracles. This version was bright and birthright-strong, as if she'd never spent a day underground.

Ash choked out a laugh. "*We?* Did Kate come?"

"Kate's fine," Natalie lied. "It's actually—"

"*Oh*," Ash whispered, and looked across the room. She tightened to a drawn bowstring in Natalie's arms. Whatever she'd seen pricked tears as easily as blood.

Natalie knew who it was, of course. The master node drew himself up from where he'd been curled on the floor, preternaturally still. He did not move as Ash pushed Natalie aside, stumbling across the messy space, her face drenched in disbelief. She went for a hug, but Len's hand shot up, work-scabbed fingers wrapping around her wrist. Natalie saw a brief moment of connection, a light in her eyes, a flash of recognition in his. Their fingers tangled together, in a moment of intimacy so bright it made Natalie's heart ache.

"It's you," she replied.

"You remember them," he whispered. "You heard them singing."

Natalie felt a sudden twisting discomfort. Jealousy twined up her back and tightened, leaving her lost in the strange, all-too-human conflict between forgiveness and revenge. *It's not Len,* she wanted to say. *He's dead and he's not coming back and he's mine, not yours, and I get to mourn him, not you—*

She felt a bright, grieving anger. *And everything he tried to stop—it all happened, exactly the way Ash told me it would. And it's all my fault. I called Solano down to the Sacrament lab. I didn't even know what he was so close to accomplishing. It's all fucked up, Ash,* she wanted to say, *all shattered and perverted and slammed into something terrible and new—*

Ashlan glanced over her shoulder. "But you're here now, and

that's what matters. Nobody asked you to disable zappers the day after you joined up. Forgiveness takes time, and—"

"Forgiveness is a fucking crock," Natalie spat, drawing an angry breath. She wanted to slap herself, to bring some sort of solid end to the panic building in whatever was left of her body. Grief wouldn't help. She didn't want to grieve for Leonard. She didn't want to forgive, either. Nothing had really *mattered* since the day she'd walked down the hill and given up one shitty life for another, and she didn't want to forgive herself for that, either. And then she realized—

"I didn't say any of that out loud," Natalie whispered.

Ash tilted her head, as if something just clicked behind her green eyes. "Didn't you?" Her eyes filled with a strange silver light, like a cup turned toward a waterfall, and the air changed around her, thrumming with possibility, as if the room itself had recognized who she was and loved her. Natalie felt that love like a warm blanket, and that care like laughter in the mess, and behind it, a clammy autumn chill that nested at the base of her spine, as if someone had just walked across her grave.

"Not a word," she said.

"I never understood," Ash said. She reached for Natalie's hand. "I do now. Oh, Natalie. You must have felt so alone."

Natalie yanked her hand away. "I'm *fine*."

"You're not." Ash blinked twice, three times, in quick succession. A chilly confusion crossed her face, and a light crawled at the tips of her fingers, wilding under her skin, beautiful and alien and wrong. "You're definitely not fine. You never have been. I know who you are, Natalie. I know entirely more than I should. I know *all* of it. All of that time on *London,* on *Twenty-Five,* and— you still felt you couldn't open up with me. To anyone. How the hell do I know that?"

The answer was obvious. Sharma had worn that light. Natalie

fumbled in her back pocket for the jewel given to her by Sharma's ghost. "She used her own memoria in the transport because there wasn't time for anything else. She—"

"—created a partition for you," said the master node. "Otherwise, Ash would have been marked as the—"

"—master node when Sharma uploaded herself shortly afterward, and she couldn't have that," Ash whispered, and it echoed in Natalie's mind like she'd spoken it herself. She *had* spoken it herself. It had just come out of the others' mouths.

"And Kate stayed for me, because that's just what she does for crewmates," Natalie said. It was Ash's thought, but she knew it like she knew her very name.

"*Together,*" Ash whispered.

As she spoke the word, Natalie was no longer entirely *herself*. Perhaps the other two had done it before and could handle the overwhelm of *together,* but Natalie was floored by light and whispers and the press of lives and thoughts and dreams that weren't her own. It was bad enough to have to live in her own crumbling body, to know what she knew about her mother, to know about all of the things she'd done wrong. It was quite another to be wrapped in Ash's wild mourning upon seeing Kate as Ingest, a breathing statue wrapped in wire, no longer entirely human.

Perhaps if Natalie had understood any of it, *together* would have felt beautiful, and not like a sick echo of Solano's hand twisting her soul out of the body she should have occupied, of the hell Natalie brought to Bittersweet, of what was being done now, as they spoke, outside this *nonspace*.

"I can't do this," she said. "Stop."

"It's all right," Ash whispered, and knelt on the floor. "I understand. You're exhausted. And I never knew you were hurting so badly."

"I—I didn't want anyone to know. And you—"

"I had *her*," Ash said. "You had—"

"Leonard and I never really—" She slumped forward. "I think that's part of it. To know what I could have had. To live with the fact that I was too small and stupid to stop any of it, that I wasn't important enough to him to convince him to stay alive."

"It's not your fault," Ash said.

"It's not yours, either."

Ash opened her hand. "Do you want to try again?"

This time, *together* transformed the space itself around them, and Natalie kept her head down out of dizziness—the walls expanded, the floors pushed wide, and the wild bone rib cage she'd seen on the ship formed above them like she'd been swallowed yet again by that great breathing leviathan. The sides of the room formed themselves of mining-planet plasteel, and the floor bubbled up in Verdict macadam and marble.

Together made Natalie feel mad and sane at the same time; in the partition, she knew Ash as intimately as she possibly could, right down to the crannies of her capillaries and her cells, as this massive shining light and this close warm companion. And the Downey-thing, the master node, the alien being beyond any name—she knew *them,* too, although she had no human words for what that meant.

She wanted to say that what existed there was love, but she didn't know, because people had used love against her before: her mother, and Xie, and Joseph Solano, whose fingers had worried apart the catch-points in her soul and convinced her that *love* was due to no one else but the Company. She didn't know if she deserved to be seen like this—not Natalie, not the person who had been used to drop a bomb on Bittersweet, the person who still dreamed of choking on red dust and terror and probably always would.

This isn't about what we deserve, she heard. Ash. And

Downey, a faint whisper. *It's about what we have to live with. I understand.*

Her voice broke. *How can you?*

I could have waited, he said,
and he showed her Natalie in the suit
in the rib cage room in her body in her blood
she was there unreachable and they were
shaking in their grief ever since
a woman in a lab
on a planet
taught them about death taught them
that each alien body was a civilization
a library a lab a memory a garden a planet

and horrified

they retreated into their nebula
because what else could you do
in the face of so much death

and that they had destroyed all of it

them
those who were life eternal
and then you forget
and forget
and forget
until a human named Natalie Chan comes to find you
and you lie to her
about what you know
of death
because you have already changed

And Ash, holding the hand of her lover and watching the dusty Tribulation sun set beyond alien trees, knew that nothing would ever make up for pulling the trigger on the Heart, even though she had been forced to by the situation she experienced—not even the hundreds of little deaths she suffered while setting off the weapons that were stored there, screamer after screamer tearing her skin and bone apart and knitting it back again, a thousand resurrections, pain beyond pain. It wasn't enough. It would never be enough.

And Natalie understood, finally: what grief could do to someone who had never known it, that the three of them had all shaken in grief so fully that millions had felt it, that enough blood was between them that they could drown in it—it brought them here, to this moment, facing down another great calamity.

She could fight it. Or she could accept it and move forward.

One left her Solano's victim.

The other option made her something new.

Something new. Natalie closed her eyes with the hope of it. She took a long breath, tasted harbor air mixed with station air and silver, the unsteady trust between them, the darkness they were leaving behind. And Natalie thought—

"Oh," Ash whispered. "Oh, that's good."

Natalie blinked. "I didn't even—"

"It's very possible," said the master node.

She hadn't even given the thought a real consideration yet—it was just a memory, just something tied up in the thought of *grief* and *forgetting* and *moving on*—a thought related to Ash, on Tribulation, being wheeled around by Sharma, and what she'd done to the enemy there. If Natalie could do that—

If she could do *more* than that—

And once she had the thought wrapped in her brain, cur-

dling there like asphalt in midsummer, she knew she could
not stay, just as she knew Ash and the node could not go. And
there would be no need for a goodbye, either, because that
had been said. Natalie simply rose and reached for the gem in
her pocket.

"Tell Kate I love her," Ash said, as the edge of the partition
swung open to the darkness.

"You'll tell her that yourself," Natalie answered, and walked
through.

27

On the other side of the partition door, the death-song of Aurora's salvaged Vai weapons hit Natalie like a knife to the throat. Her mind tipped back into her body like hot water from a pitcher, and she and the master node flowed back into the limits of her skin and bone, reentering the proxy state where Solano had control. Natalie gasped at the loss of *together*, and the fact that the node was present at all—

"I told you to *stay*!"

"I changed my mind in the millisecond before the door closed."

"This is my fight—"

He crossed his arms. "And is it not mine, as well?"

Natalie was suddenly too busy to argue. The battle raged around them in flavors of hot blood and surprise, massive cruisers and tiny fighters in varying stages of forced dissolution. Solano was winning. Out here, Natalie was still a secondary node. He almost didn't see her; his hands were alight, casting Auroran weapons into the void. And then—

"Cora!" he called.

"Seriously," Natalie said. "Can't you do *anything* without her?"

"She won't be able to help you," the master node said, and flexed his fingers.

Solano snarled, a *rattler* curdling black in his hand. "You have no power here, Ms. Chan. And—" He blinked. He breathed in. For the first moment, fear creased his eyebrows. "Who are you?"

"I am not human," the master node said. "I do not lie."

"What's that supposed to mean?"

"Then you know I speak the truth when I say that I *will* take my world back. Natalie, go."

She didn't need a together to know what he meant.

I can't leave you.

And you can't do this.

Not for me.

> *Go*, they breathed.
> They looked less like Downey now,
> and more like themselves,
> like silver and gold and earthquake-dark Vaisong.
> *I am not doing this for you.*

You'll be alone—

He'll kill you.

> *So come back to me before he does.*

Damn you.

Natalie took a deep breath.

"There's one thing about permissions that most non-programmers like Cora forget, *Joseph*. A door *in* is always a door *out* unless you lock it correctly." She barked out a laugh.

"Cora," he called, a note of panic in his voice.

"She's not going to be able to hear you."

"She's my secondary—"

"No, she's *mine*," Natalie said, and woke up.

Solano had locked down access to his brand-new Defender fairly well, but he hadn't thought to close the escape hatch to his own body, bless his narcissistic soul, and from being *together* with the master node, she knew exactly what to do next. She tunneled up into his skin like the node had shown her and felt Solano's heart—her *borrowed* heart—thudding back to life in three shuddering beats, like a hard reboot on a broken machine. She gasped for air, her lungs shoving themselves against a rib cage that felt too loose and too wide, and she fought off an instant, nauseous dysphoria.

"Sir—" she heard. *Aulander.*

She waved at the voice, coughing down the vomit. Her borrowed fingers stung with pins and needles; they'd used enough drugs to keep Solano under, but not enough to keep him from resurfacing if needed. *Coward.* Solano's memoria fumbled, still trying to reconcile flesh to consciousness. If it failed while she was here, she'd die right alongside him. And she was willing, but—

No. Not unless I have to. She picked herself out of the rig, dragging the vent from her borrowed throat, slapping an autobandage there. Solano was slightly taller than her, and he weighed more, so she nearly tripped against his foreign center of gravity. His body fit like a too-tight wetsuit; his shoulders pulled and twisted, like she'd shoved herself inside and forced the zipper to close. His rings were too tight for her taste, clutching fumbling fingers that had never had to defuse a bomb or solder a motherboard.

The board members swiveled their heads all at once, the bright flashes of the battle outside reflecting in their silver shoes and rotten golden tattoos, and she felt the undercurrent of their questions—

—*right,* she thought, *he'd noded them, too, made them secondaries. He dies, one of them will take his place. Damn it.* Solano might be a master node, but here in the real world, his human brain could only handle so much input, and his understanding of the master node's world was exclusively hierarchical, passing through rank rather than function.

So he'd delegated. He'd passed the nanotech to his board and let them have tertiaries. She could hear their doubt and their hope and their fear—and, like Solano, could manipulate that fear. She could feel the colonies lurking behind Coriolis's blue eyes and the indenture systems behind Issa's, and more beyond the others, the entire Auroran architecture. She wasn't sure as to the limits to their autonomy, and pulling the trigger on her plans right now might give them enough time to respond. The direct jack he asked Ward to install would allow her to do it, but they were using it for the chair her body was occupying.

No wonder he'd gone fishing off the deep end of the harbor. Anyone would, with this many assholes chattering on about *business* in his brain. Budget approvals and dying colonies and balance sheets and where to store the bodies—

—she looked over at the body she'd worn all her life, wrapped in the gunner's chair, and felt a wave of dysphoria.

"Sir?" asked Aulander, sliding in beside her.

Natalie jumped. Her borrowed lips took a stumbling moment to form around a reply. "I'm experiencing interface issues. My response time's shit. I need the direct jack we used for the gunner spliced over to the gunner's chair."

"Sir, you're doing fine. We need you back under now." Natalie could hear an edge of panic behind Aulander's serene exterior.

"Which should tell you that I need that jack *now*."

"Mr. Ward's already working on it." Aulander's voice was calm, but the part of her that rambled under his skin shook with nervous energy. "But you were doing so well, and the lances alone won't hold back as many fighters as they've deployed."

The borrowed memoria shot her a memory of Ward—colored with pity and mild disgust. She could feel Ward somewhere behind Vidal's skin, moving toward the bridge with his install team. *Creepy as hell.* She smiled at the assistant with as much patronizing glee as she could.

"Ward. Direct jack. Now. And—Cora?"

She felt Aulander's fear like ice on her tongue. "Sir?"

"Don't fucking question me." The words were liquid glee in her mouth.

"Sir, you always said to question you if I thought you were wrong."

Natalie spat pooling blood from her mouth onto the floor. "This isn't one of those times. This isn't *fast enough.* Do you want to keep your *head,* or would you rather get fucked in a Wellspring prison camp? I know what I'm doing."

Aulander cringed, and the satisfaction Natalie felt on seeing it was a heady, guilty feeling. The entire experience was guilt—after all, every pair of lungs that breathed air on the bridge did so because Natalie Chan allowed it. Every pair of boots on the deck, every mouth calling that their console was no longer theirs, every panicked heart—she could clutch them in her hand, gobble them down, consume their fear. She understood now how intoxicating it was. How easily it could go askew.

She thought she'd understood power. She'd been dead wrong.

This was power.

Smoke rose from some kind of broken system nearby, curling quietly to the ceiling, sucked out in disaffected swirls by the environmentals. Natalie sat back in the rig and watched the battle turn toward the Alliance, trying to keep calm. As long as there weren't Vai weapons in play, the master node was winning the fight. She tapped her index finger until Ward and his team arrived.

Ward was wearing a tight white autobandage under his jacket instead of a shirt, and she could tell from the pale, worried lines creasing his forehead that her lover was himself again. They no doubt needed his expertise to run the direct line. She almost opened her borrowed mouth to say *hey,* but she hadn't come this far to blow her cover on someone who wouldn't believe her.

Instead, she reached for Solano's rig connections. If the hovering board members thought it funny that she could attach her own belts, they said nothing—although Aulander did move in behind him, waiting to apply the neck jack herself.

Ward pulled his head out of a wall panel. "Direct connection to Ingest established," he said.

"Engage the rig," Natalie said in the most commanding voice possible—it came out strident, booming, completely un-Solano-like, and she couldn't help looking to Aulander, to see confusion in her eyes, and, *shit, here come the drugs—*

The direct connection to Ingest slammed her straight past the secondaries into the center of the Heart on the Vai cruiser beyond, into the violet-green, death-bright hollering light where time seemed to stop. She could feel Kate's light, half-conscious breathing somewhere in the background. The noise of the secondaries' chatter increased to deafening levels. She reached forward for the light, taking it in her hands, allowing it to curl around her wrists and spiral up her arms. She welcomed it. Ash had months on Tribulation to examine the Heart, to learn how to turn it from nuclear bomb to surgeon's knife.

Natalie had fifteen seconds.

Ingest knew something was wrong—Ingest, the mad, gold-soaked Heart-gate nanocomputer that was also Kate Keller—then turned the alien mystery in the rib cage room to something Solano could easily control from his comfortable chair. It burned when she told it what she wanted it to do to the secondaries, but it was a computer and she was a master node down to her skin and bone, and it had to obey her.

By now she could feel Solano's secondaries start to question her actions. Coriolis, who crawled in shouting alarms; Vidal, who was losing control of the railguns. It was no matter. The battle raged outside, and it didn't matter if Aurora lost. That wasn't why she was here.

Vidal's voice was a frantic boom in her ear. "Sir. Ingest is throwing errors. What's going on?"

"Everything's fine," Natalie said, the taste of fire on her tongue.

"Please confirm your topdown code."

What's a—She paused. She didn't care. "My topdown code is—*you're all going to hell.*"

The words tasted like sugar, and somewhere she could hear Kate's wild relief, her laughter.

And then Ingest was hers. Utterly hers.

From Natalie's perch at the top of the universe she could see the secondaries for what they truly were behind the glitter and the gilt. She could see their stories like light on their skin, could know their memories and sins in Ingest's twisted version of together. She knew all of the bloody things that had made them powerful and proud, all of the places where they'd papered over the rot in their souls, all of the circular reasoning they'd taken to land themselves in power.

And Natalie was complicit. They were all complicit. She'd known all these truths for years, hadn't she? Hadn't they all? Every single time some sort of massive tragedy would happen and she and her team would see it on the news—every single time an answer was demanded by sobbing families or desperate friends. Every meltdown and factory death and cave-in, every tragedy blamed on *mechanical failure* and *malfunctions* and the like. Each time, the board would stand in front of the cameras, telling the world it *wasn't their fault*. But if there was one thing Natalie had learned from all these years opening her veins to the corporate sky, it was that there was always a finger behind the trigger.

Slipping into Aulander's mind was easier than she thought it would be, and as Natalie settled in, she heard the woman's whisper—*please, please, I never pulled a trigger, I never*—*not once*—

Natalie smiled. *You think you're safe, Cora, because all you did was watch?*

I did what he told me to do—

I can't push off my responsibility for Bittersweet on you. What makes you think you can do the same? Show me the Bittersweet meeting—

Aulander's memory was hidden and musty, like a sip of yesterday's water, but she could see it well enough: a comfortable boardroom, hibiscus pastries on her tongue, whiskey, wine, laughter. *It's just an indenture,* they said, *and it will be presented as an accident. The test will show us if we're clear enough to go after the Vai.*

She saw meeting after meeting, the deaths rolling through her fingers in red-lined budget numbers: a closed medical clinic, a safety rule ignored, *only a dozen dead because of it, sir, it doesn't impact the bottom line or our schedule—*

And *there.* There, she's standing in back, taking notes, as they cut Reva Sharma's body open, drain Ash's dead blood—

She flashed back to their quiet space together in Aulander's memoria, where the fear in those bright birthright eyes almost made Natalie reconsider. Almost. "You justify it because you're not making the decisions yourself, you just enforce, but we both know the truth about that," she said. "What you did to Ash and Sharma—"

"They were *dead,*" Aulander said.

"They were *people,*" Natalie said. "And that's not something you're ever going to understand."

"But I do—" Aulander's heartbeat felt almost desperate. "I do."

"Do you? And then you support this madness anyway? I've done the same, and I think that might be worse." Natalie placed her ghostly thumb against the assistant's lips. She steeled herself. Remembered the indentures. Remembered that the only thing between freedom and damnation was Natalie fucking Chan, zombie princess of Aurora Company.

She had to do this. She didn't have to like it.

For a moment she hesitated. Knew that *they made me* and *they deserve this* were just her brain justifying the terrible thing she was about to do. She felt a terrible, gnawing guilt. She'd been pushing off guilt for Bittersweet, saying it wasn't her fault—but this would be. Could she call herself a good person after this? Would she want to? Was there another way?

No coup is truly bloodless, she thought. *And that's what this is. It's time I started taking some fucking responsibility.*

"Only a dozen dead, you say. I bet they have people who remember them. Let's make it a dozen and one and see if anyone remembers you." Natalie hesitated. She could stop here. She could stop.

She couldn't.

"Forget."

Aulander's eyes opened wide, and her hands clawed for Natalie's, her body stiff, her breath stopping, her cheeks sinking into grave-dust as if she'd been deleted and dead a long time. And then it felt as if Natalie had been staring at Aulander's body for months, and her name slipped from Natalie's mind, going as anonymous as the records in the dead woman's hands.

By the time the rest of the board realized what was going on, she'd yanked their permissions, one by one, then slipped into their minds, fishing around for their sins. Their minds caught fire, their bodies shook—the fear they had given so many others. Ingest erased each one of them—

Forget, she whispered. *Here is Alistair Coriolis, who revoked sixty-three Earth-based indenture contracts days before citizenship, leaving them uncitizens, with thousands of credits saved. Her lips brush his cheek and suddenly he's drowning, the water behind his teeth stinking like the dead Hudson, his skin sloughing to fish-eaten bone, forgotten like an uncitizen—*

Here is Raynor Stephenson, who left contaminants in Ryker Colony water systems, so concerned about all the lost profit if Aurora evacuates. She buries him like he did the three hundred

Ryker sick, choking on the bitterblack poison, his body going rigor-black like the children did—

Here is Aileen Amberworth, her bones broken like the suicides outside the Auroran celestium refinery on Glassheart, still breathing—at least for now, because most of them made it, I installed nets, shouldn't that be enough, and they need to die like those suicides did—

Winter Vidal, who burns like his indentures did in the cable factory, his skin turning easily to black paper, forget—

Others. Starved, boltshot, simply forgotten, like the lives they took. They'll be forgotten too—

And here is Rothan Issa, who dies of blackvein, the bogeyman illness that existed only in hushed rumors from miners with celestium sickness, because it was never given a true name, never studied, because the board said it wasn't real, so she could only guess based on his memories of burst capillaries, black tears, enlarged hearts—

And here is Joseph Solano—

She stopped mid-thought. Her tongue felt like a nuclear wasteland, her body aching—

—her body—

Natalie had gotten this part wrong. Unless she wanted to live in this murderer's skin forever, she couldn't erase Solano until she was back in her own body, when she wouldn't have the ability to do it at all. She shivered in the twisted language of Solano's nerves. Not *her* limbs. Not *her* tongue. Her tongue was across the room, her body a battleground between Solano and the master node. And the master node hadn't rejoined her. Vai slid in and out of bodies all the time, but humans—

Humans could only live as themselves.

If she finished this litany of curses in Solano's body, what would happen to her? To the master node? Would Solano die? Would she? Could she take that chance? She could already taste the blood slicking Solano's teeth, could already feel the rejection gathering inside like she was some violent disease.

She had to finish this in her own body.

She lay back. Reconnected Solano's body to Ingest, a cable at a time. Reached for the vent.

Felt the machine slide air into her borrowed body—

—and loaded back into her own head.

The battle rendered around her in brilliant black; the only light in the rig HUD came from occasional bursts of flame that died as quickly as they were born and the cones of light created by railfire. She could feel, more than see, *Vancouver*'s spinal lance spinning above her, could see the Alliance ships growing closer, moving in banding circles to box the rest of the fleet in.

Solano stood in the center, his avatar clothed in light, sweating. Whining Vai weapons lay stacked at his feet. This time, she saw the singing jewel at the hollow of his throat—the partition where Sharma had put the Vai.

"Stop," she said. "You're killing me."

"I understand that. It's a risk I'm willing to take."

The ship listed to the side, took the volley, disintegrated—and in the bright, wild explosion that remained, she saw the master node curled on the floor, bloody and broken, but still breathing. Despair crawled into her throat.

"And what about your own body?" she said.

"That thing?" said Solano. He picked up something purple and black, something that breathed out death and had no name that Natalie knew. "You think I don't have a plan for that? I've been training for this my entire life. To end it all. The competition. The politics. When we're united under one mind, there will be no end to what we can accomplish. All you have to do is let it happen. There's no shame in it. All you have to do is *move the fuck on*. And you've wanted that for so long, Natalie. I know you have. Let yourself have what you want."

Solano's words echoed, solidifying in their inevitability. Even if she were able to stop the battle, make everyone forget Solano, throw herself into some sort of suicide pact with him here and now—even if the other companies won, they'd come aboard. Find the technology. Build their own. And it would never be over. It would never end.

She feared the hundred Tribulations that might follow, the bodies that were fodder for hard work and war, the hundreds of thousands born just to upload and die, who would never see anything different from the path laid out for them. Who would never even live, because Solano could destroy them the moment they thought they could have something more.

She couldn't just give up. She was a soldier. An ordnance engineer. When you couldn't defuse the bomb, you ran. And when you couldn't run—

—you throw yourself on the bomb,
said the master node.

It was the very thought she'd started calling up herself, a terrible thought from the depths of a terrible war, and as she started to consider it, the master node stirred in the darkness of her mind. He had pulled himself toward the thought first; it was his voice she'd heard, his body curling up from the vast nothing below. She could go. She could finish this. But only if she left the master node behind. And he knew it, too.

"I thought I killed you," Solano whispered, somewhere far away.

"Humans lie," the node said, coughing up blood.

"You're not *human*."

"I'm human enough." He stretched his fingers, looked from one hand to the other.

"Impossible," Solano said.

"I had a good teacher," Downey said, picking himself up from the ground. "Natalie, go. I will hold him back."

> She reached out to say *this time you won't make it out—*
> *—and he was there,*
> *assured,*
> *as sure as the glint in his eyes.*
> *I know how to do this.*
> *Leonard taught me.*
> *He would want this.*

He would want to stay with me, she whispered.

> *Perhaps.* He smiled.
> *I don't know why it's never been clear*
> *that he did what he did for you—*
> *not just Ash—*
> *because you existed.*
> *Because he loved you.*
> *Because he wanted a better world for you.*

Her voice caught. *There has to be another way.*

> *I failed my people once.*
> *I will not do it again.*
> *Warmth.*
> *You'll only have milliseconds.*
> *Make them count.*
> *I was never going to be able to return.*
> *I have changed too much. But humans—*
> *—ah, you are change.*

Natalie ached. He lifted her chin.

When my world was ripped from me,
when I realized I could never go back,
I was ready to stop existing.

They pulled themself in front of Natalie, and for a moment she could see *them,* as they were, as they wanted to be—she couldn't quite settle on a *form* for it, for the silver and the light and the way it interacted with the world. They were a cloud and a human body and slippery mercury and a bird singing and all her broken memories of what love had once been.

"Natalie Chan changed that," said the master node. "She taught me that even when you're alone, even when you hurt, you get up. You keep going. That is a miracle. *She* is a miracle. *Humanity* is a miracle."

Solano tossed off a barking laugh. "Two master nodes can't be in the same place. You know this. And you know you can't possibly win."

And the being she had come to love smiled. "She also taught me that was a terrible reason to run from a fight."

They *moved,* in a motion that was smothering and flailing and vicious all at once. Solano reacted, and to do so, he had to loosen his grip on the world around him. Natalie didn't hesitate. She threw herself back with a bone-breaking, spraining force, emerging from the gunner's trance and hitting her physical body like she'd been dropped from a helicopter.

The bridge seemed like it was waking up from a long somnolence—with the master node taking Solano's full attention, navigators and gunners and assistants' eyes flickered open, coming conscious in their rigs. There were birthright bodies everywhere—people she didn't recognize, and after a moment she realized the code she'd written, *the forgetting,* must have worked. That she'd *forgotten.* Had she killed them? Who had they been?

Did it matter, now that she had proof the code worked?

Ward appeared nearby as she started ripping out her haptics. "Sir, if you come awake again, we're going to start losing for good."

"Fuck the sir, Ward, it's me."

"I—" He looked confused.

She stared. "The answer's still *no*. Is that better?"

The confusion on his face ceded to obvious relief. "He told me you were uploaded. That you were gone, like everyone else."

She ripped away her torso harness, tasting blood, as if she'd uploaded razors as well as her soul. She pulled herself up with all the force that her exhausted, dead muscles could bear, yanking the jack out of the back of her head like a knife from a piece of meat. Blood sprayed the seat.

"After all you've seen, after all I've told you, you still believe Solano?"

"I don't have a choice."

She swallowed blood. Her voice was coated in gravel and she thrilled to it—her blocked, Tribulation-burned lungs. *Her own fucking lungs.* It was enough of a victory to keep her going. "I don't either," she said, "but *damn* if I'm not going to fight the whole way down."

When his mouth just swung open and stayed there, she pushed him aside, leaving him in the past with everything she'd walked away from. From now on, there was only the future, and it was short and bloody and brutal, and she'd already reconciled to it. Her body felt wrong, like it was peeling away from her skin-first.

She dragged herself to the commander's rig, her fists balling. She was a soldier, and soldiers fought until they couldn't. She couldn't get off the ship, and she couldn't find her way back into Solano's head, so there was only one way to connect to the Heart to deliver the code she needed to take Solano down.

She heard the *swish* of doors opening, the whine of a cit-sec boltgun, the click of it firing.

Natalie ducked, but not fast enough. Her body had gone numb enough from her failing memoria that it didn't quite hurt when the bolt found a place next to her spine. She fell, her shoulder cracking when it hit the floor, and she smelled her own burned flesh. She'd be dead if she wasn't already. The pain came milliseconds later; she bore down on her bottom lip, climbing forward, toward the jack. There was no past—just the future, *this* future, the one where everything counted on her, where the choice was between Solano's shattered memoria or her own death.

She could almost hear the Vaisong from here, even if she was imagining it, even if the master node had left it as a memory in her broken brain, and it kept her going. Exhaustion was a dark, sodden blanket tied to her feet. A river of pain carried her along, her mouth full of muddy water, and she was reaching out when—

—when they fired again.

She grabbed for the direct jack. Missed. Fell bleeding to the ground.

And Solano woke.

Stretched.

Kicked at her, his civilized manner gone. His tough-toed boot hit her in the breastbone, and his eyes flickered up to the guards behind him. "We're going to have to rethink morgues on the big cruisers," he sighed. "Always something to do."

She tried for the jack one last time, but Solano's boot came down on her hand and crushed it to the ground, and with that pathetic showing, she knew it was over.

I'm sorry, she whispered to the dead master node. *I'm so sorry,* then, to Xie and to trapped Ash and enslaved Kate, to broken *Twenty-Five,* to everyone she'd failed, even Sharma—and when she closed her eyes and thought of *home,* she was sitting on the side of the road on Lark Street in midsummer, heat on her shoulders, eating a mango ice, the sound of atmospinners grinding nearby.

She took one last breath, held it. Tasted mango and harbor air and the metallic hue of recycled air.

Heard the clean slice of a bolt in the oxygen. Held her breath. Someone *else* screamed.

She opened her eyes. Solano had fallen back into his chair, gasping against a wide, blackening hole in his shoulder. Bolt-fire erupted from behind her, and she ducked; she looked over her shoulder to see who the shooter was. It was Ward, *fucking Ward*, she thought, his wild yellow hair sticking up hither and yon, his battered nails catching the light. Natalie saw terror in his eyes. He met hers, just once, and kept firing as cit sec kept coming—

"Citizenship is a promise," he hollered, stumbling back as the guards came toward him. "Not a gun to your head. Not this."

But Natalie was already moving, reaching for the direct jack. She yanked the cable; it popped out with a spray of blood and gold, and it jumped out of her hands and rolled away. Solano hollered, and grabbed at the shoulders of her cit jacket with more force than she'd thought him capable of, and she lost her balance. He pushed forward, punching her in the nose; she kneed him, and he toppled.

When they were both on the floor, he clawed at her, at her face, her shoulders, her jacket, while she tried to get at the jack like she was some drunken, drowning sailor and the cable was a lifeline. She was turning her face away to maneuver the jack closer to her neck when his hand popped up next to her and grabbed the memoria. She felt a tug, a pop, the strain of the connection like a wire between buildings, tugged taut. The buffer opening. The world opening for her, every thought and every dream—

But Solano stumbled back into the chair, holding the faceplate to her memoria. An inchoate *no* had barely ripped from her throat before he dropped it on the floor, slamming his heel into its curved belly. It made a desperate crunch and a pathetic little shower of broken components, and the Vailight inside shivered and went out, and with it, any chance of making her memories make sense—

Natalie saw a bright flash, like an apocalypse, and—

—someone was ranting behind where the nameless woman had fallen. Some other, *third person,* which was insane, because she knew herself and *the man with the boot* to be the only people in existence. She had been born seconds ago in smoke and plas-teel, a gangling bag of misfiring limbs against a void-cold deck, and she knew only one thing: that she was clawing at pieces of metal that had once been important before the world began, that the man with the boot had destroyed it, but she couldn't remember why she was so upset.

"Citizenship is a promise," the third person ranted. "An agreement. Not a gun to your head. You see yourself as *granting* it, of holding power you distribute, but you've forgotten. You only hold this power because we *allow* you to."

The man with the boot sighed. "Mr. Ward, *please.*"

The nameless woman coughed. All she wanted to do was sleep, and there was so much *noise.* The amount of *input* was harrowing—alarms screaming against her ear, smoke a thin corkscrew against her skin, and her only memory. A boot. A crunch. A light, skipping into darkness like a missed heartbeat. She hadn't wanted him to do it. She'd been angry about it, angry enough to fight him. Should she still be fighting him?

"How many Natalie Chans have there been? How many experiments, how many broken promises?" The yellow-haired *third* was holding something, something metal and wild-mouthed. "You can say that this was necessary, that you're *done,* but you're not. Are you?"

She looked up at the man with the boot. *He* had the thing that he'd destroyed, pasted to his head. She wondered if she shouldn't just take it. He'd taken hers, after all—

—and her body moved almost without her command, from an *intention* that almost felt alien, the one muscle memory seared into her from the moment she was born. He was looking at the golden-haired man, not *her*. A fist connected with his cheek, and she felt something hard underneath the skin give way. He stumbled back, and she used that moment to grab the metal thing on his forehead. He clawed at it, and between the two of them, it popped out of their grasp and went sailing across the room—

—where the third man raised his *whining thing* and with a crook of a finger cast hot red light, scoring straight through the spinning device.

The *other* stumbled back, blinking, as lost as she was.

The yellow-haired man was nearby in a second, and his face was full of an embarrassed relief. "Oh, my God, Natalie," he said. "Are you okay?"

"That was mine," she said.

"You were going for the jack," he said. "Come here. I'll plug you back in."

He started moving toward the seat, where the man with the boot was sitting, staring at his hands like he'd never seen them before. He tugged her hand, but she didn't move. She didn't know where to go. Her only memories were smoke, plasteel, shattering electronics, *blood*. But the name seemed familiar, like an echo in a room etched in bone, and how had she remembered *that*? "I—Natalie," she said. "Is that me? Is that who I am?"

He wavered for a moment, as the alarms clanged and jangled, then some sort of realization hit his angular face. He reached out and touched the bare metal place on her forehead with some thin reverence. "The memoria," he said. "Oh, damn. He destroyed it all, didn't he? Yes. Yes, that's who you are. You're Natalie Chan. You're the most stubborn bitch I know, the first person I've trusted since—since, I don't know, since God knows when."

She tasted that name. It seemed right. With it came the words *forget, forget, forget.* "Who are you?"

"I'm an asshole," he said, and his smile went wide. Something dark and wet passed through his eyes, and he blinked away tears. "*Your* asshole, apparently."

"Well, that's good." The bridge shook. She looked at the interface, the black outside, the moving shapes, the beams of light. "That's not."

"No. It's not."

"Death," she said. "A battle. I know about fighting, don't I?"

He rocked from one foot to the other, sucked in a breath. "You do. And we're losing. Without Solano, there aren't enough of us to handle the ship. We're all going to die. So—I'm going to do what I should have done earlier and load in to fight. I'm going to—"

She looked toward the jack. Something about it twigged a memory she shouldn't have even had, something deep, something folded into her muscle and her bone, into everything she was. Something more than her own body. Something she'd be looking for the rest of her life, however long that lasted. If she didn't go now, she'd regret it.

"No. I'll go," she said.

"But you don't remember—"

"He didn't take everything," she whispered.

Something dark and wet echoed in his eyes, and he blinked it away. He pushed back her hair with his left hand, slid that hand behind her neck, slipped her fingers into the locks, pulled her in. "I should have trusted you before."

She felt the edge of annoyance, and the words came out before she could stop them. "So trust me *now*. Just fucking *do it* already."

He laughed. "There you are," he whispered, then dropped his hand, turning back to the center of the bridge. He slid his hand under her shoulders and helped her over to the black breathing monster of a rig in the center. The man with the boot was trying to climb back into the chair, and the yellow-haired man responded by shooting him in the shoulder, then kicking him in the face. She lay back, and *fuck*, when he said *jack*, did he mean *a fucking flaming knife in her neck*—

—and she tunneled—

—to a place she'd kept in her bones, a temple to violence, with wheeling stars and the wrecks of unknown ships, boxes and lances and teardrops, silver and black and grunt-gray. And at the center: a shining, singing jeweled thing that made her ache with the brightest of choirs.

She walked over to pick it up, and as she closed her fist around it, held it roiling and shuddering to her broken chest for just one second.

There was just one word she remembered, exhaled like smoke: *return*.

A thousand voices flowing into her fingers, into her blood, and with them the memories of a million years; the conscious broken lives of a thousand stolen Auroran indentures, all of their memories, the hundred thousand voices calling her home, every single thing that had been stolen by the Heart.

Home, wherever it was, because home was the universe, a thousand walls and beds and hearths in a thousand places, the warm, close walls of a tunnel filled with silver voices. *Home* was a grand plaza and a building shaped like an egg and five tall towers, was Grenadier and Cana and the thousand bombs that could have killed her but did not, was a mine and a coffee cup and a man named Christopher. It was walking away, always walking away, from battles and blood, from Davin and Xie and a dead granddaughter in a rainbow blanket, from the guilt left behind on the fourteenth floor of a comm tower in the form of a chin that curved like hers, and *I wasn't a mistake, I was never a mistake.*

And as the tsunami died down, as the million who knew Natalie breathed her memories back into her body, she heard Ingest.

Your command, Node, said Kate's voice.

Here is Katherine Keller, Natalie said, *who after my one last request will have the power to open the partition and be with her wife.*

She heard the dead woman's ragged cry of relief. *Your command, Node.*

Here is Joseph Solano, Natalie began again, *who looked at the world and saw only himself.*

Let us know a world without him.

The world shivered, and the computer engaging the command was a wild, dark wind—

—a pulling, a wild loss of together, a pop of the jack coming out—

—and she woke.

Natalie's assistant, Emerson Ward, was standing in front of her, blinking, his hands covered in blood. *Hers? Someone else's? How did we get here?* "Thank God, Ms. Sharma," he said. "You—were overclocking, overdosing—"

And that was true. She was barely keeping herself together. The memoria was gone, somehow—that damned machine in her head that stapled her mind to her body and kept her from dying again. That was why the world felt strange and wrong and tilted and completely new. Maybe that's why she'd forgotten there was some bloody uncitizen clawing his way toward her chair, because she was sure she wouldn't have forgotten that. This man wore the signs of birthright power, the diamonds, the implants, the tattoos. He'd been shot twice and was dripping blood on *her* deck.

She had no idea who he was.

"What the *fuck*, Mr. Ward?"

"I'm not exactly sure," Ward said. "There was a battle. Apparently we're supposed to surrender to the Corporate Alliance. I simply—I don't know—"

"Well, that isn't happening."

She checked to see if the crawler was listed in the Company directory, but found herself disconnected from the main computer. She clawed at her head, and—where was her info-implant? Did she take it off? Did she have to do everything the old way? It was bad enough that someone had seemed to force through the superhaptic renovations the old board had wanted when her mother disappeared.

For a moment, she thought her memories might be wrong.

Was that even possible? It had to be—there were so many bodies. The man curled on the floor, crying. Fifteen dead, all of them nameless, all of them looking like they'd walked straight out of a *Corporate Idol* judging booth. God, it was like they weren't even *Auroran*.

"Tell them it was a mutiny," she said. Her mind felt clouded, like she was missing half her life, and she'd have to have the doctors look at it, but right now there were other things to deal with. "That's the *only* explanation."

"A mutiny," said Ward. He sounded reticent. "Of course, sir. And."

"Get medical up here."

"Right away."

The man with the curly hair arrived at the chair, slapped one bloody hand on the arm, curled his fingers tight.

"That's my chair," he hissed.

She leaned forward, rubbing her eyes. She felt like shit herself, like she'd been shot herself—had she? Oh, shit, she had—and she was far too fucking exhausted for this kind of display, even with her mother's upgrades done.

She kicked his hand away from the chair, then shoved him back with one well-placed bootheel. It was the kind of thing her mother would have done—the Sacrament traitor, the CEO who had held this seat before her, who had taken the Vai hostage and started this whole damned war. She'd been trying very hard not to be her mother, a person who had never faced anyone powerful enough to counter her desires. And a person in her position really shouldn't get her hands dirty.

Nevertheless, she really felt like punching the man in the face.

So she did.

Numerous times.

And when she was done, Natalie stood. Slapped the comm. "This is Ms. Sharma," she said, "and I have a fuckton of dead mutineers on this bridge I can't account for. Send a team to mop it up and figure it out. All directorates, report any irregularities."

"Ascanio here," came the response. "There's a . . . dead woman in the computer," said Ascanio, the leader of Applied Kinetics.

(*Why did we still have Applied Kinetics?* she thought. *I thought I had that shut down*—)

"A what," she whispered.

"A dead woman."

"What the *fuck*, Mx. Ascanio."

Ascanio stammered. "And I don't recognize any of this cabling—"

"Okay, hang tight. We'll send a team to you, as well. We'll get it all figured out."

She sat back in the CEO's chair, felt it curl around her body as it always had, as it always would—well, if she could fight off these Alliance assholes—and *why* were they fighting, anyway? Who had attacked first? Wait, what the fuck, that was a Vai ship out there, a fucking Vai fleet—

—she heard it *singing*—

—and she didn't remember—

—she couldn't remember *anything*—

—and thought: *wait, something is desperately wrong with the world—where's my memoria, where is the master node—*

But it wasn't something wrong with the world. It was something wrong with *her.* She felt a slow, dizzy ache in her stopped-up heart, felt gray and strange and gone, and a quick darkening of the world around her, and the headrush of a thousand voices and a hundred thousand memories that weren't hers, and *oh, I forgot,* she thought, *I'm already dead.*

28

By the time the gathered Corporate Alliance forces recovered enough to make a real move against the newly quiet Vai fleet, the aliens had collected their heartships and fled beyond the White Line, taking their answers—and their secrets—with them.

And as for answers, nobody found them on the bridge of *Vancouver*. Nobody on the bridge remembered the mutineers, even though they were dressed in birthright brilliance. The computer had no record of them. The CEO allowed an Alliance judiciary team to review the records, and the chief investigator found a record number of inconsistencies: the mutineers had taken over the computer core as well as the bridge, had experimented with Vai technology, had *installed* a citizen in the computer for some reason the team couldn't figure out—partially because the CEO ejected them immediately when they asked to see the crime scene.

It was the Vai, she told the investigative boards for weeks after. *They must have been in league with the Vai. I mean, we all saw the Vai ships leaving halfway through the battle, once the Alliance disabled* Vancouver.

And look what happened to the survivor, she said. The uncitizen survivor, who had stolen some birthright's diamonds and rings and even an info-implant, had gone completely insane, claiming he was the Auroran chief executive, whipping and whirling and punching until the chief investigator was forced to bind him and send him to a medbay for his own safety.

"Humans lie," said the Auroran CEO, when asked for a comment.

And there was the matter of that CEO. Everyone else swore that *someone else* was the CEO—a man from a line that had died out twenty years ago with the death of the executive Ernesto Solano and his curious lack of progeny. Proper Auroran accession had put the Sharmas in charge—or, at least, that's what the Auroran records said.

Their current CEO, listed as Natalie Chan Sharma, traced her line back for decades—there was some murkiness about her father, and about her mother's abdication and disappearance, but the Corporate Alliance wasn't allowed to meddle in Auroran accession affairs. Everyone onboard *Vancouver* swore the CEO was Sharma. Everyone at Aurora HQ did the same. The Corporate Alliance was about to write that off as correct when they discovered a few citizens who hadn't yet been upgraded with Auroran superhaptics. They told quite a wild story, but—quite honestly, the investigators found, how could it be believed as anything more than a holoshow?

They couldn't ask Sharma about it—she'd been dead when the medics took her, and was sixteen hours in surgery with Aurora's best pulmonologists, surgeons, and neuroscientists. She came out wearing a new proprietary info-implant nobody had ever seen before and would never see again, waved to the cameras, and then retreated into silence for months.

So the other companies could only speculate about the Auroran logs and records—whatever the mutineers had done, they'd left the local Corporate Alliance servers in absolute tatters, corrupting and destroying dozens of years of work. Aurora Intergalactic's records were so corrupt after the battle, in particular, that even the best programmers sent themselves away scratching their heads, talking about files they'd never seen before, about files that *moved themselves*. Similar reports started occurring in other companies that had been present at the battle, and then everyone was too busy with their own internal problems to care.

Sharma's recovery kept her away from the investigation, but as soon as the rumors started flying that she should be replaced, she dragged herself from her sickbed, leaned on a cane to walk all the way to the boardroom, and—alone, because Aurora had no board, and wasn't that strange too—made a hoarse-voiced address. She refused to send any of the Auroran bodies for common burial, citing internal investigations, then kicked out the Alliance investigators and the Alliance itself, and the broadcast that ensued was the last thing the Alliance was allowed to see for months.

My fellow Aurorans, the broadcast began. *It is time for you to know the truth about what happened at the White Line. It is time for you to know the truth about how things are going to change because of it. I call you my fellow Aurorans—because that is who you are. Every indenture, every citizen, every birthright.*

Forget those dividing words, she said, *from now on, you are simply friends.*

The Alliance executives suspected a civil war. Spies reported flames on Auroran ships, and agents talked about uploaded intelligences and other impossible things, and when the doors were reopened to the public, a number of high-ranking Aurorans had been executed, a number of others had agreed to give up their positions, and things seemed back to normal—as much as a company that allowed full citizenship, access to all technology, full health benefits, and other incredibly stupid things at the time of sign-on could be normal.

There's no way that can work, whispered the other Alliance companies. *You can't pay* everyone. *Impossible.*

I give 'em six months, they whispered.

And the CEO never looked overwhelmed or out of her depth

on-camera, even if she needed her wheelchair, her cane, her IV with that strange silver medicine she needed injected on a regular basis. There was always a bright blast in her eyes, something brilliantly enameled—almost *inhuman,* people said, that matched the inhuman profits coming out of Aurora's colonial sector.

But that's because the CEO herself waited until she was in her own quarters to break, to allow the panic to take over, the quiet anger, the constant wonder about when the ruse would be discovered—only it wasn't a ruse, was it? It was reality.

She'd done what her mother had asked of her.

They'd forgotten.

They'd all forgotten.

Only: she'd forgotten too.

At night, Natalie Chan Sharma would shut the door to her spartan quarters, hook herself up to the machines that kept her alive, and wait for the deliveries.

Ward was the one to bring them, of course. He was the only one she trusted enough. He'd arrive, push in the isolettes with the modified Heart that had once been used in the computer that was no longer Ingest, and leave. She'd open the delivery alone, and listen quietly to the Vaisong, hoping to hear a new song pointing her back toward *home,* wherever that was. He brought her weapons, too. Black glorianas. Blue screamers. Weapons that glittered and gleamed, that sucked in light and cracked open her emotions, each one opened, caressed, searched, returned.

Did you find what you were looking for? Ward would say.

No, she'd say. *They're not answering me.*

And Ward would take the weapons away, and she'd open the reports from her trusted neurosurgeons, the ones working on the Resurrection Project, and the new memoria that powered her broken brain and body. She'd sign off on the lists of Aurorans who had decided to return to their bodies, and on the lists of those who chose not to, and Natalie wondered what beautiful things her mother had built in the Vai *together* that kept them so happy they'd give up the rhythm of blood and breath.

She knew that someday she would find out for herself—they all would—but, for now, there was plenty of work to do on both sides of the veil. Natalie had plans. She had long-term goals and charts and project managers. The uploaded Aurorans poured through crackable handshakes in the Wellspring matrices and InGen computers and great Penumbran stations, and while the corporations vied for inches in the marketplaces and shoved each other around for celestium, Natalie started to build her new empire.

This was just the beginning of her plans for Aurora, for the Corporate Alliance, for everything else. In every computer in the human universe, in every new technology and dorm and mine and lounge and bridge, Aurorans would whisper songs of *change*, of *life*, of *the long walk*. It didn't need to happen overnight. That was her mother's mistake—trying to force her new world into being through blood and fire. No. Change could take centuries.

But they *had* centuries now.

She was working on their faces, as she did every night.

A graphite pen, a shaking hand, thoughts like tightly held sand: until the newer memorias were ready, she'd have to be kind to herself. She planned to draw their portraits until she remembered who they were, where they were, how she could find them.

Her family: two women holding hands, always together.

An older woman with upswept hair, who *should* have been her family, a face lost in the darkness, who gave her the name she carried and then chose to leave her behind.

And a man who always smiled—a smile that broke her heart,

only she could never get it quite correct, could never shade his skin properly, and for fuck's sake, she'd always ruin it with the tears that would run careening onto the graphite anyway, so what did it matter—

"It matters," he said.

She gasped, looking up. "How—"

He wore a familiar dusty blue jumpsuit, a sweat-stained undershirt, and an illegal indenture insignia. He was leaning against the side of her room, his arms crooked together, his head tilted to the side. He smelled of work and tight quarters, of celestium fuel and *Twenty-Five*. Her heart rioted.

"It's you," she said, feeling dumb.

The man brightened. "I was hoping you'd remember me," he said. "You were pretty hollowed out when you went up against Solano that last time."

"Went up against—who?" Natalie grabbed at her forehead, touched the place where her new memoria lay. "You're him, the one I'm missing."

He smiled. "I made a copy of myself a long time ago, when I realized I could never go back. I was waiting for the memoria to index me." He pushed off, walking over, and she felt his hands on her shoulders, as warm as her own, and she shivered. "Until you were ready."

"Fuck being ready," she whispered.

"I had to let you heal."

"I don't heal. Bastard."

He laughed, like bells. "*There* you are."

And then he was in front of her, his hands grabbing hers—

"You did it. The gates are open. The Vai are adapting to life without me—without a master node. And there are humans out there adapting to life without bodies, life in a true *together*. The corporate age is over. This is *our* age now, and those of us who choose it will no longer stand for the abuse of power. Not even from you. Not when we know how beautiful the universe can be."

"Are they here?" she said, not even daring to hope.

And over his shoulder, she saw them, smiling, tried to remember their names. Her family. A dishwater blonde with her hair in a ponytail; a dark-haired indenture who dreamed, and tried, and lost, and won in the losing. They held hands, and smiled, and she felt warm for the first time in a very long time.

"Life has a different definition now," he said. "Look at you, for example."

"My heart—"

"Needs to be rebooted six times a day. Your liver and your kidneys exist in that box back there. Your brain's getting zero-point support. But you're still you."

She shook her head. Chuffed out a laugh. "You have a point."

"Do what you can," he said. "We'll be here when you're done."

She didn't cry. She wanted to.

"I loved you, didn't I?"

"You loved someone like me."

"Bastard."

He laughed, like bells. "You can call me Len," he said, and winked. "And I have some friends I'd like you to meet."

ACKNOWLEDGMENTS

The year I wrote *Engines of Oblivion* was one of the best and one of the toughest of my stay on this planet. I found out that I was going to have a baby the day after starting the novel and handed in the final draft while covered in spit-up in the middle of a global pandemic. In the middle of it all, I am not sure I got very much sleep at all. What a ride.

Sincere thanks go out to my amazing beta readers, who picked up my sleepless drafts, brushed them off, and helped me back on the road to the finish line, especially Jane Pinckard, Amanda Williams, and the incomparable Jo Miles, all of whom read the book on extremely tight deadlines.

My thanks also go out to the MD-SPOC plotbreakers who swept in with metaphorical firecrackers and C4 when I felt utterly buried: Phil Margolies, Beth Tanner, Sydney Rossman-Reich, Martin Sherman-Marks, Jo Miles, Kelly Rossmore, and John Appel. Thank you, too, to Benjamin C. Kinney for the neuroscience consult, and to the baristas at Atwater's, who were there with my usual order on even the rainiest of days.

Of course, a simple thank-you isn't even enough for my brilliant editor, Jennifer Gunnels. When I needed to cut to the bitter, hopeful heart of both of these novels, she gave me the knife. My gratitude as well to everyone who worked on these books at Tor, including production editor Lauren Hougen and publicist Libby

Collins, and to Mike Heath, the artist who took my breath away with the cover art.

My deep gratitude also goes to my fabulous agent, Dorian Maffei, who took a chance on a PitMad post some years ago and remains a tireless advocate for my work and for myself.

And thank you, thank you, thank you to the readers. Yes, you—each and every single one of you who took a chance on the Memory War and read through to the end. You are why I do this. You are why I'm here. I hope that I can continue to write stories worthy of your attention.

Thank you, too, to my family. To my amazing husband, Glenn, and the marathon we're running together. To my parents, Sandi and Rich Dietlein. To my brother, Mike, and sister-in-law Samantha. To Jennifer, Courtney, Jacques, Margi, Fran, Jack, Bob D., Bob G., Tracy D., Caitlin, Pam, Gavin, Benjamin, Steve, Addie, Cole, Paige, Tracy R., Pete, Sandi, Tamara, George, and all the Gilsons and Dietleins. To the Osborne side: to the memory of Bill and Janice, and to Carrie, Kalli, Baron, and everyone in Nashville. You were there for me. You've always been there. And I can't thank you enough.

And finally, to my clever and amazing daughter, Claire, who was my constant companion while writing this novel: you continue to show me the meaning of love and joy every single day. Please don't read this book until you're at least thirteen.